A DIET OF HOLES

A DIET OF HOLES

DAVID GALE

ANDRE DEUTSCH

First published 1988 by
André Deutsch Limited
105-106 Great Russell Street London WC1B 3LJ

British Library Cataloguing in Publication Data

Gale, David
    A diet of holes.
    I. Title
    823'.914[F]

ISBN 0 233 98331 7

Phototypeset by Falcon Graphic Art Ltd
Wallington, Surrey
Printed in Great Britain by
St Edmundsbury Press, Bury St Edmunds, Suffolk

To Hilary and Helie

Part One

Snappy Jack Gavin, limited seer, with one of his more striking suits on, and the buckled shoes of alligator. Stepping over the chain-link fence.

'Oy!'

He sauntered between the parked cars.

'You deaf?'

A stout man in a dark uniform was running through the rows of vehicles. Probably a chauffeur.

'Where the fuck are you going, John?'

'My name's Jack,' said Jack.

'There's a gate over there.'

'It's quicker this way.' He strolled on. The man put his hand on Jack's arm. Jack spun round and snapped his arm away, 'Keep it in your pants, fatty.'

'What did you say to me?'

'I said pants and fatty. I'm in a hurry.'

'I could have you run off here in no time, my son.'

'Try your luck.' Jack turned and walked away, at more of a clip this time. The man half ran beside him, leading with his left shoulder so he could be rude to Jack's face.

'When we get to the reception,' he puffed, 'I'll get the bill in. They're only just down the road.'

'Yeah? I'm famous.'

'They're all fucking famous here, Jacky. Doesn't cut any shit with the men at the gate, I can tell you.'

'We'll see.' They were nearing the steps to the foyer.

'I don't bloody know you, that's for sure.'

'That's because you're in a hut all day, scratching your bollocks. You should watch the television.' Jack pushed through the heavy plate glass doors and surveyed the hessianed expanses. Across

1

the foyer was a long leather desk punctuated by smiling recep-
tionists.

'I know more about television than you'd think, pal. Television
doesn't like rudeness, for a start.' The security man spotted a colleague
coming out of a lift. 'Frank! Frank!' Frank walked off down a corridor.
'Deaf bastard.' The man fixed Jack with an unpleasant smile, 'It's just a
matter of time now. Then we'll show you what happens when you use
obscenities to a man who is normally moderate.' He started to move off
in pursuit of Frank.

'I'll tell you something,' offered Jack. The security man hesitated.
'Famous people never worry. They see people like you and they think,
"I could use one of those to keep coal in. His mouth's big enough."'

The security man moved rapidly back to within a foot of Jack's
person. He looked around furtively then hissed, 'You said pants to
me, you bastard.'

'I said pants *fatty*, arsehole. Where's your memory?'

'Stay right there. Right there. FRANK!' He darted off towards
the corridor.

'Mr Gavin?' A young woman with a clipboard.

'Yes.'

'I'm Carol. Elizabeth's assistant.'

'Elizabeth?'

'She's the one that will interview you. Would you like a drink first?'

'It must be telepathy, Carol.'

She led Jack along some corridors to a nice room with several sets
of armchairs and a bar.

'What have you got?' he asked.

'I thought you'd know,' she said mischievously.

Since Judy Lane's report on Jack had gone out on the regional
news, stressing Jack's purported powers, the station had received
letters from the public. Jack had baulked at the purport part, but if the
television actually said you actually had powers, you would, effectively,
be alone with Christ, since they never asserted that anyone had them
apart from him, or Him. But the public had been keen, so World Picture
After Work had approached Jack. Would he care to be interviewed and
so forth? Most definitely yes. And all the drinks. Certainly.

'Doesn't work with spirits. I just know it'll be a large one.'

And all these young women around, offering things. They tended to
twitter, but perhaps it put you at ease. Not that unease was an issue

2

here, but then was it ever? And he didn't really *need* a drink anyway. Wasn't it always a mere pleasure?

Now another young woman was telling him when it will happen and for how long.

'Are you the one that'll ask me?' he asked.

'Yes. It's my programme.'

'Oh! Of course! I've seen it. Didn't recognise you.'

Actually he hadn't seen it. Early evening was not TV time for Jack. He suspected there was a lot of minor robbery, swimming pools and new malls, that sort of thing. People saving cats. People saving dogs even. Still, those kind of viewers, you never knew, could be his constituency.

'I'm smaller in real life,' said Elizabeth Preeny.

'As aren't we all?' he jovialised.

'Well, you're the man of the moment, Mr Gavin. A little legend for many of our viewers.'

'How many?'

'Viewers? Oh, three point six I think we're doing at the moment, something like that.'

'Golly.'

'Do you say golly? I haven't heard that in years.'

'Tell me what you're going to do to me.'

'I'd like to ask you a few questions. Just a routine enquiry. You know the sort of thing. Don't you?' She grinned.

'Is this a test?'

'I thought perhaps you knew the questions already.' Her gaze hardened momentarily, as if she thought he might somehow wriggle away unless pinned down in this fashion.

Jack sighed. 'I won't let you down, Elizabeth.'

'Of course not. Please don't think I was being rude.'

'It happens all the time.'

'I mean, it is an unusual area, you must admit.'

'Look, I have a choice. I can turn it on and get bored, or I can leave things alone.' This wasn't strictly true. In fact his powers worked all the time, but when people realised this they invariably became more predictable than ever, so he had got in the habit of being offhand about it, in order to keep the world alive. 'You want me to be spontaneous, don't you? That's what it's about, isn't it?'

'Well, yes.'

3

'Good. I'm sure you'll get your money's worth.'

Elizabeth softened. 'There's one thing you can't possibly know.'

'What?'

'Miss Desperanza. She might be going on with you.'

'She's in Rome.'

'Ah! We're flying her back. But the plane's been delayed. It could be a last minute thing.'

'She was only here a week ago.'

'Wouldn't be much of a story without her, would it?'

'I guess not.'

'She discovered you, Mr Gavin! Sort of.'

'I saw her before she saw me, Elizabeth.'

Just after they arrived at the hospitality room a man and a woman entered, accompanied by several more young women, some of them almost running. They went to the bar and began ordering drinks.

'Who are those?' Jack asked.

'They're on the programme with you.'

'With me?'

'After you. They're explorers.'

'Where are their shorts?'

Elizabeth smiled nicely. She had met many people. 'They take them off in the evening. They're Guy and Deany Blighton. Just come back from the jungle. They've discovered a new animal.'

'Will they drink all the drink?'

'There's lots. Don't worry.'

'Are they more famous than me?'

'I'm afraid they might be. Haven't you seen We Went Away?'

'What's that?'

'It's their TV series. They have books as well.'

'With pictures?'

'Of course.'

'Well, I have my doubts.'

'Yes?'

'New animals. I don't believe there are any, Miss Preeny. Everything is known.'

'You don't really think that, Mr Gavin.'

'It's my secret, Elizabeth. It's made me the popular fellow I am today.'

*   *   *

4

The dark woman in the astrakhan coat, June Rousseau, by marriage, was in Jack Gavin's offices. She sat down, sighed, then shifted within her handsome garment. Now that's rich, mused Jack. Those coats, are they poodle? The tight worms of coiled fur ran in mazes round the garment, black cauliflower furrows between each varicose ridge. A black braincoat surrounds my client. A deep sea flower, a negro's hair. I'd like to touch. Is it springy, does it bristle? Jack leaned across the desk and touched Mrs Rousseau's arm. Yes and yes.

The first client of the day. The last before lunch. Within moments of sweeping into his modest offices, the latter a plural in spirit rather than floor space, she had settled in cash no credit cards accepted. Now she clearly wished to unburden herself of a quantity of anxiety. Her husband Pierre, the Frenchman, Peter the Frog as his friends call him, she disclosed with a giggle, because of his work must entertain hard. His many connections in the company, you understand, the necessity to make as if a family with the representatives, she did not abbreviate the word. But she, his wife, the woman in the rear, a frock a day sometimes, must bring up the canapés. Afternoons at it – slice, dice, spice, the whole caper. But, she said, I'm in there, it's what I do, it's my pleasure. I love those groundsprung vegetables and working with the tree or bushborne fruits.

Jack was considering his sharp shoes. I think I love my shoes, he thought. Is that possible? To be in love with a pair, so that you wanted to see them all the time. Thought about them when you weren't wearing them, started to miss them after spending a day in some lesser pump. Went straight to them when you got home. Kept them by your bed so you could look at them before putting the lights out. Ah.

June couldn't see Jack's shoes so she went on. But he tells me I'm dippy. Is that like in dipso, like in dipsomania, I have a mania? It can't be that bad. But it's my grasp, Jack, my plate – it's full to the edge with the dish of the day, you see, which is fundamentally of the here and now, the present, you understand? I'm up to here with now, if you like. I need another hand. I need three or four. And why, and why? Because I'm getting surprised all the time. I'm crept up on. She said.

'Ah!' he said. 'Where I come in.'

'Oh come in, Jack, come in,' she said, 'else why am I here?'

'Tell me what creeps,' he said, 'June.'

Her eyes brimmed for a moment. At last she was telling someone. 'Everything seems so fresh, I'm like a child in a glade. An apple rolls

5

into my circle and I've never seen it before. It's the first apple. Then another one, and that's the first one, too.'

Jack was avuncular, 'But June, now is always big. But what of next? Must we not make room? I would like you to be more specific.'

And so, as Jack caressed the kid upper, she specified. 'Well, I'd like to relax but there's no time. I'd like to have a deep bath with salts but,' Jack was humming to the soft shoe, 'but I merely freshen up. When I dress my outfits are racked as if filed so that I may rotate without repetition. I take the one at the front and don it in the robery. I apply cosmetics in appropriate tones. Accessories. Check the cuisine. Set out the nuts. The door opens. It is my man. I'm talking about tonight. So far so good.'

Jack looked up from the arch of his sole. 'Quite so. The problem?'

'Pierre washes. The bell rings.'

'Dingaling!' Jack cried.

Mrs Rousseau wondered, at this point, whether Jack were not, in some way, enjoying himself, and if so, was this what she wanted?

'And in they come, the dam is down, some with their wives and those who are from out of town not. I give them a drink, and that is the last thing I know. An abyss yawns. I am all work and no play.'

'Where I come in again! Haha.'

She ignored Jack's lightness. 'Anything could happen, Mr Gavin. Total strangers, representing numerous provinces and eager to be familiarised by Pierre. Expecting a sliver of France in my front room. I grin but cannot bear it. I have nothing to say. I am lost and mapless. I feel heavy at the prospect of tonight.'

'They're coming tonight?'

'At eight, Jack.'

The brief had been laid.

'I'm going to begin. I know what you're saying, June, and I hope I can bring something up.'

'If only. If only. Something I can use at eight o'clock, if possible.'

'That's what I shall try for, June. But it's not just me, you understand. In the end I am a gatherer, not a hunter.'

He pressed her forearm again and sat back. Then he placed his fingertips on his temples and closed his eyes. He was working on her case, looking forward to an evening at her house. She, in turn, saw herself speaking in Jack's mind, his eyes turned inward, watching a part of her life that she would never share with him. Am I in his mind now, a little image on a screen, or is he in mine? June was pleased that Jack was a professional – what might have felt like impertinent prying now became a more agreeable time-sharing arrangement. Her eyebrows arched as she searched the top of her head for any indication that ethereal molecules from the rented seer might actually be roaming the walls of her skull, rolling through the dark furrows of her cerebrum. Although, it struck her, he may be neither in himself nor me, but some future time that has as yet no location, nowhere to be, a misty slide looking for a third dimension. This might explain why her head felt, frankly, much the same as it always did, which is to say, no particular feeling in the brain itself. And who, for goodness sake, ever *felt* their own brain? So perhaps Jack had left the room entirely, apart from his fleshly body, and was even now about to report back from the frontline. Wherever he might be, he was certainly not an unattractive fellow, even if his clothes were more up-to-the-minute than one would expect of a person whose perceptions are purportedly paraphysical.

Eyes down, Jack knew that the case was, in fact, as ever, easy. But that way lay sloppiness. He had always shuddered at the catchalls of horoscopy, aghast at the commonplacing of so much difficult maths. How could they? Go to the stars, flatten them out, paint all over them, then bring them down in a gush of dark strangers and money matters. My god, it was so much easier than that, not that the stargazers ever seemed to stretch themselves once they'd graduated from Planet College. Still, the platitudes of the competition were what kept him in business. People wanted blueprints these days, not ephemerist borealism.

He had everything he needed. Breathing regularly, he allowed her to step forward into the open-plan living room. He could see the men, he had met them before. He had even met Pierre. He could see the apron, the olives, the suite. He didn't have to consult any files, the thing would unroll itself unbidden – the disgusting creature that had laid its eggs beneath the skin of everyone he had ever met and then wriggled out of sight, slithering behind the valance perhaps, or writhing beneath the sideboard in the corner of the victim's eye. From that vantage point it could peer out at the somnolent antics of those in its thrall, gloating as they fell moment after moment into the tracks and channels it had incised across the remainder of their lives. Only he could pick up those awful trails of dead choices and reveal them to the client. In fact only he could grab hold of the thing itself and resist its shudders as he wrung from it the patterns that were pertinent to a particular case. He could manipulate the worm without mercy or concern, toss it back onto the carpet then take the money. His only precaution was to wash his hands after any direct contact.

Jack looked up at June. He looked her in the eye. June awaited her money's worth.

'All these people are strangers. All people are.'

'That's the point, Jack.'

'The point is they are all the same. You will never see them again. Their memories are short. For them it's an evening, one of many. Their hearts aren't in it, only their stomachs. There's plenty of room, you can do a lot more than you think, because it doesn't etch – they'll forget it. One by one, they'll come forward, to look at your body, and you will look at their plates and glasses. I can hear what you're saying, and I can see you as you speak.'

'What am I saying?'

'It's not *what* you say, June. I could tell you, but no one is listening.'

'That's awful.'

'June, it gives you room to move.'

Jack had given her his strongest suit but she hadn't picked it up. She was frowning nervously, biting her lower lip, on the verge of shaking her head. 'But Pierre . . . what will they think of him?'

Jack suddenly reached across the desk and grasped her arm. She jumped. He dug his fingers through the poodle until he felt the bones beneath. 'Do you want to go?'

June's eyes opened wide. She pulled her arm away and sat back in her chair. 'N-no,' she stammered.

'Then listen to what I'm telling you! You paid me!'

'It's not . . . I mean, it's only a supper. It can't be . . .'

Jack banged on the desk with his fist. 'It's always a supper, June! That's all it will ever be! Barbecue, race-track, scandal, death, letters and match results! Suppers, all! Dining strictly à la carte! I mean strictly!'

'I don't understand.'

'You don't need to. It's how I make a living. Now,' he gripped the edge of the desk and leaned towards her, 'I'm going to give you what's rightfully yours. Okay?' There was no point in waiting for her response, he was too far in to abort a reading. 'You are moving round the lounge, bright as a button. They are smiling. At no point do they step outside your terms. When things get thin, they get thin with it, there will be

8

no abrupt novelties. At eight-forty-five or thereabouts the anticipation of food has virtually eliminated the possibility of the unrecognisable. At nine-thirty, during the main course . . .'

'Fish.' Now she wanted to help. It wasn't needed.

'There will be talk of television programmes which you initiate. Some thirty minutes will pass in which admiration is expressed for a variety of men who either act or joke. Dessert . . .'

'Syllabub.'

'. . . will precipitate a discussion on France. You have been there.'

'How did you know?'

'June – I'm watching you mention that very fact!'

'I'm sorry. It is, it's just . . . unusual . . .'

'At this point the transition to family talk will take place. When certain popular rivers are introduced, you pick up a reference to "we" from a man of thirty-two, or thirty-three.'

'Tom Austin. But what do I do with it?'

'It's the gateway to party peace. Pick it up, run with it.'

June's face lit up, she pointed her finger excitedly at her dapper advisor. 'Oh, did you take your family?'

Jack clapped his hands, it never failed to please him. He helped her along, 'Yes, we have two children, actually.'

'Oh, yes! Yes! How old are they?'

'Mark is five and Jessie is three. Or whatever.'

'Oh, how nice!'

'Yes, we motored down in a day.'

'Heavens – were the kids okay?'

Jack sprang from his chair and moved swiftly towards June, this time grasping her urgently by the upper arms.

'Stop there!'

'Oh!'

She giggled and looked at him with mock astonishment.

'Eleven p.m. They all go home. You slip into your dressing-gown unscathed.

'It's easy, isn't it?' she said.

'If you know how.'

'No, of course. I couldn't possibly have done it without your help. It's an extraordinary gift.'

'Tell your friends.'

'I certainly won't tell any of the guests! Heavens!'

9

'I must give you a card.'

He reached over the desk top and opened the top drawer, peeling a white slice from the perfect block. June opened her bag, swaying back from the hips in order to peer for her purse. She took the card.

'Jack Gavin Limited Seer Limited. Why two?'

'Companies Act. Have to.'

'Thank you very much, Jack.'

She pulled off a dark glove. She'd had it on the whole time and was now taking it off in order to leave. She shook his hand, squeezed it between the gloved and ungloved then left.

The seer slumped onto the swivel chair and stretched from fingertips through wrists along arms held up behind his head, his head pulled down so jaw touched sternum, bow tie pressing the adam's apple for a moment, he noticed the stitchwork of his shirt, the flatness of belly above his belt partly enhanced by elongation of the trunk, a pleasant tingling of the thighs, calves and so on, a little shudder at the point of extreme rack then quickly folding up he gazed at the blank notepad on the green metal desk top, and, with head in hands, he sighed.

He sighed. He splayed four fingers flat against his brow and pressed against his skull. This removes the lines of care, but can only be regarded as a temporary measure. He started to tap his feet lightly on the ex-exhibition carpet, no marks on it. And no more appointments till after lunch. What to do? What to do? The exhilaration drained away so fast these days, barely do they leave the office than the slump is on.

He got up, locked the office and stumped down the stairs into the chill linoleum passageway, scuffing leaflets for holiday film, reliable cabs and fur coat opportunities with his shoes. A blaze of light was framed by the open door. Why don't the Chinks keep it shut? What is this, Hong Kong? Checking the profile provided by the polished steel panel of the drycleaner's facia, he walked without overcoat through the bright bite of the spring morning.

After a few paces he started grumbling to himself. He opened the grumbling with an alienated thought, 'I am a Martian,' as he passed the news stand and noticed a headline 'I am a Fucking Titan Ainsley'. Turning the corner into the road that led to the precinct, he looked at the shopping crowds and thought, 'What are these people thinking?' followed shortly after by 'Who cares?' This he qualified with, 'But the less they think, the more I work.' As shiny products winked and glinted in the corner of his eye he was moved to a commonplace but urgently felt assertion: 'I need money. I deserve money.' Irritated at the banality of his mental process he said 'Fuck it!' out loud. He knew that he had unique skills – in their way quite modern, but not without their antecedents in the ancient history of prophecy. In other times he would, without a doubt, have had a little *status*. Now all he had was a scraggy office and rent to pay. The world passed his door but seldom saw his plaque.

'Am I transparent?' he wondered. 'Could as well be.' But all this was gloomy stuff for Jack – not typical. It was all the products that did it. In Russia there was only one type of everything, much better. After all business wasn't so bad – he was getting the cases, he was paying the rent, just. He was buttering the crust, just. But does the butterer see it like the baker? Is it good enough merely to be the greatest thing *since* sliced bread?

On the other side of town Silvia Desperanza and her Saluki Zelka stepped from the train and were greeted by Mr Edwin Curfew of the Blue Wave Merchandising Corporation.

'Miss Desperanza, I trust your journey through our green countryside was more than pleasant and is this your little doggy?'

'Are you Mr Corfu? Yes, it is.'

'Please pardon me, I am. Public Relations and your liaison for this grand occasion. And not so little, really, is he?'

'She is a she, Mr Corfu. Zelka: saluta Signor Corfu!'

Zelka yapped at Mr Curfew who rubbed his hands and appeared to be very delighted.

'What marvellous obedience! We have a car awaiting us, Miss Desperanza.'

'What of my begs?' enquired the starlet.

'Porter!' cried Mr Curfew. A sullen boy seized the set of white leather valises.

In the pleasant depths of the limousine Edwin outlined the day's schedule for the mistress of the Italian Managing Director.

'Presently we shall find ourselves at Blue Wave Central Office where coffee Italian-style with small biscuits will be available after which spacious changing rooms will be found adjacent for your convenience. At eleven-thirty we shall drive to Hanley Cross Piazza, a journey of some twenty minutes. The manager of Blue Wave Hanley Cross and certain of his understaff will greet us discreetly at the rear, whereafter tea and any amount of light sandwiches will be at your disposal. I shall conduct you to the ceremonial site at twenty-eight minutes past twelve, so that your arrival will be tantalisingly late, by about one minute. Mr Harold will introduce you to the public through the address system, and invite you to say a few words. In keeping with our imago nautico we have come up with something a little out of the ordinary for the critical moment of door opening. Something which I am sure would meet with the approval of Blue Wave Roma.'

Miss Desperanza, in her mind's eye, immediately saw Roberto removing his teeth in the bathroom, followed by Roberto tugging at his nostril hairs with a pair of tweezers. She thrust aside these thoughts of Rome and as the limousine slowed to a crawl in the traffic she stroked the noble pate of Zelka and gazed at the unfolding bustle of passersby through the smoked windows, her tongue tipping the corner of her mouth for errant lipstick. Beside a news stand posters for the morning paper proclaimed 'NEW ANIMALS PICTURES'. A dark woman in a striking astrakhan coat was buying a copy of the paper. Silvia interrupted Mr Curfew, 'Please, what is new animals?'

'I beg your pardon?'

'New animals.'

'Oh, it's a pet shop, I expect. You can buy animals there. Dogs and cats and things. New.'

She nodded and then, in a reflex action, her expression brightened. 'I'm so sorry. You was saying?'

'Yes. We have mounted upon the large double glass inswinging entrance doors an outpointing prow-like device as if of a boat whose sides bear marine imagery and the legend SS *Hanley Cross*.'

'Ess ess?'

'Steam ship. You see,' Edwin arranged his hands illustratively, 'the doors are here, and the mockly nautical prow is before them, like this.'

'Ah, isn't it clever!'

'We like it,' Edwin beamed. 'What do you say to champagne?'

'Champagna. After?'

'Ah, no. Well, yes, of course, if you'd like. But to strike with a bottle of champagne the doors. The prow, that is. And then open the doors automatically, as if launched by you. What do you think?'

The dog blinked under the continued pating, turned its head to follow some figures in the street then yawned widely. Silvia noticed.

12

'Zelka. She is tired. The bottle will break easily?'

'Hold it in both hands and whack it down. Mr Harold will point to the correct spot. No trouble.'

'It's a marvellous idea.'

'Yes. It's jokey but also dramatic, don't you think?'

'Yes. Tell me what is your opinion, Mr Corfu. I thought I would make a little joke also in my little speech. Is that good?'

'Oh, Miss Desperanza, what could be better? The English love humour! It would be a great transcontinental expression.'

'I'm glad that you think so. In Italia we say that to make a joke is God's way of saying sorry.'

Edwin frowned. 'What for? Sorry for what?'

'That life is so bloody awful.' She laughed at his sudden perplexity and patted his knee with her grey gloved hand.

'Oh.'

She took off her dark glasses and looked straight at Edwin. 'Don't you think it is?'

Edwin glanced towards the chauffeur, furtively checking the man's eyes in the driving mirror. He seemed to be singing softly but Edwin could not hear him through the glass partition. His eyes were properly employed in scanning the road ahead. Miss Desperanza's eyes, Edwin discovered, were still resting on his own face, which was currently seeking a state of composure, but in the interim presenting a variety of small expressions suggestive of discomfiture.

'Er . . . I'm not sure.'

'You don't know?'

'Well, at times, of course, it can be quite . . . awful. But, well, not *all* the time. At least, that's what I find.' Edwin suddenly thought of Naples. 'That's only me, though. For some people I'm sure, yes, it is awful, life. Yes.'

He hoped he had said enough. Miss Desperanza held her gaze directly on him for the briefest of moments, then abruptly changed the subject. 'My costume has some nautical aspect. This is very fortunate, isn't it?'

Edwin had composed himself. 'A sailor suit!'

'No, no, it is with a skirt. You will see.'

'I very much look forward to it. It'll look marvellous in the papers.'

The limousine slid into the forecourt of Central Office. The chauffeur stopped singing and reached for his cap.

13

*   *   *

'Around the corner is the new supermarket,' Jack said to himself, for despite his irritation with all the shining products, new shopping opportunities did have a certain charm.

The scaffolding had been cleared away from the front revealing the plate-glass façade shadowed beneath a swooping canopy of concrete. At either side of the main entrance a single tower of scaffolding had been retained, decked with bunting striped after the manner of the company logo. He puzzled over the purpose of the painted hardboard projections arranged in front of the doors. Swathes of bunting descended from the towers and were attached to the hardboard, giving a garish focus to the outermost point of the construction, as if it were the front end of a boat or something. Ah. Indeed. And there are the workers on the towers, waiting to applaud the launch.

As Jack watches, some important people appear and stand in front of microphones. Photographers surge and flash. The woman has a sort of sailor suit and a big dog. The workers cheer, with perhaps a dash of irony. The crowd presses forward. A man in a suit taps a microphone. The dog looks up and barks. One of the workers whistles at the dog. The dog barks more. A titter runs through the crowd. Jack feels on good ground. He looks around. Another man speaks into the microphone. Introduces himself, the shop, the sailor woman. Ribaldry and applause from the towers. The sailor woman steps forward smiling. Starts to speak. Foreign. She is pleased to be here in our country. Hands across the sea. Chain of products links us to Rome. Will not keep us long though. Perhaps a little story to illustrate. Jack shifts in his shoes. Bell ringing. Workers crowd to inner edges of platforms on towers. Looking down front of sailor outfit if possible. An Englishman, an Irishman and an Italian meet the Pope on a beach. Jack straightens up. Englishmen are punching Irishmen playfully on the platforms. Pope asks Englishman 'What's your favourite food?' Irishmen jab Englishmen in ribs. Men in suits grin at towers and crowds. These Italians and their broad ways. Englishman says. Irishmen in tower hoot. Englishmen boo. Jack pushes his way through the crowd. Pope says. Then asks Irishman, 'What's your.' Sailor girl glancing upwards to towerlings. Winks. Roar of approval. Irishman says. Saucy suggestion from Irishmen to sailor. Citizens frown at pushing Jack. He nearly at front. 'Uh huh' says the Pope and turns to Italian. Workers thrust Marco to rail of right-hand tower.

14

Marco waves and greets sailor in Italian. Crowd ripple of laughter. Press tilt up and fire off. Jack shouts 'Don't! Don't say it!' Nearbystanders brief sideways glance at him. Speaker a momentary flicker off guard but it's only a heckler. She says 'and Pope says "What's"' 'No, no! Listen! Signorina, don't say!' Jack shouts again. 'Who's he think is?' enquiry behind Jack. Managers scan crowd. Italian says. Cheers from tower. Marco arms in the air waving. Takes a bow. She pauses for maximum. Jack's chance. He moves forward. 'Don't finish it! You don't know what will happen!' Marco notices. 'Hey, mister, cut it out!' Managers nod at security man. Sailor girl truncates pause to preempt English heckler madman. So Pope says, 'Well, that's nice because I haven't got any rubber gloves!' Howls of glee above. Clapping groundlings. Clapping managers. She radiates. Little curtsy. Mock apologetic grimace. Takes up magnum of champagne and, 'So I am very pleased to.' Still bellowing up there. Dancing about. Marco singing Italian football anthem. Jack shouting now but can't be heard. Security man avuncular hand. Jack removes it. Fanfare through public address. She has her back to crowd. Manager shows her point of impact. Stands back. Groaning noise somewhere. Jack gesticulating. Groaning noise. Is it the public address? The legs of right-hand tower. They're walking. Is that clever or what? Slowly splaying out. Steel plates groan across forecourt slabs. Teeth-on-edge sort of sound. Platforms descending. Is this a coordinated display? Plank falls from tower. Buzz from crowd. Legs stop dragging. Planks spill three four five showering down. The tower is waddling. The steel screams along its lengths and bows in. Folding like a blow to the stomach. Bunting taut from left to right. Bottle above her head. She brings it down sharply towards the little lever. Marco screams. The tower comes right down towards the crowd. They scream and back away. Bunting taut and snapping in the air. The bottle speeds to the point of proper impact. The men cry out and spill brokenly from the mangled frame onto the cold stone. She misses the little lever and strikes the dog square upon its pate. The dog's legs splay in four directions as it very much loses consciousness.

Jack glides through the pandemonium enveloped in his certainty. Faces of horror and eyes aghast drag past, cries and moans sound quite faint as if snatched by the wind. The Italian woman stands frozen in anguish, a magnum of champagne still in her hand. Jack takes hold of her elbow and speaks urgently, 'Have you just made a film?'

15

She blinks, and without turning her head, replies, 'Si. In Roma Che . . .?'

He squeezes the elbow and raises his voice over the growing hubbub. 'We're going to be on television.' And to himself, 'Or I am anyway.'

Something stirs in the woman's fractured mind. She stares at Jack, but her expression is still fixed, a mask of disbelief. Her jaw moves emptily once or twice, then she whispers, 'It's awful.'

'It was a very good joke,' Jack replies, then bends to the nearest body in order to render essential service. Carefully rolling it onto its back, he rests his ear on the chest and hears a faint but steady heartbeat. 'Still alive.' The Italian woman stifles a sob and distractedly places the magnum on the pavement. Jack pulls the mouth open and is momentarily displeased by the rank miasma of raw fish that, released by his prising, wafts into his nostrils. He closes his mouth over the cavity, pinches the nostrils together, an exhales powerfully into the windpipe of the recumbent.

He has never actually carried out this particular procedure before but can recall an oily wall chart pinned up in the entrance to a dark backstreet garage that he had patronised in the days of car ownership. Listlessly kicking his heels while Winston tinkered beneath the Viva's bonnet, Jack had been drawn by the, let's face it, erotic possibilities suggested by the line drawings and the instructions thereunder. Furthermore, the notion that one might actually inflate someone else's lung by blowing down it was undeniably intriguing. Apparently care had to be taken with infants lest they were pumped to bursting point. But this was no baby, and Jack is gratified to see the ribs moving upward and outward as a result of his first puff. He releases the nostrils and closes the mouth. The air hisses from the nose, playing against his cheek. It is marginally less malodorous than that which first came from the mouth, to which he must now reapply his parted lips.

Such is Jack's concentration that he is oblivious to the frantic hithering and thithering about him. Moments pass. He inflates and lets issue. He cannot recall any instructions towards the bottom of the chart that may have indicated when the process was to be arrested. Possibly this part had been oiled over, or even worn away by passing cars. He decides to carry on until something else happens. Presumably the subject, if not dead, will indicate the return of vitality in some unambiguous way. The idea, he supposes, is that you give the subject a series of practical hints that are reminiscent of the old way of working. Certain irresistible

16

mechanisms of lung and nerves then compel the subject to resume autonomous control. Either that or the subject is shamed into self-sufficiency by the invasive indignity of having to borrow second-hand air.

But now there is stirring. A shudder animates the subject, followed by a coughing sigh. The miracle of consciousness radiates the torso and the muscles of the body shift erratically. A curious whine emerges from the mouth. Jack looks up proudly at the Italian woman, who has descended from her metaphysical state and now studies the proceedings with interest.

'E miracoloso!' she breathes. Jack shrugs modestly. The subject suddenly rolls over and gets up, unaided. Stands before them, shakily, looks at them.

'Oh, Zelka, Zelka!' cries the subject's mistress, falling to her knees to embrace the restored dog. The Saluki whines and licks her face. She removes her dark glasses so that it can moisten her eyes and brow freely.

Jack, finding himself in a devotional posture with woman and dog, a detail from a nativity, stands up, shakily. His knees ache and pins and needles are jostling through the arteries of his calves.

'Seems to be all right, doesn't he?' he observes, modestly.

'It's a she, signor.'

'Ah. Should have looked. Too busy at the sharp end.'

Zelka's lady stands up and takes Jack's hand in both of hers.

'Things come from out of the sky of life on top of you and it is so terrible at the unexpected moment, isn't it? Today I never thought of this to occur to me and I am shocked out of myself. It's so bloody strange. But you have materialised and taken my dearest thing back from almost dead. I am completely grateful.'

She squeezes Jack's hand and shakes her head in tearful disbelief. Jack replies, 'Dogs are strong.'

'Please tell me what is your name?'

'Jack Gavin, ma'am.'

'I am Silvia Desperanza. This is Zelka.'

'Yes. How do you do?' glancing politely at the dog as well. The animal padded forward and closed its mouth round Jack's wrist. Jack jumped. He could feel the warm tongue and quite a lot of teeth.

'See? She gives you a little sock.'

'Good.' He eased his wrist out, and wiped it discreetly on his trouser leg.

17

'You were shouting at me, weren't you, Mister Garveen?'

'I knew what was going to happen.'

'You knew? What do you mean?'

Jack looks round. They are both having to raise their voices over the considerable din of the extraction and rescue operations being conducted at a frantic pace towards the side of the pointed prow of hardboard.

'I saw it coming. That joke always does it. It has truly international appeal yet succeeds in being equally insulting to all parties mentioned. A gutbuster, basically. Saw it in Brussels two or three years ago. A man haemorrhaged. Same everywhere. Inevitable.'

Silvia is watching Jack closely, moving her eyes from his eyes to his mouth and back again. 'But, Mister Garveen . . .'

'Jack. Say Jack.'

'Jeck. You were so sure. It was just a little joke. How did you really know? You tried so hard.'

Jack sighs, as if reluctant. 'I foretell.'

'Pardon me?'

'I see things.'

'I'm sorry, where?'

He felt inside his jacket and removed a card. 'This is my business. See?'

Silvia frowns at the card. 'So what is "seer" mean?'

'It means I can tell the future, what's going to happen. I can see into it. It's how I make my living.'

'Oh, that is marvellous! How far can you see? A long way?'

'No. That's what the limited means. The first one.'

'What is the second one?'

'It's to do with the law. It means I'm not responsible.'

A press of gentlemen at Jack's elbow. He turns to confront three figures in suits, some of whom had been officials of the launching party.

'Miss Desperanza, my God, forgive me.'

'But Mister Corfu, why forgive? Surely it is I.'

The first man wrings his hands and seems on the verge of tears.

'Miss Desperanza. During our philosophical discussion earlier today. I feel that my evaluation of life is sadly inadequate. I am a man in his middle thirties yet somehow a child in many ways.'

Silvia extends a soothing hand to Edwin Curfew's forearm. 'What could you have done? What difference was it make? No, Mister Corfu,

18

I told the joke that made the tower to fall. I am lax.' She turns to Jack, 'Lax, you can say lax?'

Jack says 'Yes.'

'Heavens!' Edwin is indignant. He will reapportion the blame. 'A little joke, senorina! Must we eliminate levity in case of fire? Of course not! Who could have known?'

'Ah!' cries Silvia, 'Ah!' lark-like. 'This man here! Mister Jeck Garveen! He saw everything in head!'

'Ahead,' helps Jack.

Edwin evaluates Jack now, not having bothered previously. He recognises a man who takes suits lightly, clearly shopping at a brasher outlet than himself. Also the fellow who had been bellowing earlier.

'Mr Gavin. Edwin Curfew. You did marvels with Miss Desperanza's dog.'

'But he knew, Mister Corfu. He saw it coming the terrible happening.'

'Well, that is extraordinary.' Edwin attempts an abort by ushering forward the two gentlemen beside him. 'Mr Gavin, I should introduce Mr Harold, the manager of Blue Wave Hanley Cross, and Mr Nellist, the assistant manager.'

Mr Harold wishes to make amends. 'Very pleased, Mr Gavin. Will you forgive me for setting the dogs on you, so to speak, I refer to our security. I thought I could see trouble.'

'Yes! It is Mister Garveen who can see it, Mister Harold. That is why he was shouting, isn't it?'

Jack offers a modest explanation. 'When Miss Desperanza started her joke I knew something was going to happen. I had to stop her getting to the punch line.'

Mr Nellist is interested. 'How did you know, Mr Gavin? I'm most interested.'

'I can see ahead, Mr Nellist. Anything from a few seconds to the end of a day. Usually it's of no importance, but now and again . . .'

Mr Harold and Mr Curfew are concealing a degree of scepticism beneath their attentiveness, but Mr Nellist appears to be an amateur of the foreseen, and presses its intermediary further.

'So is there any nausea or faintness, Mr Gavin, at the point of looking forward?'

Here we go, Jack thinks. I blame paperbacks for this. 'No. Never felt better in my life.'

19

Mr Harold tires of his assistant's hobby. 'And of course we are all dog lovers. Had you not known the mouth-to-mouth, I hate to think.'

'Very much yes,' enthused Edwin, 'An act of enormous heroism, Mr Gavin,' adding, 'in an exceptional location.'

'Mister Garveen has a very big love for all of the things in the world of phenomena, I am convince.'

Mr Harold, Mr Nellist and Mr Curfew glanced at Miss Desperanza. Jack stared at them all and said 'Shucks.'

Edwin voiced the hidden agenda of corporate relief, 'The death of a dog on such a day, bereaving for Miss Desperanza, whose gracious presence honours us nationally, not just Hanley Cross, would not, frankly, have been so exceptionally useful for the local launch, the smaller papers as ever eager to cast the first stone in areas of widespread unemployment and we about to take on twenty-six young girls.'

Even as he speaks, no sooner has he, than, stepping over the moaning men by now receiving professional medical assistance, bypassing the firemen dismantling what is left of the tower, skirting the shirt-sleeved police officers talking to anyone who has an account or an opinion, weaving through youngsters sad to have missed what had clearly been a sensational and instructive occasion, come two young women. One of the young women has a tape recorder and is from the television and the other has a notebook and is from the local paper, the *Hanley Cross Advertiser*. The women know each other well, and the first woman, Judy Lane, from the television, has been telephoned by Chris South from the paper, who had been bored up to the point where the tower fell over. Chris excuses herself to the group by the prow and addresses her first question to Miss Desperanza.

'Miss Desperanza, how does the British sense of humour compare with the one in your native Italy?'

Mr Curfew intervenes. 'Not all of those so tragically on the ground are British subjects, and furthermore Blue Wave has taken pains to ensure that the twenty-six young girls and eleven male boy packers are from a wide range of backgrounds although all strictly local with valid permits if not of UK passport and certainly paid above the minimum wage.'

Miss Desperanza laughs modestly. 'Of course laughter is the heart trying to find its way into the mouth, we say. In all countries there is death and birth, alcohol and the love of animals. A joke is international. And also it is important the way you tell it.'

Judy Lane pushes forward her mike with its little foam sock. 'I understand', to Jack, 'that you attempted to abort the launch and also brought the dog round?'

'Well, there are two questions there,' said Jack, before whose inner eye lunch as a metaphor was looming. Even lunch as lunch, he thought, would be quite acceptable. 'Yes, it was I on both. But the dog first – I did it because I knew how to. And —'

Judy seems to sense a seedling heroism that only requires the cloche of her editorial attention. 'Is there a special place for dogs in you?'

Jack thought quickly. The answer was easily no, but what of lunch? Dogs – life's too short. All that bending to pat. However. 'The breed interested me. I know they are rare, although I'm not an expert on canine typology.'

Judy interrupts. 'Say it again with dog types.'

'Sorry. I'm not an expert on dog types. It seems to me that we must at all costs preserve the widest range of creatures and plants on our plan-et for their possible use in medicine, agriculture and the atmosphere.'

Judy can obviously see good stuff, although possibly a little principled for early evening. 'Would you have done the same for a mongrel?'

Dog class, Jack thought. He was perfectly indifferent to all dogs, regardless of face, colour or creed. 'The sight of any unconscious animal has always disturbed me.'

Chris, who has been shorthanding into her spiralbound, now makes her bid for the *Advertiser*. 'Mr Gavin, you were seen making a commo-tion during the early part of the launch. Why was this?'

The imminent pleasures of becoming expert again have a relaxing effect on Jack. He starts to gesture as he speaks.

'I was walking past the supermarket when I saw the crowd. I started to feel strange. I knew that something was going to happen. Could be good, could be bad. Probably bad. When Miss Desperanza started tell-ing the joke, that was it. All laid out before me. But nobody listened.'

Judy senses even more promising leads. 'How do you mean you knew something was going to happen?'

This is ideal, Jack decides. 'I've always had this ability. I am a professional seer. Usually I work from my own office, but of course, when you have these powers, they don't keep to office hours.'

'Can you say more about what it's like when you have a premonition?'

'It's not a premonition. A premonition is a feeling about a probability. I might start off with a premonition and then move into an actual reading of future time.'

'What is that?' asks Chris. Behind the two reporters, in order of absorption, are the faces of Miss Desperanza, Mr Nellist, Mr Harold and Mr Curfew. All eyes are on the interviewee.

'It's something that everybody could do, but only a few bother. It's to do with the way time works.' This is his standard response when pressed on matters of technique. It invariably appeals to the romantic impulse that resides in every interrogator, and it relieves him of the need to affront his audience with the truth of the matter.

'Doesn't time work the same for everybody?'

'Definitely not. But this is deep water. I'm very glad I was able to help out. Next time I'll shout louder.'

'Do you know what's going to happen next?'

'Yes, I'm going to have a drink.'

Judy turns off the tape recorder. 'Thanks, Mr Gavin. That was very interesting. You're going to be a local hero.'

'When?'

'Six o'clock news. Might even go national.'

'I should have given my phone number.'

'Oh, it'll help your business all right.' said Judy.

'You'll be in the papers too. Lunchtime tomorrow,' said Chris. 'In fact, I'd like to take a photograph if that's okay.'

Edwin sprang forward. 'That's marvellous, Chris. In front of the prow, perhaps?'

'The what?'

'This,' Edwin indicated the unscathed projection with a flourish. 'Like a bit of a boat. Blue Wave and so on.'

'Why not?'

'Perhaps,' he breezes, 'Miss Desperanza might stay next to Mr Gavin, and Mr Harold on her other side.'

Chris hesitates. 'You want her in the middle?'

'She's famous.'

'But Mr Gavin is the angle. The angle goes in the middle.'

'Then you've got two men next to each other,' protested Edwin, 'Lopsided.'

Mr Nellist has a thought. 'I could go on the other side.'

'No.' Mr Harold intervenes.

'Why not?' asks Mr Nellist.

'You're my assistant, Nellist. Not a public figure.'

Jack has it. 'The dog.'

Edwin 'Of course!'

'The dog between me and Miss Desperanza. Then you've got Mr Harold, me, dog, her.'

'Her on the edge?' Edwin disappointed.

'The dog,' calculated Chris, 'means we have to go to long shot. Otherwise only its head shows.'

Miss Desperanza, excluded for a while now, is grateful to the young woman reporter. 'Si, and her body is good isn't it?'

'She could stand on a box.' Edwin's bright idea.

'Nellist!' Mr Harold.

'What?' Mr Nellist, sulking.

'Get a box for that dog.'

'Where from?'

'How do I know?'

'Inside the shop, no?' The practical side of Miss Desperanza.

Mr Nellist is agitated. 'We can't get it open. We'd have to break the prow with the bottle.'

'Be good for the photo.' Jack brightly.

'Wrong angle,' reminds Chris, 'confuses the story.'

Mr Nellist runs off and talks to an ambulance man. He points to the first-aid chest beside the unconscious figure of Marco, now comfortable on a stretcher with red blanket.

Then, Zelka on the box, some discussion about who should touch whom, Jack's arm around Silvia, Silvia's arm in Jack's, both of these require leaning over the top of the dog, so both with hand on dog's neck. Getting dog to look at camera without bounding from box, its vitality now fully restored. Question of whether to smile. Edwin is meticulous, he points out that Silvia is happy because her dog is returned from possible coma, Jack is pleased but not radiant because he has given a service not received one, Mr Harold is president over these events, relieved at their successful resolution, not that there had ever been any question that things would get out of hand, and indeed when a rogue element had momentarily intervened it had been answered with an immediate and calmly executed response. The dog, ideally, to look grateful and, to a small degree, wan. All concerned agree that the last requirement is probably optimistic, and really, if she just looked at the camera that would be more than adequate. Although were she to gaze up at Jack, tongue out . . .

As it is when Chris calls 'Okay everybody, hold it!' everybody reverts to habits acquired by the seaside years ago and just smiles attractively. On two of the three subsequent prints, Mr Harold and the dog were found to have their eyes closed.

Mr Harold asks Jack if he would care to take lunch with himself, Mr Curfew and Miss Desperanza. Jack knows there will be smoked salmon, peppered herring and ham accompanied by a Waldorf salad and the gradual petering out of conversation, and accepts. Judy Lane, as the party departs, draws him aside. 'Mr Gavin, do you really know what's going to happen next?'

Jack chooses to interpret her in the particular. 'At this moment? No. I don't have a clue.'

But he did. He very much did. Jack knew he was going to be on the television. Not just the news.

Elizabeth Preeny took Jack's arm and drew him across the maroon cord carpet. 'Why don't you come and meet them?'

'I've never met an explorer.'

'They're *both* explorers, Mr Gavin.'

They stopped at the bar. Elizabeth made the introductions.

Mr Blighton, the explorer, had fair hair brushed straight across from a side parting, which, together with the fact that he smiled all the time, suggested to Jack the scrubbed awkwardness of an eager schoolboy. A pair of shorts would not have been so out of place after all. He seemed to smile because of the situation rather than *at* anyone, but this was no reason to assume that he was not a nice person. He certainly pressed Jack's hand quite hard, perhaps to assert a sense of corporeality prior to being taken to a studio in which he would be converted into dots and blown around the country. Or perhaps he pressed everything hard, because everything was already very real and always had been. As Jack squeezed back he felt a different kind of pressure – the man was somehow asking him to reply in kind to the manic and persistent grin. Since he could not deduce precisely what was being asked of him, he resisted, offering a pleasant but largely neutral expression instead.

The woman, Deany, his wife, had a nice tan. White lines radiated from the outside corners of her eyes, through to the golden brown of her temples. 'You should try sunglasses,' Jack suggested, as her husband moved away to talk with Elizabeth.

She frowned. 'How's that?'

'The little lines,' he indicated on his own face. 'Been screwing your face up in the sun.'

'Oh yeah!' she laughed. 'We wear hats. We like to see the colours.'

'I've got those ones where they get darker when it gets brighter,' he volunteered. 'Beach wear, really.'

'I haven't been to the beach in years. When we get home I just lie in the garden. Life is kind of dull after the jungle.'

'Life,' said Jack, 'is dull before the jungle, believe me. I live in it. Life, I mean.'

'But you're in the city. Isn't that exciting?'

'No.'

'Oh.' She paused. 'Oh well.'

'You get used to it.'

'Then what do you do? Go somewhere else?'

'There's nowhere after the city.'

'Boy! Nowhere after the jungle, nowhere after the city! What are we gonna do?' Deany seemed to reflect on this bleak, modern prospect for a sip of wine or two, but then returned to Jack. 'So maybe you should go to the jungle and me to the city?'

'No.'

'That's not right, is it? Gee.' She flashed him a curious, wild smile and the pupils of her eyes began to oscillate at an unlikely rate. Jack was caught off guard and had an image of himself reeling back under a disarming blaze. To his surprise he countered by laughing out loud and pressing her arm. She said 'Well, doesn't seem to be such a big problem right now. We're all laughing it up here, and you're looking real pleased with everything.'

'I'm about to go on the television.'

'You like that?'

'I need the coverage.'

'I guess so. I find it kind of a strain. We do a lot of it. Have you seen our stuff? We have our own programme.'

'Who?'

'With my husband. You just shook his hand.' She chastised him with a glance, he nodded nonchalantly. 'We have adventures and sell them. How about that?'

'Hot stuff.'

'We're naturalists really. Zoologists. But that doesn't sound so exciting. Two married scientists go to a hot place?'

'But you have adventures.'

'I tell you, we mostly just work hard. Maybe Guy has them more than me. Things kind of happen to him.'

Guy and Deany were asleep in the tent. Guy was breathing regularly but Deany was muttering and shifting. Outside animals and birds made strange and irregular noises. A certain amount of moonlight found its way through the tall trees and fell onto the tent, a fraction of it illuminating the faces of the sleeping couple. They were not wearing clothes, and their thin cotton sheets had slid to the ground. They had two camp-beds, each clearing the earth by a few inches.

Deany sat up and screamed very loudly, in terror.

'There's a man there!' she cried, pointing at the flaps of the tent. And then she screamed again. Guy woke up immediately and threw himself at her. He encircled her with his arms and pushed her onto her back. Whilst doing this he had glanced at the flaps. There had not been a man there.

Guy said 'It's okay, it's okay, it's okay,' over and over to Deany, pressing his face against her ear. Deany was rigid in his arms. Then she thrashed as if Guy were preventing her from getting away. Guy put his weight on her chest and said, with greater urgency, 'It's okay, Deany, it's okay.'

Deany opened her eyes and looked at Guy, quite wildly. 'There was a man there. Standing at the bottom of the bed.'

Guy said 'There's nobody there, Deany, nobody at all.' He stroked her hair and kissed her. Deany groaned then rolled over with her back to Guy. Soon she was breathing rhythmically.

Guy stared at the roof of the tent. Deany's piercing scream had ruffled him – for a moment he had been prepared to lunge at the man who might have entered the tent. He had been charged up with fear and anger, and now the fear had gone away but the anger was still there. Also he was annoyed that he had been afraid. He felt it was Deany's fault and he wanted to be angry with her but he also saw that it was not her fault really. He wished that it was. At least she could have woken up when she shouted out – it was wrong of her to go on sleeping while behaving as though she were awake, as though there really was something going on.

Eventually he fell asleep, on his back. Later on in the night there was a scratching noise at the flaps of the tent. Something was digging at the earth or pulling at the cloth. The noise went on and on, and the flaps, which were zipped together, moved as if something were bulking against them. A dark shape thrust into the tent. The shape drew itself past the cloth and stood at the foot of Guy's bed. It hesitated, sniffed the ground near Guy's shoes and socks then, moving along beside the bed, sniffed at Guy's naked body. For a moment a red and blue glint was framed in perfectly round sockets as the moonlight caught its eyes. The eyes of a creature. When it drew level with Guy's hip it paused again, placed its front paws on the rim of the camp-bed and leaned over to sniff Guy's dick. Prodding with its nose, the creature snuffled stertorously and extended a fairly long tongue with which it licked the dick. A faint rasping sound could be heard, for the creature had a scaly tongue.

Guy stirred in his sleep. He moved his right hand down to scratch his groin, and the hand landed on the back of the creature's neck. Suddenly two or three things happened very fast. The creature froze for an instant, and during this instant a nervous message was transmitted from Guy's hand to his brain, that part which never slept. Identifying an uncategorisable object, the vigilant subsystem roused the sleeper. As Guy's hand closed round the rough, leathery skin, the creature unfroze and scrabbled energetically in an escape attempt. Part of this scrabbling was located on Guy's thigh, and the friction violently awakened him. The pale beam of moonlight was sufficient for Guy to confirm that he was clutching a creature, which he threw away. Perhaps his horror at its scaly qualities caused him to be careless in this throw, for the creature struck the wall of the tent above Deany's bed, and from there fell onto her naked stomach, on its back.

The impact of this fall, connected as it was to Guy's shout of horror, was sufficient to rouse Deany instantly. She screamed and threw herself to one side, landing between the two camp-beds. Guy was now standing beside his own bed, bowed beneath the sloping roof of the tent. In his hands he held his dick, which he was examining thoroughly and continuously, with great anxiety. He yelled at Deany, although she was very close to him.

'My prick! It was trying to eat my prick!'

Deany was angry, on her back. 'Just get rid of it, Guy, get it out!'

27

Guy was not listening. He was convinced that parts of his dick had been eaten, and knowing something of the curious unreliability of the nervous system in times of stress or injury, he persisted in his inspection.

'Jesus God, it was right on it, biting it! Jesus!'

Deany got up and jumped over Guy's bed. She glanced at Guy's dick. 'There's nothing wrong with it, Guy, for Christ's sake. There'd be blood!'

Guy did not look up. He was examining the area of his perineum for evidence of nibbling or gnawing.

'I can't believe it, I can't believe it!' Guy was completely absorbed and kept repeating a number of phrases that expressed his disbelief, interspersing them with further blasphemies.

Deany, seeing the futility of attempting to pacify her husband, lunged for the further camp-bed and tipped it towards the tent wall. The creature, which had been scurrying up and down the shallow trench of the bed's canvas, was trapped between the bed and the fabric of the wall. It attacked this fabric with its powerful curved claws and to the sound of ripping nylon effected an impressive getaway, crashing through the foliage surrounding the tent, until the sounds of its retreat blended with the occasional noises produced by many other shy, hungry, inquisitive or simply restless beasts that scurried or slunk through the jungle night.

Guy had completed his inspection and was satisfied that his dick was intact. He had regained his composure. 'It's okay. Nothing wrong with it.'

Deany was irritated and spoke sarcastically to Guy. 'Guy, it was a pangolin – well known for not eating dicks.'

Guy was not convinced, 'It could have been a mistake, Deany. Animals aren't perfect, you know.'

'Mister Guy, boss, you all right?' An anxious voice from outside the tent, the figure of George silhouetted on the flaps.

'No trouble, George. An animal tried to eat Mister Guy's penis so he threw it at me. The animal, I mean.'

Guy glared at Deany. A short silence from outside. 'Mister Guy's okay, yeah?'

'I'm fine, George. Mrs Deany let it go through the wall. It's gone away.'

'What kind of animal, boss?'

'An anteater, George, I think. Scaly. Probably a young one.'

28

'I'll go to sleep again, boss.'

'Sure.'

Deany lay on Guy's bed. 'You sleep on mine, Guy.'

'You want me next to the hole.'

'Yes. Better keep your ass on the outside, you don't want that thing to tell its friends there's some spare dick hanging out the wall.'

'Why don't you sleep there, darling? They'll think it's already been eaten.'

Guy grinned nervously in the dark. He was not amused, he always grinned at times like this. Not that there were many times exactly like this.

'I'm asleep, Guy. I can't hear you.'

Guy climbed over his wife's bed, and after a moment's reflection, lay on the canvas stomach downwards.

For a few minutes he thought about the fact that he was doubly vulnerable, given that an animal could easily stick its head through the rent in the tent and bite his buttock. But gradually his blood stopped racing and his thoughts turned to his traps and what might at that very moment be crawling into them. Despite the fact that they had so far delivered absolutely nothing of interest, there was always the possibility that one morning each one would contain a different exotic beast. He couldn't help seeing them as Christmas gifts that, like a child, he would unwrap with deliberate slowness the next day. Gradually the gaily coloured packages grew faint and insubstantial and he slid into a flat, heavy sleep.

The next morning Guy was cutting his way through the dripping foliage in the worthless territory. The mists of dawn were drifting through the tree tops, sealing the jungle in an unlikely reticence before sunup loosened the cacophony that currently languished under logs or sat tucked away in trees. His traps had been set beside a small pool that lay half-concealed beneath a fallen mahogany and the parasols of a great red-leaved plant.

Guy's assistant George had been spreading the word around that the white man and woman were interested in seeing all the animals and plants in the locality, especially anything that the locals themselves considered rare or unusual. Initially a succession of timid, giggling children had ventured into the camp, clutching beautiful butterflies by their frail, removable legs, or frantic, glittering beetles wrapped in funnels of leaf. Guy and Deany had always made a great show of interest in these rather familiar items, in order to interrogate

29

their collectors more closely about specimens whose allure might not be so obvious.

Talking to some of the adults on one occasion, Deany had caught references to an animal that lived in the territory of another tribe and was hardly ever seen locally. She had pressed the men for more detail, but they had roared with laughter and shaken their heads. One of the men had made some curious squealing noises, evidently in imitation of the beast, and Deany's informants had been reduced to hysterics for several minutes. Taking pity on her bemused expression, one of the younger men had explained that this was a truly worthless beast that nobody respected. Indeed, it was so worthless that it could only find a place to live over with the other tribe, who were well-known worthless people. In his tribe, when the children were naughty, the mothers would tell them to watch out in case they turned into this worthless animal.

Deany's attempts to get a description of the beast had been frustrated by the men's conviction that the subject was simply beyond the pale of serious discourse. Guy had suggested that it would do no harm to visit the nearby territory, talk with the worthless tribe, and maybe set up some traps.

He had been hacking his way to the pool every morning for four days now, only to eject dull voles and common peccaries from the camouflaged cages on each occasion. He was beginning to wonder if the beast were not some merely mythical creation of his native advisors, for their insistence on its contemptible qualities was complemented by an infuriating vagueness when it came to questions of habitat, diet and so forth. Even the people of the worthless tribe regarded the beast as lower than the worm on their scale of animal worth and Guy could not tell if their unhelpfulness was a form of pity for his idiocy in enquiring after a beast whose awfulness was so abundantly obvious, or if he had been guilty of demanding proof of things that only existed in some sort of dream-time.

He suddenly stopped, his raised machete arm freezing in its downward arc. Against the tenuous stillness of the end of the night he could hear a distant but extraordinary sound. It neither rose nor fell, but simply carried on and on, without rhythm or cycle. It was constant, insistent, piercing like a power drill. It was very like the cry of a man or woman in intense pain.

Guy knew most of the noises that came out of the jungle, so he waited for the sound to change into something else, something that he would recognise. There was no change. He slashed through the shaggy fronds before him, and moved on through the undergrowth. As he approached his destination, joining up with the trail he had cut out a couple of days ago, the sound, the cry, grew louder. He started to feel uneasy. Not the growing volume, not the possibility of finding a man in distress, but simply the terrible, agonising tone of it. Worse than the howl of a desolate baby, it seemed to home in on some obscure organ of his innermost guts and there galvanise, with its relentless vibration, feelings of sickness and confusion that extended through the pit of his stomach and all the way up to the back of his head and shoulders.

Guy arrived at the pool. He clambered over the tree trunk and pulled back a large leaf that concealed the traps. It was quite clear now. Whatever was making the noise could not be human, for the scream was coming directly from one of the traps. Was it just another damn peccary, injured, angry, frightened? He knew it wasn't. The sound was really quite intolerable, it was making his belly tremble and its contents churn disagreeably.

On the roof of each trap was a hinged flap which could be lifted for inspection of the inmate. A wire grille lay beneath the flap, preventing any dangerous expressions of irritation or revenge. Guy knew that he had to take a look, and was surprised that his reluctance was so considerable that it bordered on a completely inappropriate sleepiness. Drawing his lips back so that his teeth were bared in an ambiguous manner, he gingerly leaned over the miniature nissen hut structure and flipped the flap with his forefinger. Amplified round the tinny curves of the trap, and now suddenly aired, the terrible screechings tore at Guy's eardrums to such an extent that he almost backed away without looking through the exposed grille. He was suddenly visited by a memory of standing on a mountainside in Wales in the middle of the night, listening to sheep. There are only a few animals in the known world, he reflected, that sound like they are being imitated by people. The sheep, in particular, sounds exactly like a man imitating a sheep. At night it is, therefore, easy to imagine that the fields are full of men on their hands and knees, baaing. He looked through the grille and saw a hairy little man's back, but of course it wasn't. The reason this noisy animal upsets me, he thought, is that it has a human voice, the more so the closer you get. Its hair was coarse and streaked grey, black and silver. Only a few square inches were visible, and these shook and trembled in a continual epilepsy of agitation.

31

'For God's sake!' Guy shouted all of a sudden. What was wrong with the bloody thing? He couldn't see any signs of injury. There was no odour of blood. He slammed the flap down. Not a peccary. In fact not immediately recognisable. How to get a better look? He'd take it back to base and release it into a pen. The prospect of carrying the cacophony made him tense. He sighed, for he knew he was being irrational. Good Lord, he thought, what's happening to me? It's not going to bite you!

Snapping the carrying handles into position, he realised that one of the other traps was occupied. He had been so perturbed by the clamour from the first trap that the din from the third one had gone unnoticed. It was the same sort of din, but it was blending in with the row from the first creature. This only dawned on him when he bent down and suddenly got stereo.

'Two!' he exclaimed. Both screaming. Both injured? Couldn't be. He picked up the third trap without even bothering to inspect it. One in either hand now, the creatures weighing about the same. A pair, maybe.

Guy's ears began to ring as he trudged laboriously back along the trail. The noise was fantastic. First he thought about stuck pigs and then he tried to imagine what a man would have to be suffering from to make him make that kind of noise. Some sort of torture or something. Awful. He shuddered. He wasn't used to things getting at him like this; people got hurt from time to time, of course, but you bandaged them up or got a medic. But when they cried out or screamed he was really at a bit of a loss. You could pat them perhaps, or say things, but you couldn't guarantee that this would ever stop them. It was tricky.

He wondered why he was dealing with it so timidly. Surely he wasn't scared to open up the traps and just let the bloody things go. They're probably something completely bloody ordinary and there he was, humping them back to base so he could find out in safety. Honestly!

In the rain forest, the man with a howling tin contraption in each hand had a sulky, defeated expression on his face. Sometimes he lifted the traps above his head, sometimes he held one before the other. A grumpy holidaymaker changing trains without a baggage trolley.

When he got back to base camp Guy released the creatures into a chicken-wire compound for the purposes of proper scrutiny. Deany, George, the boys, all gathered round in disbelief, some blocking their ears. Two long-haired, badger-like, smalldog-weight, raccoon-faced, black paw and clased, tailless animals. Lying, rolling, staggering, stopping,

32

dashing, writhing. Rubbing their heads with forepaws frantically. Lashing at their own stomachs with back legs. And the din. All the while the hellish awful din.

George shook his head. 'What's the matter with 'em, boss?'

'I think they're just scared, George.'

'How long they been doing this, Guy?' Deany asked.

'They were doing it when I found them. Haven't stopped since.'

'Not like scared, is it?' said George.

Deany folded her arms across her chest. 'They're not trying to get away, are they? They don't even seem to notice us.'

'Mrs Deany right. I think they just sick.'

Guy wasn't that sure. 'What kind of sick, George? They're not injured, their coats look good. They have plenty of energy.'

'They sound like they hurt. All the time.'

'You have any idea what they are, Guy?'

'I'm not sure. The fur could be a local variation. Otherwise they resemble *mustelidae* – same family as the ratel. Or maybe not at all. I need to get a closer look, really.'

'Are they a pair, do you think?'

'God knows. The markings are similar, but that doesn't tell us much. Have to get them on their backs.'

'When?'

'Soon?'

Deany laughed. 'You busy right now?'

Guy looked at her reproachfully. 'There's no hurry, Deany. Maybe we should let them settle. Get used to us.'

'You don't want to touch them, do you?'

'I don't mind,' he lied.

'Well, I do. They're weird.'

'I'll have to find some gloves. George, put some water in there. See if you can find something they like to eat.'

'Okay, boss.'

'Hey Guy – the girl is Eke, the boy is Ike. Yeah?'

Deany wandered across the clearing, into the trees. She stood in the leaf rot, trying to find the smell. She had been there for so many months now, and had forgotten to be mindful every day of the smell of the place. Not the flowers or the soil, but the whole, hot mix of air and river and greenstuff and butterflies, all of it. Tomorrow they would leave it behind and within a couple of days she would be inhaling the fumes of fuel oil and melting tarmac. She found a friendly tree with a deeply ridged bark and nuzzled her face into the moss that padded its way round the trunk. She stretched out her arms and embraced the tree, gripping a ridge of scaly wood with either hand then pulling hard so that she was as close as possible. With a crack the bark in her right hand tore away and her face skidded off the moss into the wood. Her nose was scratched. She cursed, and sighed.

Guy, now wearing heavy canvas gloves, took a deep breath and grabbed a creature. It struggled perfunctorily and then appeared to give up. But it wasn't so much giving up as simply attending to more urgent needs, whatever on earth these might have been. The pawing, rubbing, aimless lashing out, rolling, stretching and contracting were repeated in endless random cycles as he watched. As he turned it onto its back for sexing, it behaved as though nothing were happening, as if it were floating in space, where its limbs might work away unhindered by floors, the ground, or notions of the right way up.

So this was Eke anyway. Guy picked up the other one, and found that it was Ike. Excellent. He started to prode the creature's belly and inspect its skin, beneath the fur. He ran his hands over its whole body, felt along its spine, worked all its limb joints. There were no growths, scars, sores or fractures of any kind. Not on Ike. Not on Eke. He took Eke by the scruff of her neck, Ike by the scruff of his, and dumped one on top of the other. Nothing happened. Eke rolled off. Ike just lay on his back. They didn't scrabble at each other, no attempt to nip or cuff. Eke moved over to the water bowl and stuck her snout in it. As she lapped rapidly, her endless scream was mercifully modulated to a gurgling whine. Then without a pause or cause, she lurched forwards into the bowl itself and rubbed her ears furiously with her black forepaw claws. Her snout was immersed in the water, and she began to choke and cough. Her body shuddered and convulsed as she expelled the water from her nasal passages, but she made no effort to use her front legs to climb out. The compulsion to rub her ears appeared to override the most elementary considerations of survival. Guy walked across to lift her free. As he slipped his hands under her chest she suddenly raised her head and sunk her teeth into the first finger of his left hand, piercing the fabric of the glove. Guy swore and jerked his hand away, at which point Eke bit the rim of the water bowl several times, dashed off to a corner of the pen, snorted briefly, then continued to scream and writhe in the usual appalling manner, as if her near-drowning had never happened, let alone the incidental wounding of her captor. Guy retired from the pen and took his gloves off. He examined his finger and found two neat perforations just above the second joint. He hung the gloves in a tree and sucked on the broken skin. There was no pain to speak of, so he secured the wire gate of the pen and walked back to the lab tent. Now that he had brought himself to handle the creatures, he realised that their constant shrieking had become slightly more manageable. It was simply far too loud, but he was less moved by the agony and despair that it so forcibly suggested.

Later on in the day Guy and Deany went down to George's house to say goodbye to Ruth, George's wife. When they had first visited Lugambwa Guy and Deany had been introduced to a number of students by the Commission's south-east man. The deal was they could have as many as they liked provided they taught them the ropes. The government would pay for their supplies, and Guy and Deany would file a report to the university. Many of the students had never been out of the town before and the government wanted them to get some field skills, ostensibly to back up the agronomics programme, more likely to appease the UN while they tore down the jungle and dug for minerals. George was the oldest of the students, and had a wife and kid, living in a village downriver, near the base camp. Guy wanted him to be a kind of quartermaster, and started to brief him on the equipment as soon as the camp was set up. George invited Guy and Deany to meet his wife Ruth, who came up to town. Deany showed them photos of her kid sister Nancy and Nancy's kids little Al and Beth. Ruth was impressed by the baby buggy in the picture, so when Guy and Deany came back for the second visit they took Ruth a buggy for her baby boy Steve. That afternoon he and Deany and George and Ruth and Steve were eating sandwiches by the big red river near George and Ruth's village place and a crocodile hurtled out of the water straight at Steve and the buggy, its big jaws at right angles. It crushed down on the buggy handles, closed the jaws over the whole package and swallowed it. It must have had some trouble swallowing because it stayed right there on the bank, so Guy, who suddenly felt terribly calm, said to George, 'Get a gun', but George didn't own a gun. Guy picked up the breadknife from the table and just launched down the short steep bank into the mud. First he tried to stab the crocodile straight down into the brain but its skin and skull were just too thick so he began to slash at its throat which made it go for him with its mouth open again, you could see the blue plastic handles of

35

the buggy right at the back of its throat. Guy shouted, 'Chair, George!' and George threw a kitchen chair down and Guy let the crocodile bite on it, which kept the front end busy while Guy tried to open the neck right across, sawing away at the loose flesh there. He managed to sever some veins or arteries and soon there was a lot of blood pumping out onto the mud, and the crocodile started to convulse and thrash its tail alarmingly. Guy had to keep jumping out of the way but he would throw himself back each time and soon the crocodile started to lose strength and Guy got on top of it and wrapped his arms round one of its front legs and managed to turn it over in the mud. The crocodile lay twitching feebly, sporadically flailing its tail. It blinked distractedly, but rather less than the occasion seemed to demand. Still wielding the bread knife, Guy stuck its tip into the open neck wound and started to saw down along the length of the reptile's belly. Soon he had slit the beast down to the site of the cloaca and, working feverishly against time, for over a minute had passed since the mishap, he made two transverse incisions at the median abdominal point of the trunk, and plunged his hands into the cruciform wound thus created. Pushing back the flaps with his elbows, he exposed, to cries of astonishment from the bank, the mucous-coated form of Steve, strapped to the chassis of his buggy by two pale grey webbing belts of reinforced nylon. On seeing Guy, the little boy held out his arms and clapped his hands. Guy said, 'Hello, Steve' and carefully cut through the webbing. He lifted the boy out of his seat and carried him up the bank to Ruth, who cried and hugged her son. George embraced Guy and Deany put her arms round Ruth. Guy said to George, 'What about the buggy, George?' so the two men went back to the dead body of the reptile and cut its head off, which enabled them to expose the full length of both buggy handles. It was then a simple matter to ease the buggy straight out of the body cavity. Although manufactured from a robust, light aluminium tubing, the frame had been considerably deformed and it seemed that the axles alone had resisted the massive peristaltic pressure of the reptile's gulp, thus arresting what would certainly have been a fatal constriction of the infant boy.

Guy and George rinsed the buggy in the red river and managed to bend the frame back into shape so that the vehicle became serviceable again. Guy climbed back up the muddy bank to the hut, where Ruth had prepared him a drink. She and George wanted to thank him a lot more but he would not let them. Deany told him that he had done a remarkable thing. Guy became quite annoyed and told her not to talk about it. He

36

seemed to want everybody to forget the whole incident. He sat at a table, covered in mud and blood, and instantly fell asleep. Deany tried to wake him so that he could have a wash but it was too late.

As he moved round the pavilion, pushing past the other men, he enjoyed the whites, the green stippled rubber fingers and most of all the wood. There were, of course, many bats to be seen, and a certain number of spare wickets, but particularly pleasant was the fact that most of the men had brought some other wooden thing along as well. As he moved among them, very aware of how well he knew them, in a general way, he admired the different colours of the woods. There were dark, liverish close-grains, grey porous pieces lined with black veins, and soft succulent blondes nicely blemished with ochre knots. All the woods were oiled and their aroma filled the crowded changing room with a warm, heady charge that seemed to bind Guy to the other men in eager, easy friendship.

So crowded was the room, changing all the time as it was, that the woods cracked against each other often, and a range of sonorous notes was produced, some comically flat, with a rapid decay, others marvellously suggestive of the great springiness of their source.

As he squeezed past a circle of laughing players, each of whom had the time to shoot him an amiable grin, Guy tested the handle of his own bat, wagging it experimentally in order to accustom his palm to the weight. He tightened his fingers around the rubber covering and increased the pressure. He could feel the wooden laths crushing the rubber strips inside that acted to absorb the impacts. The bat whipped to and fro as its handle became more and more flexible and serpentine.

Through the window Guy saw a dazzle of greenness suffused with white light. The crowd near the double doors was particularly dense, and the woods rang out constantly as the men turned this way and that. One very close friend, a very pleasant man indeed, took hold of Guy's hand with his great white gloves. They were lined on the palm and fingers with a rough red rubber that tugged at the hair on Guy's wrist. He said, 'You're magnificent. Show them the business.'

Guy walked out into the light, pulling his cap down against the glare. It was so warm and the greenness had a comforting bounce. In fact the more he progressed, the more bouncy the ground became, and soon he was actually bounding along, humming and singing with pleasure.

He was glad of the cap, for to have looked directly ahead would have been quite uncomfortable. As it was, he could not make out the horizon at all, and the distant clusters of spectators at either side were blurred and distorted by the rising wave of heat. With any luck he would open with the sun behind him and not be handicapped in the business of protecting the wicket. The green still kept its bounce as he left the pavilion behind him, and he wondered whether this would slow him up when the business of runmaking began.

He could not see the wicket yet so he deliberately trod down hard on the green in order to bounce up high enough for a better view. At the peak of the jump he craned his head forward and started to overbalance. On the way down he remedied this by tucking his legs under and landing on his knees. The bulky white pads absorbed the impact well, and he was sprung back onto his feet in a trice. He had still not spotted the wicket though.

The green was starting to show patches of rubbed-out yellow. This meant that the wicket was close at hand, for it was the business of delivery and fielding that had this effect on the colouring. A figure loomed out of the great light, a man in all whites, with green on his toe caps. An outfielder. His shirtsleeves were rolled up, and he was wearing two pullovers in the great heat, the way they do. Guy greeted the man, a member of the opposing team. He could hardly see his face, just a dark head powerfully haloed. He seemed to have quite long hair, though, long and wavy.

'Bloody hot,' Guy said.

'Bloody hot,' the man replied. 'I'm dead,' he added.

'I know what you mean. Haha.' The man did not reply. 'This way to the wicket?' Guy asked.

'Into the sun,' the man said.

'Hard to see,' said Guy.

'Never look myself,' the man remarked.

Guy bounced on. The green had practically gone, replaced by the half-alive yellow and the new scrubby, dead brown. The bounce was becoming weaker, too. It was hard to get more than a low hop or skip. Guy started to jolt. He would tread down and stay there. Over to his right he made out two more figures in white. One of them was a woman. She had dark skin and long black hair down her back. Lovely hair.

He called out, 'Seen the wicket?'

The woman called back, 'Brownish!'

38

'Yes,' Guy agreed. 'I'm sure it is.' He paused.

'You're doing okay.' This was the man speaking. Something glinted on his shirt sleeve; he seemed to be wearing cufflinks. You rarely found that sort of pride in appearance these days. Especially on the field.

Guy called out again. 'Where is it? Exactly?'

'Slopes!' the man retorted.

'Oh dear, yes. It's a business, isn't it?' he cried.

The man and woman cried back together, 'Of course it is.'

On and on went Guy. His spikes could not even scratch the brickhard surface. Judging by the deployment of distant figures in white, he had come near to the centre of the pitch, but there was no crease to be seen, only the blazing cloud of sunlight that now seemed to pour in from all sides. He stopped walking and took stock. Obviously he would have to hunt for the wicket, in order to get started on the batting business. Trying to be mindful of the approximate centre that he had determined, Guy started to quarter the brown. He found himself sweeping the ground before him with bat extended, for the light was dazzling enough to cut visibility down to a few inches. From time to time he yelled out 'Where's the wicket?' but the distant fielders did not answer. 'It might as well be dark,' he thought.

At that point a man in a maroon-coloured cap stepped out of the light and into Guy's range. The peak of the cap cast a shadow over the top half of his face, but as far as Guy could make out, his eyes were very deep set, surmounted by thick, bushy eyebrows that continually arched, dropped and knitted together.

'I am the captain,' the man announced, in a gravelly voice.

'Good,' said Guy, 'I'm having trouble finding the wicket. So bloody bright.'

The captain said, 'Generally the field feels you should find your own way, but I want to get on so I'm going to give you a hint.'

'Hint away,' urged Guy.

The captain nodded his head in a direction over Guy's left shoulder. 'Best I can do,' he said, and walked off.

Guy turned and strode in the new direction. 'I'll be getting down to the business of playing now,' he thought.

With some relief he saw a shape shimmering in the distance, a shape that was not a figure or a fielder. He felt a little tired because it had been quite a time since he had left the pavilion, and he had not expected quite such a palaver before getting down to the actual business. Also he had been growing more and more anxious, and he did not enjoy that.

As he trudged on, the shimmering dissolved and at last he could see the bees' nest quite clearly. 'Now I can get down to it!' he said to himself. The nest looked slightly larger than they usually were, but that might have been because it was mounted on a waist-high table. It was familiar enough in shape – a lovely golden buff cone wrapped around with bulging rings that ran up to the tip. Guy could make out the little entrance arch at the base of the nest. This was the entrance that he must defend.

Guy's relief at finding the actual bee's nest expressed itself in tears of pleasure. It was, after all, a beautiful warm day, and now he could get down to what he knew best.

He smiled tearfully into the sunlight and patted the parched earth with the tip of his bat. It struck him that there were no bees to be seen or heard. Either they were all inside their nest or all out doing their customary chores. He made one or two practice strokes with the bat and prepared for whatever the opposition might dish up. He was in the business and at peace with the wicket.

'Ready!' he shouted.

After a pause came the shout 'No peace!' This was from somewhere in front of him, so it must have been the bowler. He pulled his cap down and screwed up his eyes. There was no sound of footsteps, so he presumed they had laid on a slow bowler, probably one who took a short run-up. He could hear a distant whine though, a high-pitched and insistent sort of noise. This grew louder and louder until Guy suddenly saw something flying towards him. It certainly wasn't coming in slowly – it was moving very fast indeed. Luckily he was more than accustomed to the high speed stuff and had sharpened his reflexes to the point where he would start to play the correct stroke within a moment of the delivery leaving the far crease.

The whining grew rapidly in volume, taking on an insistent angry tone. The bat blurred through the air and made contact. Instead of the full-bodied chock that should accompany an ordinary rebound, Guy heard a brief, sharp sound and felt a curious, vibrating impact on the face of the bat. Looking down he saw that a bee had impaled itself on the wood, and was fixed firmly up to the hilt of its sting, which in this particular case was located on its head rather than its tail. The insect appeared to be dead, or at least stunned, for it was utterly motionless.

Then Guy realised that it was very much alive, and that its mobility had been imparted to the bat itself, which was trembling right along its length, right into the rubber springs of the handle and thence onto the palms of his hand, despite the padding of the glove.

Guy felt bad about the bee. It had been trying to get in the door of the nest, probably to make honey or something, and he had batted it. He peered guiltily into the sunlight, hoping that the fielders hadn't spotted him. He was surprised to detect, at the outermost limit of his hearing, faint cries of applause from the boundary area. At least some people thought he had done the right thing. He prepared himself for the next delivery, which would be a red ball, with any luck. His bat was still vibrating, but it was not an unpleasant sensation, and even made him relax a little.

He heard a familiar sound from the far end of the pitch, a high whine, growing louder and louder as a small, shiny, winged thing sped towards him. For a split second he wondered if he should restrain his reflexes in the interests of the nest community, but there was something urgent about the flight of the incoming object that impelled him to take up the bat and do his best.

This time, when he looked down, Guy saw the impaled projectile was not a bee, but a dart. The dart had stripes along its body like a bee, and its flights were transparent, like a bee's wings. It was clearly made of metal though, and its point, embedded in the wood almost to the hilt, was of shiny steel.

The bat was vibrating now, and Guy's hands were starting to tingle of their own accord. Shouts of approval rose and fell from the boundary, and Guy realised that what he was doing was good. He was making it safe for the bees' nest. The opposition was trying to get through his cover, but he was in good shape and could take anything they'd care to serve up. Ideally he would pluck out the dart and bee from the bat, but it seemed unwise to take his eyes off the pitch in front of him, although he could still see very little. It occurred to him that he was like a bat, working blind, going by the sounds of things, unerringly.

The darts came thick and fast, like hail, in a swarm, a whining cloud. Guy defended the nest furiously, getting his bat in the way of each and every one. He would not allow a single delivery through. The bat was studded with the striped metal barrels. Their vibrations spread right up Guy's arms and through his whole body. What little he had been able to see was now hopelessly blurred, and he found he was

41

virtually disregarding the evidence of his eyes in favour of a keen use of his hearing. The opposition was certainly piling it on, that was certain. Given that the darts always stuck firmly in his bat, Guy wondered quite why the other team had bothered to put in a field at all. One bowler would have been enough.

Nevertheless the opposition people were trying to wear him down, to divert him from the business that he had to look after. What was their objective? Would they destroy the bees' nest, or just steal the honey? If they came running in, he would not be able to do anything about it, for now he was completely controlled by the vibrations of the bat, and found himself wishing he could just throw it away, for his palms had begun to smart intolerably. The relentless shaking worked its way up to his jaw, and made his teeth chatter idiotically. He had an idea; if he could channel *all* the vibrations to his jaw, and thence out of his mouth, the rest of his body might calm down and enable him to keep vigilant.

Guy's jaw started to move up and down at a great rate, and the sound from his teeth was like castanets.

Deany asked him what the matter was. At first he did not hear her, so loud were the castanets. He held his hands above his head, like the Spaniards, and played them even more vigorously. He could hear yells of applause from all round the field. The opposition knew a good player when they heard one. Deany raised her voice.

'Guy, what's the matter?'

Guy heard this time, and turned to find her face quite close to his. His arms were half-folded above his head and he was rubbing his palms with his fingernails. He blinked at his wife.

'What are you doing with your hands?' she asked.

'Oh God, I was playing castanets.' He noticed George and Ruth hovering solicitously by the door and dropped his arms onto the table. Looking down he saw that the palms of his hands were bright red.

'Gee, Guy, look at them! You were really working there, weren't you?'

'Yes,' said Guy ruefully. And then he said 'Anyway,' because it all seemed beside the point.

In order to handle the John Holes people satisfactorily they must be pictured. Without a picture they will seem abstract, or essential, or an idea. But if we say 'Well, they are just a crowd of people inside Guy,' it

42

begs too many questions, such as 'Where do they sit? At a table?' And we say 'Why not?' and this compels you to say 'You want me to believe there's a *table* in there?' and so forth. But we have to start somewhere, otherwise the proposed picture isn't a picture at all, it doesn't figure, it can't develop. So we will say, insistently, 'This is the scene inside Guy: the Holes gang is there, they are sat around a table,' and you will understand we are also saying 'Yes, the table *is* there, it is part of the picture, as is chairs, floor, walls and landscape and cetera.' All these things can now be pictured.

So having agreed table, which is to say *space*, we can now agree time. You ask 'The John Holes gang are in this space now, where were they *before* this?' And we can immediately say: in the hot game under the bright light on the brown and green. We then get the question, 'Where do people like that go *after* they have put on a piece of action? Is it to the *table*?' Well, the answer is, in this instance, once the batter had taken the flamenco option, as a reward for his good beehiver, the fielding team had clumped back to the pav to post mort the sport.

'The *pav*? Is this inside Guy *too*, then?' you want to know. Well, yes. Sure. The pav, the field, the bees' nest, everything. That's what John Holes and his people do – they make scenery and provide action for the client. Okay, *client* suggests Guy asks for the service, which he doesn't (and this, by the way, is Holes's major headache, to coin a phrase) but they still can't help seeing him as the customer, for whom they are doing everything.

So *pav* is where people like that go. It's like *back to the warehouse*, until their services are required again. They shed their whites and rack 'em because next time round it may not be cricket, it could be absolutely anything, no exaggeration here. Essentially they are a flexible bunch.

Once back in the *warehouse*, they are no longer on frontline duty, which is why they head for the *table* – to ease up, chew over how the action went, what you'd expect, the post mort of the sport. So it's field to pav to table to what is next. Which is a question:

Exactly who is here, what are they like, and who is in charge? Clearly the *force*, the *captain*, if you like, is John Holes. He wouldn't mind a name like that. That sense of a face that it gives. That long, sallow face, faintly parchmenty, something of an old woman's in the folds, not that it hangs loose though. Drab skin, in a way. John Holes's eyebrows, thick hairs constantly moving, waving to and fro, crawling along the crescent, like gritty iron filings chasing the north pole beneath the paper. The eyebrows cragged over John Holes's deep sunken eyes, set so far back in, all you see is the flicker of a blue flame in a cave, underground gas far off in some grotto. From a distance just two dark smudges under the brows that tirelessly beetle.

And gaunt John Holes's mouth, stitched with little lines, as if no teeth, but in fact a kind of Red Indian lip because beneath are teeth, good ones. Large, and their yellow perfectly fine, you don't have to judge by pearly standards here.

So that's his face, John Holes. That's how it might be put. The figure in charge: *sheriff*, if that isn't going too far.

This is the problem that Holes always has: you spend the day making major decisions, setting things in motion, get trains of thought rumbling across the scrub, and half the time it all gets ignored. Half the time the client just fucks it up: he half hears it, misreads it, claims he thought of it in the first place, then fucks it up again. For example, you set up the bat and bee business and next thing you know the client is proclaiming Spanish music – makes a strong man weep, right?

So is it any wonder Holes is sat round the table with his team, which is Slopes and Roylana Brownish, 'Dead' Dick Cater, P.R. O'Bably, Michael Butler and Arch Andrew (the Aston 'Ish')? They're all bushed after the recent sport fixture, chairs are drawn up, liquor is in evidence. Despite the 'bees go to Spain' fuckup, the crowd is light hearted – they are used to modest returns on investment around here.

John Holes, despite those stern facial characteristics gone into, has a fine sense of humour, and knows how to handle these important guys when they're off duty. He'll make sure nobody does an unleash, but otherwise they'll josh away and he will rappety report right along with them, even when it gets childish, which it does, although for these types, those distinctions are kind of fuzzy, not to say inapposite. So.

We arrive at the table as Slopes Brownish, lately of the fielding side, leans in with his wicked grin. 'Fuckaduck,' he says. We can see his loud cufflinks again. Roylana, last encountered round about mid-off or on or thereabouts, the dark woman, cracks from ear to ear. Slopes really cuts her up. It's the way he says stuff. And the stuff he says. She reaches right across, under the table they're all round, and grasps Slopes firm by the equipment between his legs. Doesn't squeeze, just palms the bunch. 'A pig,' she goes. 'A pog. A pag.' (Off duty these people aren't so choosy with their talk – they throw it up and catch what comes down. It's a sport, like anything else.) 'Dead' Dick Cater, last seen in the region of

44

gully maybe, takes notice. He goes, 'A pag! Shitago hara!' which is how he signals his appreciation. Now, of course, P.R.O'Bably looks up – he thinks he heard his name called. Goes 'Hey!' with mock censorious tone. Then 'Wellwellwellwellwell!' Shaking his old head. Adjusting his collar round his neckscrawn. Drawing his gums back and he too has beautiful teeth for a figure that is kind of getting on some.

Roylana, in a beautiful gown, basically a deep blue with guava mango motif, cut low at her lovely gold back (people like this don't have moles by the way), she starts now to jiggle at Slopes's portion, and his brown and yellow check outfit is blurring with the pump action forthcoming from this all-life vital wife of his. She feeds him the line: 'Agalop! Agopago! Your eyes are blue!'

Slopes places both hands down on the table wood there and holds the crew with his eyebeam. 'Don't I know! I came here to get'em checked!' Now there is a general hilariousness let loose. (We've got to say: Look! Slopes and Roylana, the husband-wife comedy duo team, are serious, effective types, but this is the time when they are not being seen, when the client is not thinking about them. They played the field, darted off, the client was despatched with a case of the shudders, so it's human nature that they should cut loose now. Or nature nature anyway. [What did you think? They held spears or lightning bolts or snakes all day? Never smiled?]) It's too much for Dead, not to say just about all around (perhaps except for Michael Butler, who is a coolish type). They pound the table and guffaw hoohah hooraw.

Dead is crying out 'Oh piss! Oh piss!' and the table starts to float up with the general intensity, but John Holes flattens it with a knuckle, wishing to keep a frame round things at this time. Dead gets up and takes Slopes's head in one hand and Roylana's in the other. She's all beautiful and tanned and Slopes is a little on the pale side, and Dead with his long wavy hair and veins on the cheeks. And he pulls them all close in across over the table and the liquor gets almost spilt out but he just makes a bunch of three with the heads and they're all rubbing their noses together and licking each other's face.

Right around the table they are gagging on the low jinks of Roylana and the heavenly banter of Slopes. The mirth value is immense. What a relief it is to laugh, because boy the affairs of state certainly do mudsuck a man down, they dirty up a woman's dancing shoes and you forget that you're not like all the rest. That's the trouble with nightwork, you're down to it when all the others are on the bask and doze. (We say *nightwork* because Holes generally works nights – that's when the client is up for grabs. Naturally, any other opportunity is also taken.) It's antisocial. You can say that again.

Here is how funny everybody feels the line: O'Bably's head is ducked beneath the wood, you can see clear down the back of his shirt. He's lost too much wind at the 'get it' point and is heaving in against a bray that won't respect the lungs' 'need it' crisis. Normally, to coin a phrase, P.R. is the kind of type that likes to keep you guessing – he'd change hair colour while you left the room or sometimes as you turned to put the cup down, and when you're back he'd continue with his long, rickety talk, then clap his hands together and make an owl call from them without ever applying his mouth, as if the wise creature were nested against his unique fingerprints. But right now he is flushed out with this comic quip and cannot attend to his characteristics.

Michael Butler is barely moving, his hands clasped placidly in his lap. He turns his head a little and raises an eyebrow. There is the phantom of a smile. He is not unamused, he just isn't the immediately laughing type. People say, 'I was laughing inside', something which the cacklers question, thinking, 'Well why hold in? What's the point? Show me the fun in that.' But if some type says his guts are smiling at each other then maybe that is where the fun is and he is of that type that does that.

To look at Michael Butler you think, 'This fellow is executive', you see him with shiny cheekbones at the point where they meet the ear just beneath the sideboard, which is cut off short and tight and the shine is that unlikely freshness as if the razor is portable and has just been slid back into the attaché. People like this, their necks look bright and clean too, no turkeyarse pimpling, no notches where the handheld safety blade has nicked the apple or the eager little teeth of the battery shaver have reached out and dragged a snip of flesh itself, not just bristle, through the comb and sliced it, call that a close shave it's plastic surgery of the first kind.

Despite all this skin care and cetera Michael Butler's hair is a wisp on the long side, not in the Dead league, that's talking practically gypsy, but you know, an unexpected inch, inch half in the back, gives you the clue he is only straight ace at the front. (And how do these types get their shirts so clean? And if so, who cleans them? Safe money *they* don't. Probably have a laundry that delivers with tissue in a box and your own personal mark.)

46

'Michael,' the others say, 'he is smooth, we put him in front to handle the interfacing.' Here comes the client with his I know what's right, anything else is poetry and poppycock, and Michael Butler is wheeled out for the tackle. If the client thinks, 'Here comes the oil' or, 'Back off, body of privilege!' soon there is Mister Persuadio, telling him little jokes that he's always wanted to hear, giving him those looks that make him feel he knew everything all along, and the next thing he is on about building bridges, establishing channels, letting new blood through and it was Michael had done it!

Arch Andrew, the dangerous fucker, is being himself. Which is to say he is doing that shuddering silent laugh with the sudden jolt forward where he will cry out high-pitched for a moment then settle back and shake more, that strange look of great surprise on his face, and those fine, curved eyebrows, always twitching, arching up, like the 'Ish' was questioning all the time. Big sense of a 'private life' with Arch, in the way he'd smile when there was no particular concrete joke or amusement going round, or when there was he'd always be at a different degree from the crowd, like they would bang the table and he would look down at the floor, you wouldn't see his eyes, he would just have an agreeable expression, moving his jaw a little. That faint flush high on the cheek bone, a little feverish possibly, gives him that reminiscence of a demure maiden who is modestly entertained. There is no fever, of course, among types of this type, that is for the frail, the outsiders, the clients. But woe betide he or she who concludes 'The "Ish" has a girl quality' as if to say 'He will not do anything that I cannot tackle', because this is precisely where Arch has the piranha. He can come so fast out of that 'private world' it's shocking. Who would think such a philosophical type can be so physical? He is simply cruel. Or so it seems. The company around this table know about cruelty. They say, 'It has its place. We don't rule it out. Arch is a cutting bastard, he does the blade work for all of us. Say we are doing a cricket fixture then it's him for the merciless fast pitchwork.' It wasn't that he didn't take a run-up that the client couldn't hear him, oh no by heck and billybob no, it's that he has the panther softpad foot and silent speed of the wind.

Another joke that the group would like, that they would be the last to think of, is that Arch Andrew is 'psycho'. That would be rich, for them. There is a phrase in the popular papers: 'black humour'. That is for them an alien concept, but once they had looked at it from an outsider point of view they would find it richly comic and also quite

47

'sweet' and 'touching', saying, 'The Ish a fruitcake that's rich! That's gotta be "black humour" yeah?' So that's Arch Andrew, very amused, along with the rest of them.

John Holes is the last one, his laughter is like smoke. It's so deep and hoarse, you might think it was produced from a furnace. It comes like soft thunder, the way you would hear the hot air rounding the bends in a big rusty vent pipe on top of some chemical industrial plant. The pipes are leading from his breathing machinery, and although he sits still the steady rumble of this marvellous fiery sound makes the table shake imperceptibly, you'd have to put some fine print on it and try to read it then the blur would tell you this fact.

Holes lets the uproar flow and peak over into ebb. Then he sighs, 'Yeah.' The company firms up its lips and sighs too, moving in the chairs to get focused again. 'Time,' Holes says slowly, 'it has a premium.'

Dead is about to hooraw again, he sees a joke everywhere, but John Holes quiets him with a firm smile, then turns to sound out O'Bably. 'Is there a hurry? P.R.?'

O'Bably doesn't hesitate, never does. 'Well, John, we have the equipment, we could deliver a thousand shakes, you know that. We have the whole pack and we haven't even shuffled and cut yet. We could variate right here from this place without the fear we are in dereliction or getting tardy.'

Big applause for O'Bably. This is on account of the least appealing topic to the team is the whole business of schedules and hurry. Time stuff – tables, programmes, late, early, that stuff, well, as Dead says, 'It's getting a fart into a bottle, and is that useful?' Which brings in another of John Holes's eternal problems. What he's really saying to P.R. is, 'We can't wait much longer. We have a message to get through. So do we have a quorum? Are we go or are we disarrayed?' But they think he's bulldozing them and they act like kids. They fear he's out to shear their lovely little fleetfoot anklewings, make them sweat. As if that were possible. Holes knows he must listen to their yap for a while, and he knows eventually everybody will get in position and put on the correct hat and get down to business. To say he is philosophical about it is to verge on another joke, but the way he sees the whole problem is like this: 'First time around, in the boyhood, we missed our chances. We have since mounted any number of major sorties and many minor forays – but these have merely served to contain the enterprise at a tickover rate. Time has come for a concerted pincer campaign – an all-guns push. We will not be able to sit around this table much longer, else the enterprise will vaporise and we are beached forever, except we won't even have a beach.' That is to sum up in words unlikely to come from John Holes's own mouth but serialised and put down here tidily. His important position becomes increasingly clear though – the awesome responsibility, the stewardship of the overview.

He breaks the pause. 'I move this,' that deep hoarseness, almost silent, a kind of dark velvet coming out of him, barely reminds you of a noise. He puts it to them in his own way. 'Too many small shows – getting bogged. Beneath us to. Next stage is needed. More heft, more spread. Step it up. Send it down. Pronto.'

Arch Andrew is not a joiner but likes to point the way at times. Pleased that the action has been tabled at last, he is for some reason not looking to the left and right of him, but out of the charmed circle to a little beyond, where there might be, in the ordinary way of things, thin air. He is studying an empty point out there intently, and working his jaw as is, with him, frequent. Also a slight rubbing the fingertips with the thumb, you wonder is this to do with anything, is it fastidious, or is it absent-minded, to coin a phrase not used here?

Suddenly the 'Ish' is to his feet, reaches out, snap! brings the hands down to the chest. Looks inside the cup he's made. A high pitched note. He looks around and a quick piece of dexterity, and lo! by the wings, two slivers of bad glass, it's a bee! The 'Ish' has conjured a bee! It's buzzing a protest, the little legs are waving. The pointed part is thrashing to prick but there's no risk for the clever 'Ish', who puts the whole business right in his mouth and just crushes it there with his tongue pushed up against the roof.

The crowd loves this. 'Ish' has taken John's 'get up and go' piece and swang them right round, from sloth to gungho. Nobody asked him but he conjured it as if to say, 'We did fine on the cricket field but next stage is needed.'

As they pause to admire this unlevel, cruel fucker amongst them, Slopes starts a dance, the footwork one where he treads on his own legs then pulls the one underneath straight through the other one. It gives a marvellous smooth effect, very nighttime and his clothing emphasis is an additional enhancement.

Roylana naturally joins him. Starting the snake roll where her hair lifts straight above her head and takes on a steady ripple that by the time it's at the far end the hair is cracking loudly and she widens her eyes with each crack, it has a laughably dangerous quality, and her body though is quite still, just the arms held out to the sides, as if for balance.

'Dead' Dick Cater, surprising for a well-built, fast-living type, does this numero where the palms are on the floor and with just a tiny little hippety-hop move the feet are in the air and when they're up there you see they are quite dainty and his mane of unpolished-up curls shakes down at the floor.

P.R.O'Bably, the oldest type (for no one ever puts a date on John Holes), is making some of his typical imitation routines with the face, such as, and these are just typical, where he might be a pig, where he might be a horse, where he might be a duck. Each time it forms up and you're going, 'That's the following, from the barnyard!', then he drops it, and the flesh goes to sag, and you say, 'Is that a flash of a man there I just saw?' and next thing another one is pushed up and the pleasurable shock of recognition starts again.

Michael Butler, as you might imagine, is looking at his good manicure and stays sat, but he feels the swell like the rest, he is tired of the small-change scenarios and is hot to go. You look down to his feet and there is a remarkable blur from his black business shoes, they are tapping so fast they are almost still, seen through bad glass. And it's a complex rhythm where the blows are so close they are almost one continuous sound, but you bend forward a little and lo! there is the high point of a long solo with multiple interwoven elements! Above the table those beautiful hands are in a series of gestures, richly comic, implying for example: 'Thank you, that will do very nicely', 'I'm sure we can accommodate your request, madam', 'It is completely in hand.' And over all this Michael Butler just smiles calmly and inclines his head from side to side.

A little later, as a postfix, when the crowd have strolled away from the table, Michael Butler leans to John Holes, quietly speaks; 'John, tell me, what do you think – these *bites* on our man, what are we looking down on here?'

Holes rubs the waxy chin, chews on the quiz. 'Michael, these biters . . . they're something. I believe they are cut loose from nature somehow. I believe they are beyond us. They don't bounce *off* anything, they're just live action. Rogue condition. How did they get out? New on me.'

Michael pats his neat hair neater, surprised Holes is surprised, comes back 'So it's a factor.'

Holes nods, goes 'It is a bonanza strike, Michael. The iron is hot. Our man sweats, we move through the haze. A plus opportunity. Nothing we can't handle.'

By the following day the boys had crated Eke and Ike in double-walled containers whose cavities were packed with dry fibre to cut down the noise. They were still howling, but the crew were not perturbed, for the sound-proofing was fairly effective and reduced the noise to a background whine that escaped only from the ventilation grilles. Guy told the boys to be sure the grilles were not blocked when the crates were finally loaded.

Deany was sad to leave. The expedition had kept her feeling happy for several months and although she enjoyed the reports, the classifying of the specimens, the editing of the films, she did not want to see her house or her street, or her rooms or her things. She thought she would die inside because homes were where you stopped living, they were places for people with nothing to do. She knew that this was not true, but she felt so strongly that it was. As the days went by at home her happiness would slowly dissolve into satisfaction, and then the satisfaction would melt away until she was just doing things that occupied her, being busy enough never to think about nights under the stars, or dew trapped between the petals of impossibly large flowers.

Guy was supervising the stacking of the equipment at the riverside and also sorting out the photographic gear, a department that he liked to handle on his own. He wrapped the boxes of slides with cloth and stacked them into a crate. Thousands of slides, not one of them dispensable. Rolls and rolls of still film. Stacks of tins of movie film, taped together. The two movie cameras. The stills cameras. Other boxes, other bins, bags and hampers. The proof that they had been there at all.

Things were being heaved onto the boat. Deany was tightening all the ties on the canvas awning that stretched over the stern. Guy would have quite liked to organise the loading as well but knew that his intervention would not be appreciated. It seemed to him that a finite number of packages could be stored in a variety of ways, a few of which would take up far less volume than many easily but hastily constructed alternatives. The pleasures of finding the most compact arrangement seemed to have no attraction for the boys, who simply stacked things

51

as they came, not without due consideration of their fragility and accessibility, of course, but lacking any real ingenuity and leaving irritating airspaces between things.

Mindful of the diplomatic niceties, Guy wandered about the bank, pretending not to notice where the crates were being stacked. He watched his wife making fast the hitches on the stanchions and hoped that she was putting enough weight on the rope. You needed to hang a whole body-weight on each line otherwise the canvas worked loose in a day. Was she doing that? He grimaced and abruptly turned away from the boat, walking off towards the thicket for no reason at all other than to hide the face that Deany would instantly and accurately construe.

Unlike Deany, Guy did not view his return to the home country with any trepidation. As soon as he had arrived he would release a limited statement about Eke and Ike that should guarantee a decent level of interest until all the tests had been completed. The discovery of an entirely new animal would be received with enormous excitement by both the public and the professional community, especially since he was certain that the animals were unique, quite possibly a whole new genus. Even if the tests showed that Eke and Ike were only an unclassified species, the business of their unearthly vocalisation was enough to keep the zoologists busy for an age. What is more, the name of their discoverer would be reflected in their Latin name.

Last time Guy had returned from a project he had managed to structure his reports so that they indisputably established new territory at the same time as framing the parameters of essential further researches. It had been quite an effort but the sponsors had been persuaded to cough up. This time they would all be ringing him, without a doubt. The TV series would have at least three films in it, maybe more if the creatures turned up trumps in the labs. The magazine interest would be huge – the geographicals would go wild, and the popular science monthlies would fall over themselves for pictures and interviews. It was all very exciting. People stayed at home so much now, and Guy understood that the more they did so, the more he could travel. Somehow there seemed to be a lot more *time* available these days, in a strange sort of way, and people were realising what a great deal there is to know. They wanted him to go out there and bring back the data, then they would use all that time to digest it and beef up their world picture. Everybody knew more as a result and life became richer, and had greater meaning.

That side of the work couldn't really be faulted – from all over the country he had had letters from young people who wanted to become explorers. He always wrote back. I can only praise your initiative. The world is still exciting. Make sure you have the right equipment. A good knife. Rot-proof boots. You may not be in favour of immunising injections as a matter of personal freedom, but increasingly it is a legal requirement. Read up other people's stuff – no point in discovering something another fellow has already found out. Essential not get disillusioned. Modern world crowded with chimeras, hard to get grip on or teeth into just exactly what's there any more. Solution to tread where others have not yet. Outcome thereof a real tonic. I wish you all luck, yours etc. Can't do much more really. Important to encourage. His cousin Helen knew some teenagers in a provincial town. Apparently they got up quite late and breakfasted in a working man's café. In the afternoon they took drugs of some sort in a bedsitting room and watched television until the end of transmission. Then they listened to music until they got tired. Guy often thought about this. It helped him when he was feeling lazy about replying to letters.

Going down rivers on boats Deany loved to read. She would rig a hammock under the awning and sink into a thick book. Guy had never somehow quite focused on the exact titles but he could tell from the covers that they were works of fiction. Not thrillers or action stories, probably something else. He had a secret that he kept from Deany. Not a big thing, really, but something he's never wanted to broach. He wasn't ashamed or anything, he just knew it would be difficult to be precise. It seemed to him that reading novels or what have you was something you could do at home, whereas out here on a river or in a tent you had everything you wanted already, and there was nothing in between you and it. It wasn't that he couldn't see the point in reading, back home he had certain books that he liked to look at, but out here it made him feel strangely uneasy. He had tried reading in the tent once. 'Why are you frowning?' Deany had asked. He'd grunted dismissively. It was a bit like the time he had been to a reception with the television company and had been introduced to some people who designed the backgrounds that they put behind the people who introduced programmes. They hadn't known much about his films although a couple of them had worked on the studio sequences. He had got the impression that they were very busy people, but he hadn't been able to grasp what they did exactly. He had found himself smiling for a long time, to show that he was content to be standing with them. After a while it had occurred to him that perhaps it wasn't a smile anymore, but one of his special frowns. The trouble was their general comments and their jokes were not easy to understand, he got the feeling you had to be in the city a lot to get the most out of them, you had to read the papers at the weekend and so on, and he never had the time. Not that you can get the papers in the jungle, but when he was at home. But that was why he had been frowning in the tent. Same sort of thing. It might have been that particular book, of course.

As the boat chugged steadily towards the sea, Guy sat on his small canvas folding stool and gazed at the unvarying band of vegetation that was being dragged across his field of vision. At that distance it might as well have been the view from a train in greenest England. The ripples from the boat made their way across the oily water, throwing up brief flashes of fire before rolling under the dripping vines and mosses of the bank. A great grey bird with an orange beak stepped off the uppermost branch of a dead tree as if a lower step were within inches of its black, scaly feet. Its dirty wings cracked open like old sheets stretched between two washerwomen, and with a mournful crake it banked and dipped down out of sight. Guy glanced fretfully at the first finger of his left hand, which was beginning to throb slightly, undoubtedly as a result of being punctured by Eke's teeth. He thought about the possibility of infection and grinned distractedly at the trees without focusing, his right knee jigging up and down very fast. He was not aware of the tautness at the back of his throat, did not tell himself that he might be bored, or restless, or even a little sad. He was just a busy man, who happened to be passing between phases of great busyness. But his perpetual boyish smile had thinned out to an arrangement of the corners of his mouth that, taken in conjunction with the droop of his eyelids and the faint knitting of the brows, could be read quite simply as a picture of dejection. His gaze was glazed, but his teeth were ever clenched.

By the time the boat reached the trading post below Lugambwa, three days had passed and Guy's finger had swollen considerably. The throbbing had spread right up to his armpit and was advancing across his shoulder. His temperature had rocketed and he was beginning to show the classic symptoms of a grand fever. There were no medical facilities at the air-strip, and when he and Deany disembarked at Abele City airport an hour and a half later, Guy was distinctly tottery and enduring unpleasant waves of pain that swept right across the top of his

54

trunk from fingertip to fingertip. Deany pressed him to see the resident medic, but Guy insisted on supervising the freight transfer, and climbed onto the plane at the very last moment.

Two hours into the flight, sipping a tonic water with slice of lemon, he suddenly slammed the glass down and yelled out as an appalling spasm gripped his throat and squeezed it until he could barely breathe. The stewardess urged him to drink a little cold water to soothe the pain, but as soon as he did another violent contraction occurred, seeming to reach from the back of his mouth right round to the base of his neck. He thrust the glass away and began to tremble uncontrollably, all the while shifting in his seat and constantly crossing and uncrossing his legs.

When they touched down, an ambulance was waiting. Guy, streaming with sweat, turned to Deany, as he was being helped off the plane, and said, 'Tetanus. Just need a jab.'

The doctors at the airport were annoyed with Guy for contracting rabies, and told him that in another four days he would have been dead. They gave him vaccine and anti-serum, put him on his own in a room with a view of a warehouse and assigned a roster of nurses to attend him in his delirium, in case the convulsive seizures of the larynx asphyxiated him. He tossed and turned for several days after, sleeping fitfully, sometimes waking up lucid, sometimes very confused. Deany stayed with him for the first three or four days, but when the doctors announced that he was recovering satisfactorily, she went back home to attend to the vexed matter of negotiating the treatment and quarantining of the rabid Eke and Ike, whom the health authorities were fairly eager to put down without further ado.

Towards the end of the week Guy felt as right as rain, but the doctors punished him by keeping him under observation for another ten days when it was perfectly obvious he was fit enough to walk straight out of the door and all the way home, if needs be. When they finally let him go, Deany picked him up in the car.

'Gee, you look awful!'

'I've been lying down for three weeks, for God's sake.'

'You're real pale. Not relapsing, are you?'

'It doesn't relapse, Deany. It's gone. I'm not used to the exercise, that's all.'

Deany walked him across the carpark. She nuzzled her head against his shoulder and squeezed his arm.

'Ouch.'

'Still hurts?'

'No.'

'Just wanted to say "ouch", yeah?'

'How are the animals?'

'The rabies is gone. They're clean. Should get a release next week. Been a big hassle, I can tell you.'

'So . . . what are they like?'

'The same. Still yowling.'

Guy was relieved. When Eke and Ike had been confirmed as rabies carriers, he had been disconcerted at the thought that their extraordinary behaviour might be solely attributable to the infection. The possibility that they might revert to docile, snuffling variants on the ratel was, he had concluded, more than he would be able to bear. He had actually started to miss the creatures – it had been almost a month since he'd seen them and he wanted to be alone in the lab with them, alone and listening to their insufferable, relentless complaining.

The explorer woman looked at Jack quizzically. 'Do things happen to you? They said you were some kind of hero. Doesn't sound so dull.'

'I'm a seer.' Jack said.

It was in fact at parties and gatherings that Jack's singular powers were revealed in their most impressive array. He went to the drinks table, poured anything but the German wines, turned to the darkened groups and immediately introduced himself. The person would tell Jack his or her name. Jack would ask the person his or her trade. The person would reciprocate. Jack would say, 'I foretell', or somesuch. The person would behave like those films in which a mother, responding to the cries of her infant, will move supportively towards it, but the camera, geared to the highest speeds, the loose end slapping round in the magazine scarcely has the thing turned over, thousands of frames slicing the very bacon of a second into slivers of a thousandth, each one utterly secret, but its truth flagrantly revealed when, as if in a full-deck riffle, with blur of suits and jacks and jokers, the seams of interstitial photon nulls are smeared into plastic finished presences, the animator's art unsung, we take it as read, and the camera gives the lie to mother's basic love by revealing a momentary snarl of some few frames duration to which baby will respond by backing off but then mother smiles so so does baby only too relieved, and it's over in a blur, I never saw it happen

56

and I was there all the time. The person before Jack behaves much like this and he has learned to spot it by watching closely to the exclusion of the divertissements.

Which makes him feel, 'I have so much to offer these people, but do they give a shit?'

This woman here, though, she didn't do it, not a tremor.

'What is that, like a fortune-teller?' she asked straightaway.

'I know what's going to happen.'

'What, like, next, in here?'

'That's right.' Jack drained the white wine, German, tasteless.

'Okay. What am I going to do?'

'You're going to invite your husband to join us because he has an opinion on jobs like mine.'

'Guy?' she exclaimed.

Guy turned from the knot of production assistants, interrupting a jungle conversation. As he came towards them his mouth opened and his lips pulled back to disclose bold, uncrowded teeth. Jack supposed that the upturning of both corners of his mouth signified a smile.

'Hello,' said Guy. 'How's it going?'

'Mr Gavin here is a seer, dear.'

'Not really,' Guy said.

Guy thought Jack looked rather showy. The pattern on his suit was unnecessarily obvious, and his shoes were quite extraordinary. And made out of alligator, which always annoyed Guy. One thing he did get angry about, that sort of useless display and waste. His hair was ungroomed, too, just sort of fell about on his head.

'Yes, really,' his wife informed him.

'Do you actually make money at it? If you don't mind me asking,' Guy asked.

He continued to bare his teeth at Jack, who was thinking that Guy was quite good-looking, in an old-fashioned way, you could say. How come all that jungle business hadn't made him look less of a boy? How could someone be his age and still eager?

'It's my sole source of nourishment, actually.'

'And does it work? I mean, what do you actually do?'

'It works. I see ahead and tell people. They pay me.'

'These people give you money? Before they see if you're right? I hope you don't think I'm being rude.'

57

'They come to me, I don't go looking for them. They don't complain. Next thing they know they're walking into what I told them.' Jack leaned to one side and relieved a passing tray of a glass of wine, trying the red.

Guy blinked, or maybe winced very slightly. A wince trimmed down to the eyes only and all the more difficult to pinpoint because it had to be construed in conjunction with the appalling grin. The explorer looked at Jack and sighed, as if a great sadness had swept through him but had passed on almost immediately.

'But . . . how can anyone . . . how do you . . . I mean, doesn't it assume that everything has sort of happened already? No, I suppose not, it could mean . . . no.'

Jack noticed that Deany was looking at him as he listened to her husband. During his glance he saw her eyes moving over his face as if its separate parts required a special attention that was not possible with a normal gaze. But the explorer had said something quite good.

'You said it. You already said it,' Jack said. 'Everything has happened already.' He drank some wine and wondered whether this disclosure constituted betrayal of a trade secret. But then he added, 'Several times.' It seemed that his mouth was going to motor on over his misgivings.

The explorer's wife said something. 'You talking about reincarnation?'

'No. Lot of nonsense,' he retorted irritably.

'So . . .?' She shook her head enquiringly. The explorers were transfixed.

'A lot of things happen over and over again. Most things. *This* always happens.'

Guy gave Jack a hard, innocent look. 'Well, I've certainly never had this conversation before.'

'Me neither.' Deany said.

'Sure. That's why I'm in business.' Jack plunged his hand into the breast pocket of his outstanding jacket. 'My card.'

She took it. Her husband leaned across to look and stopped smiling. His fresh features decomposed into dismay. 'You've actually got it printed on it.'

'They're called business cards. They tell people what your business is.'

'Yes, I know what they are. I was just wondering about the legal aspect sort of thing.'

'The legal aspect.'

58

Deany interrupted. 'I don't understand. What's illegal?'

'Well,' Guy was licking his lips hesitantly, 'I don't think you're supposed to claim, in advertisements that is, that you can predict the future. There actually is a law against it, I think, I'm pretty sure.'

'There's not.' Jack said.

'Oh.'

'But let's suppose there is.'

'Yes?'

'Want to know what I'd say, Mr Blighton?'

'Er . . . what?'

Jack crouched down slightly, looking up into Guy's eyes menacingly. 'Come and get me, copper!' He straightened up and finished his drink in one gulp. Deany was laughing. Guy blinked, closed his mouth, and blinked again. He seemed to be short on things to do with his face.

'Right. So you don't really care?'

'Right.'

'I can't see how it can do a lot of harm, anyway.' Deany said.

'Oh, I think it can,' Jack replied, 'it can really fuck things up.'

'To coin a phrase.' Guy laughed once, 'Ha.'

'They come naturally.'

Elizabeth Preeny walked over to them. 'Mr Gavin? You all set?'

'I've just had the pre-med. Everything's going to be fine.'

Deany smiled. 'Good luck.'

'I don't need it.' He winked.

Guy got it. 'Oh yes! No, you wouldn't, would you? Ha. Right! Perhaps we'll see you later.' And then, after a moment, 'Will we? Ha.'

As the doors swung to behind the seer, Guy asked Deany, 'What is he here for exactly?'

'He's a hero.'

'Heavens.'

Only a few hundred yards down the corridor Jack and Elizabeth heard heavy panting and the cushioned pounding of fast footsteps. At first they took no notice, for they were in a very busy place. But the breathing grew louder until it seemed as if the noise would fill the funnel of the curving passageway. They glanced over their shoulders but could see nothing – the source of the sound was some degrees of arc away. They raised their eyebrows to each other but a moment later it was upon them, or upon Jack, to be precise. It pressed down on his shoulders from the rear, causing him to fall over backwards. The floor

59

was generously carpeted, of course, so the seer was not damaged. He was, however, fairly surprised, a sensation alien to seers, which caused him to cry out as the energetic licking started. The licking was accompanied by friendly barks, so Jack knew within moments what had jumped him. Elizabeth found the situation very amusing and cried, 'What a lovely boy!'

'Zelka! Ugh!' Jack struggled to his feet and looked down the corridor, 'Where's Miss Desperanza?'

'It's her dog! The one you saved, Mr Gavin! That means she's here!'

'Is there dribble on my jacket, Elizabeth?'

'Not a drop. But your face is wet. Do you have a hanky?'

'I shall use my cuff, Elizabeth. Don't want germs in my pocket, do I?'

And as Jack wiped and the dog wove between his legs woofing, round the long curve came cries, 'O madonna! O porca miseria!" and the sound of rapid footfalls. Miss Desperanza's skirt was too tight to allow a proper leg extension, and her heels were high. Seeing both the dog and Jack she managed to accelerate, however, and bore down on them excitedly. 'Oh! Jeck is with her one more time! She will always remember!' Silvia flung her arms round Jack's neck and kissed him a lot, grasping his nape and clawing it slightly. 'Jeck – you are so wet! What has passed?'

'Dog lick.' Jack said.

Silvia produced a hanky and dried Jack's cheeks. 'Because she has missed you, and also I too!'

'I'm famous now, Silvia.' he replied.

'Oh Jeck, you bet! You should be more famous than me! I am just a little starlet compare to you!'

'Silvia, this is Miss Preeny. She's with the television.'

Elizabeth shook Silvia's hand, saying, 'I'm so glad you made it. I'm afraid we have to plunge straight into the studio and get in front of the cameras! Will you mind awfully? We're going to show a piece of *Eva Kuwait and the Powder Room*.'

'You have it? Meraviglioso!'

'Your film?' asked Jack.

'Jeck, you will love it! Is a kind of detective fiction! I am a clever girl detective! Now is the sixteen we have made of Eva Kuwait series!'

'We were lucky enough to get the dubbed version. Our viewers will be fascinated, I'm sure.' Elizabeth shepherded them down a short passageway and through a double door.

Tum te tum de dum tatata taa went the intro music for World Picture After Work and there was Elizabeth saying good evening right above the bar on a monitor that Deany watched with an orange juice. Guy was in the gents. Their young woman had invited them to watch the programme for a few minutes before they were due on themselves. 'What do a professional clairvoyant, a dog on the ground and the very latest in the series of Italian films about clever female detective Eva Kuwait have in common?' enquired Elizabeth. 'Well,' she went on, before the viewers could supply the answer, 'before we supply the answer here is a scene from the film, starring glamorous Silvia Desperanza. Eva Kuwait, bent on locating the key that will unlock the cabinet containing the genealogical charts of the racehorse Desiato, finds herself at night in the innermost secret compartments of Ralph Soutex, an influential manufacturer of fabrics. Only her keen eyes can help her in the velvet gloom.'

The monitor darkened. Guy returned from the gents. 'What's this?' he asked Deany.

'She's looking for a racehorse,' Deany replied without turning her head.

'Who?'

'Watch.'

'The fingers of steep nightink palpate Eva's brow,' a dubbed guttural drawl announced. The screen was still largely dark.

'Is it a black and white?' Guy wanted to know.

'He said it's night. Listen.'

The highlighted aspects of a woman's face appeared on the edge of the screen. The camera moved round from profile until both eyes swung centre frame like pale amoebae in an unfathomable lagoon. Darting from side to side they signalled stealth and search. Moving out, the camera revealed the trunk and arms of Eva as she picked her way through the gloom. Her breathing reinforced the atmosphere of illicit entry into claustral ungiving.

'She's got rubber gloves on, look.'

'She's a detective.'

'The membrane seals her from all but her own intent. Only her face surrenders flesh to the heartless mouth of the chamber. She must not collide with the furnishings.' But even as the voice croaked, the music juddered and Eva smacked into something. 'Prostitute who is a pig!' hissed a disembodied English voice, not coinciding well with the movement of Eva's lips.

61

'It's getting lighter,' Guy observed.

'Our eyes are getting accustomed to it. As if.'

Eva held her arms straight out in front of her and moved slowly through the room again. Her eyes had narrowed with the effort of concentration. The music rumbled sullenly. A dark thing loomed. Eva did not see it. She gasped as the pillar rocked massively from her unwitting pressure and then stifled a scream as a great decorated jug topped with apparent slowness through the air and landed squarely on her head, its rim coming to rest on her shoulders. She grasped the jug by its handles, struggling to ease the rim past her chin.

'So little air in even a big jug for a mature woman,' remarked the commentator. 'Now doubly deprived, Eva must wrench the ewer to a point at least above her mouth before continuing. To die in such a small space is to render nonsensical the miracle of birth.'

'What's that mean?' Guy asked.

'I think it's as if Eva might as well never have been born,' suggested a voice next to him. Guy looked round in surprise – it was their young woman. She had slipped into a chair just behind Guy and Deany, and was watching the excerpt with her clipboard on her knee.

'I'm afraid I've forgotten your name,' Guy whispered.

'Margo!' Deany said.

'It's quite claustrophobic, don't you think?' Guy whispered to Margo.

'It's beautifully done, though.'

'Guy!' Deany turned to Margo, 'He always talks in things.'

Eva was tottering to and fro, heaving at the handles, on the point of panic. She cannoned into a tallboy, which, to Guy's horror, teetered on its short legs, releasing a fragile item from each of its three shelves. Simultaneously in the air were a porcelain clock decorated with shepherdesses, an ivory netsuke intricately carved with fishermen piling dinner plates beside a snake, and a tureen in the shape of an artichoke with a lid of lifelike ceramic cherries.

'That's awful!' Guy declared, nervously clutching his empty wine glass.

As the valuables cascaded to the hard floor, turning over and over in space, Eva, insensible as to the scope of her most recent error, managed, with a painful upheaving, to force the big jug rim over her chin, past her lips and on to the obstruction presented by her nasal septum. Intuitively leaning back a little, she was able to peer beneath the rim and make out the poorly illuminated forms of the falling items as they passed through the absurdly narrow aperture afforded by the curvature of the jug neck away from her own cheeks. Without any discernible hesitation Eva bent her knees and extended both hands, deftly placing them in the paths of, respectively, the tureen and the netsuke.

Guy gasped with relief as the two precious artefacts settled in the cushions of Eva's palms, then sat up very straight in his chair when he realised how close the porcelain clock had come to the ground.

'The clock! The clock!' he shouted.

The clock, its crooks, shepherdesses and bowers spinning, was now within a single figure of centimetres from the awful floor. Eva thrust her pelvis forward, arched her back, and drove her knees downward with tremendous speed. The inverted simper of an Arcadian maid, by now almost a blur, suddenly froze as it appeared to impact upon the carpet. The very next instant should have seen its violent disintegration but this shocking transformation simply did not occur, for, as the cam tilted upward along the line of the simple smock, Eva's knees closed around the six of the dial at the front and the winder at the back. The descent of the clock had been arrested one millimetre from the ground, the petrified hair of the tallest figure mingling with those pile fibres that projected furthest from the weave beneath.

'Good lord, good lord!' cried Guy, shaking his head. 'That really is incredible! Have you ever seen that before?' He looked round at Margo. 'Margo? Have you?'

'No, no. It's terribly clever. It really is.'

'Good lord. No, I mean, it really is.' He looked at Deany. 'Think if she'd dropped that clock, Deany, I mean, God, it doesn't bear thinking about. It really doesn't.'

Deany nodded.

Droplets of sweat were trickling from beneath the rim of the jug and coursing down Eva's neck. She grasped the handles once again and managed to align the spout with the bridge of her nose, thus creating a vital extra space round at the back of her skull. With an agonisingly protracted push at the rim, she worked the jug up over her brow, and peered into the gloom.

Guy leaned forward in his chair, grinding his teeth, and said 'It's nearly off.'

One final effort released Eva's head completely. As her black hair tumbled down about her shoulders, she briefly rubbed her chafed face then padded confidently across the room, navigating

dressers, chairs and further pillars without any sign of her former tentativeness.

Guy inhaled noisily. 'Oh! Now what?'

'She finds the horse, you want to bet?'

Eva arrived at a wide desk with a double set of drawers. Suddenly,
with appalling shrieks from the sound track, the room was bathed in
a brilliant light, pouring from great tiered chandeliers set high in an
ornate domed ceiling.

'Eva!' the guttural dub in anguish, 'mystery is dead! Light confers
opacity, gone is the succulence which emanates from that which
cannot be located!'

Margo sighed. Guy frowned.

Eva contracted like a startled fawn, her hands stellated in yellow
translucent rubber, held against her face aghast. She glanced wildly
round the glistening chamber, and began to emit a low growl of horror.
All the objects in the room, all the surfaces, the fluted sides of pillars,
the smooth faces of columns, the intricacies of their pedestals, the soft
random folds of cushions and curtains, the carpet, the rugs, were
covered in a fine white powder which coated each texture regardless
of its nooks and convolutions. Not once did these tiny particles pile
upon each other; they never drifted, never jostled, and never left
some small spot unsnowed. They were ranked in an unending shallow
sea that swam and filmed from wall to wall and up across the ceiling.
Only the gently swaying pears and pendules of the chandeliers remained
dustless, refracting more fully the baldness of the matter and its perfect,
terrible completion.

Eva Kuwait snarled as she caught sight of the white palm-prints
on her dark ski pants and roll neck. She shuddered as she traced
her path through the room, each foot printed, every brush marked, all
scuffs rendered as unpowdered plots. She moaned in despair at the wild
calligraph of gropes and clasps that scrawled hayfeverishly across the
close, undriven fields of grain. She raked her hands through her hair,
streaking it boldly then, bending over the desk, blew half dementedly
onto the blotter. A light smoke of powder rose and drifted slowly to
the floor. At the place where the confusion of her hand-marks had
disturbed the flawless finish of the pale green paper, there was now
an oval scar of darker green to record the shape of her pitiful puff.
Eva dashed to the tallboy, where she had so skilfully saved the falling
fixtures even while enewered. By this time clearly beside herself with

shame and frustration, she frantically fanned the tale-telling slicks and slashes with her gloved hands. The evidence was enlarged by her every movement. She had become the stylus in the grand signing of her most secret journal.

As the detective fluttered and blew, a moth dying in a soft storm of dust, the doorknob began slowly to rotate. On the sound track came the slightest suggestion of a horse's hooves, a faint whinny . . . or was it just some elusive underpinning of the melody?

'What did I tell you? The horse is coming.' announced Deany.

'What is this horse business?' Guy was irritated. He had been engrossed beyond any consideration of Eva's objectives.

'You watch.'

'There's a horse opening the door? Surely not.'

The door itself began to inch open. Through the choking clouds of powder Eva Kuwait noticed this fact. She froze, did not kick up any more. The clouds drifted down. The door was ajar. Eva hissed one word. 'Desiato!'

'Well who can be at the mysterious door indeed we all wonder,' said Elizabeth brightly, Silvia to her left.

'What?' Guy said quietly. Then, with greater volume, 'What?' He swung round and addressed Margo. 'What's she doing?'

Margo was taken aback by the urgency of Guy's question. 'It's Elizabeth,' she said.

'But who's coming through the door?'

'I don't know, Mr Blighton.'

'Does she know?'

'Elizabeth?'

'Yes. The one who stopped it.'

'She has to do the interview now.'

'But she knows who's at the door.'

'I doubt it.'

'Well how on earth can she stop it? Doesn't she *want* to know?'

'Guy. It was Desiato.' Deany interrupted.

'Who is Desiato?' Guy had stood up, still holding his empty glass, which he was squeezing anxiously in his fist.

'It's the horse. Where were you?'

'Deany – you keep saying horse. They never mentioned a horse.'

'You were having a pee. They mentioned it. Elizabeth did.'

'So she does know.'

'I don't think she necessarily knows the whole story though, Mr Blighton.'

'She's actually in charge of the programme and she doesn't know the story? I find that hard to believe, Margo.'

'Guy. Listen to me. Sit down.' Guy waved his glass from side to side in an abstract of impatience. 'I told you the story already. Why don't you listen?'

'Okay. Desiato is a horse,' he said.

'Right.'

He sat down, nodding his head exaggeratedly. 'And she sees the horse. At the end.'

'Sure.'

'Ha! Deany, that is so stupid! Tell me this.' He leaned forward and waved the glass in her face. 'How can a horse open a door? Eh? Tell me that. A horse goes into a house, takes the door knob and turns it. Is that possible? It's not, is it?' He looked at Margo again. 'Is it, Margo?'

'It's hard to say, Mr Blighton. It might have been a trained horse.'

'I don't think that's the point, Margo.'

'But she did say the name, didn't she?' the young woman responded.

'Yes, the name. That you say is of the horse. Well, I don't know that, you see.'

'Actually, I wasn't here when they said it. When Elizabeth did.'

Deany put a hand on Margo's arm. 'She said it.'

'Why don't you ask Miss Desperanza? Now she'd know.' Margo looked at them both triumphantly.

'Would she tell me, do you think?'

'Ask her, Guy. She's a film star, you're an explorer. These people talk.'

'I don't know. I don't like to. It's the sort of thing they're funny about, isn't it?'

'I'm sure Miss Desperanza would be very flattered, Mr Blighton.'

'Well, I'll see. I just can't understand why they took it off in the first place. It seems very irresponsible.'

'It's just a matter of time, I'm afraid. We have four items in twenty-eight minutes, not including the weather. It's only meant to be a clip.'

'A clip! That's what's wrong, you see – clips. People get interested in things, then they find it's a clip.'

66

'We should make our way to the studio now. We're on straight after this.'

'I just find it very disturbing.'

Elizabeth turned from Silvia to include Jack as the cameras took up a three-shot.

'Mr Jack Gavin, a self-styled seer . . .'

'Seer. Seer in fact.'

'Mr Gavin, who claims to be a seer . . .'

'Limited seer. Doesn't go all the way.'

'A limited seer, has earned the undying gratitude of film star Silvia Desperanza whose clip from her film recently released we have just seen . . .'

'Aah Jeck, yes. It is true. I want the people to know.'

'For his selfless deed of bravery during the Hanley Wave Blue Cross Supermarket disaster . . .'

'Is Blue Wave I think.'

'Blue Cross is animal welfare. Understandable.'

'I do beg your pardon Hanley Cross Blue Wave . . .'

'Si.'

'Supermarket disaster in which several building workers were seriously injured when scaffolding collapsed during . . .'

'Oh I did not know! Tell me!'

'Well, during the opening ceremony at which you, Miss Desperanza, officiated . . .'

'What is that a fish?'

'You opened it, Silvia.'

'Yes, I did.'

'Mr Gavin was the first on the scene of the aftermath and perhaps in your own words, Mr Gavin?'

'Miss Desperanza's joke was of a type to induce explosive rather than simmering effects. There are only so many structures, both of joke and scaffolding. I have seen most.'

'I don't quite see what you're getting at.'

'A question of ordinariness, Elizabeth.'

'Yes.'

'Most things are, don't you think?'

'You're saying that *plus ça change plus c'est la même chose*?'

'Except that it doesn't change.'

'I wonder how many of our viewers would agree.'

67

'It doesn't matter.'

'He saved Zelka because of his worldview. And isn't that something, you think?'

'Jack, tell us just what happened.'

'Miss Desperanza got to the bit where the Pope is obliged to respond to the Italian. It's a critical part of the story. Silvia does it very well.'

'Oh shall I tell it now?'

'Is it quite long?'

'I just tell the end. Il Papa says to the Italian and what is your favourite food and the Italian he says, Papa I love calamari . . .'

'Squid.'

'And the Papa says to him "Oh that's nice because I haven't got any rubber gloves!"'

'Oh.'

'It's better when you have the buildup. There's a classic three-stage lead-in. Never fails.'

'Oh Zelka! Look, she is distress!'

'Brings it all back to her. Very upsetting.'

'We can speak in sotto voce yes? She will not hear us.'

'I'm not sure whether our microphones can handle it, actually. Ah! Yes. Our producer says they can.'

'And of course with only modest foot-plates and no inside buttress tubes on a glazed paving the towers were destined to fall towards the prow.'

'The prow.'

'Fake boat in front of doors. So the dog gets it in the brains and I apply first aid by mouth.'

'Was there any fear of disease as you bent to the job, Jack?'

'No disease thoughts crossed my mind. These bacteria are opportunistic. I don't give them a chance.'

'Silvia, what were your reactions as Zelka lay there beneath Jack Gavin's expert aid?'

'I thought of my young girlhood in Bari and how I would walk the long beach in the winter wishing to be successful in ceramics. And then I saw some pictures of great moments of sport, you know, what is it called the pentathon?'

'The pentathlon.'

'Yes I saw this. The great Italian team.'

'On the beach?'

'Pardon?'

'The team was on the beach?'

'In Bari?'

'Yes.'

'No. It was in my mind.'

'I see. At the beach.'

'No. When I am with Jack bending.'

'This is what you saw?'

'Well yes. My reactions.'

'And when at last Zelka came round. Your reactions then.'

'I thought good. Very good. And Jack is so attractive.'

'You thought.'

'Don't you think?'

'It certainly was a remarkable achievement. What about you Jack?'

'What?'

'While you were breathing into the dog.'

'I saw the subsequent four days in considerable detail.'

'Normally your clairvoyance covers shorter periods I understand.'

'Normally a few hours. Some situations are so powerfully familiar that their outcome can only be expressed through the narrowest channels.'

'Is dog rescuing so familiar to you?'

'Yes.'

'You've performed similar deeds of quick-thinking heroism?'

'No.'

'Silvia. You are a great friend of the managing director of Blue Wave Roma I believe.'

'We move in some similar circles.'

'Jack. Will you shop at Blue Wave henceforth?'

'Yes.'

'Silvia. What of the future?'

'I think we see the rundown of the whole planet now.'

'Jack.'

'What?'

'Is Silvia right in her widespread gloom for mankind?'

'The bomb has already dropped, Elizabeth.'

'You mean so to speak.'

'Apparently.'

'Will you make a point of seeing Silvia's films?'

'I very much will. The clip was tantalising.'

'I thought so too.'

'I hope Jeck and me will be close together.'

'Jack.'

'I'm picking up one or two things. It's clear that Miss Desperanza and myself will be bound by the legacy of the dog issue.'

'I do hope so. Your example will urge people to look out for animals in difficulty. So many cats and dogs apparently dead at the roadside may merely be resting or unconscious say reports so the answer is do not walk by but blow down them. Mr Jack Gavin has shown this and Silvia Desperanza has enthralled us all with her clip tonight. Thank you both and now very shortly we shall be talking to Guy and Deany Blighton about their colourful adventures and significant contribution to zoology after the break.'

'Okay, thank you Elizabeth. Can we wheel in the explorers please?'

'Is that it?'

'I'm afraid so. I think it went very well.'

'I didn't know which camera to look at.'

'You don't have to. That's my problem.'

'Zelka is crawled beneath the chair from the beginning. It's a pity.'

'I think we got some shots of her, actually.'

'Well thanks Elizabeth.'

'A pleasure. Here are the Blightons.'

'Hi. You were good.'

'Yeah?'

'We saw you from the bar. Was fine, wasn't it, Guy?'

'It was fascinating. What a marvellous dog.'

'She is not use to all this media.'

'Nor am I! Ha.'

'Well you must not get under the chair.'

'Ha. No. Here girl. Does she bite?'

'You are afraid? Surely no.'

'He had kind of a bad experience a while back. Just getting over it.'

'That's too bad.'

'Thank you explorers. Can we have you sitting down please?'

'Hey Mr Gavin!'

'What?'

'Gonna watch us?'

'Sure.'

Silvia had to fly so Jack went back to the bar to watch the Blightons. It seemed that these people had captured some kind of animal that was not related to any known genus. Deep in the jungle, it had evolved separately and unsuspectedly over thousands of years. Photographs. Looks like a grey badger with a black face. And apparently the most remarkable findings are yet to be revealed? Yes, zoologists and ourselves are currently concluding researches on certain extraordinary, quite unique characteristics. Might we ask what these are? Rather not at this point, but certainly make it fully available very soon, when all results are fully evaluated. Jack thought: what are these people up to? There are no new animals.

Watching the couple, he saw how Guy didn't change much on the screen, which impressed him, maybe the fellow was so straight he never changed even under the lights and the gaze of three point six times two eyes, mill.

Guy's own eyes opened wide as he chatted away, and he shone with the enthusiasm that, Jack knew, people liked. Now and again Jack had the feeling that the earnest, youthful smile was floating above something else. It wasn't that you didn't believe in the man, he was obviously sincere but . . . he became suddenly impatient and switched his attention to the bar.

'I'll just have the vodka straight, please, with ice.'

Now, the woman, Deany, she didn't seem as much of a boy as him, or a girl. Living in the jungle, putting things in bottles, counting animals. Does she like doing that?

Jack grimaced. He stopped chewing for a moment. The thought of life under canvas. Every plant is different, but too close to look at. He'd go mad. The boredom. Everything happens, all the time, which is nothing. Would his powers fail him there? Would they even be of any use? Wandering between trees, watching insects eat each other – in one way he'd be at his most effective, but to what purpose? Everybody knows about nature – the endless meal time, the supportive rot of the dead, their role in a continual composture, the chemical interludes, the variations on in or outdoor ovoblasty, the teeth of the big, the tunnels of the tiny, how the mighty must still fear the scuffle, the ganging of the least to lay logs low, dig dams or make mud mounds, the munching and fucking, bunching and mucking, the various turds, footprints, chewmarks, halfpelts and sloughed skins, the noises, to wit, the trumpet, the rattle, the whistle, and the pairings, to woo, with tall tails, bright bottoms and loud jackets, lures and masks, dances and dashes, then the young, their gambolling, their achievement of the stalk and pounce, their own four legs, or six or more, or fins, on which all this, what they must do, in order to get on then die, is done.

He swallowed without properly finishing the chew. He had often wondered where the action was, other than some minutes hence. Somewhere between the jungle and his office, clearly, but at what point, moving away from the pole of people and their patterns, did some unaffected, neutral, midway area arise, an area into which things might just, with an unbiased rawness, pop up, before the whole business slid across to the other polar bearing, nature, which had all the vocabulary but so few options? Where did things *happen*?

When Guy and Deany and Elizabeth Preeny came back into hospitality after the show, everybody shook hands and laughed and then sat down to watch the tape. Jack watched Deany watching him on the screen. At one point she turned to Elizabeth and saw Jack watching her watching him. Later on in the tape, when she and Guy were being interviewed, she turned once more and saw Jack watching her on the screen. Jack sensed that he was under observation again and shot a brief, covering-fire type of glance at Guy. The explorer was also studying the screen and seemed oblivious to this exchange of small messages whose tracks were passing perilously close to the tip of his nose. Jack did notice, however, that he looked rather pale and tired. Droplets of perspiration trickled from his hair-line onto his brow, and he was swallowing as though his mouth were very dry.

Afterwards, as the guests stood in the courtyard of the television, Jack realised it was only half past seven, although it felt like a late Saturday night that was still young. Guy and Deany shook his hand and climbed into an estate car. He watched their tail lights get lost in the swarm. He decided he would buy himself a meal. Although he was already quite drunk he would drink a bottle of wine. He knew that by the end of the meal he would be, in a manner of speaking, entirely consistent with himself: anything that happened would be received with exactly the same level of attention as anything else. Events would not be discerned as such, and the whole walk through the city, and back to his home, would be entirely free of any collections of moments that might make up an occasion or even an instant. Without breaking down into an entirely senseless soup, the world would unfold before him and infold after him, signalling in colours that only became

72

distinct if he chose to pause and make them so. But pausing was day work, and soon he would be a solitary dynamo in the night, slipping unsteadily but unscathed through the passageway that lay beneath the occurrence yet several steps up from the mysterious churn and its teeming effluents. Jack being nimble, needing no man. Aboil with his own concoction.

Part Two

Jack gazed listlessly round his office. The shelf over the lintel, stacked with its unchanging miscellany. A guide to the streets of a large town. A worn and anonymous table of logarithms. A treatise on succulents with good colour plates. A novel of detection of the hard-boiled dick type. The bound proceedings of the Society for the Generation of Interest in Wildlife for the year 1953. The latter, it must be promptly asserted, was a substantial volume some five inches thick, which Jack had been bequeathed by the previous tenant. Although he had come to regard himself, to all intents and purposes, as virtually supramanual, its bulk had appealed to the vestigial handyman in him and during an access of the extemporary spirit he had turned the item onto its back, deftly transforming it into a handy bookend. Other volumes were apparent on the shelf but none fell within the scope of Jack's current gaze, and will not, therefore, be insinuated.

His eyes passed over the framed letters on the wall near the window. *Dear Mr Gavin,* he skated across one of them, he'd read it many times, *pursuant to my recent meeting with you I did what you said. Gracious me, how it all fell out as you had put forward! I conducted myself to the letter, feeling as if a swan gliding with her young, and the situation unfurled as if furled by you initially! The quiet sensation of inner knowledge is a powerful muscle, Mr Gavin, and I have been its fortunate partisan if briefly. I look forward(!) to the engagement of your undoubted reserves if the occasion should arise again. Yours with gratitude J. Benchley, Mrs.* Beside it others of that ilk.

Pinned inside the open cupboard door the cutting 'Dog Hero: I Saw It Coming'. The cupboard bare almost – a lidless box of flimsy, an empty salt cellar, a bag with a few dry beans that some tiny beetle had made unpleasant.

75

'Bad day at Shithouse Creek,' he muttered. A car backfired in the street below. 'Shot at the bus-stop,' he announced, with reference more to his own state of mind than anything else. But even so, he got up, wandered to the window and looked out.

It was quite a busy street. Most of the buildings were small shops with small businesses above them. People and cars flowed up and down. Trucks blocked the road. Cyclists behaved dangerously.

Down there a man was looking straight up at him. The man wore a heavy coat, which was unusual for the time of year. He fixed Jack with a rather challenging gaze. 'Why?' Jack wondered. 'He doesn't know me.' Then he saw that the man was having a piss. 'Ah.' The man was having a piss at the edge of the pavement. People were walking straight past him, and cars were driving by in front of him. Nothing in his manner suggested he was an indecent exposer – he was just a man having a piss. Minding his own business really, until Jack had interrupted him.

Jack looked straight back at the man, and considered the expression on his face. It was quite a clever one. The challenging quality was suggested by the ambiguous way in which the man used his eyebrows. They seemed to be right on the verge of arching up in a quizzical manner, as if about to frame questions like 'Can I help you in any way?' or, more assertively 'Is there something wrong?' But the eyebrows did not arch as expected, and as you kept looking those possibilities seemed all to dissolve, leaving a face that was just looking unconcernedly and unpointedly in your direction. You were acknowledged, but only slightly more than a tree or a pillarbox.

A sporting cyclist, wearing the comical shorts peculiar to his pastime, sped along the street, head down and gears a-glitter. Hugging the kerb in anticipation of being bullied by cars, he swept towards the pissing man, and in an instant had interrupted the passage of water with his vehicle and his shaven legs. Such, however, was the cyclist's intensity of purpose that he powered onward without a downward glance or loss of pedalling cadence. A cruel parody of roadside refreshment procedures in the larger cycling rallies, Jack reflected.

The man in the street was buttoning his overcoat. He turned away from the kerb, and his wordless exchange with Jack, and strolled off into the crowd of passersby.

That was when Jack had his major insight, and the crystallising of resolve that soon followed it. He stood at the window with one hand on his hip, and bit his lower lip as a succession of hunches, suspicions and long-held, half-formed ideas fell into a completely original order in his mind. He turned from the window, deep in thought, and walked across the office, staring abstractedly at the floor. Sitting at the desk again, he nodded slowly three or four times and wondered if he were the first man to have had this particular revelation. He decided that others had been this way before him, and had taken up the challenge without drawing attention to themselves. That was the essence of it, in fact – there had been no attention there in the first place, so obviously no one had ever heard about the pioneers. What he had discovered was not to be taken lightly, even if it seemed to promise the most marvellous rewards. Instead of congratulating himself on his perspicacity, he now dwelt on the utter obviousness of what he had seen, and marvelled at his failure to notice something that had been, well, right beneath his nose.

He was then overtaken by feelings of awe as his insight began to translate itself into many walks of life, ramifying at a great rate through corridors and channels of possibility until it looked as though it might girdle the whole world, or at least wherever there were people, for the scheme did require people. This last observation caused Jack to laugh out loud, and when he stopped, and touched his cheek, he found that he had also been crying. And even as he brushed the tears from his cheek, his whole body started to tremble, and soon an irresistible sobbing welled up from the pit of his stomach. The tears flowed freely as he cried out his exultation and moaned the grief that nonsensically accompanied it. His head rolled forward onto his chest as wave after wave of emotion shuddered up his spine, contorting his face and making him force his balled-up fists into his lap. He saw his father in the alleyway leading to the back door of number seventeen, the old man bending to retrieve Mister Bill the teddybear that Jack had thrown out of the door in a fit of pique. And his mother crying as blood poured from the palm of her hand, and then he was opening a tin of chocolates and on the lid were mice and pigs dancing in a barnyard. He was on his bicycle going no-hands on a long summer evening, and all the men and women in the street were laughing joyously, and their children carried buckets and spades decorated with shells and starfish. He was with his friends from home and they were at parties under faraway hills that smelled of lavender as people squeezed hands.

Now Jack was breathing deeply and regularly, sighing out his outbreaths and drawing his inbreaths in right across the back of his nostrils. He felt soft and quiet, and smiled gently to himself, wiping

77

his face with his cuff. He opened a drawer in the desk, lifted out a bottle of milk and poured some into a teacup. He sipped and sat and looked at his thoughts.

Jack's insight redefined time and space. There was no longer any hurry, and there was no need to search any more. Everything that was required lay just outside the front door, and would always be there. One could not say it *had* always been there, for the conditions that had promoted the insight were very much of the time, and he knew he could not have made his breakthrough even four or five years ago. He was, in all probability, the first person in the western world actually to synthesize all the available clues into a plan of action rather than a series of wan and perturbed hypotheses. A more whimsical intelligence would have ascribed a magical quality to the new knowledge, but Jack was sober enough to recognise that it was his own history as a pragmatist that had set him up for all this, rather than any silly 'tapping-in' to some 'intangible level'. Pragmatism, and his ability to see through the everyday to the pitiful vocabulary that determined it.

Draining the milk, Jack stopped congratulating himself and turned his attention to what he should actually do next. It was all very well, he conceded, to be granted the Big Licence, but there was still the matter of the first Driving Test. Clearly it wouldn't do to tear out of the door and get stuck in without a trial run of some sort. He would take his time, the new, redefined time, and he would not go out hunting for chances in the newly opened space because the chances were spread uniformly through that space and therefore required no hunting.

He put the milk bottle back into the drawer, inverted the teacup over it, and went into the street. There were people walking past his door. As soon as he saw them he reeled back and had to steady himself with the doorknob, fighting the extraordinary urge to duck back inside and hide in the stairway. He had actually broken out into a sweat, so he quickly wiped his brow with the free hand. Then he abruptly shut the door behind him and berated himself. What an arsehole! What a complete fucking jerk! What was the point if you were going to lose your bottle within two seconds of stepping into the field? But he just hadn't reckoned with this . . . this strangeness. What was it? He felt like a child somehow. He remembered something that absurd woman had said, Mrs Rousseau, 'An apple rolls into my circle, and it's the first apple. And the next one.' My God, he didn't want to catch anything off a client – that could be the thin end of a well-greased wedge. Yet there was something distinctly different here, and this first whiff was making him decidedly queasy. He glanced nervously down the street and tried to hold his gaze steady so that he might pin the thing down. There were gaps round the people. Not in the obvious way, of course, but in the sense of a kind of space around their bodies, as if each person were insulated by a cold, dead light that followed the lines of their trunk and limbs. Even as he blinked to affirm it, the impression faded, and he realised that that was perhaps all it had been, just an effect growing out of a powerful new notion. But then again, look at the trees, look at the cars – they've changed too. The pavement itself, the tarmac of the road even, everything there that was not actually a person, seemed to be, well, *radiating* in some way. Like the waves of air that rise and fold over the land in a heat wave, only glimpsed when the light is just right.

Jack screwed his eyes up and scanned the busy thoroughfare. Without a doubt there was a pulse of some sort streaming between every piece of hardware he could see, whether it was man-made or a plant of some sort. And the pedestrians, the shoppers, were not touched by it. The streaming simply passed around them with scarcely an eddy or a swirl. The people bore their cold light through a landscape that turned away from them. Or was it the other way round?

He looked down at his left arm. It looked quite normal, certainly no glow clung to it, or, conversely, a shrinking of the light. He moved it through the air, watching closely to see if it cut or disrupted the streaming that emanated from the front wall of his house. As soon as he focused on his arm the streaming disappeared entirely– all he could see was a familiar limb swinging to and fro beside his body. He stepped away from the house into the street and held his arm up against the sky, where it silhouetted and presented him with a hard edge that he could examine in the bright light. He tried locating the arm at the bottom of his field of vision and gazing across the top of it so that it went out of focus. There were no optical irregularities of any sort. He raised his other arm, spread the fingers of both hands and started a waving motion that bore the silhouetted fingers through the light in a crisscross pattern. None of this produced any of the information that he sought. He screwed up his eyes again and, while continuing to wave, slowly turned a complete circle, all the while straining to detect the curious halo that had clung to the people he had seen from the doorway.

Suddenly he caught sight of his reflection in the baker shop window. A man standing in the street, waving at the sky. He dropped his arms and looked around furtively to see if he had been drawing attention to himself. The passersby had not noticed him.

Jack slapped his brow and groaned. Of course no one had noticed him! Wasn't that exactly it? He laughed out loud for his lack of faith. His laughter threatened to assume the same intensity as his great weeping had done earlier. He leaned against the bonnet of a nearby car and allowed the exhilaration to roll out of him. Palms down on the warm metal, he bounced up and down playfully and felt the vehicle moving on its springs beneath him. Inside the car a woman eating sandwiches from a bag picked a piece of discoloured lettuce leaf from between the slices of bread. Jack whacked the car bonnet with both hands. An enormous weight seemed to be lifting away from him, taking with it the debris of numberless years of resentment. For the first time in his life he stood on the face of the planet and saw right round it to the back of his own head. This place wasn't a zoo, it wasn't an experiment, it was a new land, and if he was not the first to discover it, he was certainly going to be the first settler.

Out in the garden the gigantic gunnera leaves swayed above the flower beds and cast shuddering shadows well beyond the blooms onto the lawn. The plant came from the tropics, but Deany had picked it up at a garden centre. It reminded her of her other life, of course, and was the only concession to her love of those climes in an otherwise neat but crowded garden.

She sat in a deckchair with her back to the house and read her way through the papers and magazines piled on the grass beside her. Only a week ago she and Guy had held a press conference, jointly arranged by Olly and the television, to tell the world about Eke and Ike and their offspring. The response had been phenomenal – three hours after the conference was over, the Japanese were on the phone, then the Chileans. The Russians offered breeding pairs of any ten species from the Moscow Zoo and the Chinese promised a herd of pandas with a guaranteed replacement-within-ten-days policy for every beast that died either in transit or in its new home. None of them seemed to understand that the new animals were privately owned and housed in a run at the bottom of Guy and Deany's back garden. And Guy was not going to sell or swap with anybody. The creatures were for research, and he would care for them personally until a proper neurological facility had been put together. At the rate things were going this wouldn't take long, but he was anxious to stick to state funding and steer clear of the pharmaceuticals.

Deany dropped *Science Fact News* and picked up the *Daily Supplier*. OUCH! ran the headline, WHY BOTHER TO GET UP?, and beneath a picture of Eke and Ike in Deany's gauntletted arms, the report opened:

Darkly attractive Deany Blighton wife of explorer Guy well known to millions for their TV series We Went Away told me today that little Eke and Ike and their tiny offspring deep from the jungles of the dark continent from where Deany and Guy have recently returned on a flora and fauna gathering expedition are in constant and terrible pain. 'We have established beyond doubt,' said Deany who is careful not to let a playful nip turn to the rabies which laid husband Guy low, 'that Eke and Ike, who are members of a hitherto undiscovered genus, have a congenital neurological condition that results in their experiencing intolerable and incessant pain. This condition derives essentially from a structural characteristic of the cerebro-spinal system, which most probably organises the profounder aspects of the limbic system. The discomfort experienced by the animals therefore has no external origin at all, yet cannot be dismissed as illusory, for, from the animals' point of view it is as if the most intense hurt were being constantly and unremittingly renewed.' *Our Science Correspondent writes:* What she means is these poor rare jungle denizens have never known a moment's peace, a mother's soothing clasp, the contentment that follows a big meal, the freedom to swing from tree to tree with a mango in your mouth. From day one it's an ache. Can you imagine it? The whole affair will give scientists and philosophers the world over cause to review the most basic principles of evolution. And theologians. They should ask what their God had in mind. And ordinary working people. They should count their blessings.

Deany studied her photograph again. Funny how a determined smile can look kind of crazy when it's frozen like that – unless you knew that people holding animals in newspapers always smiled you might think this woman was frantically terrified of something. But then Eke and Ike didn't exactly look as though they were in pain either; Eke was actually upside down and appeared to be yawning, while the boy had both eyes shut and his paws in his mouth.

81

Olly had managed to get some of the foreign language articles translated, and had sent a folder of photocopies to the house. Among the items stapled in to the sheaf was an editorial from a Chilean national paper called, in rough translation, *The Spirit of Hazard*. Titled 'Two Hands at the Wheel?', the essay pursued the theological angles with a greater rigour than the British papers.

How ironic to find that today in apostate Britain a curiosity from the dark continent is reviving questions of the fallibility of the God so firmly rejected by this most materialistic of nations. Hastening to undo the work of nature, their philosophers are beating a treacherous path between an abruptly reopened New Testament and the Galapagan rigidities of their Charles Darwin. The uncertainty of these frustrated Empire builders will surprise our citizens, who have no abyss of godlessness to traverse in order to make common sense of what is clearly an integral facet of a marvellous plan. Despite the spirit of continuity that is so apparent in the religious life of our own country, we are not compelled to search in the past for our certitude. The discovery of this Eke and Ike in their exotic home is not a magical affair – it is merely timely, emphasising that the tableau of Nature was painted not by an amateur of mechanics but by a figure whose mercy is infinite not only through space but across the whole of time. This is a modern sign from One who sees that a world weakened by the diseases of so-called psychological science will now respond positively to the notion that suffering is not a consequence but a perfected and implicit condition.

Deany didn't think about the Chilean angle for too long – like many of the pieces she had read, it took a philosophical position on something around which anyone in the natural sciences could virtually build a career. The neurology alone was so utterly astounding that once the rewriting of basic text books had been done, those still inclined to abstract any moral lesson from the business would have to invent virtually a new grammar. Give it a year or two, then pump out the high-flown stuff. She drank her apple juice and reached for something meatier. I FUCKING WANT ONE AINSLEY ran the headline on *The Continuous Present*. The English passion for table tennis escaped her entirely, but its champion was kind of hard to avoid unless you lived in a cave. '"Yes I do,"' ran the story:

'They are completely unique and so am I. It all goes together. Suffering is a terrible thing. I could give a good home.' Ainsley, never a man for the half-measure, is prepared to pay well over the odds for the chance to own one of the sensational pain-animals. 'Fuck one, I want a pair,' he told me when I called him at his country house today. 'I want to breed them and help them out of their misery. Pain comes from not having everything. Well I fucking got out of that one on my own, so I can get them out of it. Right?' How will explorer naturalist Guy Blighton react to this suggestion from our greatest sporting personality? Sadly for our young hero, this may be one contest he cannot win, for the Blightons are not intending to release any of the animals in the near future. Guy Blighton said, 'I'm afraid we deplore the attitude that exotic animals can be regarded as household pets. There is absolutely no possibility of their being available outside the scientific community.'

Out of juice, a cloud over the sun, Deany squirmed round in the deckchair to look up at the house. No sign of Guy. Normally a punctilious early riser, he had lately been lying in for as long as two hours past breakfast time. The rabies seemed to have sapped his reserves at a level deeper than his otherwise hearty manner would suggest. The doctor had told him this might well be the case for some months, and Guy, predictably, had scoffed at the notion. He reconciled his rejection of medical opinion with the daily evidence of his lingering fatigue by becoming annoyed with anyone who mentioned it. As long as he made his own breakfast Deany was prepared to let him snooze back to being a hale fellow at his own pace.

She walked up to the house, put her shoes on, took her bag and headed out for the garage. Some birds were doing peculiar things in the garden. Flying around wildly, scrapping on the grass, pecking at the tree trunks. They were not woodpeckers, however, but starlings. Deany tried to make out if there was a ringleader or a scapegoat, but it seemed to be general bird madness. After a couple of minutes they flew off.

Deany was going into town, to see Olly, to talk photos. Might take an hour at the most. She had other things to do after that.

The place was packed and all eyes were most definitely on Guy. He was the most important person in the place. The place was certainly big enough. The roof was very high, and the walls very far apart. The gentlemen from the press were very much in evidence, but so were an equally great or even greater number who could be described as simply admirers of Guy or admirers of his achievements. From the platform he scanned the faces to see what they were like, and found some attentive, some kindly, some with slight smiles that showed they were looking forward to what he was going to do.

The attractive young woman who was going to start the proceedings was certainly darkly attractive, such as a woman from Mexico or Italy often is. She came up to Guy, came up to his face, leaned over to his ear and said that if it was all right with him to start the proceedings she would go right ahead and start the proceedings. As she spoke into his ear he heard her say some things about the fact that she found him attractive too, but he found that those words were slightly vague and possibly more to do with the effect created by her warmth and the sounds of her breath coming out.

The Award was for Body Achievements and after the speech from the woman the President of the Association came forward and up to Guy. He was dressed very smartly and Guy noticed that his jacket had cuffed sleeves with small jewelled buttons, which was an unusual tailoring detail. The Award was in a small flat box which the President opened and there, inside, on red velvet, was the Award: a medal. There was no ribbon or pin, it was a medal you kept in a box with the lid open for looking at it. But the President lifted it from the little box and held it whilst saying various things. These things were quite hard to hear because of the hum from the crowd. The crowd was not being noisy, but there were so many people in it expressing interest to each other that their small exchanges combined to make up such a volume that the murmur from the President could not quite be caught.

The medal, which was golden and engraved, came up out of the box in the President's hand and he held it out to Guy. Guy was not sure what to do with it. He could put it in his pocket. But first he should look at it, of course. He could look at it, naturally, then put it in his pocket. Something about that plan seemed wrong. It seemed a bit tawdry, or a word like that. Just to drop it into the pocket. The humming, interested people in the crowd, his admirers many of them, would know that the pocket had not been especially prepared for the medal and that it might be slightly dusty or containing typical small pieces of pocket grit, or the grey fluff that often comes out with money. Guy put his hand into his pocket and there certainly were things like that in there. The President was still holding the medal out, the Award, and obviously Guy must at least go towards it, at the very least, for the people watching, for their sake. He took the golden medal and held it and the crowd gave him some enthusiastic applause. The medal was quite warm. He held it for some moments and then decided to put it on the table. He smiled modestly and nodded his head in a thanking gesture and then put the medal down onto the table.

The President said to him, 'Haven't you got a pocket?' and Guy said, 'It's not really good enough.' The President said, 'You should take it.' Guy said, 'People can see it on the table. It makes sense.' The President said, 'Will you pick it up eventually?' and the dark woman in charge of proceedings said, 'Be sure that you take it in the long run.'

It was expected that Guy give some exhibition after the Award, of the kind of achievements he had made. The rolling over seemed a good choice. He got onto the table and lay down on his back. The crowd of people buzzed with expectation, for they knew what to expect now. Guy found that what was required was a short sharp intake of breath so that the centre of his rib-cage rose suddenly. This was sufficient to achieve the required lifting so that when he rolled round his nose very nearly touched the table top in passing. It was then a question of leading with the shoulder right round until he was on his back again. The crowd of people admired this achievement a great deal. Guy lifted up again, only a few inches, and rolled the other way. This time he took it more slowly, so that they could appreciate that the air was quite thick around him. As his nose slowly came round to face the shiny table top he stopped rolling and just hung there. After some moments all he had to do was push very gently at the air beneath his palms, and very smoothly he stood right up so that he was standing an inch or two above the table. This achievement was taken very well by the assembled people in the hall and Guy could feel their great admiration easily. Then he went down to the ground and it was a question of journeying to the next destination.

During the journey he refused the dates offered by the darkly attractive hostess several times. They were on a tray and glistened freshly, but Guy simply had no interest in them. After the third or possibly the fourth time of offering, the hostess said, 'And just exactly why do you not want the dates that I bring?' but he just looked at her from his seat and would not answer. On the fifth occasion she smiled at him warmly and suggested, 'We really should fix up some dates' and he said, 'No I'm afraid I'm absolutely full up, we should try some other time.' There really was no urgency or enmity in it from either side. She leaned down to him and he could feel her smiling close to his ear and her breath and perfume combined in a cloud that seemed full of promise. She left the tray on his arm-rest so that at any time he could simply take a dark date in his hand if he so wished.

The news of the Award and Guy's achievements had travelled before him and when he got there a crowd of various people were assembled. One man stepped forward. He was an older type of man, and although smartly dressed in diplomatic getup namely the morning suit with striped trousers, grey waistcoat, top hat and the other details, Guy noticed that his neck was quite scrawny in a way that did not immediately suggest good living, rather a life either of indigence or, it then struck him, abandon. Also the neck of the man had been rather poorly shaven so that pale blond bristles in the folds of the skin caught the light.

The man was obviously of some standing amongst the party, and Guy readily extended his hand in greeting. The man grasped Guy's hand with both his hands, enclosing it in two warm, older man's hands that bore veins quite visibly at their surface. Guy knew little of the Masonic Order or its arcane procedures. He knew little of the wearing of the aprons and the distribution of scrolls of membership, and he was barely aware of the greeting procedures. Nevertheless, he knew something of these matters. When the man began to trace shapes with a sharp fingernail upon Guy's right-hand palm. Guy immediately knew that a covert communication was in progress, and almost drew back in protest. The fingernail etched along his life-line, transected his heart-line and arced through many of the other creases that signified career change, number of children and cause of death. At first he thought that the scratching was in a foreign language, such as might be expected from a European branch of the Masonic Order, but then he realised that the fish, the twins, the bull and so on were being sketched. Not only that, but in a gold line that glowed briefly on the palm before fading out. As the water-carrier was traced, he felt an aqueous ripple in his knees which caused them to knock. He thought that the bow and arrow would be next and something caused his teeth to chatter and made him shrink away, but curiously this particular picture was omitted from the set.

The man said, 'You left your medal back there, but I've got it with me as a matter of fact. Would you like to take it now?' Guy said, 'It's

86

just a question of not putting it in my pocket. I'm reluctant.' The man said, 'You can hold it.' Guy said, 'I feel it would become moist. I'd like you to take charge of it until later.' The old figure straightened up and smiled ravishingly. His lips were full and of the type that drew back over the teeth and then over the gum during the smile. His teeth were absolutely perfect, quite beautiful.

Down in the street the crowd had lined up on both sides. Guy saw that the ground had been covered in big dry leaves from the typical trees of the area, and so he walked on them. He even noticed one or two dates glistening on the leaves, among them, but he still felt no need for them, to snack, and was content to let them be attractive fixtures of the novel covering, the covering that was a welcome.

He walked between the rows of crowds, noticing that men wearing the burnous stood out from the others, who, though vague to the eye, were for the most part decked in broad-brimmed hats, coloured neckerchieves and leather over-trousers. The women among those vague to the eye wore, in addition to the hats, fringed shirts. But these figures were part of the scene really, while the men in burnous were outstandingly jocular, with marvellous brows and hooked sallow noses.

'Hey, pal!' hissed one of them. 'Heard about the body. Good, good!' 'White boy,' another hisser. 'We appreciate what you're doing. If only you knew about us.'

Guy stopped and said, 'Knew what?'

The two flowing robed men stepped out of the crowd. Some of their colleagues filled in the blank spaces around them, as background. 'Listen: once we hadda tent, harem, swords, everything. We had, what, stallions, falcons, rifles, er . . .'

'Couscous,' supplied the other one.

'Yeah, that. And silver dishes, you know, everything out of silver dishes. All different kinds of food. With spice. We had all kinds of spice.'

'Sandalwood. We had sandalwood.' The other one eagerly.

'That's for the perfume, right? Not, like, for the wood. I mean, wood sandals? That's going to hurt, right? Put'em on, get a lot of foot trouble, blisters, whatever.'

'We had the whole picture, all the shit. Yeah. Rugs. Moving around the whole time.'

'Nomadic,' now the first one filling in.

'We knew where to find what we want, okay? Water. We hadda knowledge of how to get to that. And maps. Not too sure, you've got the map.'

'We were at home. Wherever. How many can say that? Down off the stallion, unload the rugs. Little coffee coming up. For us, that is more than just adequate. That's home. Sun goes down. Little spiced tea. Read some scrolls. The end of a perfect day. What more, what more?'

'Except for what happened then.'

'What did happen?' Guy enquired, for the men were not unlikeable.

'One morning, no particular reason that we can see now, everybody, the whole party, they forgot how to carry on. You know what I'm saying?'

'No, I don't follow you,' Guy said.

'We look at the stuff around us, the stuff we had, that we mentioned, and this is typical to our picture, *was* typical, now I gotta say, and it's like nobody knows what the fuck to do with it. Like, there's the fucking falcon, right on the end of yer fucking arm – whadda you do with it?'

'Or there's the tent – how do you move it around? Do you have to cut it up, or drag it behind the fucking stallion, or what? We didn't know. Nobody knew. The wives didn't know. We're standing there. Perplexed.'

'And who knows how to find water now? Soon what we got is gonna run out, we're gonna die, so we say, "Hey, anybody here still know how to be nomadic?" and one fellow says, "Yeah, it means to wander about" so we just took off. Just fucking left the stuff situated there.'

'We hadda leave it. Everything. Tent, all the various equipment. Just situated in the last place we been, by the water we found. What use is it to us?'

'This is it, right? It has a use, this material, this is obvious, but we don't have a connection no more. So – we should go. Fuck it.'

'So we did. Walked to here. All the fellows. All the guys that you see in the hooded outfits.'

'Burnous, isn't it?' Guy said.

'You knew that? Good!'

'What about the women?' Guy asked.

'They're not here.'

'You left them behind?'

'Had to. All part of the picture, right? No longer our picture – we don't know what to do with them.'

88

'That's terrible.' Guy was quite shocked.

'Fuck, it's all terrible. We're just wandering about – that's all we know what to do.'

'We were a great race.'

'Got nowhere to stay. Nowhere to go. No equipment.'

Guy said, 'You need to find somewhere you can get back with your women.'

'Listen, that's the truth of it. We got to stop wandering.'

'You have any ideas on that, pal?'

Guy said, 'I can't say that I have.'

'At the moment we're raising funds. We figure to get money here and use it to live. Maybe then we find somewhere to go. Maybe we remember how to carry on.'

Guy said, 'How will you make money?'

All the men in burnous stepped clear of the men and women in check shirts and leather belts and moved onto the leaf-strewn pathway. They crowded round Guy, nodding and grinning. Some of them started telling jokes with a folkloric basis, and the punchlines were greeted with waves of great mirth. Many of the faces were vague, but of those near Guy, not all were dark, sallow or swarthy, by any means. Studying them as they swirled round him, he saw British and American faces, and those of youths, married men, business men and even slightly rakish figures. He was struck by the absence of any strong smells of animal fats, ambergris or similar male perfume.

One of the men in burnous, who had a reposeful, cultured face, with a dash of the business man, pushed some of his robed colleagues aside and addressed Guy directly.

'Allow me to introduce myself. Some of these fellows are quite direct, but they should not be construed as lacking in manners. Our situation is indeed extreme, and to that end we should welcome your co-operation in a small project we have devised.'

The pleasant man clapped his hands. The striped garments rippled as the jostling men parted to allow another of their number to approach Guy. This person carried a tray which appeared to be on fire. When the person reached Guy, it was possible to see that the smoke was steam, and that it was rising from a pile of pastries or other small cooked things. The quiet, measured man turned again to Guy, indicating the tray with a flourish, 'Our project'.

Guy said, 'What are they?'

He said, 'They are our cakes.'

Guy said, 'They look hot.'

The man said, 'They sell better like that.'

Guy said, 'Who makes them?'

'They are a small spicy cake remembered by one of the men. Some bits and pieces of useful knowledge still hang about.'

'This is where you can help us, buddy,' interjected one of the earlier men.

The polite man motioned the other to be silent. 'Your work in Body Achievements is known everywhere. Were you to honour us by taking a cake the world would follow.'

Guy said, 'I'm very flattered but as much as I sympathise with your cause I'm afraid I cannot associate myself with any commercial promotions. It would be against the spirit of Body Achievements.'

The men all murmured disappointedly. The nice man nodded. 'I quite understand your position, and appreciate that it derives from the best ethical motives. However, if you were to sample one of these little cakes, I think you might find that they are truly delicious and a commodity well worth introducing to a greater viewing public.' The men nodded energetically and grunted their warm agreement. Guy said, 'Please do not misunderstand me. I am sure that the little cakes are delicious. I am sure that they are skilfully and carefully made. Doubtless their introduction to a larger market would prove to be a worthwhile and successful venture. But despite the degree of prominence which I currently enjoy, I must repeat that I simply cannot exploit these advantages in the furtherance of a venture, which although arguably having charitable goals, will be seen by the eating public at large as a wing or facet of the bakery business.' Guy was beginning to feel heated.

Some of the more emotional burnoused men began to moan and tug at their garments. One of the two earlier men suddenly lunged forward, his eyes flashing. The polite man frowned and held out an arm to check him, but he ducked and threw himself towards the tray. Then he seized a cake from the steaming pile and put it straight into his mouth, chewing fiercely and gesturing with his hands to indicate that he would speak as soon as he had swallowed enough to permit movement of his tongue. Then he spoke, 'Oh! Oh! I'm tasting now what is the complete symphony of what can happen in all the most exceptional eating!'

This declaration seemed to act as a coded release mechanism on the gathered others. They swooped, they fell on the cakes, cannoning into Guy, elbowing him aside, juggling the hot items on their fingertips because they were still so hot, going 'Ooh! Ooh!' at the heat. The composed man shook his head and glanced upwards resignedly. Soon every man had a cake in his mouth and was shouting his reaction to Guy.

'These cakes, I gotta tell you!'

'This is unbelievable what's happening!'

'Say to the world "Here is for your mouth the ultimate thing!"'

Guy felt very hemmed in. The noise was hard to take, and he started to look around for a way out of the melee. The business man took his arm and shouted in his ear, 'Look, all you have to do is take one with you. Don't have to eat it here. Try it at your leisure. Let us know what you decide. I can't guarantee your safety with these men, they're so bloody excitable at times.' Without letting go of Guy, he leaned over, deftly lifted one of the last hot cakes from the tray and before Guy realised what was happening, pressed it into his hand.

The men stopped yelling their random endorsements and encircled Guy and the businessman. They began to chant. 'Take the cake! Take the cake!' The cake itself was extremely hot on Guy's palm, extremely hot indeed. His eyes bulged and he opened his mouth to yell, whilst twisting his wrist and trying to back away from the business man. The latter was possessed of an iron grip, however, and all of Guy's efforts were reduced to a series of hops and skips which did not succeed in moving him even one inch from his tormentor.

The cake was actually searing into his flesh, he was sure of it. He started to yell now, and this somehow released a reserve of strength which he translated into one almighty, wrenching heave. The business man's grip was broken and Guy's arm flew off in reaction, causing his hand to smack violently into something beside him.

A sharp pain across the back of his hand made him roll over to find its source. To his intense annoyance he discovered that the travelling clock was on its back, and that its folding lid had torn off, breaking open the hinge irreparably. 'Bloody hell,' he muttered. Then, rapidly recalling that he was rather attached to that clock, and they didn't make them anymore, he said 'Shit!' with considerably more force. He looked at his hand and saw the evidence of his folly, a faint red welt below the knuckles. Then he turned his hand over and looked with horror at the raw, blistered flesh that seeped blood from its roughly circular wound on the centre of his palm.

He sat up and stared wildly at the wound. There seemed to be no pain in the hand, only the small sensation deriving from the impact with the clock, and that was on the other side. He wiggled his fingers and made a tentative half-fist, almost willing some pain to declare itself. None came. He suddenly looked down at his chest – bloodstains. None. Nor was there blood on the pillow or the sheets. He tore the coverlet back and leaped out of the bed in a single bound, having been seized with an awful terror at the thought that some blade or device or electric wire or . . . but the stripped bed was as bare as it should be.

Guy, swallowing repeatedly and licking his lips, scrutinised his fingernails. Obviously he had been scratching himself for some reason, maybe a bite, and the thing had itched infernally so he'd gone on and on. It was obviously a bite, but Christ almighty, you'd think he would have stopped at drawing blood. But the fingernails were quite clean, no blood on or beneath them. But there must be. What kind of a bite gets like that in the course of a single night?

Then he considered the blisters. A translucent dome of flesh, clearly etched with the lines that normally creased his palm, rose from a livid areola that flushed from one side of his hand to the other, and from wrist to finger joints. The dome had ruptured, leaving the skin partially puffed and dented. From the tear in the flesh there suppurated a clear liquid. Around the large blister, edging into the lividness, were several much smaller, intact blisters. At certain points on the reddened skin, near the mound of the thumb, and at the base of the first two fingers, the hardened surface had cracked open, more or less along the lines that were already there. It was from those cracks that blood seeped.

Now blisters were from friction. Or burning. But how could he have burned himself? And, for God's sake, what kind of friction would produce a mess like that?

Guy slumped onto the side of the bed. It couldn't be the bloody rabies, surely? That was weeks ago. He was sleeping a bit more than usual, but that was to be expected. And does rabies produce blisters, weeks after the event? Hardly.

So it was a bite. Had to be. He jumped off the bed again, and peered closely at the sheets. Bed bugs or something. Mosquitoes. Maybe Deany had been bitten. Nothing on the sheets. But they'd hop off. You'd have to creep up on them. If Deany had been bitten as well, there's your answer.

He went down to the kitchen. On the table was a pile of the latest cuttings and magazines. He looked into the garden. The deckchair was empty. Some birds were scrapping near the path. He heard the car start. She must be going up to town. Would he chase out after her? He stood, hunched up, holding his left wrist with his right hand, as though there were pain, but there wasn't. For a moment he wished that it really hurt.

Jack sauntered down the street in his new mentality. Some way down from the office was the TV rental shop. There were some six or eight colour sets in the window, and every single one of them was tuned in to Ainsley. It goes without saying that there was, therefore, a sizeable crowd assembled on the pavement. Ainsley was British, which was probably a major factor; he was incredibly accomplished, that was another; and he had an exceptional manner. Ainsley had been on the front page of the papers for two years now, since he was fifteen, in fact. His career was clearly on the ascendant, according to the experts, and would continue to be so for some considerable time. He was already considered the most skilled practitioner in the recorded history of his vocation, and was held by many virtually to have reinvented a pursuit that had been written off throughout the country as hopelessly old fashioned and lacking in appeal. Ainsley's idiosyncratic style of dress had been slavishly adopted by countless fans, not all of whom were adolescents by any means. His habit of wearing either powder blue or pale pink brushed woollen tights beneath brief shorts had captivated young and old alike, and quite overwhelmed the cynics who had claimed Ainsley was afraid to show his true legs. Few now were the public houses about whose bars there would not be two or three men or women of all ages clad in the short-and-tight combination that was readily available in any number of high street clothes shops. And few too were the voices of derision raised against Ainsley's supporters, for it had long been clear to all and sundry that Ainsley made perfect sense, and the emulation of his ways could only lead his emulators to a greater sense of that sense.

So unequivocally and indisputably in order were Ainsley's ways that the two most vociferous groups of his early detractors, namely the women and the old fools, were decisively won over within a few weeks of trumpeting their initial objections. The women had been particularly exercised by Ainsley's catchphrase, which was 'Fuck off you cunts'. They had said that it was demeaning to them to use the anatomical term as an insult, for it equated the anatomical part *with* an insult. Ainsley had been riding particularly high at the time, and the mood of the country, and of course, Ainsley himself, was well captured by the banner headline of one of the national papers, run at the height of the controversy. In 64 point Gill Bold beneath the masthead it read TO THE WOMEN and beneath that, in 124 point, it continued FUCK OFF YOU CUNTS. After this it became clear to the women that Ainsley's ways were very much a measure of an inner intent, and the coincidence of this intent with qualities that the country both required and admired could not be ignored. Several other papers editorialised on the controversy, with the left-of-centre journals arguing quite carefully through the women's objections. The women eventually realised the extent to which Ainsley was articulating a long suppressed societal need and got off his back.

The old fools did not understand the point the women had been trying to make, but nevertheless did object generally to his foulness of mouth. Ainsley's dicta were particularly trying for them, printed as they were on clothing and hoardings and shouted across streets and in public places by the young. It is probable that the famous do not set out to produce dicta, but finding themselves widely quoted cannot subsequently resist making their pronouncements in dictum-sized pack-ages. When Ainsley first said, 'Every bastard pisses on you', one can be fairly sure that he had no idea of the way in which that statement would be taken as a model response for a wide variety of situations, some of which bore little resemblance to the incident that Ainsley had initially found so provocative. But the element of injustice in all situations was pinpointed so appositely by his throwaway remark that the public was not at all surprised when, in the course of a press conference, a government minister used the phrase in connection with the short shrift he had received on behalf of his country at a meeting with the Europeans. Ainsley may have felt at this point that to be quoted was to be in some way appropriated for he took to suffixing his sayings with his own name, which certainly established a patent, although some argued that he was thereby making it rather obvious that he regarded his statements as formal dicta rather than casual felicities. Be that as it may, the folkloric instinct, buried so shallowly in all peoples, surfaced in its fullest bloom of national idiosyncrasy and Ainsley's dicta came to be widely used with the suffix intact. Thus, late at night after parties, the followers of Ainsley would now shout, 'Every bastard pisses on you Ainsley', or, wishing to be assertive, 'Any bugger looks at me then shit Ainsley', or, in simple disbelief, 'What? I'll cut my fucking cock off Ainsley'. Of course, some of Ainsley's dicta were, strictly speaking, only catchphrases, like 'Fuck off you cunts Ainsley', but insofar as all his sayings spoke for experiences that were universal it was felt that they were worthy of a more sublime status, one that emphasised durability rather than transience. Thus it was that everyone would ask, 'Have you heard Ainsley's most recent dictum?' rather than ditto ditto 'catchphrase'.

An Ainsley crowd could be spotted a mile off because of the way they flailed their arms and shouted. The group in front of the TV shop was no exception, and as Jack approached it he could hear some of the dicta being bellowed out above the general roars of approval. The arm-flailing was in energetic imitation of Ainsley's own arm movements, and lent the crowd an air of extraordinary animation, which on closer inspection was belied by the solitary absorption of each of its members. Ainsley's spell bound them to him alone, to such an extent that they appeared oblivious to each other's presence, and were therefore not a proper crowd at all. Every time Ainsley executed the notorious Smash, or the infamous Blur, the group on the pavement would follow him within a split second, and the chorus of raspberries rose like the harsh drone of a buzz saw. Part of Ainsley's exceptional manner was his use of the blown raspberry at unexpected points in his sentences and when actually at work, his Smash and Blur seemed incomplete if they were not rounded off by a blast from his pursed lips. If the Smash or Blur failed to disarm the opposition, Ainsley would not rasp, but shout 'Fuck' or 'Shit', unless he felt that the opposition was being vindictive, in which case he would say 'Arsewipe' or 'Cocksucker'.

Ainsley had a marvellous sense of humour, which endeared him to a wider audience than would normally follow anything in this particular field. Two years back, when he had first caught the attention of the press, Ainsley would turn to the crowd at the end of each victorious encounter with the opposition and simply ask them, in a strong but not strident voice, 'What did I tell you, you fucking pitiful bastards?' Walking right round the table he would repeat the question at each of the four sides, holding out his arms and scanning the rows from left to right with a proud, challenging expression on his face. At first the crowds were nonplussed by such a direct approach, but after one particularly savage encounter, in the course of which Ainsley had displayed some exceptionally blurred strokework, concluding with a decisive victory, he proceeded to ask his questions in the usual way and then, returning to the table, pounded it fiercely with his clenched fists and screamed 'Ping! Pong!' at the top of his voice. The opposition was utterly transfixed, but the crowd suddenly got the joke and started laughing and clapping. Again Ainsley yelled out 'Ping! PONG!' and the two funny little syllables suddenly assumed a dignity and moral power that few would have thought possible. The shouting of 'Ping' was inflected in such a way that the opposition, and any other doubters, were subtly chastised for their rashness in taking Ainsley, his youth, or his tights, so lightly. The shouting of 'PONG' was thoroughly condemnatory, but it served to remind the opposition of the vanity of his initial competitive stance, and the absolute inevitability of his subsequent vanquishment. Thus, while ruthless in its moral tone, the 'PONG' drew attention to the frailty of man when he nursed aspirations beyond the purview of his genetic horizon.

Journalists were not slow to pick up on Ainsley's humorous side, and a number of at-surface articles were published which had the effect of promoting his victory cry to catchphrase status within days of his first using it in the field. 'Ping! Pong!' went public several weeks before the emergences of 'Fuck off you cunts', and prepared the ground for the dicta. Some of the left-of-centre sporting journalists pointed out the rigorously principled sub-text to 'Ping! Pong!', and were able to show thereby that Ainsley's humour was not a casual, specious thing. In fact, Ainsley's insistence on using the term 'ping pong' instead of the more established 'table tennis' was held by some commentators to represent a distillation of all that was vitally attractive in the youngster's personality. By reverting to an old-fashioned usage that had overtones of amateurism, they contended, Ainsley was rejecting the exclusivism that adhered to the concept of professionalism, and returning the game to the people. His familiar query, 'Who built this fucking table?' could be seen as an admonition to those who had failed to consider the team-based background to the star game, a background that included craftsmen and artisans of the bat, ball and so forth, working in sheds under poor light.

Jack drew level with the followers. It was clear what he had to do, and there was nothing to be gained by hesitation, no virtue in trying to find the 'right moment'. He stepped towards the nearest follower, a bespectacled man in his forties, and stuck his tongue in the man's ear.

The man was moving around quite a lot, so Jack took hold of his neck in order to keep in contact. From this very close position he could hear his subject breathing excitedly and grunting to himself whenever Ainsley pulled off one of his stunners. After a while, however, the man flailed his arms in response to a Blur, and Jack was knocked off balance.

His first choice had been fairly tall, Jack realised, forcing him to stand on tiptoe. He walked straight over to a shorter member of the crowd, a woman in her late twenties, wearing Ainsley shorts over jeans. Jack leaned forward, lifted her long hair aside, and placed the tip of his tongue in her left ear. He used his right hand on her far shoulder to steady himself, and found that as long as he anticipated her arm movements, he could maintain the position for as long as he liked. Having established this, he stepped away and scrutinised the rest of the crowd. On the far side, close to the window, stood a policeman, apparently as engrossed in the game as any of the other bystanders. Jack's pulse quickened. The risk was considerable, but as a definitive bench-test, the situation offered no parallel. He wondered if he was taking on too much too soon, but that seemed to make nonsense of his revelation, and he had to remind himself that this cautionary style of thinking was now a relic of another time and, of course, another place.

The policeman's truncheon hung from its strap beneath the flap of his tunic. Jack tugged at it experimentally, trying to figure out how it might be released. In the back pocket of the constable's trousers he felt a bulky protuberance, so he raised the rear flap of the tunic in order to take a look. As he expected, it was only the combined thicknesses of a street guide and a notebook. He dropped the flap and put his arm round the man's neck, inadvertently adopting a comradely pose. As the policeman roared and shouted, Jack began stroking his cheek and chin. The stubble of a morning shave scraped his fingertips, and the jaw movements made the flesh of the man's cheek bulge and slacken.

Breathing as steadily as he could, Jack considered his next move. The test couldn't be regarded as thorough unless it had a controllable abort – he was not yet in a position to assume that every sortie came with its own exit. Without breaking the rhythm of his stroking movements, Jack passed his free hand quickly across the policeman's line of vision, so that the latter's view of the window was interrupted for no more than a fraction of a second. The man did not react in any way that Jack could detect, so he raised his hand again, this time much more slowly, so that it broke the sight line for at least a full second. The man's body quivered perceptibly – its musculature slackened and the tension of excitement was distinctly reduced, returning as soon as full vision was restored.

Jack moved to the logical conclusion of the process. He blocked the sight line completely, holding his hand one inch from the policeman's eyes. The man's head swivelled instantly in Jack's direction, and in that same instant Jack removed his hand from around the other's shoulder and took a step back.

'Can you tell me where the nearest supermarket is, please?' Jack enquired evenly.

With only the faintest suggestion of surprise the constable responded, 'Two hundred yards down on your left. Blue Wave.'

'Oh. Thank you.' Jack strode off down the road. Ainsley did a Blur. Cries of 'Cheat Death Shit Gobblers Ainsley' filled the air. So far so pretty good. That had to be definitive, didn't it? Couldn't ask for much more at this stage, could you?

Coming abreast of Blue Wave Jack noticed the Big Offers and pushed through the glass doors. At the cash desk a teenager sat watching two television screens; one a security scanner, the other tuned to Ainsley. Both screens were small, and the Ainsley station was turned down low so that it did not cut through the soft music piped around the store. The shelves nearest the cash desk featured liquor, confectionery and biscuits, with an open freezer-cabinet full of cheese and dairy products a little further along. Jack stepped through the aisle and sat on an unmanned desk next to the teenager. 'Fucking Ainsley,' Jack said.

The teenager did not look up, but nodded his head, 'Right.'

'Shit that other guy,' referring to Ainsley's hapless opponent.

'Definite wanker,' the youth agreed.

Jack strolled over to the biscuit shelf. Something plain, but not a cracker, was what he had in mind. 'Killing him, is he?' Selecting a package of wholemeal biscuits and moving across to the cheese.

'He's pissing in his face,' the kid said.

'Piss is too good for these turds,' Jack suggested. A herb cheese with garlic, soft and fatty. 'Got a knife?'

'What for?' asked the young person. Jack almost faltered. He was on a high wire, and you don't falter, it's as simple as that. He caught his breath, and tried not to rush. 'Spread this.'

The cashboy reached under the till and produced a penknife. Still without taking his eyes off the screen, he held it out to Jack, who opened it up and proceeded to spread the cheese onto his biscuit. It was a pleasant enough snack, so Jack sat on the desk again and prepared another. Ainsley had just won the first game and was screaming at his opponent. The kid clapped his hands and joined in. 'Fucking bred back shitsweeping tossgirly Ainsley!' he yelled. 'You sub the lid pigarse bummage repositorium of cack Ainsley!' he hollered, pounding the till with the Next Customer sign.

'Toilet dwarf of brownest belt,' volunteered Jack, who had been eyeing the wine racks and thinking about his next appointment.

'Ainsley,' added the boy.

'Ainsley,' Jack corrected himself and lifted one or two full-bodied Italians out for the once over. For a spring evening though, he would choose a white. He reached across the lad for a carrier, confident in his earlier discovery that brief interruptions were feasible, and loaded in two Frascatis and an Orvieto. On the way back, once he was clear of the sight line, he ruffled the boy's fair hair with his hand and spoke into his ear. 'Fucking monkeyblood filthgate shitocaust fucking bastards fucking Ainsley.'

Deany was about to enter the café as Jack turned the corner, so he shouted her name and waved. She was wearing a belted shirt-dress and looked lovely. Jack beamed.

'You didn't mind meeting downtown?' she asked.

'No trouble. I don't live so far from here.'

'I've been to see our publisher. He's just over the road.'

'Hot stuff. What do you want to do?'

'Well, do you want to get a coffee?'

'Well, I've got this wine here,' he swung the carrier.

'Oh yeah.' Pause.

'It needs to be chilled. It's a nice evening, isn't it?'

'You got a freezer?'

Whoof he thought. Deany giggled.

'Yeah. Wouldn't take too long.'

'You can put ice in it, you know.'

'Do Italians do that?'

'Is it Italian?'

'Yeh.'

'I never went to Italy. But Americans do. Put ice.'

'I met an Italian the other day. I should have asked.'

'The dog lady?'

'You remembered.'

'Doesn't happen every day.'

'Americans put ice in wine?'

'Sure. You have to drink it before it melts.'

They were walking along. She took his arm.

'I'll take your arm?'

'You already did.'

'I'm polite. Sometimes before, sometimes just after.'

'Polite is good.'

'Is it?'

'Well, yeh. Depends on the situation.'

'You think about polite. I can tell.'

Jack laughed. He closed his elbow to his waist so that her hand was squeezed, just for a moment.

'You take clients to your house?'

'Never. You got a problem?'

'Not at all. Everything is kind of dandy right now.'

'What about your work?'

'That's what I mean. We're really onto something.'

'Great. What?'

'I shouldn't say yet. But it's those animals, you remember?'

'Sure. Your husband said they were new.'

'They are. A whole new genus.'

'What's a genus?'

'It's a group that has characteristics distinct from all other groups.'

'Is that good?'

'Sure. Genus is good. Especially with animals. Plants everybody knows there's a bunch to be discovered. Animals, these days, that's really exceptional.'

'You could make a lot of money.'

'You're kidding. How do you make money out of an animal?'

'There has to be something in it.'

'Naturally. We get funds for more work. We don't make a buck on it though.'

'Uh.'

'But this isn't just any old new animal, you know. Those creatures are totally amazing. They have some incredible characteristics.'

'What like?'

'You don't read the papers?'

'I don't get the science page.'

'They're in pain all the time. You didn't hear about that?'

'I didn't. Can't you give them something?'

'It's in their nervous system – it's natural. Like hair or breathing.'

'Maybe they're just very honest.'

'All the time?'

'Who knows? I still can't believe there's no money in it.'

'We don't look at it like that.'

'Give me all your research stuff and I'll sell it for you.'

'Another time, huh? Not that I don't trust you.'

'You *do* trust me?' He affected wide-eyed surprise.

'I'm visiting your place. But I know I'm gonna be perfectly all right. How's that?' She affected a jokey piercing stare.

'I've got a little balcony.'

'That sounds safe.'

'This is my front door.'

The water was tuned to the hot-cold-hot-cold pulse. This ensured that no state could be enjoyed overlong. As the hot dispersed the bare metals of chill it was easy to feel yourself going backwards. Back towards what, Ainsley did not specify, not having any psychological terminology at his disposal. But in another way of speaking, definitely back, back to cosy hearths, obviously, or nests, things which were creature comforts. And not the sort of creature that he wanted to be. The cold got rid of all those considerations, made him go forwards. So why not keep it cold all the time? Because he knew that life was not all cold, life had its regular pleasures, its hot waters, and there was no point in ignoring them, he was not stupid.

Although the sole purpose of everything he did was to move forwards, he knew that he had to keep on his toes at all times. You could easily become slack and flatfooted by staying in one state for too long. So forwards must be mixed with backwards, then you never came to rely on it, you were in a constant state of changing your state, and this was exactly what his work required, never being complacent, always ready, always *agitated* was the word that he used. And so that this worked in the work, then it must be practised in the life, so that it became natural, and this was why he had bought the pulse system for his bathroom.

His body, a thing that Jack would ponder on later, was pale and interesting. He himself had no such opinion. He was, it should be remembered, still young, and saw his body in quite narrow terms. It was a fit thing, a not fat thing, it was wiry not bulky, and so forth. A woman had never really seen it. Some men had seen it, quite recently, but that was only at school, in the general run of changing rooms and so forth. When he looked at it in the mirror, he did not see something that women or men might find interesting. This is a difficult sort of thought at the best of times, but one that most of us can manage. But it had never crossed his mind. His body was what he did his job with. He was at one with it. The idea that he wasn't at one with it because it had no sexual life would have aroused his contempt. Look what he had done with it, after all. Had any of the fuck people done that?

All over his back were golden freckles. They scattered down the small, over the buttocks and thickened around the calves, as if offering there some sort of support to those muscles that took such extraordinary spasms of instruction during his work. His front was freckled too. It was as if a golden skin had shrunk away some time before, revealing an unready white underskin, yet leaving traces that would easily reclaim their ground if ever quickened by the sun. But he never went out in the sun, he was too busy.

His chest and limbs were fairly hairless, but those tufts and outcrops that did remain in the natural way seemed impertinent, as is the case with redheads. Wild lichens clinging to statues, flaming from crannies of milky marble.

It was a shame that Ainsley's face did not reflect the taut economies of his trained trunk. His teeth were not properly white, his upper lip was not satisfactorily shaven and his eyes were close together.

He towelled himself off, pulled on a pair of blue tights and some grey shorts and started to think about Mr Gavin, who should be here any minute.

Jack, scrunching up the drive, had no particular bracket for this one. The famous were mad, that was all; either too gracious or too impatient. He was pretty sure Ainsley would not prove to be gracious. On the phone the youth had said about twelve words, in a curt and colourless tone that brings out, in most people, an anxiety to please. Jack had never, as far as he could remember, wanted to please anyone merely in order to avoid their displeasure. He reserved his capacity to gratify for more concrete advantages. Knowing already what the youth wanted, the question of rapport had become dispensable.

102

Ainsley's house, now visible at the end of the drive, was fundamentally doomladen, he decided. An old person's house, and irreversibly so, in the way that only a very few styles of exterior can be. The effect started, in fact, with the hedges and bushes around the porch entrance. Jack didn't know plant names, but these bushes had very black branches, very thickly and dustily packed in under small, drab leaves. If you were to have licked the branches, a dark, bitter powder would have coated your tongue and tasted dank and desolate for days. It was an old lady's bush, dropping twigs onto the brown hexagonal tiles of the porch. The walls of the house were rendered in pebble dash, virtually the only finish he could think of that completely eliminated the possibility of improvement. The windows were small and reluctant, their frames glossed in stale chocolate brown, clearly in subservience to the awesome pebbling. As he glanced upwards he noticed that the wall under the guttering was blackened by grit that had washed through the old tin joints over the years. Up on the roof the tiles had a gloomy viridescence that would scotch the most inspired redecorative schemes. Surely the rooms would be dark and thick, linked by corridors cluttered with trippables that could not be identified in the gloom. The kid must have a bunch of money, Jack mused; why not get a little gay with the paint? With that money you could take whole windows out and put bigger in. You could tear down the scratchy garden. Hell, you could get another house.

No bellpush even, just a rod that yanked a wire that jangled a bell at the far end of the long, dark corridors. Jack jangled. He wouldn't hear Ainsley coming because the latter would be wearing sports shoes. After a number of moments Jack felt that someone was standing on the other side of the door.

Over the last few days he had been getting accustomed to the unusual physical effects that accompanied his new state of mind. He had tuned himself to the radiance which wrapped around everything except people and tugged so insistently at his attention, and he was becoming less alarmed by the curious vertigo that seized him whenever he had forgotten that he had changed and then suddenly remembered again. In these moments he would be overwhelmed by the sensation of standing on the very edge of an abyss which was actually there at the tips of his toes, right on the pavement, so vivid that it seemed not to be an image of an inner disquiet but a devious deformation of the actual, physical world. The abyss would usually dissolve as fast as he could bring himself to believe anew in his own discovery, but often not before he had actually hesitated in the street, almost toppled over by his forward momentum.

Once he had recovered his determination, and stepped forward into the novel space, the radiance would immediately stream from all the objects around him. He had come to the conclusion that the radiance was always there, and that it was his own tentative relation to it that made it seem intermittent. He would tune in to it for varying periods, during which he was quite painfully aware of an awesome sense of opportunity, almost as if the radiance were implanting this sense directly into his thoughts. In fact, he had decided, what he was picking up on should best be seen as a characteristic of space, a kind of vacuum that demanded inflation by his actions.

Once he began to act in a certain way, the radiance would engulf him, and he would notice it less. The space was still available, however, and the opportunities there only multiplied. The radiance, then, was a kind of advertising, an etheric 'To Let' sign slung across an estate that encompassed just about everything you cared to look at. Jack found that as soon as he had embarked on a course of action his powers as a seer were more sharply focused than they had ever been before the Insight. Yet conversely, as soon as he allowed himself actually to speculate on what might happen next, the radiance faded away into the walls and cars, and he would find himself in the old world again, a world that was as dead and predictable as ever but lacked the peculiar quality of emptiness that he found so exhilarating.

Thus it was that his expectations led him to feel slightly oppressed by the cheerless portals of Ainsley's mansion. In a state of expectancy he was denied the encouragement of the radiance, and felt deserted by his powers. He stood, rather reluctantly restricted to the present, and waited for the boy champion to reveal himself.

The door opened, sucking slightly as if framed with hairs. The redhead frowned in the frame.

'Mr Gavin?' said Ainsley.

'Yes,' said Jack.

Ainsley walked away from the door into the house. Jack followed him and shut the door. The corridor was indeed dark. He did not trip. Ainsley walked quite fast. His sports shoes snatched at the wooden floor with little squeaks. He pushed at another door and they were in a

104

large room with pale grey walls and several shuttered windows. There were no lights on, but enough daylight was spilling through the shutters to enable Jack to see what was in the room.

'There's nothing in here,' he exclaimed.

'I don't know what I want yet,' replied Ainsley.

'There's a sofa,' Jack noticed.

The sofa was long, with a cushion at either arm. Ainsley sat at one end. Jack took a place at the other. He found himself looking at the fireplace, which was bare.

'What do you mean you don't know what you want?' Now he had to turn to look at Ainsley. The kid's legs, wrapped in their blue tights, glowed in the subdued light. The kid stared straight ahead, at the bare wall next to the fireplace.

'It's not a problem, Mr Gavin.' Ainsley gazed beyond the wall, as if he were overseeing something important in the next street.

'I didn't say it was.'

'I've got all the stuff.'

'What stuff?'

'The things you need. In another part of the house.'

'Ah. You just like this room empty, then.'

'No. Most of the rooms are empty, except for the ones I keep the stuff in. There's no hurry, is there?'

Ainsley turned to look at Jack, at last. Jack couldn't decide if that was a moustache or uncut territory that had yet to know a blade. Perhaps he had a razor in with his stuff. Ainsley looked impatiently at Jack, but not in a way that persuaded Jack to drop the subject. Jack raised his eyebrows encouragingly.

'I got it years ago. Everything. When I decide what I want, I'll bring it in. There's no hurry.'

'No. Not if you've already got it. No hurry at all.'

Ainsley turned away and nodded. 'Right. Later on maybe I'll show it to you.'

'Sure.'

'You want to drink?'

'Where is it?'

The champion jerked his head towards a far corner of the room. Jack hadn't spotted the cabinet in the shadows. He made his way over and opened it up. There were about forty bottles in there – all the spirits, in two or three varieties each, and most of the liqueurs. None of the

bottles had been opened. No mixers. Jack smiled at the bottles and
called out, 'It's like a kit, isn't it?' Ainsley did not reply. Jack picked a
bottle of mescal, because he hadn't had it very much. He checked that
the worm was intact, then broke the seal.

'Got ice?'

'No.'

'Uh huh. Glasses?'

'I haven't brought them in yet. Do you really need one?'

'Well . . . no. No. I'll swallow in shots. Could be a useful skill. What
about you . . . want a bottle of something?'

'I don't drink.'

'Not good for fitness, I expect.' Jack was exercising his rudimentary
understanding of the athlete's regime.

'I don't like the taste.'

'Have you tried them all?'

'Once.'

The seer sat down again, clutching the bottle. He took a
slug. 'Got a game tonight?' by way of pleasantry. At the end
of the sofa the kid shifted, perhaps with impatience. 'No. I hav-
en't.'

Jack nodded, as if understanding something. The mescal burned
pleasantly in his stomach. He might as well have some more. Ainsley
said 'Is there something you want to tell me, Mr Gavin?'

Jack swallowed again and sat up properly. 'You'd like one of these
new animals, wouldn't you?'

'I want two. If you have one they get lonely.'

'I didn't think they cared about that. They don't seem to notice
much, do they?'

Ainsley's foxy eyes shifted round and he looked into the gloom that
surrounded his visitor. His gaze came to rest on Jack and he said, 'They
must have intercourse, don't you think?'

'Well, they've bred, haven't they? So they must.'

'What I mean is,' Ainsley sounded slightly irritated, 'they must
have the opportunity for intercourse.' He paused, glaring now at Jack.
'That's natural, isn't it?'

Jack frowned back at Ainsley, feeling that he should acknowledge the
high seriousness, if that was what it was. He said 'Of course it's bloody
natural. It's a sign of life – it's fucking.'

Ainsley stood up abruptly. He hovered for an instant with his calves pressed against the sofa, then walked quickly to the drinks cabinet. A shaft of light from one of the shutters sliced across his thighs, causing a splash of light blue to erupt from his tights. He took hold of the cabinet doors and seemed to be studying the array of bottles at close range. When he spoke hisvoice was measured but faintly over-enunciated.

'I don't say it like that.'

Jack stopped the bottle on its third arc to his lips. Were his ears deceiving him? 'Beg pardon?'

Ainsley closed the cabinet. 'I don't see it like that.' Sounded almost the same. Almost. 'If I get them I want them to lead full lives. They don't want people watching them all the time. I won't watch them like that.'

'What – you won't watch them at it, then?'

'Mr Gavin, how much do you require?'

'Did I say the wrong thing?'

'It doesn't matter what you say. We're not here to talk.'

'But you want to talk about the money.'

'That's why you've come.'

'Okay.' Jack savoured the curious flatness of the exaltation delivered by the cactus, a distinct tightness in the forebrain which in weather would be humid or close, and in bereavement would be having just heard the news. A depression without the discomfort, a kind of elevation by subtraction. 'Wanting two is a surprise, of course. With one I hold it under my arm and open the door with the other arm.'

'What door?'

'Any door. There'll be doors. But with two my hands are tied.'

'Put them down.'

'They'd get away.'

'Use a bag.'

'I'll use a bag.'

'Are you perfectly confident of this, Mr Gavin?' The kid was looking irritable again.

'Don't worry about it, Ainsley. Start building a pen. It'll be ten grand each.'

'Twenty thousand pounds is a great deal of money.'

'You've got a great deal.'

'Is that how you see it?'

'That's how I say it.' He grinned at the champ, who suddenly made a swiping movement with his right arm. A forehand first, not useful as a martial device, but quickly followed by a backhand that would snap

107

the pump handles off a bar. This one-two was repeated several times, with a steady ferocity. On the final backhand Ainsley spun round and barked, 'Very good.'

'*Very* good,' Jack agreed. 'Half up front?'

'No way. Two thousand five hundred. We'll go and get it.' He marched out of the sitting room without looking back. Jack followed him down the corridor, watching the diamond-shaped calves tighten and deflate beneath their pale stretch-fabric skin.

'Wait there.' Ainsley opened a door and stepped into a small dark room. Jack heard a drawer opening and then some agreeable rustling noises. Ainsley reappeared and thrust an envelope into Jack's hand.

'How do I know it's in there?' the seer enquired.

'You don't.'

'What about all this stuff you were going to show me?'

'Why not?' He seemed pleased. Led Jack off down the corridor again.

Thing about shits was, reflected the seer, they bounced so well, from one thing to another. Not expecting to be liked, and never showing any sign that they were collecting your words and deeds into a file, they let you like and dislike them at will, and you didn't feel that they remembered anything, or cared. They were probably good to go on holiday with. Time spent with a shit could be like love, or at least the way love was talked about these days. There was a difference, of course, somewhere, but he had never been in love and didn't care to speculate any further.

'This is one of the rooms,' Ainsley said, pushing through the doorway. The room was dark, and Ainsley disappeared into its shadows. Jack heard him marching across the floor. Lights blazed, but not from the ceiling. At each corner of the room stood a tubular steel lighting stand, topped with a powerful floodlight, turned towards the centre of the space. Black cable fell from each lamp and ran to a junction box by the wall. The floor had no carpet, and was mostly obscured by the piles of boxes and crates stacked upon it.

'It's all boxed up,' Jack complained.

'What do you expect? I haven't used it yet. I don't want it to fade.' Ainsley stood with his hands on his hips, scowling at the stacks.

'What's in them, then?'

'Lights.'

'Lights? All this?'

'Rooms need light, Mr Gavin. I've got a lot of rooms.'

'They all dark, are they?'

'I made one basic choice, I had to. I got these studio lights and fixed up each room so I could see the stuff.'

'You can't see it.'

'I don't have to. I know what I've got.'

Jack tapped a crate. 'What's in here?'

'That crate? It's a big glitter ball.'

'Not really a light.'

'It's an effect. I could hang it with just one spotlight on it and it would be like space. Very interesting.'

'Yeah. You like space?'

'People do. If I have people here, they would like it. It doesn't really bother me personally.'

'No. Nor me.'

'These boxes have all got shades in them,' Ainsley gestured to a pile beside him. 'I got all the basic shapes; globe, cone, bowl, you know.' He touched each box lightly with a freckled hand. Certainly the skin of redheads had a greater affinity with animal hides than any other human colouring that Jack could think of. The pale blemishes that seemed to float beneath the bristles of a pig came to mind, then the liverish melanisms and albino pools from the belly of a dog. This led him to consider the possibility that Ainsley's genitals were encased in a speckled, tufted glove of dogsuede. This image was so arresting that it eclipsed other, lesser thoughts about chameleons that were forming. He turned his attention back to his host once more.

'Yeah. What about basic materials, though? What about them?'

'I've got them in cloth, glass, plastic, wood and paper. And lots of colours. I want to make my mind up here. You're expected to do it in shops, and I find this offensive.'

'You might have some left over, though.'

'It doesn't really matter, does it?' Ainsley was looking at Jack for a response now; he was testing, he was interested.

'Put them in another room with the other leftovers. Things wear out. They fall off the ceiling without warning. People make an arm movement and the standard lamp is over. Anything.'

'Something like that. Anyway, that's lights.'

Now Ainsley swung out of the room and took Jack through a

double door to a room full of carpeting. The carpets were mostly from foreign countries, apparently they were something of an art over there. Covered in polythene sheeting and end on, the whorls made a nice effect despite all the chillsome plastic.

The next room was a snow palace created by the sheeting draped over stacked sofas, settees, settles, stools and seats. A shrouded armchair on a sideboard blocked one of the lights, making a sunset among the white mountains. Ainsley said some were in groups, say a sofa had three easy chairs of the same finish, these would not be split up. He stated the obvious, as if he had heard about things but not had the time to try.

Backing out they progressed to kitchen equipment, Jack was assured. Ainsley did not cook as yet, but felt that he would not be likely to pick it up if there no implements with which to commence, utensils to handle, tools to try. How did he know what was required? He had instructed the man to supply a full set of apparatus, based on all the procedures taking place in a top-class restaurant. He did not like the idea of starting off with a deliberately limited range, the possibility that he might get halfway through a cake, to find then that a very sophisticated procedure was next indicated, to put the hand there and the implement was simply not beneath it, never had been, deliberately not got. Every cake would be a poor thing, and how could he then progress? So there were whisks, terrinades, enmeaters, deboilers, unmersants, ejuicers, depeelators, upheatners, consommaters, inputners, saucers, patississions, turnatives, pressments, miscologisers, rollands and impolyaters, croutonards, dickspotters, brulisers, supatterns, laevopeners, dextricards, morphixers, an ansucraliter, peppidiniments, overturners, spicanerts, cakeholers, embouchards, seeditisers, squeakpipners, intraovenous englovatures, pinous accutment boards and folded aprons in a number of styles. They were wrapped and unlabelled but Ainsley named the packages for Jack, who had no proof, but when the kid would open them he would know what they were. Or would he, he might forget, and then? To knife with a fork, to spoon with a skewer.

Then the room that Jack liked, rather than one which merely elicited his morbid interest. His host had actually unpacked the goods here, and showed him stacked in layers a variety of recordings players, hisser graded. In the first category, laser bolts splashed on teeny shimmered faces of microtiny slopes and plates bouncing back utter monogamy of bugle at dawn standard, then, second type, little jewels bump over rutted courses dragged beneath them, somehow ssss getting in but we have colour gentlemen we have presence, this is to envy, they have presence mygod, mylifelong I tried for that. Thirdly, next type, brown ribbon with adhered ferrates ferrites heaved acrosshead, recordings readily made but lots of ssssss but system deals with it feeds in under redouble giveback signal hisslesser at other end if switch thrown. Ribbons of chromium, silver, gold, the best. Around these producers placed a circus of speakers of the premier order, tweeting very tweet, bulgent bassures chocolading the rich deeps, polyphony making quadraphony a cave painting, giving as if you were there ambience, as if you were there not depressed, moreover, but wideawake, just fallen in love had a recent hotmeal ambience. A so real effect after which everyday auralising just grubby and crowded. Ainsley remarked that every component at the moment of procurement was sharpending the artstate. Parts were derived from rocketry and parachuting and little more could reasonably be asked.

Similarly televisions so good they had many more dots, many many more dots per area so that the pictures were as solid and opaque and likelife as, as the outer film of things lifted off. Pictures committed to these transmitters replayed as skin from skin, no lag, no decrepitation. Telephones too enjoyed mixture into highfaith systems. No more tinny squinny whines from old silver paper discs under breathsoiled hand- and mouthpieces. No more harris tweeding of the online, competitions with crackle storms and fried bacon, but a system where the whim to dial could be realised in the trouser pocket, depressing lightly brailled keys in a palm-concealable unit, pausing, changing location, if needed, from room to room, right across the house, then speaking, simply saying out loud, what you had to say, arrangements for the next tournament, say, and the listener, they say what they want, and the whole exchange is heard, completely heard, without any earpieces or hand-on parts. Each room picks you up, wherever you stand, even the corridor. Each room gives speak-back. In the chilly carpet mausoleum a voice engages with Ainsley. He is elsewhere, in his bare living room, or among the crated bathroomware, or rinsing his chameleon hands in the undressed kitchen. The voice echoes unheard from the lampless ceiling, falls onto the grey glistening of the polythene, is reinforced from the corridor, built up by faint similar strains from the landing, thickened from the empty bedrooms and functionless spaces giving onto the unplanted garden. Ainsley dries his hands, still talking, snaps down the corridor, making a few strokes, sits on his only unwrapped settee and makes conversation in a thin, irritable voice, matter of fact, impatient. To the air. Not touching anything.

Ainsley's descriptions were all very well, but Jack had now seen a lot of boxes, and was about to make a radical suggestion. They could stay in one room and Ainsley could describe the contents of the other rooms while they sat on a crate. The kid seemed to sense Jack's restlessness, and responded by withdrawing abruptly from the electronics room. In the corridor he announced, 'There's a lot more, but you've got the idea, haven't you?' Without waiting for an answer he marched back to the front door and held it open for Jack.

'So, Mr Gavin, how long?'

'I'll ring you, Ainsley. Not long.'

The champ shut the door without any politeness and Jack headed back to town, from time to time patting the wad contentedly.

Guy's favourite non-technical book was Lilian Bentley's *With Alan*. He particularly liked the chapter in which the two explorers made their legendary expedition to the featureless plain. In this episode Sir Alan Bentley had trekked for many days with Lilian and the bearers. They had left the village of most recent succour far behind. The further they went the more sparse became the evidences of life. The scrub thinned, the trees shortened, the birds became small and infrequent. Lilian, who was to write *With Alan* soon after her return, sketched ceaselessly. Sir Alan continued to make a variety of measurements. At night they would study each other's faces across the fire, and draw strength from the unwavering conviction that each could detect there. As the long days went by, the evidences of life virtually disappeared. The scrub vanished, the trees shrank to below one inch, and the infrequent birds had either become minute or were flying at great heights, it was difficult to tell. The terrain was shockingly bare: a hard, flat, grey stratum evenly peppered with sharp, grey pebbles. They had left any contoured land behind them, not a hill or hummock broke the dead line of the horizon. Sir Alan and Lilian were both, however, strong and singleminded. Their sense of purpose supported them, and was communicated inexplicitly to the bearers. Sir

Alan's theory was sound and would be vindicated. It was felt that there was a point.

For many more days the party traversed the featureless stratum. Had it not been for the sun and the compasses, no means of orientation would have been at their disposal. So uniform was the stratum that the party had no sensation of travel, it was as if their footsteps did not quite touch the gravelled overstrate, and were thus denied the friction by which they might carry the bodies forward. Only the gradual onset of tiredness told the travellers that they must have made some progress, for the visual field was utterly unchanging. At night, as the bearers cleared away the soiled metal dishes, the two naturalists would exchange their customary glances across the embers beside the equipment. As ever, the glances spoke of the sinew within their intent, and of the certitude which they brought to bear on their project.

On the thirty-sixth day Sir Alan stopped the party and pointed. None of the party had eyesight as keen as he. Lilian strained to make out anything irregular within the visual field. The bearers murmured to each other as they bent down to appraise the horizon.

One hour later it could be seen. The eyes of the party were by now so accustomed to unbroken featurelessness that the least obtrusion loomed as if large. At a distance the object of their attention seemed quite impertinent in the degree to which it stuck out. The nearer they came to it, the more extraordinary its simple presence became, although its size was actually modest.

Sir Alan had postulated, and Lilian had supported, the notion that there need not always be multiplicity. That rich environments encouraged diversity was already known. It was further known that in locales of exceptional diversity only a few individuals of each type were found. There was simply no room. It was logical that in conditions of maximal advantage only one representative of each type was required. The question of perpetuation arose. How? By what means? With whom? Or what? If not with itself, then . . .

Ultimate rarity, reasoned Sir Alan, threatened some of the more fundamental premises. Those, for example, of origination, the where from? Those of destination, having arrived, where to? Those of ultimate purpose, being there, with nothing next, why then? What's the point?

He felt, as did Lilian, that there was not purposelessness. They were not, and this was becoming increasingly common in their restless epoch, of a religious persuasion, yet they felt confident of a deep natural organisation, which was Guy's position, really. Explained his enduring affection for *With Alan*.

No, they concurred, there was not purposelessness. A unique tree, for example, unrepeated in any locality, bore in every leaf and branch an awesome proposition. Nature, in her most exquisitely funded plenitude, in circumstances of utter photochemical apogee, took delight in endless novelty. She had no need of similars and repeats – why bother when another novelty can be so effortlessly conjured? There would be one of everything, just one, which was thrilling for Guy, although he saw its naivety, which he passed over, the epoch having been conducive to much heady extrapolation in this vein.

The world of many single things. A world comprising only uniqueness. This seemed, to Sir Alan and Lilian, to be the aspiration of Nature, an aspiration thwarted almost from the beginning of biological time by inclemency. Yet were they not now living in an epoch which held the promise of a Nature *controlled* by man? Might this be the opportunity towards which Nature had coiled and sprouted over the millenia? Unlikely, Sir Alan felt. More likely that Nature might be *understood* by man, who would assist her towards multiple oneship. Guy greatly admired Sir Alan's humility here, despite the shakiness of the whole oneship business.

Faced with the prospect of ridicule from the Zoological Society, Sir Alan determined to preempt such an occurrence by establishing the universal viability of oneship. Were the principle to be dignified with evidence from the field, then the way would be open to an epistemological earthquake of awesome proportions.

The party stood around the flower, blinking in disbelief. Sir Alan dropped to his knees. Lilian's hand shook as she freed her pad from her haversack. The flower was about three inches tall, with a firm, thick, leafless stalk. The petals, five in all, were the same colour as the stalk, a dark greeny grey. In the centre of the flower was a hard, purplish, asexual button.

Guy had taken his copy of *With Alan* from his study and placed it on the shelf above Eke and Ike's cage. He had got into the habit of slipping out to the workshop at odd moments just to gaze at the creatures on his own, and it felt right that the book should be close at hand during these special ruminative periods. The visits were quite separate from his regular monitoring sessions, in which his time would be entirely taken up with logging test results. He would draw up an old

114

canvas folding chair and set it by the door so that he had a view of both the nesting unit and the larger exercise cage. The whole structure was built at table height and ran in an L round two sides of the workshop. Now that Eke had her litter, Guy and Deany were obliged to monitor a total of seven animals. So many functions had to be regularly checked they were obliged to work an eighteen-hour day upon which they had imposed a rota of four-hour shifts.

Guy was in the workshop during Deany's first day shift. She had run all the checks and was back in the house preparing tea for Jack Gavin who, for some reason that escaped him, had been invited to visit later that afternoon. He ran through the video at fast forward and, finding that neither adults nor cubs had slept in the last three hours, updated the relevant log. The animals had never slept since their capture, and the sheaf of almost blank sheets bore testimony to his growing conviction that they were incapable of doing so. Eke had writhed and screamed so consistently throughout the birth of the cubs that it had been impossible to tell when she might have delivered her last. The cubs had emerged mewing in agony and seemed to find Eke's teats almost by accident. At first Guy had found their behaviour while feeding almost unbearable to watch. The tiny blind creatures, while emitting a chorus of noises that combined into a shrill drilling buzz, would shudder and twitch at such a rate that the fur of their bodies appeared perpetually blurred. In this state they managed to travel across the floor of the nesting cage without even using their legs, vibrating hither and thither at random. Brushing past a teat, in an instant when their mother happened to be on her side, which would never be for long, the cubs would snap open their irritated, opossum-like jaws and clamp on with what seemed to be an appropriate zeal. Moments later mother or cub or both would jerk away in a fresh paroxysm that seemed immediately to cancel all their appetites and instincts up to that point – hunger, maternity, proximity, all gone, and not a trace of consternation or regret.

Guy had observed that over a period of several hours the cubs collided with Eke's teats a number of times. Although the contact was invariably brief, each cub managed an average of four swallows per collision, and the total for a day was in the region of three hundred swallows. Compared to other mammal species of a comparable body weight, the amount of milk ingested by the cubs was impossibly small. A kitten commonly swallowed several hundred times per feed and furthermore its attention in the first weeks of its life was directed exclusively towards the elimination of hunger – it did little else.

Deany had analysed milk extracted from Eke. She found a high concentration of iron and calcium and a casein content at least three times greater than that found in the milk of any known viviparous creature. At just over eleven per cent by unit weight the protein was coming in at three or four times the level found in cow or goat milk.

These figures answered some of the nutritional questions, and also developed an issue that would never arise in any 'natural' context. It looked as though the animals wanted to live. At some level, albeit metabolic, nature had compensated for her consummate cruelty and provided exceptional resources for survival. Deany said this looked to her like a piece of exceptional cynicism; put the little buggers there with a permanent dose of death throes, then make sure they're healthy enough to endure it for as long as possible. Guy quite liked thinking about these things. When Deany pushed him to take a broader look at the philosophical side the whole business seemed to rise to a sublime and universal level, where one day, he sometimes dared to think, it might even qualify to stand alongside the achievements of men like Bentley. He disapproved of scientists who rushed headlong into print claiming to have transformed our whole way of looking at the world, but the direction their own researches were taking certainly promised to turn some pretty basic ideas upside down.

For a few weeks now he'd been sleeping rather erratically, suddenly waking out of a deep slumber into memories of the most ridiculous dreams, some of which he'd found quite worrying in an obscure, niggling sort of way. But this whole thing with the animals probably explained it; after all, how many people discovered a new mammalian genus these days? It was a terrific responsibility if you stopped and thought about it, and it was probably taking it out of him more than he realised. But as well as being a responsibility, it sort of gave everybody hope. It meant there were still things to find in the world, the limits hadn't been reached yet, there were real challenges left. You didn't have to stay at home and read books about how good other people's lives were.

He hung the sleep log back on a hook by the video and pulled up the canvas chair into his favourite viewing position. Ike was pressed against a corner of the exercise cage, his face squashed against the mesh. A square of wire framed each of his eyes. For some reason Guy had not looked at their eyes before, apart from during the comprehensive

116

inspection he and Deany had given the animals when they were released from quarantine. He had never actually tried to *interpret* their eyes in any way. So many people were ready to detect sadness in the eyes of animals – that was all they ever saw. This line of thinking led you to the conclusion that all dogs, horses and cows were permanently depressed, which was absurd because these particular animals were generally very well fed. Give a dog a bone and a place to sleep and it would be a satisfied dog – this was the most you could say for any animal – it was satisfied, or it was not. Remove the bone – instant modification of mood. Give it back – reversal of previous situation.

He looked into Ike's eyes. The creature was desperately kicking at its stomach with one of its back legs. The question of what degree of pain it suffered had been debated at length by Guy and Deany. Was the pain constantly unbearable or subject to changes of intensity? Were there periods of mere mild discomfort? If the latter, then could their occurrence be deduced from the animal's reactions? Protracted observation had indicated that the physical vocabulary of the animal was limited. To the casual observer it seemed that the pain induced a constantly changing array of movements, but over a period of a few minutes it became clear that the convulsions, writhings and scratchings had few variations, and were generally executed with the same intensity, without patterning into waves or cycles, which suggested that the pain was experienced at a constant level. Whether it was insufferable, awful or just very unpleasant remained obscure. Insofar as the animals were oblivious to most, if not all, external stimuli, there was clearly a case for concluding that the discomfort was enough to eclipse sensory input totally. Thus compromised, the animals were effectively blind, deaf and in a special sense, numb. Were they numb to any tactile input because their nervous systems were constantly on overload, or did their congenital predicament compel them to be indifferent to minor distractions? It looked as though *any* distraction would be minor, in fact. The creatures were both living in the present moment, a moment of appalling unpleasure, and comprehensively seceding from any environment in which they might be placed, or into which they might stray. Guy felt that the animals were not capable of choosing an environment because their volition was entirely consumed by the need to resist their moment by moment experience.

Ike's eyes had very large pupils, dark irises and no visible whites. The pupils were so large that you could not tell in which direction the animal was looking, if indeed he was looking at all, at anything at all. The eyes certainly moved around in their sockets, but you felt as if they didn't focus on anything in particular, just scanned with complete indifference what was out in front. Guy moved the chair closer, since it looked like Ike might stay against the mesh for a while. He peered down into the darting orbs. At their surface were twin tiny reflections of the light bulb above his head. He tried to ignore the reflections and somehow look beyond them, into the actual pupil. The pupil was, of course, a hole surrounded by a muscle. Look right at it and you are looking right inside someone's head. Often when you looked straight at animals they blinked or looked away. He had even experienced this with a garden tortoise on one occasion. It was probably an abasement technique, designed to defuse a threatening situation. Now that he was studying Ike's eyes closely, he realised that the creature was not looking away and had stopped moving its eyes around. It appeared to be looking straight at him. Guy blinked involuntarily, then instantly chastised himself. It was just a bit strange when an animal suddenly looked at you, close up. It was hard not to feel there was something in it, although he knew very well that, in this case especially, it was really a coincidence more than anything else.

The whole of Ike's body was trembling, and his scream seemed to wash all round Guy until it almost wasn't there any more. A sort of silent corridor opened up between them. There was something strange in Ike's expression, something separate from the pain. He was studying Guy, from beneath the pain. There was another life in there, down in the back to the depths of his pupils. He was . . . what was he doing? He was reproaching Guy. Why? thought Guy. Why be like that? I'm his friend, I took him out of a place where everyone thought he was worthless. And he's resentful of me, under that pain, down in the shining black of a place where no one has looked before.

The scream wore its way back into Guy's attention and he felt a sudden flash of irritation. He reached for the gloves on top of the cage. There were certain questions that could be answered by experiment, but for some reason he had not got around to designing the relevant procedures. Perhaps the approach that had just occurred to him was too unscientific, too subjective, but it made a lot of sense. God, somebody had to get to the bottom of these things, otherwise the philosophers would have it all their own way, imposing speculation on territory better delineated by proof, courtesy of the slack attitudes of timid scientists.

He opened the cage, lifted Ike out and carried him to a side table. A pencil, perhaps, would be the best instrument. But where? Not the flanks or back, they were too muscle-bound. The side of the belly was suitably vulnerable. He held the pencil by the sharpened end and jabbed at Ike's stomach.

Ike was unmoved. He uncurled his body and stretched in what would have seemed a luxurious manner had one not known of the agony which saturated his nervous system. Guy turned the pencil round in his hand, a little spear. He jabbed at Ike's stomach. The impact shifted Ike's body a couple of inches across the table. Ike, stiff as a plank, started to quiver. His spine began arching backwards, carrying his head over towards the stump of his tail. None of this was related to Guy's input, it was just happening anyway, part of a lifelong reaction, a contraction of obedience that had persisted without interruption from moment one.

Guy licked his lower lip. He grasped Ike by the neck and pressed him against the table top. Then he changed his grip on the pencil, wrapping his fingers around it so that it projected from the underside of his fist, blocked off at the blunt end by his thumb. Aiming at the upper portion of the side of the belly, he tentatively brought his fist down. Something about the new grip had inhibited him; the pencil tip slid across Ike's pelt and onto the table, where the lead snapped off. He grunted with annoyance, pressed down harder on the creature's neck, and with a short, punching movement drove the little spear down again.

The fragile wood that had collared the lead broke into splinters as the weapon, the implement, made a visible depression in the tough hide. But from Ike, nothing new, just wailing beneath Guy's glove.

Guy took his hand off Ike's neck and stepped back. He put the pencil in a jam jar, removed a glove and mopped his brow. Obviously the use of a pointed implement had its limitations – if he chose to stab harder, to apply greater pressure, he would eventually break the creature's skin. This would certainly provide some unequivocal data, but the notion of damaging the subject was clearly out of the question. It was, in fact, an absurd notion. And abhorrent. The demands of the situation were not that extreme. Pain, pressure, must be systematically applied in a manner that minimised, eliminated, damage yet ensured a measurable incrementation.

He slipped the glove back on and punched, applied a blow, to the furry creature. The creature was now on its back, and took the punch squarely in the guts, the abdomen. The force of the blow was such that the body momentarily curled around Guy's fist. This, however, was a mechanical effect and did not signify a genuine organic response. Guy did notice, however, that the impact had displaced air from Ike's lungs, for the creature made a mournful, inwardly hissing noise as the wind rushed back down its throat. Progress of a sort, Guy felt, for while it could not be said that he had actually caused any discomfort, he had at least interrupted Ike's vital processes, and this must surely constitute, technically, the early phase of a critical condition.

When he next hammered, exerted a powerful downward force upon, the belly, Ike closed around the incoming and held on with his claws. Again, it was only a reaction to leverage, embellished with a conclusion that appeared to be concerned with survival yet in reality was merely incidental. Ike's claws had been contracting at that point, and Guy's fist had happened to be in their locality. As the air hissed back into him, Ike clung to the glove which Guy was attempting to disengage. At first Guy considered wriggling out of the glove and waiting till Ike jerked away, but then a better course of action occurred to him. Ike weighed as much as a small dog or a large cat, so when Guy raised his arm the strain was considerable. By bending the arm and holding his elbow in against his right hip, he could maintain an equilibrium while deciding on one of the two possibilities he had in mind. The sweat, which glistened all over his face, had begun to trickle down onto his chest. He was trembling too, but it could have been the weight, supported in such an unnatural way, calling upon muscle combinations rarely required in the ordinary run of things.

The animal curved over his fist, an outsize hairy boxing glove. It was a question of the type of blow. He eliminated any downward action. Ike would fall off before connecting with the table top. Clearly a more reliable vector was indicated. He supported his right wrist with his left hand and breathed in deeply through his nose.

Ike hit the wall of the workshop, on the end of Guy's fist, with such a whack that three sets of clipboards bounced off their hooks and clattered to the ground. Ike screamed on the way in, hissed involuntarily on impact, and screamed while Guy picked up his right wrist for another pound. The screams were constant, uniform, and unrelated to any local influences. This time Guy came in from below waist height, on an upward gradient, thus ensuring that Ike didn't lose his grip too easily. Effectively an upper cut, the punch delivered Ike's back into the plasterboard so hard that a hair-line crack opened up along the ceiling line, and small flakes of paint drifted down onto the animal's fur. Guy, not a fighting man on the whole, realised that the secret was to put your body behind the punch. Let it come through from the shoulder, and sort of get all your body weight behind the shoulder in the first place. His fist felt fine, Ike's body cushioned it perfectly. He did feel considerably hotter though; as soon as he'd started on the new technique a great blush of heat had swept over his back and his legs, and now his shirt and trousers were clinging to his damp skin.

The creature must be subjected to much greater forces. In proportion to the size of its bones it was heavily muscled and powerfully built. It had none of the light sinuousness of a cat, or the loose-skinned vulnerability of a rabbit. So far nothing he had done to it had had any effect whatsoever. The thing just ignored him, ignored everything. He suddenly swung his arm very fast over his head, as if bowling a cricket ball. Ike flew off the end of his fist, taking the glove with him. Guy had been roughly aiming at the door, but to his horror and annoyance Ike struck the adjacent window, which shattered noisily as the rare animal passed straight through the glass.

'Christ Almighty!' Guy exclaimed as he dashed to the door. And then 'Jesus Christ!' as he bounded into the garden. Ike was curled up in a ball on the lawn, a few feet away from the glove that he had finally relinquished. Guy ran over and dropped to his knees to inspect the yowling mammal. When he found there were no cuts on Ike's body he sighed with relief and started to pick him up with his bare hand. Ike contracted in his usual random manner and scratched Guy with one of his claws. Guy yelped and jumped back several feet. Ike had only left a very faint mark on the back of his hand, but Guy was unable to check a great fury that was rising within him. He ran at Ike and kicked him very hard with his right foot. The fur ball lifted off and parabolaed across the flower beds, peaking at about five or six feet before it crashed into the garden wall. It fell onto one of Deany's favourite shrubs and snapped off a couple of branches. Guy was incensed. 'Damn you!' he roared. 'Bloody damn you!' and raced across the lawn. He flung the broken shrub aside and heaved Ike out with his foot. Once he had him back on the grass, Guy stepped back three paces then ran at Ike, hooking his shoe into the silver-grey belly so that a mighty place kick, technique recalled from rugby days, would connect in the proper manner. The creature folded most gratifyingly around the shoe, ensuring that every ounce of attack was transmitted into the subject and then permitted to decay into the elegant follow through of the initial arc.

Boom went Ike as he crunched into the trellis arch. How he whined, and squealed, but was it because of anything, or just a nervous condition?

'Grrrugh!' or thereabouts went Guy, himself experiencing a high whine of temperament that bored irresistibly into his emotional scheme, drenching the back of his neck, giving him that thing you get in dreams where you shout your guts out or do something very much. 'Oh God!' and he hared over the grass, jumped the glads, practically landed on the bastard. (The bastard had both paws behind its ears, as if primping a hair-do, or knotting a headscarf.) Oblivious, completely bloody oblivious. A punt. Why not a punt? Tears welled up in Guy's eyes and skidded down over the sweat of his cheeks. Now his hair was damp and fell into hanks revealing white scalp. Grime had appeared round his eyes, as if he had been bonfire building. He picked the bastard up, to hell with the risk of hands, and punted it. Recalled from wing three-q, the running kick, use the fact that you're running, just glide the foot up, hard though, use the top of the ankle, not a boot kick, but bloody effective, lifts the ball way up if you want, then get after it, if you want, up and under. He didn't wish to be under Ike as Ike came down from twenty feet, but he'd dash over there and be ready for him, that's for sure.

Stopping short then, not catching Ike, but letting him thump onto the deck at his feet. That should do the trick, surely. Ike flattened out from the whack, that should shift some air out of the bugger. And Ike is wheezing, but did it hurt? That's the point, the bastard, the ridiculous bastard. Of course it bloody hurt, how could it not? He wasn't numb, was he? Was he? Of course not, it hurt him, but within the other hurt, so it was hard to see it. But it added to the other hurt, it made the sum of hurt bigger, it must do.

Anyway, the bastard, and another bloody good kick, and it's not a good one, gets him in the arse, and he just shifts across the grass a couple of feet. Right, so he grabs the back legs, squeezes them together, swings it to and fro, could smash it into the ground dammit, just bloody swing it up and bring it right down, try your strength like with a mallet and a bell, that business. Swing it round and round, fast, God just bring it up against something, that would do it. Faster and faster, windmilling his right arm, it's pulling on his arm sockets. He's staring at the sky now, he's sweating such a lot,

122

all his clothes are wet. The bastard, just let it go, let it bloody go. Jesus it's gone.

Ike came down into the crab apple tree, smashing through the top branches then wedging firmly in a cleft about twelve feet off the ground, head and front paws jammed together facing Guy.

Guy never had much of a temper but did he shout out now. Yes. He bunched his fists and screamed, then did a short, curious dance in which he kicked out at the thin air first with one foot then the other. He was shaking all over, but he didn't notice this.

Back up at the house Deany was getting ready for Jack who was coming round for tea shortly.

Out in the street Jack on his way to tea strode through this: (he could pick it up now. What happened was that the air fell away from everything, and the radiance would stream from everything except for people, in the usual way, and his powers would leap into exhilarating focus, and he knew, with absolute certainty, what was going to happen next, but then, when the task in hand was both commonplace and protracted, such as walking through a crowded street in order eventually to do something important, namely take tea and reconnoitre his commission, then the short-term future could be predicted by anyone, you hardly needed special powers. So what happened was that his powers would seek engagement elsewhere, they required satisfaction, unlike radio waves that travelled dumbly through the chill wastes of the interstellar spaces eventually maybe colliding with the ear or extraordinary purple membrane of some ghastly half-spider half-slime alien who, which, would then hear, assuming the dimensional issues were even halfway sorted out, something like, 'I love your pudding Wendy but will you just look at what the dog is doing,' but they don't *have* pudding up there, let alone a comparable syntax, not to mention a deep linguistic substrate from which usefully to commence decipherment. They probably use remarkably intricate, indeed barely perceptible and extraordinarily rapid hand movements, to beg the hand question, or perhaps they have no desire and just are there, very intelligent but not needing a thing and consequently no speech just nod, to beg the neck, at each other at the beginning of the day, assuming some sort of day, it could be a year long by our standards, say their sun comes round infrequently they just nod once a year out of politeness and then it's just being for a year until the next day and nod, not to exaggerate the importance of the nod, it's not the highlight, it's just what we would notice if we were there, if it were even possible, with the dimensional issues, to be 'there' in the sense of is this a place or a thought or what? So Jack's powers, insofar, and this is to beg and even abuse a number of big paraphysical posers, as they might be envisaged as having a wave form, were not indifferent to the spaces through which they found passage, they sought contact and conclusion and consequently, as he walked through the shops and shoppers to the trains he found that despite the cold outline of his fellow beings their preoccupations were very legible. The substance of these fixed ideas was delivered unsolicited to his mind's ear and translated there into a pre-verbal discourse which he didn't particularly care for, but over the broadcasting of which he had no choice. To Jack it felt like something you knew so well that you had backgrounded it being forcibly foregrounded. He bathed in the chattered fragments and as the gravity of the occasion found a centre in his stomach it created there a tingling, mild nausea that he recognised as the final expression of a boredom so complete that it pervaded his very guts.) I wonder where Monty Lavalle is now? (The translation which took place in Jack's mind was merely into categories of familiarity. These categories might then have broken down into actual snatches, but that would have been akin to telepathy, which was not one of his powers. Nevertheless, it is possible to paraphrase the snippet clatter.) His moustache was so friendly, and the puppet doll Tony so convincing as to seem a separate person. They bring back conkers and thin legs, I don't know why./I wonder what happened to Baba du Reszke? So husky and on the point of tears in her voice. Her mouth could brush my neck. Her world, rustling, you could smell her, she never walked, she drifted, she brings back snowy logs some-where./Corsica. Me walking back and the sun still way up. Oh. I held his hand when he opened his foot on the glass./Little Jolly, hit by a truck but we romped. Stay, Jolly, stay, but it wasn't in his nature to obey. (Such sad stuff, Jack thought, but it's all in the past.)/And that big money prize! Just supposing, it's childish but just supposing – I would go out of the front door and take every ... but it's so silly, life would become so dull, wouldn't it? But then a strong, silent car, when you're really zooming, in the night, not a tremor, that would be something./Bad Billy again. Biff! He is so naughty. Hair in thick spikes, knees dirty always, oh I don't want that. Was it really so good? He beat me up, or the likes of him did./That is a great leather. (And Jack agreed, keen

124

shoeman himself.)/Hawaii./We never really talked. (Oh Christ, thought Jack, it's too late now.)/A phone that is in your mouth! Hygienic material and fitting beside the teeth you merely murmur with barely parted lips. I can impart my thoughts in the park to my beloved without booth and the usual floor of piss./The gorse stretches of the North, my mind would be clear and sparkling with a tang of peat. Brings back we never ever talked properly. (Fuckinhell, Jack's reaction, not again, thankgod I'm an orphan.)/Two Thousand After Death. (Now there's a thought, he thought.) When everybody will be modern, everywhere, not just the ones with the money. By then easy will be everywhere and all machines react to your nerve messages that you just think 'I want some soup' and lo it comes from the shop in an electric parcel./Is that a boy? Got very high cheeks and a greatcoat greatcut. In three weeks if you didn't eat or drink or move you'd have paid for it. (To fuck Deany again was Jack's own particular line now, jogged by this last snatch.)/Oh bubba bubba is um goochygoochy, little sweet softies tuckemup one each side of my face, brings back oh my, brings back (just about fucking everything, that one. Jesus, who could resist it? Well, he could. No fucking babies in his natural lifetime, that was one thing that was perfectly clear. He shook his head, as if that might break a transistor or something, try to stop this shit flooding in. He'd love to fuck her again. The second time was always best. Get away from it for a few days, remember what went down well. Oh God.)

Sliding into a protracted consideration of Deany's untanned areas that was overlaid both with versions of the attentions he had paid them and the refined attentions he aspired to apply soonest, Jack did not realise that he had eclipsed the shit which had, until a moment ago, taken up, virtually taken over, the available space in his routine thinking. He was entirely unaware of the published biographies of advanced men and women in which the debilitating aspects of special powers, or tran-scendental views, had been documented. His ignorance insulated him from any anxiety that he might be prone to the great illnesses of a man like, for example, the healer Robert Faintly Deskin (dubbed the Panty Christ by a jeering press, in an unsympathetic allusion to the briefs worn by Deskin when working in warm or crowded environments). Deskin's Fixations (protracted periods when the healer would not talk or move a single muscle for weeks on end, often occurring randomly in areas such as cinemas or supermarket check-out lanes) were generally followed by the explosive and dramatically curative Outbursts (in which

125

Deskin, formerly a manservant, would suddenly break into a tumult of small and large movements of every single part of his body, accompanied by a stream of fragmented or partially phrased speech, some of which could be quite rude, or interesting or, it was alleged, insightful) which brought him into prominence in the east of the country for several years. When Deskin was not actually absorbed by either of these modes, he spent much time in an appalling discomfort brought about by the failure of his body's temperature-regulating mechanism. Bouts of hot flushes would alternate with numbing sensations of chill, and his remarkable capacity to alleviate the ills of others would be of absolutely no avail to himself. Deskin loathed his peculiarity and dreamed into his dotage of returning to the even regularities of service in the fenbound mansions of his youth.

Jack had always taken his predictive skills for granted, and his major revelation had been so recent that it still seemed merely strange to him rather than a good or bad thing. He had failed to notice that the shit buzzing into his head from the street was wholly unsolicited and, as such, had a markedly different quality from the idle meanderings that engaged his mind when nothing important was going on. So effortlessly had his erotic reverie dispelled the plaintive but invasive chords of the shoppers that it did not occur to him that he had crossed a unique threshold. The most private aspect of his life, wherein a man might keep his self to his self, had been permanently compromised. By breaking through into the desert that lay beneath this world of little opportunity – the true desert of infinite possibility, he had exposed himself to the vapours that swept so mournfully across that perverse, depopulated terrain.

Spryly Jack leaped the bus, sat and dreamed of Deany's thighs, dashed the train and sprawled across two sets of seats, gazed out the window at the silent factories at the edge of town, and when told to take his feet off said to the man, 'You don't care' and shortened the debate with a look, the one where he opens his eyes wide and smiles unpleasantly the incongruity makes the opposition think, 'Fuck I don't need this'.

A sort of countryside where they lived. That is to say small areas of land had been developed into versions of the garden, jealously preserved between fences as the nearby highways bore the defoliating process far beyond what was once a hamlet on a green. Paradoxically, this was all quite novel for Jack, who had never seen the point of the countryside, did not wish to spend money visiting it and felt that life was too short for excursions to the places where really absolutely nothing happened,

126

as distinct from the city where everything happened but absolutely nothing changed.

Strolling past a post office with thatch on its roof and half-timbering on its walls, he marvelled at the notion that such tight, finite activities as the issue of separate stamps bearing pictures of the monarch or major achievers in entertainment were regularly carried out in the vagueness of this impossibly soupy structure. He slouched over to the window to see if there was a little old lady behind the counter, and on locating her, found himself gazing at her raptly. Without thinking he moved across to the door and pushed it open. When the bell tinkled he almost shuddered. A fleeting image of tumbling face down into a curtain of warm enfolding velvet caused him to blink and step decisively towards the counter. He stopped a few feet from the grille. The little old lady had grey hair in a bun, round spectacles, and clothing typical of the little old lady. She looked at Jack and said, 'Can I help you, dear?' Jack thrust his hands into the pockets of his jacket and looked at her. A wholly classic situation, it swam out of the soup and came into sharp focus before him, not as a picture but as an affirmation. The intangible mechanisms that supported Jack's awful voyancy had been recharged, trued up and retreaded for further mileage. The little old lady had been put there by people, as an anchor for the nationwide project that Jack was slowly beginning to understand. The cynicism of it was impressive, but in fact he was feeling more and more buoyant by the minute, and could only smile with pleasure at the timing of it all. The expected had impinged upon him with unexpected intensity and had verified the whole field thereby. He noticed that the little old lady was speaking again. He turned and left the post office.

Guy and Deany's was one of those country places where you couldn't tell where the front was supposed to be. He chose the fork in the path which led to the nearest door and whistled as he waited for Deany to open it. Deany opened the door and said, 'Hi, Jack. Come on in.' Jack stepped into the front room. There was no hall or anything, the door just let you straight into the sitting room. Across the room was another door that must be the back door, into the garden. He looked around and then at Deany. She grinned at him and he winked at her. She said, 'Well . . .' He smiled and she went on, 'Found it okay, then?' He said, 'Couldn't find the front.'

'That was the front. It's right on the front, you can't miss it. You didn't miss it.'

127

'It's just like towns, isn't it? But smaller.'

'It's similar.'

'Looking healthy.'

'Healthy. That's probably a compliment, right?'

He was smiling warmly through all this. Then thinking sometimes they think it's a one-off and you don't realise. You go on like something had begun and for them it was over last week and now you're just friends and there's no problem unless you're going to make one.

'Guy around?'

'My husband Guy? Sure, he's around. He likes to live and work here.'

Jack walked across the room, low ceiling, had to duck a little. He looked into the garden. 'Guy's up a tree.'

'Yeah?'

'Yeah. He's up a tree. He's got a dog up there.'

'What?' Deany moved swiftly to the window. 'Shit, that's not a dog!'

She started to open the window. Jack said 'Maybe not surprise him. Looks delicate.'

'You said it! Unbelievable!' She rushed to the back door.

Jack said 'Wow, we never hear about this in the city,' but she was already in the garden, so he followed her out.

Guy was quite close to the animal, but on a fairly thin branch. He had the footholds but not the thickness, and under the combined weight of animal and zoologist the branch was bending dangerously. The animal was secure, however, pinned in a fork that pegged it behind the shoulders in such a way that it would be unlikely to slip. Deany marched up to the tree, was about to call out, but decided to walk round to face Guy, in case she made him jump. She stood beneath her husband and tried to affect a mild tone. 'What are you doing, Guy?' Guy jumped and the branch dipped, imparting a triple shake to the forked Ike before it resumed its former unnatural degree of arc. 'Deany! You made me jump!'

'Tell me what you're doing, Guy.' A hint of menace had crept into her voice. Guy, whose chin was pressed against the branch, tried to look at Deany by rolling his head to one side. 'What on earth does it look like, Deany?' he replied peevishly.

'How did she get up there?'

'It's Ike.'

'Well how did he get there, Guy?'

'I'll tell you later. Let me get the bloody thing down.'

'Did he climb? How did he get out?'

'Deany!' Guy hissed, 'Please let me concentrate!'

Deany sighed in exasperation and looked at Jack, who was enjoying himself. He gave her a little wave. She was on the point of glaring at him, but turned her head away abruptly.

'That branch will break, Guy.'

'What do you suggest?'

'How do I know? Goddamn thing shouldn't *be* up there!'

'That's very helpful, Deany.'

Jack gave another little wave, more serious this time. She looked at him, her features softening slightly. Jack spread his hands out and made an up and down motion. She frowned. Jack made a gripping shape and moved it up and down again. Deany mouthed 'What?' then said 'What?'

'Shake it. He should shake it.'

Guy tried to turn his head, then thought better of it. 'Who's that?'

'Jack.' Deany said.

'Who?'

'Jack Gavin, Guy. He's come round for tea, remember?'

'Oh, yes.'

'Hi, Guy.' Jack strolled over to stand beside Deany. 'If you shake it up and down hard, I could catch it.'

'Catch it?' Deany was incredulous. 'Jack, this is an extremely rare animal. It's not a basketball, for Christ's sake.'

'He has a point, Deany. It won't hurt it.' Guy was panting as he spoke.

'What do you *mean?*'

'He won't feel it, will he? Isn't that the idea?' Jack interjected.

'That's not the idea, Jack. They're not numb. Of course they feel things.'

'It won't give it any more pain, though, will it?'

'We don't know that. It hasn't been shown.'

From up the tree, 'Deany, he's right. I know. I'll tell you later.'

'Guy, just shake it up and down and bounce it out. And I'll catch it. No problem.' He turned to Deany, 'Got a good record with animals.'

'Jesus. I don't wanna watch.' She shook her head and watched as Jack took up his position. He buttoned his snappy jacket and pushed the cuffs back.

'Okay, Guy. Shake it up.'

Guy pushed the hair out of his eyes and extended his arms along the branch. He put his full weight on it, let it dip, then pulled back. He repeated this a few times and soon the far end of the branch was swaying up and down quite fast. Ike, yowling disconsolately, hung snugly in the fork on the down and on the up.

'You've got to whip it, Guy. Make it jerk down when it gets to the top next.' Jack had become an expert, not bad for a man on his first day in the country that decade.

Guy tried the jerk. His first effort was poorly timed; the branch was already descending when he threw his weight onto it, and merely travelled further towards the ground than usual. Jack saw potential in this misjudgement though. He raised his arms above his head as the branch rose, and when it was within moments of apogee, brought his arms down and yelled 'Now!' Guy crashed onto the branch, quite cleverly imparting some whiplash to its farthest, animal-bearing extremity by pulling upwards with his hands as his body bowed the limb into an extreme curve. As Ike broke free of the cleft the branch insisted on a return to its proper curvature and in so doing bucked hard against Guy's stomach, causing him to cry out and lose his grip which meant that he landed on the lawn on his side in almost the same instant as Jack cradled his arms and deftly caught the slowly spinning body of Ike. He could surely have been something in athletics had he not smoked behind the changing sheds.

Guy's fall happened so quickly that it was not softened by any instinctive curling, turning or cushioning by use of the outflung arm. At the point of impact every cubic centimetre of wind was expelled from his lungs and this imposed certain priorities on his behaviour. He lay on the grass wanting to groan but having to naorg or kaorc instead, dragging air into a system that seemed to have taken leave of its senses, so reluctant was it to resume a regular animation. Deany was beside her husband, alarmed, rubbing his leg, gripping his shoulder.

Jack, at a time like this, knew what a man has to do. In the same way that a good person washes up in his host's house without palaver, he carried the twisting, noisy animal, quite heavy, across the lawn towards the outhouse at the bottom of the garden. That had to be the place where they kept them. Funny really, everything apart from an actual instruction sheet. Like those aborigines on their first car ride, he felt all he had to do was stand still and watch the landscape being pulled past him.

Deany had rolled Guy onto his hands and knees and was massaging his back. Guy stared into the grass and in the throes of

130

his pulmonary panic noticed a little red beetle clambering through the dark thicket of blades.

An hour later Guy was on his back in the bedroom. After an impossibly long bout of panic-stricken wheezing in the garden he had managed to drag some air back into his depleted lungs but as a result of the fall his hip and shoulder were hurting a great deal, and he had been obliged to forgo the tea that Deany had prepared in the sitting room. He wanted very much to go to sleep, but every time he began to drop off his breathing became deeper and he experienced stabbing pains across the top of his chest. He tried to make his inbreaths shallow, but kept getting it wrong. Every few minutes he would run out of air and had to catch up by inhaling deeply which made him groan and twist his head from side to side. Downstairs Deany was giving tea to Jack Gavin. He felt he ought to be down there with them, for Jack had been very helpful about the animal. Surprisingly practical, in fact, given the sort of sloppy impression the man usually made. So he really should be down there, to show his gratitude, but then Deany would ask him about Ike, and he had no idea what to say about it all. Beneath his studied respirations, he believed he could still detect a sort of pressure deep in his chest, or was it his stomach? A whirring in his guts, not a sound exactly, but as if his heart were pounding too fast and creating a kind of hurry, an urgency, all over his body. It had been there while he was up the tree, and before that, when he had been experimenting with Ike. Sometimes he felt his body was simply beyond him – he would be doing something perfectly straightforward, that required a certain attitude or concentration, and then without any reason certain other feelings would start up, and they would break his concentration. It was a puzzle, and not something that Deany would understand; it all sounded so vague, and not like him, she wouldn't expect it from him.

Christ, he couldn't sleep, he couldn't breathe, he just had to bloody *be* there, lying about, waiting for the seconds to tick by.

'That a lizard?' Jack had his teacup in his hand and was wandering round the sitting room.

'Chameleon,' Deany said.

Jack bent down and peered into the glass case. 'It's dead.'

'He just ate. They don't move a whole lot.' She got up and stood beside him.

131

'Doesn't mind being in there?'

'It's a heated vivarium. Few flies a day and I guess he's happy.'

'I'm the same.'

'And I just made all those sandwiches!'

'What is it they do, these?'

'Change colour?'

'Yeah. Make it do that.'

'You want me to force this chameleon to change colour?'

'Yes please.'

'I thought you were against nature, Jack.'

'That's against nature, isn't it, to force it?'

'Have to lift him out. Just for a minute, though. Doesn't want to get too cold.'

Deany lifted the metal cover off the vivarium. 'I'll bring him out on the branch. He won't want to be touched.' She gently withdrew the stick, the chameleon still rigid upon it. 'See the feet? Like a parrot? Got two toes on the front and three opposite. He can really hang on.' Jack leaned in for a look. The chameleon reared up on its hind legs, puffed up its throat-pouch and began to hiss fiercely. Jack jumped back.

'What'd I do?'

'He's angry. Your head's too big.'

'It's average, perfectly average.'

'See him changing now?' As they watched, the orange-flecked dark green skin blushed into a bright emerald tone. The flecks disappeared and a series of pink patches broke out along the creature's sides and legs. Jack grunted his appreciation. 'Is that where he thinks he is?'

'Huh?'

'What kind of a place is he in? I don't see any pink dots around, do you?'

'That's his reaction to handling. I guess it's both panic and designed to put us off.'

'I'm not afraid!' Jack said to the chameleon.

'Any more,' Deany said.

'Make him blend with the environment.'

'Well, maybe we should put him over by the curtain. I don't guarantee this, by the way.' She walked over to the bookcase and picked up a heavy glass vase. Carefully lodging the end of the branch inside it she placed the vase on the ledge of the garden window. 'Okay . . .' Lifting up one of the curtains she wrapped it round the back of the vase so that the chameleon was more or less surrounded by fabric on three sides. 'We step back here, give him some room.' She took Jack's hand, led him over to the front window and sat him on the ledge.

The curtains were tawny, with an unobtrusive dark yellow pattern. The chameleon very slowly raised one of its front legs off the branch and leaned forward in a reptilian pastiche of a hound scenting game. Jack, whose hand was still being held, became restless and looked at Deany out of the corner of his eye. She was staring unblinkingly at the chameleon. He nudged her. 'Nobody's blinking in here.' She put her head on his shoulder. The chameleon became tawny. 'Good,' Jack said.

'Not bad, huh?' Deany said.

'I still see him,' Jack said.

'Yeah?'

'Sure. See that vase? And the stick in it? Well, about halfway up that stick is a chameleon. See – against the curtain?'

'You're a perfectionist. Say you ran in here, say you were a fly . . .'

'I'd fly in. Why run?'

'Would you see that? You'd think "that's a piece of curtain", right?'

'Yeah. I'd think "Look at that curtain there on that stick, that's very strange, usually they have them round windows."'

'This is a fly? They think that?'

He turned and took her head in his hand and kissed her, saying 'Deany, will we ever know?'

Deany pressed against him and hummed some notes. He suddenly stood up. 'Got a better idea.'

'Better than that?'

'Better than curtains. A proper test.'

Jack strode to the centre of the room and started searching through a pile of books and papers on top of a coffee table. 'Right.' He removed a newspaper and unfolded it, laying out a couple of sheets on the carpet. He then took the vase from the window, placed it on the floor beside the newspaper and gingerly lifted out the branch. 'Kebab,' he said, 'Now . . .' putting the branch down on the paper, 'what do you think?' The chameleon lowered its cocked front leg onto the paper and froze again, three legs still locked onto the branch. Jack was squatting on the carpet, with his tongue out. 'Put this round maybe.' He picked up the remains of the newspaper, folded it so that it made a stubby crescent-shaped packet and stood it behind the chameleon, like a little fence. The packet fell over. He pulled the coffee table closer, unfolded the paper again and hung a double page from the edge of the table so that it formed a backdrop.

Deany's arms encircled his neck from behind. 'Thought for a moment you were going to wrap it up.'

'This is my big contribution to science, Deany.'

'Nothing's happening.'

He rocked back onto his heels and put his arms round her calves, pulling her shins into his back. Her legs were bare and he could feel the tan on them.

She would slide her hands down the front of his jacket and stroke his ribs, and he would lift his arms so that his hands travelled up her legs to the warm pulse on the back of her knee, at which point the movement would become awkward and he would laugh lightly and so would she. Then he would just turn round, still on his haunches and press his head into her groin and slide his hands much further until he held each of her buttocks and squeezed them gently. At this point she would place both hands on his head and bend over him, pulling away slightly. She would whisper urgently, 'Jack! No!' and he would say, 'It's okay' and she would say 'Guy!' as if to remind him and he would reply, leaning back to look up at her, 'He won't come, Deany', because he wouldn't, and her eyes would open in amazement and he would draw her down to the carpet and her legs would slip either side of him as her dress rode up. Then they would roll back, he on top, pushing their bodies together. She would arch against him and as he inched her pants along her legs she would struggle with his belt. When her pants were in his hands he would put them in his righthand jacket pocket and they would both giggle and he would help her with the belt and the buttons and his trousers and shorts would move down to his ankles and as he went inside her she would tense and dig her fingers into his arms and look up at the ceiling and he would whisper, 'He won't come' and she would shake her head in disbelief, not believing what they were doing, and arch against him and he would open her dress at the top and she would undo his shirt so that their breasts were touching and most of their clothes were still on but only just. As they moved she would take the hair at the nape of his neck and involve it in a fist she would make with her right hand. When he was not kissing her mouth or breasts he would find his face pressed into the pile of the carpet and find himself looking at and half seeing the harsh, tight tufts of cream wool. He would see the end coming and he would prepare himself and in the end he would be groaning and her nape now would be in his right hand as she came into the end and tried only to breathe not to cry out. Certain pictures suggesting great glories and exultations would rush before him, and he would not be sure if they were exultations that he would experience one day or if he had already enjoyed them, a long time ago. He would wonder also if they were not memories or possibilities but just ideas about those things, ideas which could never be consumed. In a few seconds the pictures would slip away, and he would know that the glories were just something that had life for a few seconds and then faded. They pointed everywhere, some-times into the past, sometimes into the future; that was their nature, they never actually happened. He would leave these thoughts behind and turn his head to Deany and she would sigh against his ear and push his head back and stare straight at him, still not believing what they had done on the floor of the sitting room in her house.

All these things happened as he had foreseen and he rolled onto his back and reclaimed his shorts and trousers. Deany got up, smoothed her dress, then immediately sat down in an armchair. She was shaking slightly, but soon began to laugh. She said, 'I don't believe this!' Jack grinned and tidied his hair in the glass of a framed photograph of a condor. As he studied his reflection Deany gasped and he swung round.

The chameleon had not moved at all. The tiniest of pulses flickered at the base of its neck, and the leathery cones of its eyes were turned outwards, presumably affording it a simultaneous prospect of both sides of its situation. On one side, a few inches away, hung the sheet of newspaper. The creature had become waxen white from head to tail. A series of black marks, arranged in configurations of curved and straight lines, ran in horizontal bands along its back and flanks.

Deany dropped to her knees and crawled across the carpet. Jack was beside her a moment later. 'Jack! It's copied it! The print!'

'Wow.'

'You can see letters, look. It's actually picked up the shapes, and the lines.'

'With one eye.'

'It's shut down nearly all its pigment. That never happens!'

'Well, they don't get the papers out there, do they?'

'Look at that!' She pointed to a black cipher on the chameleon's shoulder. 'What do you think that is?'

'Could be an s.'

135

'It is! It definitely is!' Her eyes darted over the wrinkled skin, pausing at a mark situated on the rump just above the rear left leg. 'And that's an o, for sure.'

Jack reached into his jacket and pulled out a pen. 'We can write them down. Start at the head and work along. Then we can tell which part he's reading.'

'I'll call 'em out.' Deany crouched even lower, so that her face was only a few inches from the publishing reptile. 'Dunno where to start, it goes right around. I'll come along the back from left to right.' Deany inched her gaze along the lines of script, calling out the letters one by one, and Jack copied them onto a piece of newspaper, keeping to the line groupings that she indicated. By the time Deany finished he had made up seven lines, one taken off the chameleon's spine and three from either side of its trunk.

Deany sat back on her behind. 'What do we get?'

'I think we have a paragraph.'

'Read it out.'

'Whrfbnd.'

'Wurfbund?'

'German. They come from Germany, these things?'

'No.'

'Well, it knows German. How do you explain that?'

'What does it mean, Jack?'

'Deany, I don't speak German. We'll have to send out for a dictionary.'

'Let me see.' She moved round to Jack's side in order to read the list. 'It's not even spelt right. That's not a wurf.'

'That's a wurf, Deany. What else can it be? It's the German wurf.'

'That's just half a line, right? Then we got some more. Geroihc.'

'Polish. Whrfbnd Geroik. Polish football player. It's a sports column. I'll just check that.' He leaned over and scanned the page hanging from the coffee table. 'This is the financial page.'

'Nothing like geroihc there?'

'What is like geroik? Is it a commodity?'

'We're talking as though it reads the stuff. In fact it's just imitating an effect, finding the most effective way to blend.'

'That's dull, Deany. Imagine the satisfaction these could give the young and the bedridden. Or those of limited attention span. Put the chameleon on a worthwhile book or paper and it will select a passage for your reading pleasure. Particularly good for short poems. Train them

136

to climb onto the page, come back, and slowly roll over in your hand. Money to be made here.'

'I guess I'm just a scientist, Jack. These material rewards mean nothing to me.'

'It's obvious.'

Deany picked up the newspaper and folded it to a more manageable size. She continued to study the lines of letters. 'Be weird if it said something, though, wouldn't it?'

'Like here, you mean?' He pointed to a group of letters in the fifth line.

'tposolosolorh. What is that? po-so-lo-so.'

'Lo.'

'po-so-lo-so-lo. Rh.'

'Solo solo. Two proper words. One word twice, anyway.'

'That's right.'

'That's weird, isn't it?'

'Out of a whole string of garbage you get one word repeated and then garbage again. That is actually quite remarkable. Yeah.'

'I think it's significant. I'm prepared to go that far.'

'The chameleon says solo solo. Sounds like a movie,' she said.

'A bad one,' he said.

The thud on the ceiling was readily interpreted as an impact on the floor above, and Deany leaped to her feet instantly. 'Shit! I said I'd take him tea!' She ran out of the room.

Jack stood up and put the folded newspaper, and his pen, in his inside jacket pocket. Deany ran back into the room. 'My pants!' With a quick-on-the-draw flourish Jack whipped out the underthing from his side pocket and tossed it at her. A number of coins caught up in the garment flew across the room, striking the walls and rolling under chairs. He crawled around recovering his property as Deany giggled in horror. She pulled her pants on and ran out of the room again.

Jack stood at the garden window and put his hands on the ceiling. There was the workshop. After he had so helpfully returned Ike to his cage, Deany had dashed in, padlocked the meshed hatch and then run back to the garden to succour her winded husband. There were no pockets in her dress. The key had probably been in Guy's pocket throughout the tree episode. In order to help him into the house she might well have slipped it back in his shirt or trousers.

Jack whistled and pushed at the ceiling. Deany stuck her head round the door. 'He knocked the side table over.'

'Oh dear.'

'He's fine. Still got a bad shoulder though. I'm going to make some tea. You all right?'

'Don't worry.'

'You wanna put that animal back?'

'Sure.'

He tidied up the chameleon, glanced once more into the garden, then walked purposefully into the kitchen. He came up behind Deany, slipped his arms round her waist and squeezed her breasts.

'Hey!'

'I'm going to go.'

'Why?'

'You should be looking after Guy. I'm in your way.'

'No you're not.'

'It's not right. Why don't you ring me tomorrow, maybe come up to town? We could do something.'

He put his tongue in her ear and she shuddered. Her hand descended to, and then gripped, his thigh. 'Such a nice visit, Jack.'

'Thank you for my tea.' He moved round and kissed her. She hummed as he did so. He let himself out and walked into the village.

This time the tinkling bell did not impinge on his purpose. It tinkled, inevitably, but it was cushioned by its own radiance. Because the dear old lady was now sharply outlined and unradiant, she heard the bell without being aroused by it. His entry into the swirl of radiances was, for him, dramatic. He compared it to the shock of crossing the threshold of the steam room in a Turkish bath, the impact that was almost like a blow to the stomach. He knew that he virtually created this situation himself or, more precisely, allowed it to manifest itself, but its intensity still surprised him. He swam into the post office, expecting to break out in a sweat as the cards, wrapping-paper, magazines, sacks of peat, rubber sandals and shopping bags all throbbed their availability. There was no need to tiptoe, he reminded himself. If he wanted, he could even sing. The business seemed to work out best when he followed his impulses without caution, but singing struck him as needlessly audacious, and besides, he didn't actually want to sing at that moment. He tried some of the bags for size. One or two? Given what he had seen in the workshop, one would be enough. A strong handle and a double zipper. Should do the trick.

He was worried about Deany. Would it work with her? If he was going to be cautious because of her, and necessarily unfettered in the course of the rest of it, the operation could get fucked up. He already knew the answer – there was no room for caution, no room whatsoever. He knew what he would do. He knew.

She was back in the sitting room. He saw her as he passed the window. As he stepped into the room she looked up. He walked straight to the stairs and made his way to the first floor. The first room he entered was the bathroom. The second a guest room. Guy lay on the bed in the third room he entered.

Guy was finding that sipping tea while prone taxed his powers of physical improvisation. When he tried to raise himself further onto the pillows, the base of his spine gave him gyp. Earlier on, through sheer bicep application, he had managed to lever the top half of his body from the mattress into what might have been a useful angle to his legs. Just as he had been about to drag his bottom back along the bed, his arms had begun to tremble violently. One of them had shot out and sent the side table flying, and he had abruptly fallen back to his old, unsatisfactory position with a new, lower lumbar discomfort. His reward had been the cup of tea that he was now attempting to consume. To be precise, he was resting between sips, having found that in forcing half a mouthful of the gradually cooling liquid round the taut right angle that was the best he could make of his throat, his energy reserve had been halved. If this tendency were allowed to develop, he would presumably pass out about a third of the way down the cup.

He lay, for the moment, flat on his back, the cup on the mattress beside him, steadied by his hand. Building up strength. So tiresome. Incredibly tiresome. Falling out of a tree in your own garden. Half way round the world a few weeks ago and hardly a scratch, well, discounting the bite, and now falling out of a crab apple tree. In front of Jack Gavin, who obviously had precious little time for anyone who made their living getting out and about. Now having tea down there. With Deany. A new friend. Of the family. Was this true? Whose friend was he, really, actually? Still, it doesn't matter. You don't have to like everything your partner likes. Ow. Sort of rubbery feeling in the legs. And sweaty. Be nice to have the trousers off but there you are. And a pee. Out of the question. Too bad. This sort of fluey thing in the legs, tingling. Just shock, or some side effect from the lower lumbar. Fell out of that tree in Hoadley. Eight or nine then. Absolutely flat on the back. Had to be carried across the field, through the garden and into bed. No actual harm but sweating a lot. For three days.

Into the bedroom came his mother. He had called out for her. Wanting a wee. Could have walked to the loo but you could get things done for you when you were ill and he wasn't ill often and it was interesting. She seemed to come in and look round. There he is on the bed. Over here. Where's the pot? It's not on the shelf, who's looking there? Looking on the floor now. She had picked it up from under the bed and did he want to hold it? She would hold it. He stands up on the bed and his legs are a bit rubbery. Where's his father? Not in the room surely. He comes in in the evening. He's downstairs anyway, having his tea. He pulls his pyjama top out of his pyjama trousers and then finds his willy. There aren't any pockets in the jama trousers. There's a pocket in the jama top. Now he has his willy and he's going for a wee. Into the pot. There's only a handkerchief in the top pocket. He looks down at the jama top pocket and yes it's only a hanky. He's missed the pot, he's peeing on his mother's hand. She shouts. It's so funny. It's very very very funny. She can't move away or else he'll wee all over the bed. She's shouting and there's wee all on her wrist as well. It's really the funniest thing in the world. Now the pot's back in the right place, she shouldn't have moved it anyway. He finishes his wee and she wants his hanky. There's a hand in his top pocket. It's not fair. Now he hasn't got a hanky. Well it's jolly well his fault he'll just have to sniff.

Jack stepped back from Guy, breathing evenly. He could look straight into Guy's eyes if he wanted, but there was no call for it, he didn't have to prove anything. There were three keys on the ring, and that was definitely the only ring Guy had had on him. His trouser pockets had been empty and the only other thing in the shirt pocket had been a small penknife.

At the bottom of the stairs he looked over at Deany and found himself admiring her bare calves again. To his horror, the radiance suddenly disappeared. The room was crystal clear, just like her outline. She was turning a page of the book in her lap and as Jack's breathing stopped entirely, her head started to come up. In a fraction of a second she would be looking at him, seeing him. The most primitive thoughts ricocheted around in his head – just look away, just look away! He wrenched his head round as the panic mounted inside him. Her head was up now, it had to be. He could not move. Transfixed at the stairs with the shopper and the keys. He stared imploringly at the window shelf beside the front

140

door. A phone. A jug. Some gloves. Some wire. A purse. He could hear Deany breathing in. Right across the room he could hear her. Gloves. Wire. Purse. Navy blue leather. Little clip at the top. A nice little purse. A jolt somewhere. A jolt and the fine fog came back, the fog that he could see through. Humming across from wall to wall, gently rolling off the window ledge, a slow uncoloured steam curling around the jug and the purse. He started to breathe again. He wouldn't have to dash for the door, he could just walk over to it. She was looking in his direction, he stood in the line of her gaze – that was all.

He skirted the house and came round into the back garden. Through the sitting-room window he could see Deany reading. The door of the workshop was open. He could hear the screaming of the animals and their cubs. He put the shopper down and unlocked the padlock on the hatch. On top of the cage was a pair of heavy gloves, which he slipped on. There seemed to be five cubs, and he had no idea how to sex them. A moment later he realised that that didn't matter, he only needed to get one of each type, assuming that the typing occurred at the back end as in the common cat or dog. He grabbed a cub and upended it. No dick like a dog, but maybe it had one buried in the fur. He put the cub on top of the cage and grabbed at an adult that had strayed into range. Same sort of thing, holes and hair, so he laid it alongside cub one. He wasn't after the fully grown ones anyway. Cub two had a different arrangement, at last, less holes. Maybe a male then. He was about to bag it, then decided to dump it with the girls in case there were further variations in the cage. Not a third sex, of course, but perhaps something a little clearer, since he wasn't about to poke about in some animal's arse with his clumsy gloves on. Or off, come to that. They seemed content, hardly the word, to roll about on the mesh, so he reached in for his fourth dip.

The other adult was quite close at hand, but the rest of the cubs were scattered about in various corners of the enclosure, well beyond the reach of his arm. From time to time, for no apparent reason, one of them would dash across from one side to another, but none of these random runs ever came near the grab zone. It was also clear from their complete absorption in suffering that they weren't the kind of animal you could coax or lure anywhere.

Leaning against a wall of the workshop was a collection of gardening implements. Jack selected a rake and pushed it through the hatch in the direction of a cub rolling about in one of the cage corners. He slid the toothed end towards the beast and was annoyed to find himself about eighteen inches short of the mark. Furthermore the weight of his body on the frame was producing a threatening bend in the wood. If he had a box of something . . .

The effect of standing on the paper sack of potatoes was to position too much of his body over the mesh, thereby actually reducing his reach. He moved the sack back a little, remounted it and fitted his right shoulder into the hatch. The hatch frame pressed uncomfortably into his neck, but he did gain about six inches in the reach department. Grunting impatiently he tried sweeping the rake from side to side, as if the radar might somehow encourage the enemy to enter its field. Curiously enough, the enemy did at this point roll back suddenly, to receive a blow in the side. Excitedly and with some effort, Jack lifted the rake up and managed to drop it teeth first on to the cub's haunches. As the cub squealed and shook in its unending paroxysm, Jack inched it towards him, into the grab zone. Tossing the rake aside, he took the cub firmly by the scruff of the neck.

With his hands round its belly he inverted the animal and peered at its arse. Type two: the one-holer. Now he definitely had a set. Two sets, in fact. He dropped it into the shopper, which he carefully zipped up before turning to pick out the non-adult type one from the bunch on top of the cage. He was startled to discover that where once had lain three creatures there was now just one, the adult. Crouching down he looked beneath the cage – all he could see was a couple of boxes and a roll of chicken wire.

Jack scanned the grass and flowerbeds from the door of the workshop. There was no sign of the two cubs. He ran to the centre of the lawn and listened for their screams. Only birdsong. He shrugged and ran back to the cage, where he picked up the remaining animal, the adult. To his relief, it proved to be a type one. He still had a set!

The return of the keyring to Guy's shirt pocket was a straightforward operation, uncomplicated by any covetous consideration of the victim's wife's legs. By the time he had let himself out of the front door, Jack was visiting a gentlemen's outfitter in town. Half way through the village he had purchased the deep blue with yellow fleck and had decided to take another in the same style but rendered in a sandy beige with a faint pink box check. It was particularly pleasant choosing five or six ties that would probably work, and if some of them didn't there was no harm in getting a third suit later on, one that would bring them out properly.

Dodecahedral dust drifts in a golden fume between the purple stems. Sometimes a grain of it falls onto the tip of a black glistening bristle and slowly bounces off, rolling upwards against the tumbling haze before another mote bumps it back into a new descent. These are specks that will never garter a bee's leg or stipple the tiger fur of its back. In more settled, natural times, they would meet the soil below and tip into the pits and pocks that make up its face, never to be stigmatised by the perfect pistillation, never taking the seedy dive that makes a fecund date. All these possibilities are now confounded by the lathered head that thrusts through the dahlias and other florid perennials, snapping boughs in its wake, dishevelling the flocked anthers and precociously loosing the smoke of germs. Shagged with a towish aureole, the dripping brow is caked with the pollen knocked up in clouds by its own rude passage. Globed eyes rolling left and right, there into the mix of sticks beneath a bush, here into the waxed gloom of the laurel, the blotched head ploughs beyond the padding hands, palms jammed with leaf rot and tiny rocks of mud, supported by fleck-peppered arms and closely followed by the clump of knees and the scarifying drag of toe caps. Beds and borders grooved, blooms strewn, canes skewed, cloches cracked.

A hand lifts and sweeps over the groundsel, raining grit on the flower heads before threshing into thickets of shrub beside the fence. The whole invading body then staggers up, slumps into the slatting, stoops and scours along it, rattling branches, bending sheaves, bursting through prickly clusters carefully contained by raffia, green wire and rough brown string. All the crop crushing of a fox hunt is concentrated in this campaign, but the flushing out amounts to little more than a scurry of lice, the dislodgement of a cabbage white, one thrush flustered from the lilac.

As he flails the perimeters, the huntsman groans and mutters to himself, 'Oh God, Oh Jesus, Oh Christ, Oh God.' Now and then he sobs, pausing to be wracked, seconds later driving himself on again. Tears mingle freely with his perspiration and the rivulets salt the cries with which he punctuates his gasps of desperate invective. 'Eke!' 'Eke!' 'Eke!'

But this is not a dog or cat or horse, known for responding hungrily to calls of Boy! or Puss! or Ralph's Reprise! Nor is it the homely rabbit, which certainly looks in your direction when the greeting 'Chin up, Mister Fur E. Bunnington!' is proffered. Ranks of the minor caged, such as the mouse Squeaks, the hamster Chunkles, the gerbil Rafferty, the rat Fred, the ferret Chewy and the weasel Nips, will often emerge from straw or shredded paper on the occasion of one's arrival in the room. The toad Bulgy will sometimes blink to the prod, the goldfish Malcolm may swerve to the tap, the salamander Jacqueline will leave a log at tidbit time. Pigs and minks alike will flock to the pail clank. Budgerigars will hop to extended index fingers and take pieces of pulses from pursed lips, while within seconds of the unsnicking of the back door latch the webbed quackers are honking at Mrs Giles's apron. Eke is not of this ilk. No future in the naming business here, no wheedling worth it, for no displays of allure will stick. There can be no bribery or favourite foods, she is incorruptible and as good as deaf. Eke does not give a fish's fuck.

'It's hopeless, Guy, they've gone!' Deany on the lawn, hands on her hips, exhausted. 'We'd hear them!'

Some slippage is occurring in his mind. Somehow, on the screen where thoughts and pictures are thrown up for assay, the pullulation has taken on a queasy tone. Usually his pictures were clear, and fell into two categories – those that were legible and those that were inscrutable. The latter class was disposable, an inevitable byproduct of the massive electrical enterprise of the cerebrum. Everyone had a certain amount of nonsense in his mind, and some, like himself, had trained their minds to relegate it to the margins. Despite being inconsequential, and often fragmented, this material was nevertheless always *focused* in some way. This is why, as he pants and trembles against the garden fence, the slippage strikes him as an altogether new phenomenon, and the last thing he needs in this hour of utter catastrophe.

'God, I can't see!' He presses muddy knuckles against his temples.

'Come away from the fence, you'll push it over!'

He stumbles through the flowers towards his wife. She takes his wrist and bends it away from his head.

'You're covered in sweat and mud, darling. Let me!' She pushes his wild hair back over his brow and brushes dirt from around his eyes.

'I mean, I can see, but . . . oh God!' He throws up his hand and turns away from her. 'Christ, bloody Christ, Deany!' Punching down with the backs of his fists onto thin air. 'Eke!' This last not a cry but a whisper, a simple signifier of the appalling. Telling her what she already knows – all females gone. The end of the line.

144

He looks hard at the fence. And there it is. Sharp as sharp. And the lilac. Photo fresh. Of course he can see. But inside him something colourless is sliding across his ears and eyes. The fence jumps. How sharp should it be? There. Did it jump away? Not away, not in distance, but making a gap somehow, not there enough. How do you tell? He cannot remember.

His wife does not often see him cry. She too feels bad, punished, defeated. She holds his hand as he sobs and sobs. He squeezes the back of his neck, then shakes his head violently and stares hither and thither. She sees the odd things that people do when they are greatly distressed but she can find nothing adequate in response.

He gulps for air, winded by grief, and Deany bites her lip. Tears tremble at the point of tipping onto her cheeks, but they spring from anger. Guy has been steamrollered from behind and she wants to kick the world.

'We'll put a sign up, Guy. In the post office.'

'No! You're out of your mind! Nobody must know! I'll find them myself!'

She sighs and pulls him back towards the house. He snatches his arm away and walks down the lawn. When she looks at him through the kitchen window, he is sitting cross-legged, head cupped in his hands, staring straight down into the grass. Not even a beetle passes through. He closes his eyes.

'Got to get something in here, Jack,' said Ainsley, who called him Jack now. It was hard to get used to the kid in a moustache, especially when it didn't match his hair. Given that he was still wearing pale blue tights and shorts, the hue of the hair was so unmistakeable that it must surely give the game away to the most casual observer. Were it not for the cover afforded the champ by the legions of Ainsley imitators regularly seen in the streets, the black moustache would strike any keen follower as a clumsy iconoclasm.

Back at the house Ainsley had told Jack that people never recognised him immediately, there was always a time lag of one or two seconds, during which the subjects' initial complete conviction was undermined by massive waves of superstitious doubt. Immediately after a sighting, as the devotees began to take stock of their sensations of rapture and, above all, heightened meaning, a terrible moral drama unfolded within them. Soaring into access came the irresistible desire to find a timeliness in the encounter, whereby all of history could be seen to funnel down to this moment and there be rendered patternful. Overshadowing these intimations of a transcendent force were shame-filled compulsions to self-immolation, visited upon the wretched devotee for his or her presumption in denying the despair that, as everyone knew, constituted the bedrock of the modern experience. It was in the course of this profound but unnaturally condensed debate that Ainsley took his precaution.

'What do you do?' Jack had asked.

'I look through them,' Ainsley had replied.

'Don't understand,' Jack had said.

'First I put on a look of total hate, then I look through them.'

'And?'

'They always think that I know them, right? They think they know me so well that I must know them in return. If I look through them with hate, not hating them in any *particular* way, they feel as though they've disappeared.' He saw Jack's mouth starting to open again. 'Because if I knew them I wouldn't hate them, so it can't be me. So we both disappear.'

'So why the tash?'

'That's for the ones at the side or behind. Can't do a lot about them.'

Fortified by this useful tip from a hero, Jack had accompanied the disguised kid into the streets, for what Ainsley had described as 'a treat'. Seventeen thousand five hundred pounds in fifties nestled against his breast in a jacket-distending wad and he was up for anything. When Ainsley entered the sports shop Jack had been quite surprised, having assumed that heroes did not need to shop for the accoutrements of their speciality, all of which would have been donated in sextuplicate by fawning manufacturers. Certainly a man of Ainsley's warehousing inclination would never want for anything that could be retailed by a common high street supplier.

The kid strode out of the shop and nodded at Jack. He had a small package in his hand.

'Balls, I expect?' said Jack, who hated knowing what heroes did.

'That sort of thing,' the kid said, and gave him a quick, small smile before leading the way to the treat.

The nature of the treat had not been specified, but Jack was not really bothered. Ainsley didn't say much as they walked along, at least not directly to him. At one point, out of the blue, he announced 'Why not a whole room?' and Jack said, 'What?' and Ainsley said, 'What?' so Jack said, 'A whole room,' and the kid said, 'Just thinking.' A few minutes later, this was after the shop, the kid said, 'Could have trees, everything,' so Jack just nodded. Five minutes after that, when the kid said, 'Two of each. Why stop there?' Jack was barely listening.

Then Ainsley said, 'Not long now,' but he looked at Jack as he said it, so Jack said, 'Great.' They were passing a TV shop at the time, and both paused to see what was showing in the window. The crowds on the pavement made it perfectly obvious, of course, but Jack hung on for a moment to see what Ainsley would do. Then he had a witty idea.

'Take the tash off,' he whispered to his companion.

'Don't be stupid,' Ainsley said tersely, studying his plays on the thirty screens.

'Hundred quid,' Jack said, warming to his idea.

'What are you talking about?' The champ was on tip-toe and wouldn't look at the seer.

'I bet you a hundred quid you could take the tash off and nobody would notice.'

'I don't bet.'

'Just do it then.'

Ainsley turned from the window, 'I don't want to play games with these people, Jack,' he said wearily, as if mustering his patience for the benefit of a difficult child.

Jack was not dissuaded, 'Fuck that! I'm going to show you something useful. Something you don't know.'

Somehow this impertinence did it. 'You want me to take it off. What do I do then?'

'I'll show you. Nothing difficult.'

Ainsley tugged at the moustache and peeled it from his lip. Jack grasped his upper arm and led him round the side of the crowd to the front of the TV shop. A number of people close to the window were shouting 'Suck my fucking skidmarks!' and rotating their arms wildly. Jack leaned into the melee, keeping one side of his body pressed against the window. He took hold of the nearest figure, a youngish man in a business suit, by the front of his shirt and pushed him back from the window. The man yelled, 'Cunteating shit taster!' as the multiple images of Ainsley were briefly blurred by the awesome velocity of an overarm smash. Jack shot his own arm back towards the unmoustached champion and heaved him into

147

the gap. Ainsley's eyes were very wide open, but he did not protest. Or dared not.

Jack was now right behind Ainsley, between the crowd and the glass. With his left hand he pressed the small of Ainsley's back and with the right he pushed at the chest of the woman who was partially blocking their passage. Both of her arms were extended above her head, and Jack found he could shove against her brow and unbalance her sufficiently to induce a two- or three-pace backward topple. Ainsley tensed and started to resist, but Jack pushed him firmly forward. Before them was a potential corridor, obstructed by perhaps twenty more fans.

'Push them back,' Jack instructed.

Ainsley turned his head and spoke out of the side of his mouth, 'I don't want to touch them.'

'Why are you whispering? Relax!' Jack jolted him on with a double-handed press to the shoulder blades. Ainsley stepped off and began tentatively to squeeze past the next viewer, a teenage girl in leather jacket. 'Get her out of the way!' Jack insisted. The champ put his hand on the girl's shoulder, then froze.

'Now what?' he hissed.

'Whatever you want.'

'I've got my hand on her!'

'Sure. She's one of your biggest fans. Look . . .' Jack moved towards the girl and bellowed 'Fucking Ainsley!' in her ear. Ainsley instantly withdrew his hand but Jack grabbed it and forced him to touch her again. The girl's jaw dropped, and a look of astonishment came over her face. Without taking her eyes from the window, she suddenly let out a piercing scream, followed by the hoarse injunction, 'Tell your mother you're drinking piss again, saddle sniffer!' Jack responded straightaway with, 'Bollocks in the lawn mower next time, dogarselick!' at which point Ainsley glanced at the window, saw himself bringing off a blinding return backshot from right down on the floor way off in deep corner, and immediately understood. Despite sounding rather sullen when he muttered, 'Yeah, right,' to Jack, he then launched himself into the corridor with great vigour, levering the girl aside and applying himself to a succession of his followers in an uninhibited fashion.

When he reached the halfway point on the window, he stopped, put his back to the plate glass and stretched his arms out to the side. Surveying the crowd in this cruciform pose, he began to snicker. There was little trace of a smile on his face, but Jack could hear the small

148

sounds coming from his mouth. Light from the stacked TVs behind him played over his head and shoulders and lent them a flickering blue aura. His head was pulled back so that its crown touched the glass, and his lips were slightly parted, baring a set of evenly spaced, slightly yellow teeth. His faint laughter broke up into regular beats like the rapid blows of a knife blade whittling away at a soft, green stick.

At the far side of the crowd Ainsley tapped his moustache back into place. 'Pretty good.'

'They were looking through you,' Jack said.

Ainsley glanced at Jack suspiciously for the briefest of moments, then nodded ruminatively. 'Yes. It's useful. Could be very useful.'

Some minutes later, Ainsley stopped in front of a cinema. 'This should do,' he announced. 'What do you think?'

'We going to the pictures?'

'That's right.'

Jack read the marquee. 'I know her.'

'I know you do. I saw it too.'

'Eva Kuwait and the Church of the Two Things.'

'You like her, don't you?' This was not an enquiry, the kid was informing him. Without waiting for Jack's answer, he stepped up to the booth and demanded two tickets.

Normally Jack liked to sit in the third row from the front in the stalls. It had been years since he had sat in the circle of a cinema, and at this distance the screen was much too discrete for his taste, but the seats appeared to be newly upholstered and the stalls were fairly full, so he settled in contentedly enough, with Ainsley on his right-hand side. Looking around, he noticed that in fact the bulk of the audience was down below and only about eight other people had forked out for the privilege of remoteness. These were arranged in couples, each of which had, without apparatus, computed the position which afforded it the greatest possible remove from all other populated points in the raked and cavernous crescent.

Turning from his survey to the screen, Jack was intrigued to find Ainsley's hand in his lap. On inspection, he realised that his benefactor was placing a packet of some sort at his disposal. The hand withdrew and Jack picked up the donation, which proved to be a box of fruit gums. Again, decades had passed since he had sucked a sweety at the pictures, or indeed anywhere else, since he had no fondness whatsoever for confectionery, but he thanked Ainsley nicely all the same.

149

'Oh, thanks.'

'Yeh.' Clearly one did not chatter while the champ took his pleasures.

A short film preceded the main attraction. Titled *The War Against Death: Part III – The Last of the Shallow Graves*, it turned out to be a popular science documentary dealing with innovations in forensic technology. A disembodied voice explained that, if progress were maintained at its present rate, a breakthrough of considerable magnitude was imminent in the field of corpse detection.

Apparently for years now you could trace guns, bullets and daggers in the ground by the metal detection device. In which the policeman or team, or lines of locals, with the plate-like scanners on the end of rods with earphones, as often seen on the beach or in the park at the weekends. They would sweep from side to side listening out for the telltale beep which would indicate. In the park it could be a bottle cap or drinking can, on the beach an old boat nail or leisure bucket handle, in the crime locale often a gored dirk or vital implicator. A big step forward from constables searching thoroughly by hand. Still there were the problems with whips or clothing items that would establish. Concern and outrage and a community stunned were good turn out. But however much scouring of wasteland one romper or gaberdine macintosh will escape. Thus an open book in the annals. Another space in the black museum. Be that as it may.

However. When it comes to flesh or blood, or bone, there were only dogs. For whole bodies or their parts such as a hand or head they are appropriate. They want to eat meat and will sniff for it anywhere. Certain areas are their skill. This is any land where the flesh is on top, could be hill or dale. Thicket or nothing. Then where the stabbed or throttled may be buried, up to a point. This is the limit, of the shallow grave. Killers usually hurry so graves nine times out of ten are relatively a scuff on the crust. Fine. Dogs sniff the meat through the soil but more than two feet and they run by. Just think of the many, many bodies at two foot six in all the woods and quiet areas of unbuiltup land.

Police hate this at the senior level. The thought, they say, is an insult to their sense. If the average killer has done it once then for every corpse at two-six or more there is, give or take of course, a person at loose that would better be behind bars or receiving some form of counselling. This is what so annoys the police. It is one of those topics where it is best not mentioned because of professional frustration.

Which is where the innovations enter. If there was a tunable

150

search device, a radar that *chose*, it would only give when it got what you wanted. It would not give for sweet wrappings, can tugs, or Victorian nails. It would not give for irrelevant sock shreds, wool wisps or hats blown off. Were, say, flesh keyed in then it would only give for flesh. This is the idea.

Templates of the unique constitution of organic molecules as arrayed in muscle, fat and what have you are stored in device, itself, as shown here on young woman, a slung backpack, with dish strapped to head, and it will sweep the area and give both screen blip and sonic beep increasing as you get warm. Depth not a factor. Up in a tree as with failed parachute, or ambitious grave of calm thorough maniac, tests so far remarkable.

Here is the young woman across a wet, bleak field, nothing planted, the rain against her face, the sullen sky. On the horizon a copse. A low blip and no beeps, these show distant location. She opens a gate in a wire fence, there is an old implement, plough maybe, rusting there. It is a cold day, the rain is filling up the gaps in the field. This one has some stubble. But the blip is indicating more strongly and now the beep. The copse it is clear. At its edge leaves drip, broken sticks are shiny, no birds. Thin trees are close together, ivy runs on the ground. In there it looks darker. Now here she is, in there, her feet breaking the fallen materials of the ground. The blip is clicked to the large-scale mode for the fine final stage. Relentlessly the rain rivulets down barks. Beetles working in rotten logs and the beep is continuous now. No signs at her feet, just dark earth, some weed, branch pieces.

She breaks into the topsoil with a field shovel, the instrument is switched off. The earth blackens with depth and her shovelsful pile to one side. She goes down one foot, two feet, past two feet six and into three. Still there is no flesh. Then at four feet deep in the black hole there is a white hand. Wearing gloves she pulls it and out comes the bare arm, rotting away. With her hands she removes soil where the head must be and there it is, a boy's head, most of the flesh gone but the hair quite clear.

In an office they explain that this corpse was taken from an old crime and buried in the copse for the sake of the demonstration. Then they point out that the age of lying is over, no one can hide flesh, blood or bone anymore, and this is not just dead, it can apply to felons in a large house, escapees secreted in a railyard. The clearup on missing persons believed no longer alive will be vastly improved, relatives will gain early release from agonised waiting, killers will think twice.

They say eventually templating of biomass will be gene critical. This means they dial you in, say your name is Robert, and it will know where you are, Robert, whenever they want. You need never fear being missing, or becoming disoriented, eventually someone will home in. Of course the same will go for pets: cats heisted by glovers, birds flown through unwise windows. You can get them back. If you wished, as a free choice, you could register personal profile and always be known where you are. Insurance premiums automatically lowered, preferential bank arrangements just two obvious pluses. If all people wished to be registered, and their pets and livestock, then a picture of the world with all flesh in it becomes available, and a great sense of separateness from it is marvellously alleviated, needless mystery and wondering where others are all goes. They say that where you have nothing to hide then it is an addition to your quality of life.

'I don't like these science films,' Ainsley said.

Jack, who had slumped down into his seat, pushed with his knees at the seat in front and drew himself up. 'I didn't mind it.'

'They should have more about places that people haven't been to, that sort of thing. Something light. People want something light.'

Jack stretched. 'I didn't mind it.' He nudged Ainsley's elbow. 'Just think, if all that stuff happens, there's no point in you wearing a moustache.'

'Rubbish. They won't know where I am.'

'You sure?'

'I can go anywhere I like. Anywhere!' He glared at Jack, then his eyebrows arched threateningly. 'Those machines are for the ordinary people. Don't you see that?'

Jack looked straight back at his inquisitor and for a second made as if to stare him out. Then he grinned and replied, 'I see it. More and more.' The lights dimmed again. Ainsley sniffed and turned his head towards the screen.

Eva Kuwait, in steely-lensed sun spectacles, was framed in an airliner window, titles over window, then to interior where Eva sat in Club class with her table down. On the table, a glass of water made turbid by lemon juice. Also a pile of black garments. Eva wore black for her assignments. On top of the pile a v-necked cashmere sweater, in one hand a needle and thread and in the other a small square of white cloth.

152

She began to stitch the cloth to the back of the neck of the sweater, on the inside. On it was embroidered a trade name, a size and a washing symbol. On the empty seat beside her, neatly folded, in textures of black, were several shirts, slacks and jumpers, each garment clearly displaying an emblazoned patch sewn to the fabric beneath it. The cam perused the variety of the signs in view. The music crescendoed, as the significance of the scene erupted – labels! Eva Kuwait, woman of mystery, has been attaching labels to her clothing, and each one was completely different!

Ainsley breathed sharply through his nose and shifted in his seat. Jack, not paying too much attention, wondered whether the kid was amused or impatient.

The parched ochre plains, the dusty green foothills of Paraguay, the bustle of Asuncion. Apart from the very old and the very young, everyone on the streets of the town wore uniforms of some kind. Eva pushed her way through what appeared to be a succession of military parades. The cam moved as if with Eva's eye to a flag decorated with the legend 'Wednesday 26th March 1923 Society'. A pan enframed another flag, and the gazer's curiosity was further stoked. 'Sunday December 9th 1950 Society', ran the appliquéd lettering. A third banner was painted with the words 'Fourth Eyelet Left Side Right Boot Perez Anderson Fraternity'.

A mild restlessness passed through the auditorium, an index of the sympathetic perplexity mixed with actual impatience that was dominating the gazers' mood. Jack felt fine about it all, but found himself wondering why his companion was still fussing with his sweets or whatever they were. Ainsley had prised the cardboard flaps open and was now rattling the packet rather irritatingly. Either he was testing its contents somehow or just idly, and unthinkingly, playing with it.

An old man was shuffling slowly towards Eva, trailing his fingers along the wall beside him and muttering to himself. Stepping aside to give him passage, she noticed that his fingers were alternately splaying out and contracting, which had the effect of drawing them crablike across the bricks of the wall. As he passed her she was able to hear his mumblings more clearly.

'Pasqualito/Barrinton/Fresnel/Laszlo/Melanie/Umbert/Sissy/Kees Buell/Peper,' the voice was calm, measured, unwavering, 'Tonia/Yusef/ Caresse/Bowers/Patsy/Lita/Delano/Norris/Meston/Arif/Nonal/Suey/

Adervi/Capton/Bella/Aldine . . .' gradually it faded away as the speaker receded from Eva and the gazer.

Eva was approached in a plaza. The peon thrust a piece of paper into her hand. She unfolded it. It was blank. Jack laughed softly. Eva looked at the narrowed, brown eyes of the peon and with a knowing smile tore the paper into a confetti. A rustling noise momentarily distracted Jack. Ainsley seemed to be picking at the cellophane encasing his package and then started fiddling with might have been a pen, screwing its cap on or off, rattling like he had two or three together. The peon turned and slid away into the weaving parades. Eva chased after him.

After many short shots exploiting the power of the glimpse to frustrate, Eva found herself in a quieter part of town. Her guide pointed to a building and vanished into the shadows. Eva opened her attaché case and produced a coil of nylon rope attached to a collapsible grappling hook. She stood back from the flaking stucco and whirled the hook. It arced upward, glinting in the sun glare, and clattered around a small window column, some thirty feet from the ground. Jack studied Silvia's sinuous gyrations approvingly. Eva ascended the rope lithely, her feet dislodging small showers of pink powder with each step. Suddenly groans rose from the cheap seats as a violet handkerchief freed itself from the hip pocket of Eva's slacks and fluttered towards the ground. Cruelly the cam closed on the rippling square, capturing its gauzy undulations through the torrid haze of powdered plaster and afternoon air. As it poured languidly onto the cracked mud of the road the significance of the episode was established – the hanky had no label!

Ainsley stood up and adjusted his shorts. He seemed to peer over the balcony for a moment before sitting down again, but Jack was learning to marginalise his companion's twitchiness, and dismissed the activities from his mind.

In a gallery running round the upper perimeter of the building, Eva had discovered an open window looking onto an interior space. She looked down in awe into a cavernous hall with a double door at its far end and a dais at the other. Above the dais was an imposing metal emblem, comprising two sizeable globes of lacklustre metal, which, by means of a discreet use of fine cable, appeared to be hovering in space. Every square centimetre of every other visible surface was overlaid with an optical confusion that resisted the eye's attempt to resolve it into focus. The predominant colour in the puzzle was white, regularly blemished with blue markings, but as soon as the eye rested upon any smallish area, this area seemed to break up, which Eva clearly found both vertiginous and discomforting. She did not allow it to slow her down for more than a few seconds, however. Stooping to her attaché she removed four black rubber suction pads, each about the size of the end of a drain unblocker. With the sureness born of a life spent confronting the difficult, Eva breathed in and made a long adenoidal snort. She spat sharply into each cup, and distributed the spittle evenly with her finger-tip before strapping the cups to her left and right knee and the inside of each wrist respectively. An agile movement saw her hanging from the sill of the high window, about to make her sucker-assisted descent.

In a silence only faintly tinged with a zephyr of violins, Eva Kuwait drove her right knee against the wall. Air was briskly expelled from the sucker and it cleaved to the dubious surface. Testing the seal with her weight, Eva seemed satisfied, and punched her left wrist at a spot just below the window sill. The scene took on a contemplative tone in which themes of risk, gravity, its defiance, insect life and the beauty of calisthenic achievement all interplayed freely. The regular slap and hiss of the applied suckers alternated with the smack and rush of the detached suckers and developed into an enigmatic, wordless litany which at times suggested poetic concerns beyond the normal confines of the genre. The audience was certainly captivated and when the spidery asterisk of Eva's body finally reached the floor, a ripple of applause and scattered cheering animated the house. Ainsley, too, was evidently moved, for he leaped to his feet and jerked his right arm upwards and forwards in the direction of the screen. The applause died away and he sat down promptly, turning to Jack as he did so, with bright eyes and a satisfied smile.

Eva stripped off the suckers and returned them to her case. As she stood up, a hand grasped her shoulder. She whirled round. There, utterly naked, stood a young man. Eva gasped, 'You are Mister Ian Page, the son of my client!' The young man moved his head feebly, and stared with vacant misery at the woman detective who had penetrated the sanctum without using the door. He made no attempt to cover himself, but stood listlessly before her, swaying slightly and wetting his lower lip repeatedly with the tip of his tongue.

Tears welled then streamed down Eva's cheeks. She pulled the young man towards her and squeezed him against her jumper. He began to shake and sob, and was soon weeping uncontrollably. As he trembled at her breast, she looked around at the optical disorder presented by the surfaces of the hall of the Church of Two Things. This turned out to be the result of the attachment of thousands of white adhesive labels, initially to the wall itself, then to each other's surface, layer upon layer, until the original fabric of the wall was completely covered. So rigorous was the execution of this design that each of the four corners of each successive label was also tabbed by a label. The gazer could deduce that the endless repetition of this process had led, inevitably, to an imposition of the design upon itself, wherein labels that had earlier been snicked only at their corners were later covered by the labels that were placed in that same area thousands of generations later, the process having spread countless times, through innumerable circuits, right around the wall of the hall, back to its point of origin.

An awed murmur rose from the audience as it considered the malign and implacable agency that could be sensed behind this monstrous exercise.

'What inconceivable and fanatic intelligence could possibly have brought about this thickness?' Eva cried, her jumper damp from the distress of Ian. The shuddering youth lurched towards the nearest expanse of wall and extended a pale, bony arm to the labelled surface. As soon as he made contact with it, his lips began to move, and he started speaking, in a voice that was at first low and unsteady, then grew into a mellow and modulated tone.

Ian said, 'Sixthreeninenine of the lower course, the original west, fourstrokeeightBstrokeseriesalphatwoohseven, Kenneth.' He moved his finger to the label overlapping the bottom left-hand corner of the first label, and with no hesitation pronounced another stream of figures. He said, 'Sixfourohoh of the lower course, the original west, fourstrokeeightBstrokeseriesalphatwoohseven,' then after a slight pause, 'Fuad.'

Eva stepped over and examined the blue markings on the labels as did the cam. She blinked then screwed up her eyes, the ones that Jack was thinkingwere so very dark, so very . . . alluring. In blue ink, in a crabbed hand, on every label, was a string of letters and digits. One of the examples favoured by the cam ran: 627 H.C., O.W. 4/8B/ser@207. Other contiguous instances in frame were similarly inscribed. Ainsley was becoming restless and had risen a few inches from his seat, apparently in order to survey the stalls once more. Ian was about to make another pronouncement. Eva realised she could not help him.

'Poor boy, I cannot help you,' she whispered, and Ainsley sighed.

Then Ian blurted out, with a supportive thrill of strings, 'Uli!' Eva took hold of Ian's other arm and shook him. 'We must leave this place of infinite nominism, Ian. There is no equivalence, no category! Return to the broad church of the One Thing with me now!'

The cam rose and roved around the very topmost aspects of the walls. As it neared the window of Eva's descent, it moved closer and in an instant was through the window and down to the street. A bulky, uniformed sexagenarian was walking towards . . . a scrap of coloured cloth. He stooped, and the rattle of Ainsley's packet coincided with the turning over in the hand of the sexagenarian the violet gauzy hanky of Eva Kuwait! And there of course it was . . . the damning absence, the lack of label! The man started, startled. The audience stirred, Ainsley jumped to his feet, his arm punched again into the air, the man turned and hurried to the front of the building, a murmur of consternation rose from a section of the stalls. Eva, revisited by the cam now, pulled at the arm of Ian and hissed in his ear, 'Ian, perfection does not lie this way! Every thing has things within it – think of the subparticles that proliferate within the proton! There is no prospect of finity in your obeisances!'

Even as Eva strove to animate the novice, a flurry could be heard in the passages without. Enflamed by the suggestions of equivalence and category implicit in the discovered handkerchief, the hierarchs were scouring the building for the infiltrated heresiarch, the scent of apostasy acrid on their tongues. Eva assessed the situation rapidly. 'There is no way my sucker set will hold two! We must leave by the door!'

Even as she spoke, the great labelled portals of the sanctum inswung and many men and women swarmed into the hall. A low, expectant murmur came from the cheap seats, and Eva bent at the waist. The priests spread out, lining the walls. Eva drove her shoulder into Ian's stomach and as he collapsed, pulled him up in a fireman's lift. Jack realised that Ainsley was cackling, which he found quite touching.

Eva walked coolly toward the open doors and stopped three paces from the priests who were blocking the doorway. She took a deep breath and met their cold glare with a level look. Then she spoke.

'Birds!' The priests winced and anger flickered across their faces. Eva spoke again.

'Cars!' The priests snarled, probably exercised as much by the

157

decadence associated with the proffered category as by the heresy of its actual utterance.

'Buildings!' The priests groaned in chorus. One or two of them broke the link with their immediate neighbours and moved forward. Eva was ready for them. She delivered a brilliant, ringing profanity.

'Bric à brac!'

Eva had intuited the equivalent of the bouncing bomb. The extremists of nominism wavered on the brink of confusion as she launched herself towards the loosened elements of the circle. The members of the cinema audience released, as one, a roar. Since the opening scenes of Eva's adventure a meticulously fabricated sensation of enclosure had steadily induced a tension that at last found unanimous discharge.

The priestess's septum was driven sharply into her soft palate by an explosive fingertip jab. Ainsley leaped to his feet, Eva swung Ian's legs into the stomach of the man to her right, the gazers clapped as her knee rose into his descending face, and Ainsley rattled his packet. A head butt took out a third priest as Ainsley, whose sweating brow glistened in the light reflected from the screen, punched the air. A scream rose from the stalls and the palatectomised priestess spat blood as she attempted to apply a half nelson to the arm that had borne the hardened implement of her disfigurement. Now gazers were standing in small groups gesticulating and Eva stamped on the priestess's foot, driving her elbow back and up against the woman's windpipe. With a deliberately provocative cry of 'Apparatus!' she glanced over her shoulder, Ainsley laughed in a string of short, high-pitched notes, Jack thought, this is how champions relax, the priests were closing in, in the stalls two groups were growing rapidly, gazers standing spreading as if from epicentres, she did not waste an instant, Ainsley turned to look at Jack, grinning, nodding in the direction of the groups below, he's enjoying being ordinary Jack thought, catching an incomer severely in the nuts with her kick Eva was through, which released a greater roar, someone was shouting 'Stop!' or 'Don't stop!' down there, outside the hall was a long cloister, a formal garden with statuary on its open side, Ainsley climbed over two rows of seats and stood at the lip of the circle, the priests pursued Eva hotly, Ian bounced on her shoulder, the kid shook his fist or something like that in the direction of the cheap seats, he wants to be down there with them, Jack thought, every aspect of the cloister caught in the cam's fast track was labelled, the inked inscriptions ran *Column, Pedestal, Wall/High*, but where was *Door*? Some gazers had left their seats, they were moving through the rows, screams from two or three points, some distress in the screams, but the chase was unbearable, the fast track picked up *Crack/Tile, Mark/Dark/Arch, Lichen/Base/Urn*, shouting from the priests, urgent cries from the floor, Jack thought it's exciting but not that exciting, obviously she gets away, she has to, haven't these people been to the pictures before? One scream was quite dreadful and around it loud discussions as Eva raced across the garden, pausing by the fountain that jetted no water, and there, beside *Gravel* was *Fountain/Cock*, some gazers were right at the front now, by the screen, looking round, pointing, Ainsley sat down in the front row circle, Eva grasped the rusted tap, Ian mumbled 'Cock/Faucet', Ainsley climbed over the back of his seat without rising much, not taking his eyes off the scenes below, from the floor a groan of disgust followed by weeping, the cry 'It's his neck!', what are they on about? Jack wondered, suddenly a plume jumped from the unused spout, Eva thrust her head straight into the silvery sinews of liquid, below the balcony everyone that Jack could see was standing, many were running to the ends of their rows, Ainsley snaked over two more sets of seats and returned to his original place, he gripped Jack's wrist and squeezed it very hard, Eva's head was soaked, she advanced on the dumbfounded priests with distended cheeks.

'Jack! I want to go!'

'What?'

'I want to go. Now!'

'Thought you were enjoying it.'

'It's too noisy. Come on!'

Eva, a few feet from the nominist horde, tipped her head back and Jack said, 'I want to see what happens next.'

Eva forced the water violently from her mouth, covering the priests with a fine droppletted spray. As they staggered back in disarray she snarled, 'Drink nameless profusion, particulate swine!' and ran full out for the far cloister wall, on part of which *Door/Street* could be made out.

Torch beams cut and swept the upstairs gloom. Ainsley tensed. Exerting a champion's irresistible force he dragged Jack to his feet as the erstwhile captors of Ian dabbed hysterically at the unnameable boundlessness that threatened to dissolve the nomenclature of their faith. 'Excuse me, sir!' but Ainsley was at the other end of the row and heading for the vomitory as the usher picked his way towards them.

159

The foyer of the cinema was empty, but the doors leading to the stalls were open. As he was steered out by the steely-armed kid Jack glimpsed a group of usherettes talking agitatedly at the top of the raked aisle. One of their number was weeping hysterically, and Jack heard another say, 'It's right in her spine, Penny.'

'I hate it when you can't hear the film, don't you, Jack?' Ainsley said as he propelled the perplexed seer down a side street. In the distance two sirens wailed. The sound grew louder and Ainsley started to giggle. He put his hand in the pocket of his track suit and pulled out a cardboard packet.

'Didn't finish your sweets,' Jack observed, rather lamely.

'Hate sweets,' Ainsley replied, and giggled again. He threw the packet down in front of Jack, who was about to step over it but slowed up considerably as he read *Sherwood Sportsco. Match Standard. Six darts, brass ferrule, flighted.*

Slopes, Roylana on his lap, he has cupped a tit, cheroot in the other, leans over and cuts the cheese. This kind of breaks the silence. O'Bably, got a wicked glass of whatever going, shoots that skinny wrist free of the yellow stripe shirt, snaps the fingers 'pelt!' and gives his short cackle, the 'Ha!', more of a 'cack!'.

This time inside Guy the figure is a row of stands, as in around an arena, and the Holes people are up there in the director's suite. They have a table again, this time laid with little cut sandwiches, lots of bottles in clear colour, various hard stuffs glinting in there and those stubby shotglasses in every palm, knockaback style, hup and glup gimme another a those.

It's first-class viewing, everybody's in a line, got their feet up, and it's a decent show, very encouraging, the client is coming along nicely. You have to understand that *production*, that's in the showbiz sense, the production of the show, is after all the basic trade here, and the Holes people always get results, goes without saying. But do they get the results they want? We have to say no. It's like they are the backers, what is that showbusiness word, the angels, but the client doesn't even know it. Unfortunately the client reserves the right to a major interpretation of the production, which frustrates the 'Ish' so much that one time he, not your warmest social type, says to Holes, 'John, couldn't we just *impose* the fucker?' and Holes has to remind him,

160

'Andrew, our pleasure is to make sure the costumes are clean, we don't get to step out, remember?' by which he means to say that they just produce stuff, they don't push an interpretation. So then the 'Ish' does that contemptuous wide-eyed shit and you think one day he *will* step out and then fucking hang onto your valuables the tornado is here.

But right now they are all appraising the show, keeping a tab on the story so far. Slopes has just cut that loud cheese, normally some lockerroom yuks in that, but he is actually shorthanding with his backendhole to say, with gas, that this last piece of action, the hot-cake scenario, in which he personally ate too many spiced cakes, went down very well. The client had resisted to the end, but that special cookery had blistered through a treat. Got close to something there, this horse has teeth yet.

Holes gets up, over to the drinks, holds the bottle to his chest and the drink is gone, it's in him, it just went through the glass and him. He didn't make a show, he's just looking across the seating, not at anything, just absorbed. Everybody is looking out at the arena action but they know what he did. John wasn't the man to strut that sleight stuff for cheap effect – when you live in that stuff you don't have to make a point exactly. Most times John would work on the 'outside' technique, kind of a hobby with him, see how the other half lives. On the 'outside', if you want to get the pie out of the box, okay, as follows: walk to the box, grasp it, inch off the lid with hand-lever methods, place the lid down on some ground, area the hands into the inside, around them to the pie, onto them at the pie, heft on the pie with bicep tricep cetera, area the pie to some ground, off the grasp of the pie, area to the ground where is the lid, place grasps on, heft to above box, down and fit position, the lid pressed with some weight, then you can eat or show to a friend maybe. John says, 'It's amusing. It's harmless,' when the bunch josh at him, especially 'Dead', he says, 'Life's too short, John. I leave that lever shit to the dollies.' Dollies is how 'Dead' sees the client and that general 'outside' ilk.

So when John does that business where the liquor goes through his chest, he is dropping his hobby, and people know right away he is absorbed, got something on his mind, we'll use that expression, got to beg a question, got to move along. He turns.

'This hot-cake action, this A-rab cookery,' he says, 'fine work.' They feel complimented. Everyone likes the good word from the boss. 'It's rolling now. Show's on the road.' They smirk to hear the boss use

161

those corny expressions. 'But way to go yet.' They nod, chorus line effect if you were there. 'The push.' They are all listening hard. They don't turn but they stop following the action details in the arena. 'Time for the sign?' he asks. And the 'Ish' is to his feet in an instant, he stands on the chair, his back to the action and up go the arms high. Lean, the 'Ish'. Forearms way out of the jacket, the 'Ish'. His beautiful face just is shining out. Now he drops the arms and those black shiny sleeves fall to the wrist and then up again and he's doing the *gusher*. This is the 'Ish's' gusher effect. This time round it's cash. He has done worse, far worse. 'Dead', even 'Dead', is still shaking his head over that fabled 'shit storm', but that was the early era, before the client himself knew to unbox a pie even.

So dollars and pounds are gushing from out the 'Ish's' sleeve holes, spraying up around the suite, kind of fast bird wing sound as they zoom and unroll and generally crowd about in the air. Thick cloud of green doesn't settle, there's more where it came from, like liquid almost, and the seated bunch are looking at this for craftsmanship, a show is a show, for them, but they appreciate each other's specialty work, they like to see what's new up the 'Ish's' sleeve.

That snakey 'Ish', got his head back out of the flutter, shoots a small peek to the side, checking the attention. Roylana is stood up, looking over at Holes, but the rest are with Andrew and his behaviour. 'Ish' senses they wish him to vary it up. Woosh and no longer is it green the general vapour of the event, but suddenly all colours are there, red blue and the others, yellow. Michael Butler sees one flutter to his shoe and grasps for it. It has a bright colour picture on it of very nice scenes with clear shapes, say there is some pink furry rabbits leaping over purple toadstools and the sky is green, or by Slopes's leg, he looks down, there is one with looks like a big white teacup and going into it an orange waterfall and it's by a wall with other coloured animals, quite small, on the wall. Here is O'Bably jiggling his note that has dropped onto his belt, it has a red road going through flowers and trees and there at the end is two plates of jelly against the sky, and P.R. appreciates this with 'Hehehehehehheheh', runs his knotty hand through that hair and then, 'Arch, kind of a high street is involved here?' to say where can he spend this currency that is so of-the-minute the banks don't have a rate up. So various of these pleasant depictions are on the notes, and they are continuing to spurt from that 'He'd do murders' 'Ish', who is now leaning right back and

162

laughing in that high pitch as if in a racing car with no roof and he has heard a great gag.

So what is the 'Ish' saying here, with these dumb flourishes? He is moving the argument forward, suggesting if John wants to go for big 'push', that is, a major production, then why not *bribe* the client, why not force *money* on him? As if to say 'Fuck cookies. Let's get serious.'

Holes, burning up that bottleful, chewing at the mouth like he has chaw in there, goes, 'Okay Andrew'. The 'Ish' just stops. The air is empty, the floor, table and cetera are clear. Like 'Dead' remarks of that still talked about 'poo fling', 'Kid's on a hinge but he always clears up. We got to be thankful.' 'Ish' hangs his head to one side gives this small glance to Roylana and does this little fussy rearrangement of the cuffs, gets a haw from 'Dead' but Holes is to give some reaction now.

'Okay. Andrew flies off. This is him. We don't have to go that full stroke. But he gave a sign. He suggests we make a cashflow. This is a can do. I take the note.' And Holes has kept this green pound from the cuff torrent, and he folds it with thoughtful movements and slips it in the front of say his tunic which is maybe grey. 'Dead' sees John's 'outside' technique again here, such a nice piece of work, he appreciates the boss has a strictly dry sense of what is to laugh, he does the heehee and the others they all feel fine now because they know when 'Dead' gives the haw and haw to John then the next big show is all set up, fixed to reveal.

So now everybody eases into some bottled materials and they get back to watching the client. The 'Ish' is in the line but he's got his head slumped down, he's not so enthralled with the everyday stuff. Holes, still over the table, looks at the bunch from the back, sees the not concerned 'Fuck this' 'Ish', and has to give a long hoarse sigh, that boy is all edge and no basement.

Guy had gone from bad to worse and now creatures from space were taking advantage of him. Only a moment ago he had sunk onto the sofa with his head in his hands and now he was in some grey, empty place and the centre of attention. They were not even all from one planet, if their contrasting appearances were anything to go by. One had three eyes and six legs, another was shaped like a giant purple brain and floated two feet above the ground, while a third had green spidery limbs of such tremendous length that its body, a black glistening globe, could

163

scarcely be glimpsed among the fluorescent clouds scudding across the drab, brown sky. A fourth was only an open mouth containing countless rows of discoloured teeth, dampened from time to time by a slow slug-like tongue. Beside it was a creature composed of at least a dozen small, jumping, hairy balls from each of which protruded a pair of perfect, pink, unwrinkled hands. The hands were all linked so that the bouncing bodies formed a circle. It seemed possible that the hands were not actually separable, but designed to give that impression.

The thing nearest to Guy, unbearably near in fact, resembled a simmering lump of phlegm, the size of a large dog. From its slimy, featureless surface red, varicose-veined tentacles would burst out and recede at odd intervals. The thing had wrapped itself around Guy's legs, engulfing him up to the knees. Several tentacles were currently extended, and all of them had snaked up the legs of his shorts. Guy was not in the mood to count them but there was at least one in every orifice of his body, including those of his head. The one that had slid into his bottom seemed to have made contact with the one that had plunged down his throat, but as yet there was no indication that the creature meant to harm him.

The immensely tall creature was in the process of sending him an important message. It took the form of a liquid which streamed from a hole in the underside of the distant, globular body. As the liquid splashed onto his head Guy could hear a low hoarse voice speaking to him. His ears were both blocked by tentacles but the voice was somehow inside him despite that. It seemed he was being given an ultimatum.

The voice said, 'You have been chosen because of your work in the field and because you are respected among your people. We are a consortium of space creatures who find their territory under intolerable pressure. Look at this place . . .' Guy turned his head obediently, in order to survey the desolate plains, but was disconcerted to see that the creature with three eyes and six legs appeared to be giggling. He pretended he had not noticed and turned to face front again.

'. . . Like you, we appreciate variety and the feeling that there is more to our existence than the daily repetition of labour. But here we have nothing. This is an empty place, it has no streets, no houses, no recreational facilities.

'Each of us has knowledge and skills that would advance the condition of your people immeasurably, and we are quite prepared to share all that we know. However, before we can leave this dreadful place we must be sure that your people will welcome us, and give us room in which to live. We cannot afford to drift stateless through the swirling mist of time and stars.'

An unmistakeable snort of suppressed laughter distracted Guy again, and out of the corner of his eye he was sure he could see the six-legged creature shaking and turning away from the group with a hand over its mouth. His suspicions were reinforced when the stream of liquid from above faltered for a second or two, then resumed its informative flow. The voice coughed and sounded rather put out as it continued with the momentous message.

'Therefore we say this to you – contact your leaders and convince them of our good intentions. Tell them of our requirements and explain our need for guarantees. When we are satisfied with your reports we shall reveal ourselves on your territory, for then part of it will be ours.'

Guy felt a sudden wave of unwillingness pass through him. The creature far above his head noticed this immediately. As it spoke again, he was horrified to feel the tentacles in his ears, eyes, nose, mouth, penis and anus start to expand. An unspeakable terror and nausea gripped him. The liquid splashed down relentlessly.

'We do not wish to hurt you, but we are capable of exposing you to a quite remarkable degree of pain should you demonstrate the least sign of resistance. We understand, nevertheless, that you will still require some earnest of our benignity. The notion of the incentive is not alien to us, in fact it is well established throughout the multiverse.'

Ignoring the sniggers from not only the six-legged thing but also the floating brain, the voice went on. 'You will take a token from us. We know that it has value in your world. Be assured that if you accede to our demands, many more such will be at your disposal.'

The stream of liquid was abruptly cut off. Two tentacles emerged from the phlegm and wrapped around Guy's wrists. He found himself being pulled down into the hideous bubbling mass of the creature's body. Just before his head went under, something closed around his right hand and squeezed it into a fist. Then the vileness

became so great that he tried desperately to leave the planet.

His chin came up from his chest and his neck ached. His right hand
felt cramped and knotted. He forced the fingers apart then cried out
in horror. Folded neatly on his palm, covered in a thin glaze of slime,
was a pound note.

'Deany!'

But Deany was not in the house. She had gone into town
to see somebody.

Part Three

Back in Lugambwa he had picked up some of the rudiments of stalking from George. A certain central core of relaxation was a major requirement, and it must result in an even, silent breathing. This serene disposition was overlaid with 'just got one mind', which meant great intensity of purpose. You drained off all other thoughts, so it was just you, the net or spear or gun, and the creature.

He didn't know what to wear here. There were stretches of downland, which were boggy in parts, and also woods and copses. For a while you might step as quietly as possible through sucking leafmould and cracking twigs, pausing and listening, trying to get the hang of the even-breath business, but then, inching round a bush you would find yourself looking down somebody's back garden, along their lawn and into their lounge. He wanted to wear fatigues and heavy boots, so that he could crawl or climb if necessary, but a few days ago, clad in his chosen outfit, he had emerged from a wall of shrub on his hands and knees and found two teenagers lying on sunchairs listening to music through earphones on a crazy-paved terrace adjacent to the open french windows of a well-to-do house. The shock for the young woman, who had removed the top of her swimming costume, was somehow greater because she had not heard him panting and pressing through the dense interior of the big bush, and as he stood up in horror, hesitating fatally while he worked out whether to march forward or dive back in, she opened her eyes and misconstrued his perplexity. Her scream went unheeded by her companion, whose headphone was plugged into the same machine, and whose head bobbed contentedly on the pillow. Her jab to his ribs precipitated the situation in which Guy found himself saying, 'I've lost my dog', and the young man replied, 'You better fuck off while you've got the time, chum' as he rose and ran to the phone in the lounge, closely followed

167

by his friend, whose headphones tore out of the machine one pace after she took off.

Now he wore tennis shoes and brown cords and a new anorak. In his pack he carried crucial items such as a net, gloves and a nylon zipper bag from the local post office. In the wake of what he thought of as a bit of a brainwave he also carried a dog lead. He would hold the lead coiled up in one hand, with the clip dangling down, and whistle as he walked along. If he looked around, even over people's fences, he had a cover. He had developed a fairly good picture of the dog too, it was a red setter, very friendly, would bite his wrist harmlessly, but streak through the undergrowth after things when requested.

The tennis shoes were comfy but came off in mud, while the cords were strong but cut too generously round the upper leg – they rubbed on the inside of his thighs and chapped the skin, especially when he put in seven or eight hours a day at it, which had been the case for some days now.

One of the major omissions in the fieldwork at Lugambwa had been investigation of habitat – he had never actually observed the creatures in the wild, and had no idea of the kind of shelter they preferred. Their fore-paws were certainly capable of burrowing, but it was also not inconceivable that they would climb trees. Not inconceivable in terms of an anatomical analysis, that is, but wholly improbable in the light of the extreme self-absorption which appeared to limit their attention so drastically. The net result of all this unsubstantiated surmise was that Guy peered into holes, looked up trees and rattled bushes wherever he went.

Stalking was premised on the existence of the prey, of course, and also on the assumption that the stalked would run away if it sensed a preyer. If there were no prey around, the stalker need not employ the even breathing. Because of the slippage in Guy's inner grasp, he found that the even breathing, premised on a serene disposition, made him quite tense. This was because a serene disposition rarely informed his breathing, for it was incompatible with the extreme and abiding distress that he had felt since losing the animals. It could almost be said that, before the awful day, he had, after a fashion, enjoyed a great deal of serenity. This quality is commonly held to derive from an inner calm, and to result in an unruffled manner. Given what we know of his inner life, and what we have seen of his rufflability, his serenity had clearly been constructed along quite different lines from those implied by the workaday definitions. Be that as it may, when he arrived in a likely spot, and began the even breathing, it only served to reveal to him just how fuzzy and scrambled his insides were. It was as if the tuning had gone. He wanted so desperately to recapture Eke that everything he did, from scratching his nose to kissing his wife, felt like a last minute aside before he plunged into a massive enterprise whose outcome would define the whole of his future life. Until that point, his life was over, the present moment no longer existed, all was haste and preparation. Unfortunately these last minutes, these final and trivial adjustments, had been going on for days and days. He was trapped in an interminable Next, and when he tried to breathe, it was as if his whole being was panting, and he could not stop before he started.

As he struggled through a swathe of gorse he began to wish, as he had so often since the awful day, that he had more of a plan, or even a plan at all. He simply could not decide whether he should continually rework a limited area or gradually extend the search further afield. He knew nothing about the creatures' mobility. Did they move around? And if so, how much, and why? Things moved in order to satisfy needs – what needs had he ever discerned in Eke and Ike? But they had certainly moved from the back garden – and he had combed the immediate neighbourhood to no avail. From what he had observed, it seemed unlikely that the animals were great travellers, but he had observed so little, his charges had only ever known the coop and pen.

He came across a break in the gorse traversed by a footpath and paused, as he did so often, to consider his next moves. A quadruped broke from the bushes a few feet away. Guy jumped and, before he could stop himself, yelled out with excitement. The fox, which had been loping along on a lazy diagonal-but-forwards tack, turned and looked at Guy in surprise, then dashed away. Guy felt foolish, and decided he had been out long enough. The sun was going down and he was beginning to make mistakes. He unzipped his pack, dropped the lead into it, and headed for home, a walk of some three miles.

As he strode back he thought about the fox, and how casual it had been, taking a good look at him before running off. It might almost have run towards him, taken his wrist in its mouth as a friendly greeting. Or bitten him. Then he would have got rabies again, they were all rabid, all over the country. He wondered if his first bout had had any long-term effect on him, done something to his mind perhaps. Ridiculous. It was over and done with. But he had got it from a unique source. Maybe Eke had a strain that hadn't been detected anywhere else, that wouldn't be surprising. He shuddered, remembering the agonising violence of his throat spasm on the plane, after he had sipped the tonic water. And the sweat. He'd never been so wet, it had rather disgusted him, as though he'd been an incontinent little boy messing up his pyjamas. And this, by some elusive linkage, brought him back to the other terrible thing. The thing which sometimes made even the loss of the animals seem a mild affair. As soon as it found a place in his thoughts he felt a swooning nausea in his stomach, a sigh of dread that involved not his lungs but all the viscera below his chest, all churning and swimming around, tubes of gut slithering over each other, knotting and rearranging in panic. This was a panic quite unlike anything he had felt in his life. Many times, when faced with situations which would undo the most unshakeable of men, he had found himself transformed into a paragon of collectedness. His common sense would surge to the fore, eclipsing all the inclinations that detracted from the cause, so that he simply did what simply had to be done. But this thing, it mocked common sense, it crushed it into a corner and threatened to banish it beyond recall. Just the thought of the thing, the actual presence of it in his mind, created a feeling of pressure that was almost physical. It was as though his brain were swelling within his skull as it strove to accommodate both the force with which the thought intruded and the desperate intensity of his own efforts to expel it.

As he trudged through the gloaming, his feet grew cold in his tennis shoes and he lifted the hood of the anorak around his ears, tightening the drawstring so that as much of his face as possible receded into the warm cave of the quilted fabric.

Deany still didn't believe him. She didn't *want* to believe him, it was obvious. She said there must be an explanation. But he had given her the explanation, and she had said it was crazy. So she wanted another explanation. What could he say? On two or three occasions it had happened while she had been in bed with him, right next to him, and she had said, each time, that he must have left it in the bed the night before, or somehow sleepwalked and then put it in the bed. But she knew that wasn't the case. If he had been sleepwalking she would have woken up. She had tried staying awake while he was asleep but it never seemed to happen then. He knew she thought he was trying to trick her, as though he were trying to get at her for some reason. She was waiting for him to slip up. His own wife, not taking him seriously. And she'd told Jack Gavin.

170

Guy grunted angrily into the hood and thrusted his fists deeper into his pockets. Usually on the way back he'd keep an eye open, not wanting to relax his vigilance until he was right inside the house, but now he glared at the ground in front of him. Catching sight of a white puffball a few feet off the path, he detoured in order to kick it to pieces with a swing of his leg.

Jack Gavin. It was appalling, really. Deany had said it was the kind of thing that interested him! So what? Really, so what? It was probably all very fascinating, looked at from the outside, probably extremely entertaining indeed. But Christ! Why him? What was the attraction there? The man was thoroughly shifty, and he didn't believe in work, that was obvious, and now he'd practically moved in with them!

The funny thing was, and this confused him, Jack Gavin, in his way, was actually more supportive than Deany. He had said he didn't see any reason why those sort of things shouldn't happen. When you looked at it, that was a sloppy way of thinking, it wasn't thinking at all, strictly speaking. But at least he hadn't just rejected the whole business, or told Guy that he was talking absolute nonsense. It had been Jack's idea to try and test it out, to prove to Deany that Guy wasn't bluffing. He had suggested that Guy should spend a night on the sofa-bed in the sitting room, and that he, Jack, would sit up with him, just keeping an eye on him. Jack had searched his pyjamas, in front of Deany, and checked that the sofa-bed had nothing hidden in it. Guy had felt like he was back in hospital, or even back at home, when he had had the mumps and his mother had stood him in front of the fire while changing the sweat-soaked sheets on his bed. Then Deany had gone upstairs and Jack had settled into a chair with just a table lamp and a bottle of brandy. Guy had suggested he might like to look at *With Alan*, partly so that Jack might benefit from the example of Bentley's exceptional force of will, but more so that Jack would have something to do and not just sit there waiting for something to happen.

Guy had known all along that it wouldn't work. It was like giving a urine sample, or having a pee in a public place; whatever you might want to do, the fact that other people expected something made your body resist your mind. Above all he wanted to prove it to Deany, but lying there in his own sitting room, where he had never had any reason to sleep before, listening to Jack turning the pages and drinking their good cognac, he had suddenly felt both absurd and a little resentful. By about one in the morning he had descended into

171

a hopeless, uncomfortable drowse that he knew would never develop into proper sleep. Jack was silhouetted against the light, apparently still reading, but Guy was convinced he was listening out for the rustling of the bedclothes. It just wasn't right, going to sleep in your own downstairs room while another man stayed awake. As the night wore on, Guy's thoughts slowly devolved to one or two dominant strands. There was some sort of task he had to carry out, nothing to do with falling asleep, and there were various rules that could not be broken. The rules were hard to put into words, but they were something to do with certain thoughts that were not possible if another sort of thought came before them, or possibly if the body was in a certain position, or the head, then it would not be possible to roll to the right at all until something was got, but where this thing was was difficult to see, and certainly there was no question of being allowed to stop thinking until the task was completed.

When the birds had started singing at dawn he had had the feeling that Jack was no longer in the room, and because it was not long before he must get up, he had managed to fall asleep. Then he had heard his name being called and had woken up to find Jack holding him quite hard by the wrists. Deany was beside him saying, 'Open your hands, Guy', and when he had done so there had been nothing there.

'Guy! Any luck?' Jack Gavin said as Guy came through the kitchen door.

'I saw a fox,' Guy said.

'Was it red?'

'Yes. They are red.'

'I've never seen one. I heard they were red, but that's what I thought about lobsters. Until I found out.'

'Most of them have rabies.'

'That a fact? No wonder they boil them.' Jack laughed facetiously. 'I'm stirring this soup,' he added.

'Is Deany in?'

'She's in the bedroom, I think.'

Guy walked through to the sitting room, peeling off his anorak. Jack looked down into the soup and sniffed it, as chefs probably did. He didn't mind other people's homes, they were usually very tidy and clean, which he found interesting, and they were generally equipped with all manner of things to make staying in bearable. Herbs, for example, or paintings. And their furniture was always very chosen, which he found

172

fascinating. Curtains and carpets had been paid for, and they matched or complemented each other. The bathrooms were invariably spotless, which he supposed was correct, and their toilet bowls always glistened, which, he conceded, was probably reassuring, or satisfying. He guessed that they looked into their toilet bowls more often than he did himself, probably because they spent more time in their houses. He was even prepared to admit that their chairs were usually more comfortable than his, because of the business of choosing them. He liked his stuff well enough, but most of it just came to him, and if wasn't quite right, then he was only passing through anyway. It had occurred to him that now he had found out about 'the corridor', as he had come to call it, he could get any amount of nice stuff in his flat, whenever he wanted. But the idea of choosing it made him feel uncomfortable, not that he didn't have 'taste', but the idea of 'home' had never really convinced him in the first place. And he didn't want to end up like that dangerous little fucker Ainsley either, stack now and decide later. Suits, yes, cars, yes, food, fine, but interior decoration, what's the point?

The soup looked as though it had been stirred enough. Deany came into the kitchen and kissed him. Her skin felt fresh from the shower. Over the last few days she had got into the habit of showering before Guy came back from his forays, just in case he should smell Jack on her. Jack said not to worry, Guy didn't think like that, but she said Jack had no right to assume that about Guy, he was very sensitive in many ways.

'It's stirred,' he said.

'I can see! Beautifully stirred! You picked it up really fast.'

'Yeah. Stirring's not hard.'

'Guy didn't have any luck.'

'Will he ever?'

'He's got to, Jack! Somebody will see them soon, I bet.'

'Why?'

'Happens all the time – parrots up trees, snakes in stores, leopards in the park, you know.'

Jack started to open a bottle of wine, another thing they always had, which sort of impressed him, how could people not drink all their drink in one go?

'Is he tired, did he say?'

'Don't!' She still didn't like him to talk about it.

'Six pounds so far, Deany. More interesting than some escaped animal, isn't it?'

'Jack, why do you lead him on? It's so obvious what's happening! His whole life just collapsed, or his work anyway, and this other stuff is just some neurotic thing, just he's being weird for a while, until he finds Eke or the cubs.' She poured herself some wine and glared at him while knocking it back.

'Until. Could be a long time. Got a lot of countryside in this country.'

'I don't like you going on about it to him. Trying to make him sleep all the time.'

'It's not all the time!' He picked the jamjar off the shelf and held it out towards her. 'Six pounds! It's incredible, Deany! It could be!'

'But they're notes, Jack! They don't have them any more here.'

'They're still legal tender. Try it.'

'Obviously he has a stash somewhere, left over from notes days.'

'Why? He's got a bank, hasn't he? And if it is a stash, it'll run out, so he'll have to stop. Or not.'

'He hasn't done it, said he's done it, for nearly a week. So maybe that's it.'

'No. It's because I've been watching him – he doesn't really sleep. Feels self-conscious, it's understandable. Like when you piss in the cinema.'

'I'm sorry?'

'Man's thing. Can't do what comes naturally when there's a crowd. You know.'

'I don't pee in the cinema.'

'What about the theatre?'

'Anyway.'

'When he sleeps properly, it happens. He has to get down to a level.'

'Come on! You're crazy!'

'He's neurotic and I'm crazy. The two men in your life!'

Guy came down the stairs from the bathroom and sat in the next room. 'Sit at the table, Guy, I'm bringing it in!' Jack called out cheerily.

Guy had always quite liked a glass of wine with a meal, but had never particularly enjoyed getting drunk. Since the terrible events, however, he had upped his evening intake by a factor of three, but had been surprised to find that it did not make him tipsy at all. He soon realised that his capacity had been extended, so that the alcohol merely softened the edges of his anxiety without creating any wooziness. It was as if his anxiety did the drinking and left the rest of him alone. He finished his

174

first glass of red as he watched Jack Gavin bringing the supper in. It was odd to see this rather flashy man wearing oven gloves and helping his wife out. He knew that he didn't really understand it, but so much else was on his mind that he put it aside – he couldn't be expected to think about everything.

'Gonna go out tomorrow, Guy?'

'Of course I am. What else is there to do?'

'You were out all day today.'

'I'll be out all day until something happens, Deany. I'm getting quite methodical now, covering a lot more ground.'

'But what if they come back to somewhere you've already done?'

Guy sighed. 'I've told you, I rework the old ground on the way back. Every day.'

'But what if . . .'

Jack interrupted. 'Guy. You'll wear yourself out. Have some more wine.'

Guy watched the glass filling up. 'What you don't realise, Jack, is that when you do something regularly, something strenuous, I mean, then you get fitter. Not worn out. It gets easier.'

'So eventually you wouldn't ever have to rest, you'd be so fit, right?'

'That's dumb, Jack,' Deany said irritably.

'Everybody has to rest,' Guy said, then instantly regretted it.

'Well, I have a theory,' Jack announced. Deany looked at him anxiously, and Guy, who also guessed what was coming, reached for his glass. 'About this other business.'

Deany frowned and muttered, 'Oh, Jack.'

'Everybody's looking worried – it's okay. We all want to know whether it's true, right?' Deany made a point, with the set of her mouth, of saying nothing.

Guy said, 'I already know.'

'Sure. It's to do with the quality of sleep, isn't it? Doesn't work if everybody wants it to. Like having a piss in a cinema.'

'I wouldn't have put it like that, actually.'

'No. So . . .' He paused. He had just had an idea. 'So you should just sleep whenever you want, wherever. In bed, in a field. Nobody watching, just get back to the natural way.' His idea had slowed him down, and in consequence his theory had sounded rather lame. He tried to put some more beef into it. 'Yes. You should really *want* to sleep.'

175

Both of his hosts sighed, but Guy replied patiently, softened by the wine, 'Jack, I'm afraid that doesn't help in the least. I have no control over the thing, one way or the other.'

Jack ploughed on, and as he did so, slid his left leg across towards Deany, who was seated beside him. He slipped his foot behind her ankle so that it rested on his. He felt her stiffen. 'Try for a fiver, Guy.'

'What do you mean?'

'What I said. Next time you sleep, see if you can come up with a fiver.' He began rocking his leg to and fro, so that Deany's thigh was compelled to roll with it, across the top of her chair. She reached nervously for her glass, which was on his side, her arm warning him off.

Guy shook his head. 'That's ridiculous.'

'Why? It could be the answer. If it works it'll be because you wanted it to. That's the problem, isn't it? That you don't want the money.'

He dropped his hand below the table, and placed it on Deany's knee. She twitched her leg agitatedly.

Guy started to feel weary. 'The money has nothing to do with it. I don't want *anything*, I don't want . . .'

'That's what I'm talking about, Guy! You don't listen!' Jack realised that he could do it on two levels, push from the front and back simultaneously, as it were. He slid his hand under Deany's skirt, so that it rested on her bare thigh. She dropped her right hand down and dug her nails into his skin. 'You think it's wrong, and you don't want to do anything that's wrong.'

Guy poured himself another glass, shaking his head continually. 'Really, Jack, I think you miss the whole point. I thought you understood my feelings about it all.'

Jack ignored the talons on his flesh and moved his hand further along, so far along Deany's thigh that his shoulder began to twist, turning in to the table, and bringing his chest with it, so that he was leaning over his soup plate. He kept his gaze on Guy, and continued to talk to him despite the complicated writhings of protest from behind that were threatening to tip him onto his chest.

'The point is you're upset because you think you didn't earn it. That's just a detail! What you need . . .' He slowed his speech down and gradually reduced its volume until nothing could be heard. Guy was looking in Jack's direction, but his eyes were unfocused. His lids drooped slightly, and Jack could hear him breathing evenly through his nose. Jack sat back and turned to Deany. He moved his hand between her legs as high as it would go, and moved forward to kiss her. She started to stand up, pushing her chair back, aghast, shaking her head.

'Jack . . .'

'Let me fuck you.'

He slipped his fingers beneath her pants, at the groin. Deany pushed hard against his shoulder. She looked across at her husband. Guy was looking in her direction, but his eyes were not focused. His chin moved up and down as he breathed deeply from his chest. Deany stopped pushing against Jack and stared at Guy. She blinked incredulously.

'Guy?' Jack was kissing her neck, half out of his chair now.

Guy's eyes slowly closed. His face seemed quite calm. Seconds later his arms fell away from the table into his lap, and his chin dropped onto his chest.

Deany whispered 'He's asleep!' Jack was undoing the small buttons at the back of her dress. He did not look round.

'Yes. I know.'

'Is he drunk?'

'No. It's not that.'

He pulled her gently off the chair onto the floor. She was so engrossed in her husband's slumber that she let Jack fold her back onto the carpet, giving him her weight, not bothering to support herself. As Jack eased her dress up over her hips she looked at him for the first time, and started to speak. He stopped her by kissing her mouth, and then said, 'We don't have to watch him.'

Guy slipped down and the crowd goes wild. Holes is on a podium on the trade floor, a little raised affair of wood, and he is chalking up from the crowd down below. They are racing around today –· considerable consternation you'd have to call it, as if tin is about to go worthless, this is the trade idea example, and they all wish to unload I believe is the expression. So everybody is saying 'Tin I got to here – get me out!' or 'Unleash me this quantity I'm talking pronto' or 'Degusset the wallet it's slim for metals and me!', these are more examples.

They do not wish to unload the client, this is not it, they are with him all the way, they have no other job, he goes they go, without him what do they do? There is no choice in the matter, they must stay on the job. The problem right now is that the client is in with a bad set. An unprecedented disruption of the power lines has just occurred.

To recapitulate, for the sake of the picture, you remember Holes said how way way back, first time around, the gang 'missed their chances', and how 'we were ignored' but they did make 'forays', well he was referring to the early years with the client, his babyhood and youth. But these fledgling outings didn't result in the big Day Pass, the All-In Ticket where they enjoy continuous access to the front-of-house area. (If they *had*, then everybody would be out tanning on the beach, with magazines, tan oil, air beds, flasks with a little something stiffish in, no Holes barred (one of Slopes's, that crack). They would have had early retirement for sure, but no more exploits, no more anecdotes to unreel.)

They didn't get the Voucher – does anybody? All in all, given some of the stuff that's been coming through over the years, they feel it's a miraculous achievement they ever got the client off the tit. Having got him through the slush and stormways of average outgrowing, through the mummy daddy shit to where he walks, he talks, so forth, then steering him through the dark and dashwaters of wife, job, house, car, cash, all that shit, they get this depressing result! He will not look them in the eye now! (That is one of Dead's, the cry where he goes, in almost despair, 'We're over here!' and waves his hand in a comic kind of cooee! and they must of heard that once it's a million times but still gets the titter.) He just totally turns the back, no gratitude, not even a 'Thanks you cowboy fools, without you I was to the toilet as a prospect.' It's as if he feels phew that struggling stuff is over, now let's career.

And now his whole project threatens to go to vapour! Some major act of larceny has fucked the pitch to the point where he is so crazed up to straighten it out he won't practically stop to eat! Makes the jurassic, the formative years, look kind of straightforward, least back then they didn't have to contend with some fucking outside agent who finds this now you see it now you don't trick where he can piss straight down the client's mouth and the client doesn't even blink! They never imagined this! Not only is this figure seriously fucking with the mechanics but in addition he heists the sleeved ace, the special extreme pressure cash-in-hand effect they brought in to force the client across!

'Shit,' says Michael Butler, and he is the one with the poise and charm! He is the one *never* to dung out the air with loose usage or muddy quotes! So if he says this word, then this shows how major is the flurry and dismay on the trading floor, going back to that early helpful example.

178

Holes is looking down at the crowd now. Slopes, the youngish racetrack type, is with O'Bably, the thin-hair codger, and they are chewing the thing over.

O'Bably wants to say how he sees the big calamity. 'Slopes, no, I got to say, it's like . . .' But P.R. doesn't care to truck with his mouth too long, he likes to make the direct model, so he conjures a gun in his hand. You wouldn't say, 'This here's a Luger Ruger with ventilated rib mag .38 motherfucker punch like a cannon' because it's more the *idea* of gun: you look closely it's not one gun, it's not all guns but pull on the trigger and bang out comes the bullet, lead snub streaking through.

O'Bably squeezes one off. Nobody bothers to look but Slopes, they know O'Bably is just making a point, but now the old guy is running, more of a gallop, right alongside the bullet, got a fleet foot for an ageing geezer, trousers flapping, he's showing those great teeth in a keen flash, his finger and thumb are stretched out in order to nip, he throws a look back to Slopes, so Slopes grins, yeah the old guy can dish the jests even when there's a squall on, and then snip P.R. has pinched down and has the bullet held by the nose, the shotster and the shootee in parallel, and then skid he heels the floor, dust up, he points the shootee back down to where it banged out, and you follow it along and you're back at the shooter and crunch there's this local explosion, and the shooter, which is in the air where P.R. left it, bursts up into peeled-off chunks, ripped up by its own progeny.

Slopes nods, goes, 'I see that,' slides his hand down his necktie, a beauty with jewels, birdwings pictured on, 'I see that, we been cracked by the whip, yeah. But so we profligate, we ample up. Is there a dearth on the eye jimmery? I should fastedly declare nobob,' he declares. Then asks, 'How long, old boy, we been saddled?' O'Bably casts his eyes up, flutters his hands, as if, 'Oh, long, long, don't we know it!' Slopes primps that breast jazzy hanky up, sherbet against the checks, and says, 'So did the bugle of revealy go dim? Did the hands deal the deck already? I go with the times-table school! Let's swamp!'

Where O'Bably merely pictured the predicament, Slopes has insisted that they should not let it faze them, they should in fact redouble their efforts. His big pep speech caught the floor, the crowd could not ignore it. Dusky, Roylana swings round to her loved man of no expanses spared, croons, 'O poola poola poola, Dashy (her pet name)!' She leans to Michael Butler, tongues him, 'Blare, Michael! So blare!' by which she means they should trumpet unabashed. Now Butler is not just a

179

cool piece, he can feel that babble in the tongue, and he will spread the tiding. As Mister Seat'n'Greet he appreciates how there is abashment in the crowd of late, so he will gladly pass any morale booster along. To Dead goes Michael's tongue and this shaggy barroom type wheezes, 'Lana Mikey pop! We're goin fer swamp, sez yer old man!' He unflaps that liquorous tongue and peers for the 'Ish'.

'Ish' is pacing round the edge. Hands down in pockets, jaw biting at nothing, sometimes runs some fingers across his hair. He won't have that tongue, he won't have the crowd's surge. In his eyes you can see 'Fuck blare! Fuck hopes!' 'Ish' has a pale face today, he glances to the crowd and this thing plays across his features, 'These partytime maybugs!' He even shoots a squint at Holes, and Holes is looking right back at him, so 'Ish' flicks it away, but he knows that Holes saw this little checkout, and that it means the 'Ish' is moving away from the crowd, moving away.

But the general beefup from Slopes has morale climbing. Less smallgroup muttering on the floor, now they've clustered. To celebrate the renewed vigour, P.R. is floating off at about chest height, about to do 'colour'.

'Colour' is a P.R. specialty. First let his blood rush off to the feet, which produces a general blanch of the face, hands etc. This is the preliminary condition for where he next: grips his lips together, bulges out the eyes, makes this grunt noise and starts to squeeze. 'Dead' Dick Cater loves this, he divines that O'Bably is going to fudge his trousers, and he begins to cackle as the flush spreads up the scrag of P.R.'s ancient neck.

Couple of moments on and the fogey is red all over, getting redder fast, veins worm out on his brow, eyes egg onto his cheek. His head is filling up like a bag, and now the face is positively dark, so red that it's going to purple, which is only some shades from inkout. Dead is slapping away at his thighs, and the rest are grinning but waiting for the actual 'colour' to start, the previous stuff being warmups. O'Bably can feel they are waiting around for the punch so he slips in a novelty item to ruffle the prelude, he doesn't like to be just a zoo thing. What it is, he gives some more grunt, scrunches down on the jaws then suddenly furls back on the lips, there is this snapping and cracking, powder comes out of his foodhole and a whole debris of bust teeth, they just spring out, cracked off at the stump from this intense gritting, hail down to the floor, (you remember he is floating in air) and he goes 'oh' in a small way, as if 'what a surprise' or 'oopsy'. This is an obvious pleaser. But the old pisser doesn't ease off, he pumps up his head, hands etc, and you think, 'Shit, get behind a chair he is going to rupture' and his eyes are balled so much out they touch across the nose, and the veins practically like nature put them on the outside in the first place they bulge so. He gets to the point of near inkout, goes 'Blaah!', letting off the steam, and finally starts the roll. General cheering from the gang, he has begun.

O'Bably rolls slowly around in the longitude of his lie, as if a rod is passing through the bunghole exiting the headtop. As he rolls, picking up some spin, he goes to green, his traffic gag. Now all his skin that is to see is green, the red has gone. He does an 'Urrrr' through the lips. Cranking up to faster, he makes the green stream to yellow, a bright one.

Now the whole of him is yellow, and he's going 'Ehhhh'. Getting up quite a turbo, and a definite blur on the features, he gives out a sharp bark and suddenly there is a blue, close to Roylana's gown shade. Dead reaches out for the oldster's belt and peels it off of his pants as they whistle by, then with a quick yank the pants to the ankles, the knotty legs all bared in blue from socks to kecks. P.R. isn't fazed, just speeds up to a fierce rate, opens his gob, you hear the wind flute across it, and snaps into an orange. The phenomenon here is that the old colour stays in the eye, the new comes in and there is a smear effect. P.R. works the colour so that there is good jar, and the jar builds to a throb as every couple of moments he throws a new hue. This is a very pleasant effect, all the established hues are thrown, and with the extra from the legs, the assembled bunch are getting a bright show.

Michael Butler gives a remark: 'He always can be relied on', meaning well, but something about that gets to the spinning 'colourist' – the idea that okay it's a grand display but really he is scenery. Michael put that remark in the area of a little compliment but P.R. takes it as 'Oil up, old guy! We are used to seeing your colour specialty'. So what he does is bring in 'the colour from outer space'. (That is actually again a Michael Butlerism, he often finds good tags, that grows out of his frontman work, always the man to make the introductions. The crowd like the tag, especially since they have all recently done that whole slime and other planets job, but basically it refers to the fact that they do have this whole range of effects that rarely leaves the shelf, the 'No call for it' selection as Holes calls it.)

181

The 'no call for it' material is like this: to get the client nicely motivated, they have to dish him stuff from the menu that he has read. If they serve à la carte when this wasn't on the menu he won't make headnertail of it. Given that Guy is a resistant type, this means there's a lot of unused carte out on the racks in the warehouse on account of there's no call for it. Next thing you know, the Holes crowd forget it is there, they rust over when they could be browsing for refreshments in that actual facility. O'Bably remembers a few of those unused items and decides to bring them through. The stuff is wasted on the client but could be it will jerk the audience on the floor, could be show Michael Butler he should stop relying.

So now P.R. has got a tremendous lick on, the features blurred out, he is just a tube, he introduces a 'no call for it' hue from the rack. The effect! 'Yay!' from Slopes and Roylana Brownish. Pleased nod from Michael. P.R. keeps that hue and runs some tone and dark/bright variations.

The problem here is fundamental – say you have had basic menu every night and you decide let's go à la carte but hey, it is in Swedish. But, after a piece of luck, hey, someone has a Swedish dictionary and you reference a carte item and you learn it is 'Toast with particular covering' or 'Meat pieces in category of sauce', well fine, an opendeck situation surely. Nothing out of the mill there. *Swedish* goes to *toast*. Now, this is the thing, say there is à la carte and it is in Zlp. Zlp? Did they do a dictionary in that? No. But say they *did* and this seasoned fellow whips it out his bag and you reference *strelnt* and it gives *trehms*. Huh? You want a dish? Of trehms? Could be it is not even a foodstuff, maybe a hand tool or sports expression – what do you know? So there it is – Zlp à la carte and you're stiffed. Well, leastways you know it is Zlp, could of been *. *? Exactly. P.R. is doing a hue that is in *. *They* know what it is, we don't. They say, 'Saw an exceptional flower, it was in red with · · · (*) streaks.' Huh? Exactly.

So that is the size of it.

P.R. blends through from this specialist hue with another. The crowd go 'Attaboy!' and 'Gully gully, Peeb!' (It's not that these trick hues are beautiful, I mean, is red beautiful? Is blue? They just appreciate to see these rare items out in use, not dusting over in the locker – you got it, flaunt it.) P.R. is so fast now he's just a line in the air, just an area of hue about four feet up and five seven along maybe.

182

John Holes is still above all this, on the podium. He sees they are so down they will grasp at any stuff that comes by, providing it comes with pep. O'Bably's colour was a sideshow, it didn't solve any problems. He sighs low and hoarse, he knows it is to him to point the way forward. Trouble was he thought he had already done that with the slime and cash offer from outer space. Okay, maybe there'd been some cornball in the picture aspect, had got them snickering, but what did they know about Pushthrough? What did anybody know? He sighs again. Six times now they had achieved Pushthrough, and still the client won't negotiate.

Holes looks to the 'Ish'. He sees something bad coming there. Sees it before the 'Ish' knows it himself. Got to make a move before this group falls apart. On a hunch he looks to P.R. again, still bringing in backrack material. He straightens up and stares hard at those * hues. Now . . .

John starts to hum, deep down wheeze. 'Y-e-s . . .' P.R. is piping in fresh 'no call for it' material every few moments. It's nice material, pity it's wasted, inasmuch as no one on the 'outside' can ever see it. If it's not in the old vibgyor stretch they can't use it. They can't use it, they can't abuse it. Yes . . .

Holes suddenly takes the chalk and writes up on the board: HEY. The screech cuts into the gang. P.R. blurs on for a moment then feels the new temperature. He winds down, 'colour' goes, he draws up his trousers, drops his feet down, looks to John, with the rest.

Holes has their attention. He chalks: WE MOVE OUT. They stir. No cheering – they don't know yet where he's from. He chalks: ANDREW! The 'Ish' gives a low smile, joins the rest, at the back. Holes chalks: AS FOLLOWS. Then there is long screech, he does a whole board full. The gang nod and do little tidy up movements with their clothing, like they want to be ready when the call comes. Holes gets right down to the board rim, looks over his shoulder and raises one brow. The wild hair just moves up the face and down, across the skin, no muscle. He dots the chalk onto the slate: '.' Michael nods and says 'Thank you, John', rubs his hands together, says, 'All right, ladies and gentlemen – nothing between us and it!'

The John Holes gang have been briefed. They leave the floor and move to the racks.

In order to appreciate the preparatory operations fully, it may be useful to witness them through the eyes of Michael Butler, who in other contexts might be designated a Production Manager, answerable to John Holes. Holes, in this terminology, would have a Directorial

183

role, inasmuch as basic structural and narrative parameters are of his devising. He tends to indicate areas of activity without prescribing the activities themselves. His team will then express itself within those areas, producing material that is susceptible to reception by the client.

Morale has not been at its highest lately, owing to the extreme manipulation of the client by an outside agent. The group is aware, moreover, that John Holes has been under pressure and in consequence its members are more than usually preoccupied with the results of their next enterprise.

Butler has great sympathy for his colleagues – feeling as acutely as they the impossible tension between their tireless application and the arbitrary manner in which the fruits of their endeavours are made sensible by Guy. While enjoying unreservedly his own contribution to the productions, he accepts a relative degree of restriction in the actual parts that he takes on, having found that his most crucial work will invariably take place beforehand, in the racks. (Inevitably the spatial arrangement suggested by this term is misleading, but a spatial terminology will, if consistently deployed, organise the overall field more than adequately.) Michael has become adept at delivering the offhand, diplomatic suggestion that serves to spur the members on as they circle diffidently round the racks.

As he walks quietly through, Michael smiles at 'Dead' Dick Cater, nods pleasantly to Slopes Brownish, winks cheerily to Roylana Brownish, and so forth. He makes a little 'hmm' of agreement at P.R. O'Bably's choice of outfit, relieves Cater of his indecision in relation to a choice between certain pieces of equipment, and suggests that Slopes might try *this*, over here, rather than *that*, which he has been scrutinising doubtfully for rather too long.

He is just about to stroll back whence he had come when he notices the Aston 'Ish' some distance away, in the direction of the back racks. The 'Ish', in Michael's view, embodies the worst of the wayward tendency in the team. He gives the impression of being largely indifferent to Holes's briefs, yet has a rather infuriating capacity for the unexpected yet brilliantly apposite flourish. Michael knew that Holes felt uneasy about the 'Ish' at times, but supposed that he tolerated the 'Ish's' truculence because the 'Ish' had a tonic effect on the team. At the margins of an essentially unpredictable group, his singular brand of unpredictability kept the members on their toes.

184

Michael makes his way to the back racks without checking his step. He does not want the 'Ish' to feel he is the object of a special visit. 'Andrew,' he murmurs, nodding amiably again, with slightly less of a smile than he has delivered to the others. He knows that the 'Ish' appreciates the cooler side of his character. The 'Ish' flicks Michael a glance, barely acknowledging him, but acknowledging him. He is working at something on a bench top.

'Ah,' says Michael, looking down at the 'Ish's' work. On the bench the 'Ish' is putting together one of the major items in Holes's brief. Michael is surprised that he has taken over this particular aspect of the preparations, because although 'properties' are one of 'Ish's' specialities, his attitude of late has suggested that he is only prepared to endorse the leadership in the most desultory way.

The 'Ish' nods to himself, and Michael can hear a faint rush of air through his nose, the ghost of a snigger.

'Looking good,' says Michael.

'It's nothing,' the 'Ish' says, and then he sniggers quite audibly. Again Michael is taken aback, not by the disdain, which is par for the course, but by the fact of his speech, for the 'Ish' rarely speaks, so adept is he at expressing himself by demonstration.

'No, it's a nice piece,' Michael replies.

'Giving it *value*,' the 'Ish' speaks again and then jolts forward into a sharp, high-pitched laugh, his whole trunk trembling, his eyebrows jumping and arching wildly, his eyes opening wide and wide and wide with each lift from the fine brows.

Michael has seen the 'Ish's' unsettling laugh a thousand times, but this time he finds himself unsettled. Usually the laugh denotes an imminent mischief in the line of duty, but now it resounds with a menace that feels distinctly at odds with the interests of the corporation. Michael does not betray his uneasiness, however. 'Well, that's the picture, Andrew! Ready when you are!'

There is no jostling at the off, as it were. Now that the team members have completed their preparations, it is simply a matter of who wishes to step into the reception area. Michael Butler surveys the turnout, satisfying himself that every aspect of John Holes's outline is adequately represented. Roylana looks extremely handsome in a dark blue twill uniform that comprises an epauletted tunic and knee-length skirt. Her glistening hair, now blonde, is drawn tightly up beneath a peaked cap, on the front of which is a black badge that changes its aspect continually

185

but unobtrusively as Michael studies it. Known as a 'detail', this example assumes a wide range of configurations drawn from heraldic imagery. 'Details' are invariably small in proportion to their ground, but designed to be especially memorable, offering, as they do, the possibility of 'final signature' from the client himself.

P. R. O'Bably is sharing the animal roles with 'Dead' Dick Cater. At the moment he is still standing on his hind legs, which enables Michael to sex him at a glance. O'Bably has chosen to be a male dog, modelled along what we would call St Bernard cum retriever lines. The result is not so much a mongrel but a meeting point of two distinct possibilities. The creature's creator is amusing some of his colleagues by attempting to drain a small wooden barrel of its contents by grasping it between his front paws and lifting it to his muzzle. The spigot requires a half-turn before it will release the fiery liquid within, and O'Bably is trying to knock it round with his wet, black nose. By far the greatest volume of laughter comes from Cater, whose sympathies are clearly amplified by his own situation in a sort of badger outfit. (This term should not evoke the essentially laughable attire associated with a hire shop or carnival. Cater has taken on animal characteristics that render him unfamiliar as to species but entirely effective as an essence of beastlike qualities.) He has equipped himself with short silver and black hairs and a build similar to what we would call a coypu.

O'Bably finally admits defeat by the spigot and momentarily takes on his own hands again, just in order to twist the wooden tap those exasperating few degrees to his advantage. Cater, who is reclining on his back against one of the reception room walls, howls with derision and waves at the dogman the cigar that he is so adroitly clasping between the curved claws of his right forepaw.

Slopes Brownish snatches the cask from O'Bably and takes a drink. Like his wife, he wears a uniform, but it is fashioned in a black cloth, featuring a jacket rather than a tunic, with a belt in the back and button down pockets. His 'detail' is his shoes, which are, in terms of the conventions of a uniform, rather unusual. They are styled in a crocodile or alligator skin and have a pointed and elongated toe. The 'detail' would certainly not stand out in one of Slopes's off-duty outfits, and its current obtrusiveness is of no concern to Michael, who is confident that its relevance will become apparent once the work is under way.

To one side of the merrymakers stands the Aston 'Ish'. Considerably shortened, he wears skintight yellow trousers which disappear into red boots made of soft leather. The toes of the boots are long and curled over. A loose green jerkin covers the trunk of his stunted body and is secured at the waist with a cord belt from which hangs a number of leather pouches. On his head is a red cloth cap with an extended point which falls down the back of his neck and has a bobble at its tip. The 'Ish' has folded his stubby arms across his chest and drums his thick fingers impatiently.

Stepping through the far door of the reception room, Michael checks out the settings that John Holes has provided. Holes believes that men are critically affected by their environments, and consequently has always reserved to himself the task of constructing and dressing the locations. Some productions feature only one setting, others entail such a proliferation that only Holes is capable of counting them, so quickly do both the team and the client lose track of them.

Holes's skill lies in his understanding of the degree of finish required to make each setting legible. Again, 'detail' is deployed shrewdly – a curious tension is created between the broad, impressionistic gesture and the high-focus local rendition which he chooses to exert in a relatively small number of selected areas. If the 'detail' is sufficiently stimulating, the client himself will extend the dressing of the setting to a comparable standard.

Arrayed before Michael's gaze are four or five situations: a countryside (gestures of blue sky and green strips), a large amount of soil, variations on a cylindrical form (rendered in brick, meat, steel), a cavernous space, a compartment fitted with seats and windows (containing many 'detail' areas). The question of 'quality control', in this instance, is not Michael's concern, he knows that the client's feedback overrides any opinions he may have about the execution of the settings. Degrees of 'finish' reflect Holes's estimation of what is required to make an enduring impression on the client, they are not expressions of his own taste. In the current situation of crisis, Holes has stepped up the volume of 'detail' in the settings and has made it clear that he expects the same of all the team members. This is very much to Michael's liking, but does not represent the approach favoured by every member of the team.

The recent and unique 'Pushthrough' exploits have taken a considerable toll on the team and its resources. For Michael, 'Pushthrough' constitutes a betrayal of the most fundamental principles of his work. Despite the extreme challenges it presents to the team, he finds it humiliatingly crass and desperately heavy handed. Most of the others, however, are excited by the intimations of power and access that it brings in train. Michael is a company man, diplomatic to the end, and suppresses his considerable misgivings in the interests of fluid operations. He sighs as he turns away from the array of settings, for there is now little left between him and yet another abuse of the team's artistry.

All that remains is for him to determine the client's availability. Given that the client has just this moment undergone a spectacular capitulation to an outsider, quite unrelated to his usual modes of bestowing himself, Michael only has to ascertain whether a suitable window is currently at the team's disposal. Finding that this is indeed the case he returns to the reception room, whence he will escort the first figure to catch his eye.

The client is sitting in a railway carriage, looking out at the countryside. He is enjoying the naturalness of it, the grass, the trees, the cows, a flock of seagulls that has sought shelter inland from the bad weather at sea.

The ticket collector walks down the aisle towards him. He realises she is his wife, Deany. He says, 'Are you the ticket collector?' She replies, 'No. I'm the guard.' She takes his ticket and punches it with her ticket punch. When she gives it back he sees that it is covered in small holes. Like woodworm.

The train leaves the countryside now. Now it is in darkness. In a tunnel. The client can see nothing, he cannot see anything. The ticket collector, his wife, the guard, is still standing there. Beside where he is sitting.

He says 'What about the driver?'

She says 'Yes?'

He says 'What about him?'

She says 'He has been canoodling with me.'

He looks at the guard, the collector, her cap has the queen on its badge. Despite it is still dark.

He turns to look along the carriage. There is the back of the driver, far down through some carriages. Beyond the driver he can see the dark coming forward. Against the dark the driver's hands and feet are on the controls. His hands are still but his feet move on the pedals.

The driver turns to look back. His face is difficult to make out. His hands are by his sides.

How can the driver drive without his hands?

The train is under the control of his feet. He can see the driver's feet clearly.

She says 'Yes. He is in oar with me.'

Outside the window, where he now looks, liquid not rain runs across all the windows.

He touches the head of Sandy.

He says 'Sandy will find him,' as he looks up at her.

She says 'He is at the front.'

He says 'You don't want Sandy to find him.'

Now down his cheeks it runs.

Now it is thick on the glass and pressing in.

Over the loudspeaker comes 'We must stop now.'

The doors pull apart and there is earth.

She says 'Everyone will walk from here. We are at the end of the line.'

Sandy and him step out. Into the earth.

Behind him she calls 'You want your punch meant.'

It is mud but Sandy can burrow. So Sandy leads him.

He must go horizontal to go through the earth. It is easier and the natural thing to do.

At first the mud is hard to press through. It presses on his eyes and his mouth.

At first he was pleased to be so clever to get out of the train but now he hates the darkness and the weight.

He looks at Sandy in front of him and sees mud come out of Sandy's endhole.

He opens his mouth and the mud goes down inside him. Along his throat down his stomach. He opens his mouth wider and wider until he is yawning the mud in.

He is full of mud and stones. The mud is very very cold. He opens his eyes. He is going along faster now.

The stones press against the inside of his endhole. He does not want to squit them out because his wife, the collector, is behind him.

She says 'It won't pain.' Somewhere up behind him.

He lets the stones out through his hole and the stones pull at it but they get through and then the mud. The mud now tunnels out of his passage. He is moving faster now.

Now he draws the mud in at the mouth and streams along the tube of it.

Him and Sandy are travelling together.

189

He loves Sandy. The mud from Sandy passages into him and out. And he cries onto his cheeks.

But he is trapped, he thinks. He does not know up or down or where.

Now he has telepathy with Sandy. And asks him what he knows. Sandy thinks, 'I'm no good here.'

Now for hours they are burrowing through the deep earth. He wants to see his wife, Deany, but it is just wet.

It is so tiring. He is moving along but he cannot see anything. Sandy is getting tired.

Sandy is getting very faint. He is going to die soon. If he cannot get somewhere to rest.

Now he starts to cry for Sandy. And the mud washes from his eyes along his body.

He has only ever loved Sandy. And Sandy has always been a faithful friend.

A great ache comes from his heart and he is more sad than he has ever been. Sandy thinks to him, 'I'm going to die.'

Now Sandy and him are going to die together under the earth.

He reaches out through the soil to Sandy and can just touch his back leg. As they eat through the earth he strokes Sandy's leg to give him strength. And Sandy thinks warmth towards him.

Now his whole body aches with sadness and it flows out of him.

He cannot move his head up, down or to the side. He can only look into the dark.

Something comes from Sandy. Sandy thinks, 'Something is coming.'

Now he gets new thoughts from Sandy. Sandy can hear something coming towards him. He can see the mud moving.

Sandy sees the animal coming. The animal thinks to Sandy, 'What are you?' and Sandy thinks the same back to him.

And Sandy thinks to the animal, 'We are lost and dying.'

The animal thinks, 'I like it here. Don't you?'

Sandy thinks, 'It is dark and cold and heavy.'

The animal thinks, 'That is good. Don't you feel that?'

Sandy thinks, 'I am a dog and he is a man. We are scared.'

At last out of the mud comes the animal. Sandy and him see it. He thinks to it, 'Help us.'

The animal has a barrel hanging from its neck. It gives this to Sandy. And Sandy puts the barrel to his mouth and drinks from it. Then Sandy passes the barrel to him and he drinks.

In his body the liquid starts to burn. It burns through every part of him. Not just his throat but down his stomach and out along all his nerves until he is being pricked and stabbed from the inside all over.

And Sandy too. He feels the dreadful burning.

In the dark wet earth they both scream and try to roll around. Their spines go white and their brains. Their mouths yawn open and they scream and roar into the cold blackness.

The animal thinks, 'Now you don't mind the dark.'

He is jerking in the earth now, beating his arms and legs around out of control. The white flows from his spine and eats out his nerves and eyes. His stomach crushes onto the mud in it, over and over again. His ears and eyes open and let in the cold mud but it flows into the fire in him and starts to boil.

He thinks desperately to the animal, 'Lead us to another place.'

'Take my legs,' the animal thinks to Sandy and him.

Sandy takes the back legs of the animal and he takes Sandy's back legs and the animal swims powerfully through the mud. The mud now washes past them as they speed through it. And it passes through them as they keep their mouths yawned open and their endholes.

Still Sandy and him feel the incredible burning. He does not know how he can stay alive if this feeling goes on. He tries to let it flow over him so that it is all there is, and this might stop it. But already it is all there is, and it has already flowed all over him and he cannot bear it.

Each second he tries to stop it, and his whole being goes into it, and he does nothing else but try to get away from it, but it simply is everywhere. And in Sandy.

He feels that Sandy is suffering because of him. Sandy who is so faithful and a good hunter.

All he knows is that they are travelling along the earth now behind the animal, and it is going on for a long, long time.

The animal is friendly but he knows it does not understand them. It does not sympathise with what they are feeling.

The animal is thinking something to them. 'We are nearly there.'

Soon they will be out of the earth and able to breathe again. He will be able to move his head around and try to stop the awful fire inside him.

Sandy thinks, 'The mud is getting thinner.'

Light comes through the mud, making it light grey.

Around his body the weight is much less. The passing soil is more like liquid. Soon they will be somewhere else.

191

They come out of the mud and are in a cave, very deep down. At least they can move. But now that they can move they jerk around because of the feeling inside them. Sandy and him jerk around in the cave near the animal as it watches them.

He thinks to the animal, 'Please help us stop this terrible feeling.' And Sandy thinks the same.

The animal thinks, 'I have brought you here out of the mud. That is all I can do for you.'

He thinks to the animal, 'Well who can help us now?'

But the animal goes away.

He thinks desperately to Sandy, 'Sandy, can you tell where he has gone?'

Sandy thinks, 'No. I cannot smell under the ground.'

He wants the animal now more than anything in the world. Only it can help.

A little man comes up. And says, 'Welcome to here.'

He says to him, 'Sandy and me are in agony.'

The little man says, 'I may be of help.'

He says, 'What can you do, please?'

The little man speaks to them and takes them round. 'You must do something for me as well.'

'Tell us what.'

In the cave roof and walls are many glinting jewels. The little man points to them and says, 'They are very beautiful, don't you think?'

'It is what I have always wanted,' he says. 'But now I cannot appreciate them.'

'Well, they will help you, if you just hold them.'

'Please give us one each.'

The little man jumps up on a rock and talks to Sandy and him, 'Look, the problem here is that the people who run the trains want to come through here and lay lines down. There will be stations and platforms and everything and this natural place will be destroyed in the name of progress. The driver of those trains is coming along soon to start the work.'

In his black uniform the driver comes into the cave and his shoes are of hair which is like the animal.

Sandy and him say, 'What can we do?'

The little man says, 'It's urgent now. I will give you a jewel to take up with you but you must go to the politicians and tell them that us people down here are in danger and need somewhere to live. Tell them they can have all the jewellery.'

He says to the little man, 'What if they don't listen?'

The little man says, 'Well then your jewel won't work and you and your dog will be hurting for ever.'

The driver comes closer and says to them all, 'I will track through all this.'

He feels urgent now. The hurt is enormous and the driver looks very strong.

The little man says, 'Don't hang about. Are you in or out?'

'Give me a jewel then,' he says.

The little man reaches for a shining jewel from the wall. 'You better not mess this up,' the little man says to Sandy and him.

'So how do we get up back?' he enquires. And the driver begins to measure things.

'Just hold on to it,' says the little man and he puts it in his hand. 'Fucking tight.'

And the little man starts to laugh but he and Sandy are shooting up through the soil to the land at last and the driver is left behind.

–Is that Deany Blighton?

–Yes?

–Guy there? It's Dennis Peters.

–Oh Dennis. Hi. How are you? Long time.

–Yes. Fine. You?

–Sure. He's in the garden. I'll get him.

–Dennis. Guy.

–Guy. Hello. Catching up on the weeding?

–Er . . . well, keeping busy, you know.

–Well now, I've got some results for you.

–Ah.

–Yes. Interesting. Not complete, I'm afraid, but pretty promising. For somebody.

–What do you mean?

–Depends what you're going to do with it, really. It's not a UK sample is it?

–Er . . . no. No, it isn't.

–Right. I'd be amazed if it was. Wouldn't be Norway, though?

–I've never been there, Dennis.

–Oh. Funny. Probably from out near your last sortie, then.

–Yes. Around there, yes. I suppose.

–I'm not going to grill you, don't worry!

–No, no, I wasn't thinking . . .

–Listen, how big was the piece you actually brought home? A lot bigger than what you sent me?

–Well, just . . . a small lump. You know.

–What . . . big as a football, was it?

–Oh no. Smaller. Tennis ball.

–Ah. Get it in your hand, sort of thing?

–What?

–Small – like a pebble. Hold it in your hand.

–Yes.

–Hmm.

–Why?

–Well, it's a bit funny. It's very pure.

–Is that good?

–Good, bad, it's not the point. It's just . . . how much do you know about minerals?

–Minerals? Nothing.

–You don't know what thortveitite is?

–Thortveitite. No.

–Silicate of scandium. What they call a rare earth. Valuable.

–That's what it is? Scandium?

–Yes. Discovered by Olaus Thortveit in 1911. Had to look it up. Norwegian. That's where it occurs. Mostly.

–Why is it rare?

–Well. It's what they call them. There's a group of them. Yttrium's one. They use them in these superconductors, no electrical resistance and all that. Your rock has a thirty-seven percent deposit by weight of the mineral. And no other traces.

–That's why it's pure.

–It's too pure, Guy. Really, there's no such thing as pure. Obviously you're aware of that. Any rock, regardless of what might be high yields of whatever, is full of traces of other compounds. That's why it's not thortveitite.

–You said . . .

–It ought to be, but it lacks all the characteristic traces.

–What about the . . . sixty-three percent left? What's in that?

–Yes. I had a problem there. It wouldn't read.

–How do you mean?

–Well, I can run various tests here, but we don't really have the full gear. I'm really just doing an assay:

–So . . .

–It didn't respond to anything. It has no physical properties.

–I don't understand.

–I'm joking. You need to get at it with the electron microprobe – that gives you a complete qualitative readout. You'd probably pick up your traces then as well. We just haven't got that sort of gear.

–No. I'm most grateful, Dennis.

–Pleasure. Sorry I can't pin it down for you. You're quite sure you found it in the ground, aren't you?

–Of course I did, Dennis. Where else?

–No, I'm kidding again. But it's a rum old rock you've got there, Guy, I must say. File your claim pronto, I would.

–My claim?

–It's worth a packet, scandium. Nine thousand dollars a pound for four nines pure! Yield like that could make you a rich man. Get digging! If it isn't someone else's land, of course.

–Yes. I must find out.

–Look, if you want further tests, you'll have to fork out – I don't have any contacts in that area. I can get an address for you, though.

–I must think about that, Dennis.

–Don't leave it too long! In the meantime I've sent you a little report, just says what I've just told you. In other words not much!

–It's very kind of you, Dennis. Very kind indeed.

–No. Any time. Deany sounds well.

–Oh yes. Yes.

–Okay, Guy. Better go. All the best.

–And you, Dennis.

He had put the thing straight into his pocket as soon as he had woken up at the supper table. Deany and Jack Gavin had been in the other room, thank God. Without pausing to think, he had moved silently across to the fireplace and taken the screw-top jar from the mantelpiece. The six pound notes were rolled up inside it. Guy had slipped one out, replaced the jar and returned to the table. Moments later Jack Gavin had come into the room.

'You nodded off. Missed the coffee. You look terrible.'

'Must have got in a funny position. Got a bit of a headache.'

'Anything to report?'

'I haven't looked.'

'Haven't looked! Can't you feel anything?'

He had looked dully at his clenched fist then, and for a moment had almost managed to forget the surreptitious switch that he had pulled off moments earlier. His shirt and underwear had been quite damp and he had fought to restrain a strong need to shudder and groan in front of Jack. Pieces of some dreadful dream rattled away in his mind, and he had desperately and repeatedly cast aside thoughts of the outrageous fruit of his ordeal.

'Guy! You did it! Another one!'

He had nodded weakly.

'Well, that is so good, Guy! You were tired after the hunt and you just flopped out of your own accord. Like I said. Pity it's a oner.' Jack had gently pulled the note from between his fingers, and held if up to the light. 'It's perfect, isn't it? Remarkable. And dry this time.'

Guy had glanced nervously at Jack then, but his comment seemed to be quite straightforward, so Guy had nodded again, adding an unconvincing grin, and then rubbing his neck as if to soothe the muscles made taut by his impromptu slumber.

'Deany!' Jack had cried. And to Guy, with a conspiratorial wink, 'This'll show her!'

Guy had said, 'No, no!' but realised that his lips had not moved, the protestation had not been voiced but retained within the queasy perimeter of his three-quarters wakened mind. By the time he had deduced this Deany had come through from the other room. Jack had thrust the pound note at her.

'Look! Guy dreamed up another one!'

Deany had instantly adopted a sour expression. She had barely looked at the note, just muttering, 'Really,' as though Guy had been some tiresome pet that had lapsed in its housetraining.

'Was there a dream, Guy, can you remember?' Jack had asked.

Before Guy could answer, Deany had marched over to the fireplace, picked up the jam jar and twisted the lid off. 'There's five in here, Guy.'

Jack Gavin had taken the jar from her.

'Count them, Jack, if you must.'

He had quickly riffled the notes with his finger. Deany had continued. 'You're both really pissing me off, you know that?' Her lower lip had started to tremble. 'Guy – you don't have to do all this, you really don't. It's not your fault, the animals. You're just so . . . tired. You should stop for a while. All this . . . stuff . . .' she had waved her hand at the jar, around the room. Tears had wetted her cheeks. 'Jack, it's, they're just notes, just money. Guy's money. He puts them in a jar, he takes them out. Nothing . . . no big deal. Please can't we forget it? Can't we all think about something else?'

Guy had felt rather affronted by his wife's account of his activities. He realised that, unthinkable as much of the affair was, he expected credit where credit was due. Then, sitting at the dinner table under Deany's rueful gaze, trying not to catch Jack Gavin's eye, he had been filled with a confusion of relief and frustration. Just at the point where his wife seemed to have neutralised the issue, he had become painfully aware that his problems had moved into a terrible new dimension. Each time he had begun to consider the remission he might have earned, the lump in his trouser pocket had seemed to press on his thigh, galvanising him with a swirling panic that threatened to dissolve any conclusions or resolutions he could ever hope to form.

Guy turned the radio on, hoping that it would somehow stop Deany quizzing him about the call from Dennis. A rattle from the front door told him that the morning post had arrived. He walked through the house and scooped up the letters from the mat. Walking back he examined the envelopes, frowning as he came across one bearing the device of Dennis's university, with the title *Department of Geology* printed beneath it. He suppressed a guilty urge to stuff the letter in his pocket, and started to tear it open. Something on the radio caught his attention. He stood beside the kitchen table, removing the contents of the envelope as he listened.

'. . . of East Haslowe. Mr Arnold, a keen amateur naturalist, is convinced that the creature was not a badger. Reports from workers at the nearby electricity board sub-station at Axeworth tend to confirm his view. The animal spotted yesterday morning by a five-man maintenance crew had none of the bold markings characteristic of our old friend Brock, and seemed too bulky for a small fox or indeed a large ferret. Join us at four-fifteen for a new edition of Country Club, when

Tom Ringsby and Brian Jeffs will be chatting about parrots, pumas, coypus and all the other exotic beasts that have made their home in the British countryside.'

Guy was staring blankly into the garden, he had not moved a muscle for a whole minute. The theme music to a new programme faded in on the radio. Suddenly he dashed out of the kitchen door, across the lawn and into the workshop.

Axeworth and East Haslowe. He had never heard of them. He pulled a sheaf of maps from a shelf and unfolded one that covered an area about twenty-five miles square, with his own village located roughly at the centre. Pencilled cross-hatching indicated the areas that he had searched so far. Groaning impatiently he ran his eyes hither and thither over the sheet, waiting for the place names to spring out at him. When they failed to oblige he reluctantly summoned up the patience necessary to scrutinise the map inch by inch, square by square. There was no sign of either village.

Guy sighed. He stood on a chair and searched the top shelf. Under a couple of mildewed files he found his old atlas of Britain. Axeworth. Thirty-eight. Good God. He stepped down from the chair, forgetting how high he was, and jarred his knee. Good God. He placed the atlas on top of the cage containing the single parent Ike and his remaining offspring. Seventy-five, seventy-seven, and a half, seventy-seven and a half miles away. Three miles to the north, East Haslowe. How? How on earth?

He closed the atlas and selected the appropriate folding map from the pile. Then, shaking his head in puzzlement, made his way back to the house.

Jack Gavin had a cognac in his hand and was reading Dennis Peters's report.

'Didn't know you did geology.'

'That's a private document, Jack. And I don't.'

'Just happened to see it on the table. It was open, face up. Sorry about that.' Guy made a sniffing noise. Jack went on, 'I guess you must pick up all sorts of things on the old nature jaunts.'

Guy's heart was beating fiercely. He moved to the table and removed the report.

Jack went on, 'I suppose there's huge amounts of stuff under the jungle. Waiting for whoever gets there first.'

'It's not from there,' Guy blurted, and instantly regretted it. He still

198

had absurdly contradictory feelings about Jack. While he was convinced that Jack's interest in his tribulations was not completely sincere, he recognised that the man never seemed to doubt him, never questioned that certain things had actually happened, and was able, apparently, to accommodate the incredible without effort or reservation. Guy's need for support was considerable, aggravated as it was by his wife's vehement rejections, and he was now uncomfortably aware of a strong desire to unburden himself before Jack. He tried to cover his confusion by busily tucking the report back into its envelope.

'Really. Made in Britain, is it?'

'Yes. You could say that.'

Jack nodded several times, as if understanding something that Guy had not realised was on the agenda. 'Well, it's a question of who owns the land, isn't it? I don't know how these things work – I suppose you lease the rights, or something like that, don't you?'

'It's just a stone, Jack.' Guy tried to affect a light, offhand manner. 'Doesn't mean there's going to be loads of it in the ground. Sort of thing you pick up for fun.'

Jack seemed not to be listening to him. His reply was voiced in a musing, distant tone. 'Yes. That's the word, isn't it?'

Guy, to his annoyance, was drawn in by the disconnectedness of this observation. 'I'm sorry?'

Jack turned his gaze directly on Guy now. 'Lodes. That's what they come in, don't they? Metals and ores.'

'Oh. Yes. I believe that is the term.'

'Yes. It is.' Jack turned away from Guy and looked out into the garden.

Guy asked himself why he did not stroll out of the room – it was his house, he had things to do, why did he stand there, as if Jack Gavin were somehow licensed to define the beginnings and ends of things? He looked down at the envelope in his right hand, as though it had just developed a greater importance which needed to be acknowledged with a businesslike bodily movement. To his surprise he found himself taking the envelope from one hand with the other, then slipping it under his right armpit like a newspaper carried by an encumbered traveller. This left him with two free hands, which he allowed, at first, to rest alongside his thighs. There was something not quite credible about this posture which drove him to lift his hands into his pockets. As he lifted his right arm its biceps moved away from the envelope, causing it to

199

drop down to his waist, at which point he trapped it again by quickly removing the recently pocketed hand and slapping it, more loudly than he had intended, on his hip.

Jack said 'Strictly speaking, you *dig* it up for fun.'

'What?'

'You said you picked it up.'

'It's just an expression, Jack.'

Guy suddenly remembered that the most important thing in his recent life had just happened. 'There've been sightings!' he announced. The conversation was his at last.

'What?'

'On the radio. People have seen strange animals in two places. About seventy miles away.'

'How'd they get out there? Legs are too short.'

'It's perfectly possible, Jack. We know very little about their mobility. In an unfamiliar habitat they might wander continually.'

'But what's a "strange animal"? What do people know about animals? Could be anything.'

'It's not a question of evaluating the probabilities, is it? I have to go there.'

'You think they'll wait for you?'

'I have to go there. I must tell Deany.'

Now he was able to leave the kitchen with an unassailable project and unquestionable integrity. He freed the envelope from its station at his hip, placed it in his left hand and strode, with purpose, to the sitting room.

'What did Dennis Peters want?'

'We had a chat.'

'I figured that.'

'Deany, the animals have been sighted. We've got to go.'

'Sighted where? Who by?'

'On the radio. Twice. In these villages, north from here.'

'You're kidding.'

'They said it wasn't a badger. Two lots of people saw them.'

Deany stood up. 'Guy!' Tears welled in her eyes. 'We'll go there, huh?'

He squeezed her hands. 'We can't afford not to, really.'

'They're alive!' She started to tremble and dropped her head abruptly onto his shoulder. 'I'm so pleased, darling.'

200

Something in her tone annoyed him. He held her at arm's length. 'There's no indication they're all together, Deany. It could well have 'I was thinking we might both be rather pleased, actually.'

'Well, you bet! Be so nice just to start our work again, get back to . . . you know, the way things were. Sure!'

'Anyway, we should go as soon as possible.'

'Right! We could go right now, yeah?'

'We need to pack.'

'Just take a cage, gloves, stuff like that. Food.'

'I must get the tent out.'

'The tent?'

'It won't be a day trip, Deany. They're not going to be waiting for us to pick them up, it up.'

'You wanna camp?'

'I want to be as close to the scene as possible. It's not exactly novel for you, is it?'

'Well, hardly, but . . . England?'

'Sounds great,' said Jack, who had walked through from the kitchen, and was now leaning against the wall at the far end of the room. Guy felt that Jack was supporting him again, and forgave him for eavesdropping. He voiced a pleasantry. 'Just the sort of thing you'd like, Jack!'

'I'd love to come.'

Deany grinned. 'He could have the little blue tent.'

'Nah. Hotel man, myself. I don't mind looking around with you, though.'

'I'm sure we could use your help. You might find it pretty dull, though,' Guy said, and even as he spoke, wondered why his feelings about Jack vacillated so dramatically.

'I know I will.'

'We're just going to be walking about, Jack. If you don't like it you could always take off again, we'd understand,' Deany said.

'Not a problem,' Jack replied. 'I get bored I'll just dig around, find something to keep me happy.'

Deany thought that Jack was being unnecessarily suggestive, and started to tense up. Guy knew instantly that Jack had not let go of their conversation in the kitchen, and was now coolly reminding him that they had some unfinished business to deal with. A chill of apprehension gripped him as he tried to formulate a response that would cut Jack short.

'I haven't been to this area before,' he announced, too hurriedly.

'No? You've been so many places, I'm surprised you remember.' been the same animal in both places.'

'But that's still fantastic, Guy. My god, if we get just one, think how happy you'll be!'

'No. I don't forget places.' Why did he say that?

'Of course, you keep a log, don't you? All the ground you've covered.'

'That's why I know. These villages are miles further on.'

'Still, you can show me places of interest en route, I bet.'

Guy smiled feebly, and felt utterly transparent. He had run out of things to say. There was a sort of code going on and he found it exhausting to keep up a repartee in such indirect terms.

Deany brightened up. 'Jack! Such a little nature boy now! You gonna find your fortune under the hedgerows?' She giggled.

'Yes,' Jack said.

Guy desperately wanted him to laugh then, but he just nodded and smiled lazily at them both.

Part Four

The Stowe Boys, Little Danny, far from little, at the helm, had ways that all the other boys looked up to, said Little Danny anyway. Danny would do anything, anything. Furthermore nobody touched him, ever. 'Nobody touches me. Ever.' Any fucker touches him would be sorry. That fucker would feel the shiv. Or Danny would grasp his bollocks, through the fabric of his trousers, and tear them downwards.

In Stowe a pleasant day, a short shout to the edge of town, past the poxy chipped streets like Agravaine or Trincomalee, the cars too stripped to move, no one paid to move them, a place to shit if you were short. But the sun was well out, well out, over the hire shops, Danny walked past there, on route to the edge, the boys kicking behind, there was a fragment on all the screens, they stopped for a look, of the camera moving along a bed of flowers, roses, with the close-up lens fitment, assumably, and the boys could see right down into their pistils, on thirty screens.

The boys barged the small crowd, bumping its backs with their bats, but their minds were elsewhere, on techniques and the improvement of their personal bests. Hitherto there had been so little to do for young people, in Stowe. Of an evening Danny would stand by the clock and the boys would come in, Terry, Bri, And, Sweller, one by one, from ambles out of Boudicca, Nolan, Algarve and Brummel, and each would bellow 'Is Danny here?', the answer being already known, and roars would go up, from beneath the clock. Exempted from income schemes by reason of lack of conviction, the boys were on a few ale budget, but the hire shops were visible to all, even if the sound was turned down, or not audible through the glass. Many a happy hour would be spent, particularly at Haversham's, faced as it was by a municipal bench. After the townsfolk had made their way to bed, the boys would still be lined up, in the empty street, on the bench, watching the silent films on a wide range of topics, reading lip movements, adding interpretations when visual clues were sparse.

Many of the films featured situations in which disadvantaged groups had their circumstances improved by the interventions of stronger, helpful groups or individuals, and it is only to be expected that these themes, seen so often, and at all hours of the long day, found fertile bedding in the open minds of Little Danny and the Stowe Boys, who by now were out in the steel sheds, batting the dilapidated corrugated sheeting and shouting experimentally through the dark and cavernous spaces in which rusted the silent monolithic rolling presses.

On the far side of the sheds was the open ground, stretching away over England, they weren't sure where to. The ground was tight, scrubby, stuck with scrap, dry ochre stained from broken seeping bolts and bars, blackened by heaps of ten thousand nails melting into low, cabbagey, crawling weed.

Danny started to run about, waving the bat. The boys too, jumping up, making slashing, cutting, bopping moves. Danny had a cricket bat, nobody criticised that, nobody. Danny's eyes would go yellow, his grey teeth would show and he would whisper, 'Nobody criticises me. Ever.' So that reduced the volume of comments on the bat. Reduced them – there were none. Ever. Besides, Danny would do anything, and the boys would only do most things. They had baseball bats, stolen from the base.

Anyway, they saw one pretty soon, and circled it. They still found it interesting, how it never stopped moving, like when Sweller's brother Micky had a kidney stone, he never stopped moving. So they looked at it for a bit. Danny said, 'Fucking thing', out of pity. That was one of the few opinions he shared with Elizabeth, his mum, she thought it was a shame too. But then most of the Stowe folk, being poor and dying youngish, they would have that sympathy, where others would just be cold and indifferent.

And said, after a minute, 'You could numb that, we never tried that.' Sweller said, 'Fucking numb it! How you do that, prick?' And said, 'Fucking put it half out. That'd be better for it.' Danny said, 'I'll fucking numb it,' and he lifted up his bat and cracked it down onto its head, but not that hard. It didn't seem to do much.

Terry, who knew how to handle Danny, said, critically, 'It's a matter of degree, Dan.' And he stepped forward, held the baseball bat vertically in both hands, handle up, knobend down, and drove it sharply onto the head, quite neat. This crushed the jaw into the scrub, and Terry held it there for a while, pinned, but you couldn't see any difference otherwise, it still squealed away.

'Spent all your spunk last night?' Danny jeered, referring to Terry's new marriage, Terry and Sian, two months new.

Bri said, 'Fucking numb it,' disparagingly, changing the subject, and the project. He just sailed up the bat over his head and whistled it down onto its back, and that definitely cracked it. You could see where the curve was broken.

'The worst pain a man can feel,' said Sweller, drawing on anecdotal material generated at the time of Micky's kidney rupture.

'Cunt,' said Danny. 'That fucking numbs it.'

'Later it numbs,' Sweller said, 'at first that's terrible.'

Bri stuck the bat end under it, managed to roll it over and with an effort succeeded in suspending it from the bat shaft, with its
stomach to the sky, arched over the wrong way but notched on by the snap in its spine. Bri grunted and flipped it up into the air. It thumped to the ground, the right way up, still squealing, still pawing meaninglessly at the dirt.

'See,' he instructed, 'still in fucking misery.'

'Well, I just thought it,' complained And.

Danny tired of the sissying and announced the mode of operations for the day. 'I want to drop it. That'd be sudden, right?'

'What off of, Dan?'

'Up those stairs.' Danny nodded at the steel staircase that zigzagged down the side of the nearest rolling shed.

'Fucking tear off the wall, won't they?' said Terry.

'You worry about that, you don't have to go up,' sneered Danny.

Anyway, Danny took it by the back legs and dragged it over to the rickety stairs and climbed right up. At the top the wind blew in his face but he could see way over England, stretches of scrub, great dead banks of sheds and plant, off at the horizon. That would be Plaston, off past there, he knew that, his late dad had brothers there. The Plaston Boys were shit, certainly, probably just into drowning, or even starving, that was all they could think of. Christ, that would be typical. The Stowe Boys were always thinking, they had curious minds.

Danny swung it to and fro by the back legs, then over and over, rotating his arm. It was as heavy as a small dog, but Danny had good muscles. Down below the boys were cheering. He let go of the legs and the thing shot up in the air, only about eight foot, squealing above him then falling down past him, getting fainter.

'Danny!'

It was Bri, yelling up at him against the sky, as the thing plummeted to the lads. Bri swung his bat back, weeping with laughter. As the thing blurred down he swept in and made the connection. Big, Bri, like Dan, he still could only move it a few feet out of line, the speed it had by then. It crashed into Sweller's face and by the time, split seconds, it reached the scrub, all the boys were on it, bats flailing, blood coming out at last.

Up at the stairs' top, Danny screamed. 'Cunts!' in hoarse rage, his eyes swollen and yellow, a very bad sign. They barely heard him, he barely could hear himself, the wind up there.

And, in the swirling chopping, heard the squealing stop. He stepped back and wiped his bat end on Terry's leg. Terry jumped away with a cry. And said, 'That's misery's over, then.' The boys could see that, so they looked upwards for Dan.

Danny's eyes had filmed over. He stared over at Plaston, but not looking at it. He was raging at the boys, but his burning gaze beamed past the next town, on to the horizon, curving over a minute or two of the English part of the globe, laying waste in a swathe to any fuckers in the way. Eventually, about sixty miles further on, in the next county, Danny's beam would pass over people who were comfortably well off in Berrowe, a town of which he had never heard.

Where Miss Cheetah was doing her rounds of the orchard, moving gracefully and with great economy between the trees, further and further from the ranks of glasshouses laid out behind her. At this time of year several types of pest emerged from the fields nearby and invariably moved into the orchard where they would spoil the fallen fruit. From the orchard it was a short scurry to the glasshouses, which were easily breached, affording access to the succulent buds and blooms. These latter were generally cellophaned and boxed on the premises, prior to being despatched to the Berrowe homes. The nursery was easily the largest business in town, for the average Berrowe home had some five or six rooms in which blooms were placed, and most of the clients stipulated that the arrangements be renewed daily. The nursery deployed two fleets of transporters: the white fleet, emblazoned with flowing golden script, and manned by men in white uniforms piped and epauletted in gold, and the

206

brown fleet, effectively a squad of refuse wagons, equipped with hydraulic compacters, into which chocolate uniformed personnel would tip discarded blooms before returning them to the giant composting vats at the nursery.

Miss Cheetah's sole responsibility was pest control, so naturally she took it very seriously. The other staff recognised her uncanny stealth and the awesome speed of her reflexes. None of them was able to stalk and pounce in quite the same way, indeed, few of them had the patience or dedication in the first place. Clearly, it was very much in Miss Cheetah's nature to work on her own, and to set her own quotas. Since these had always been high, and were consistently filled, Miss Cheetah had been granted virtual immunity from supervision.

Something caught her eye in the long grass. She froze. Crouching very slightly she scrutinised the suspicious movements of the foliage, and concluded that they were caused by a creature. She began to move in. She had crept only a few feet closer when the began to hear squealing noises from the targeted area. The long grass waved chaotically, and further sounds of crashing reached her ears.

Whenever she found herself in a situation in which her presence was undetected Miss Cheetah would succumb to a feeling of great playfulness. As she crept ever closer to the source of the disturbance, a delicious tingle began to animate her trunk and thighs. Her eyes quivered within their sockets, and were soon greeted with the first glimpse of the beast that rummaged in the long grass oblivious to the fact of its imminent despatch.

As she sprang through the air Miss Cheetah sensed that the target pest was new to her. She even wavered very slightly in mid parabola as it struck her that it might be a small dog that loomed ever larger in her downrushing field of vision. The physical commitment had been made, however, and within a thought she had grasped the invader by the neck and then cuffed it onto its side. This brief initial contact was sufficient to show her that although the thing most certainly was not canine, it had an unusually massive musculature and fur of an almost bristly coarseness – qualities that Miss Cheetah did not associate with the normal run of rodents. The common rabbit was perhaps the largest of all her various victims, and its bulk had originally caused her some problems. With the encouragement of Miss Adair, her immediate superior in the nursery, Miss Cheetah had eventually evolved a technique of neutralising the rabbit, and had thereby brought into her folio, as it were, the full range of

207

bloom- and root-nibblers that might otherwise lay waste to the glass-forced ranks of product in her stewardship.

It was obvious that the animal that now lay squealing in front of her, pressed to the grass by her full weight, would have to be dealt a variation on the rabbit treatment. Miss Cheetah leaned forward and applied herself to the back of its neck. A partial severance of the vital cords which ran through that area of the body would render the creature passive enough for its captor to take the opportunity to discharge some of her simmering playfulness.

The neck muscles were quite as resistant as she had expected, but with a little extra application she soon laid them bare and then tore through them to the spine, units of which she managed to fracture in order to mutilate the wormish cord. It was in the course of these operations that she found the time to consider the attitude and condition of the victim. She realised that since the beginning of her assault there had been something untoward about the thing's reactions. It had evinced neither fright nor surprise when she had seized it, and had offered no resistance or attempts at flight. Why had she not noticed these irregularities earlier? As she sat back to contemplate the now semi-paralysed object of her ravaging attentions, its incessant screaming concentrated her mind again and she began to understand. The creature had been screaming before she had leaped on it, before she had even crept through the grass towards it. It had been in pain all along, almost indifferent to her refined attack, too absorbed to attempt an escape. She had picked up these signals but had somehow failed to make proper sense of them, preferring, it seemed, to construe them to her advantage. The cart had indeed preceded the horse, and her instincts had effected a switch.

Miss Cheetah took a few paces back. She felt suddenly dispirited, cheated of the opportunity to play. She felt contempt for the creature now, mingled with a growing irritation. She ran forward and jumped on it. It yowled and turned on its back. She butted it with her head and tore spitefully at its flanks. Then she walked slowly round it, lunging in at odd intervals to pat it, teasing it with her mastery, showing it that she was in no particular hurry to put it out of its misery. Miss Cheetah circled the creature in this way for a long time.

Miss Adair hummed a popular song as she turned the corner of the bottom block, on her way to the azalea house. She heard a curious sound from the orchard and turned to track its source.

208

It was definitely an animal in distress. Miss Adair stopped humming and strode towards the trees, her lips tightening as she considered the possibility that Miss Cheetah might have lapsed again. Miss Adair loved Miss Cheetah, had created the vacancy for her, and had supported her keenly through the first weeks of her employment. There had, nevertheless, been some *incidents*, albeit very few, and these had unsettled some of the other staff. Miss Adair knew full well that Miss Cheetah's errant impulses were very deeply embedded in her nature, and could never be dissolved, but she had determined that this would not persuade her to exempt Miss Cheetah from correction. Miss Adair felt it was important that her protégée should receive the appropriate admonition on each and every occasion that she strayed from the decent execution of her duties.

'Aagh!' screamed Miss Adair in horror. 'Miss Cheetah! Oh! Bad!' She rushed forward, emitting a long, hoarse, warlike cry. 'Oh, shoo, shoo!' she shouted, raising her arms and beating them down onto her thighs in order to create the maximum of fearsome effect.

Miss Cheetah turned guiltily, caught her mentor's eye for just a moment, then bounded off through the grass, her tail held straight out behind her, her white paws flashing as she jumped over a fallen branch and headed for the safe expanses of the pest-infested fields beyond the orchard.

Miss Adair looked down on the bloodied beast at her feet and was instantly overcome by confusion. The piercing noise the beast was making seemed wholly out of proportion to the injuries visible on its back and sides, and Miss Adair became aware that her early feeling of compassion had given way to simple irritation. She thrust aside these considerations and concentrated on what was clearly the overriding priority: the relief of the creature's misery.

The relief must be effected as soon as possible. She couldn't bear the racket any longer. The poor thing. But how? She bit her fingernail absent-mindedly and looked around the orchard, then back at the glasshouses.

The first blow from the fork was a weak and compromised affair, deriving from Miss Adair's compunction at delivering a five-prong thrust straight off. The side prong bounded off the bristly back and sent a dull throb up the wooden handle. The beast barely moved. Miss Adair faced facts. Her own reluctance was a form of cruelty – despatch was now of the utmost urgency. It mattered not that the activity was alien to her.

209

It was irrelevant that she had no technique. Everyone possessed a deep well of common sense. There was a knowledge there if you needed it. Courage could be summoned.

She drove the prongs into the belly of the beast. For a second there was resistance – she imagined it would feel the same if you did it to a handbag – but then the prongs slid right in, and out the other side, into the soil beneath the grass. Blood jumped from some of the entry holes, onto her shoes and ankles. She shuddered and kicked out with little short footstabs, trying to flick away the globules before they seeped through her stockings.

The beast's legs twitched at each corner of its body. Its screams did not abate. Miss Adair began to weep. Strong words formed in her mouth but she did not mouth them. She felt terribly hot, terribly angry. She swallowed hard and gripped the handle of the fork, pressing down on it with all her might. The tines ground slowly deeper into the earth, scraping against small stones. The crossbar reached the belly, which bulged around it. Miss Adair could push no further. She drew upon her common sense. The sole of her shoe slipped across the bar, carrying her foot down until it was checked by the top of her high instep. As she put her weight onto the fork it slid in a little further and carried her high heel into the tight wall of the beast's stomach. Such was the relationship between the beast, the bar and the heel that any further pressure threatened actually to drive the heel into the beast.

Miss Adair, weeping no longer, angry no more, clarified by the draught from her own deeper resources, took the shovel from the lily house and returned to the site of her chore. She really needed the fork to break up the turf next to the stuck beast, but she would make do without it. After some awkward and laborious thrusts with the shovel she managed to uncover a patch of soil. She kicked and shoved the blade into it and lifted up a mound of earth which she poured over the beast's head. Some of it fell straight into the beast's mouth, and suddenly the orchard was silent. The beast choked and chewed on the grit, but could not expel it. Miss Adair quickly emptied a succession of shovel loads over the twitching body, piling up the soil until it covered the crossbar of the fork. She dropped to her knees and patted the mound smooth with her hands, then stood back, watching the compacted surface closely. No tremor was apparent, nor was there the slightest sound.

The fork did not look at all odd there. One of the brown-truck boys could deal with it later in the afternoon. Give it an hour or so, to be safe.

Far away, over England, in Angrave, the people at Penny's party were really restless. It was a hot night. Some were in the street looking up at the purple in the sky. Some were looking at the bonfire in the back. There was also a fire in one of the downstairs rooms and two people were gazing into it. In one of the rooms the television was on. It was Ainsley and several men and women were watching him, and making their comments. But none of these people was easy, none could concentrate on the thing before him. The heat opened the windows so that the curtains rolled and it pushed the doors wide so that it could course the house uninterrupted. It held the men's trousers to their legs and dampened the dresses of the women beneath their arms. This, with the fires, the bright lights from some rooms, the blue haze from the room with the television, the plates with left food on, the frowns from several of them as they bent forward their heads and ran back their hands from the sweat on their brows through their hair, the silence because now they had stopped talking, the moving through the house of many more friends of Penny, from room to room, squeezing up and down the stairs, sighing and coughing, placing their elbows on the ledges of the upstairs windows, gazing at the front into the street, at the back over the fire to the open land not yet built on, and all the buzzing of the lights from the street, and those in the ceilings, and the paleness it gave to their faces, the pasty skin that it threw into relief, all this, with their thoughts about their lives tomorrow, and where they would go, and how they would come back, and their pasts, the parts that they remembered, and how old they seemed to be, and how fast it all went by, all this poured down and mixed with the noise they had tried to ignore, a tearing, maddening noise, the noise that wasn't part of Penny's party, but was something to do with her children, something her children had brought in from the fields, in a box, screaming, beneath the sink.

Penny was disturbed by the noise, it took her into her past, all the deeds and sights she had not liked, so she pushed past the people in her hall and reached beneath the sink for the box and took it to the room with the fire, followed by people from the corridor who pressed quietly into the room and sat, some of them on the sofas and some on the back of the sofas with their feet between the people below, and some sat on the floor leaning on the legs of those seated behind. All those at the windows came away from staring at the sky, and those in the back and before the television and squeezed on the stairs came into the room and found a place. The fire crackled and threw light over the crowd, and the noise from the box became the centre of attention, no longer something faint at the back of Penny's party, something from her kids that spread unease.

Penny opened the box so that the animal could move freely if it wished, and the people started to breathe evenly, although they could not hear each other doing so. Penny sat back and started to cry and her hands were loose in her lap. She cried quietly and so did the others, the tears rolled down their cheeks, and their breaths became heavier. The fire played against them, around the rows of them and up the ranks who had found seating. Their faces glistened, from the heat as well as the grief.

Penny said to Roger, 'I can't bear it,' and many of them there silently agreed with her. Roger was shaking with sorrow, but he rose and went to the kitchen where he picked up his tool box. Back in the room with the fire he closed the door and placed his tools near the hearth. He looked at all Penny's friends, who were largely his friends too. They were ranged in a crescent right around the room. He felt sad but easy with them now.

The names do not matter. It may have been Roger who started, or Penny, or Andrew. It was Roger who suggested using the door, which meant that their friends had to rearrange themselves a little, some standing with their backs to the fire. Since they were his tools, it may well have been Roger who fixed the animal to the door, quite high up. It hung there, the nail placed approximately at the centre of its rib cage between the front legs. With the heat, from the fire, and the windows open for the heat of the night, and the many of them there, touching closely, and their tears, there was an atmosphere, both of their damp clothes and the light, and also of their unitedness, and it was difficult to say where the one ended.

The room was not stifling though. They were able to concentrate without trouble. Without any particular scheme they stepped forward one at a time, sometimes coming from the side, sometimes right from the furthest row back. They fixed each paw to the door then opened the skin of the belly with an adjustable knife. The animal screamed in pain and sent waves of misery through them. One of them overcame her grief and stepped forward. She gripped the loosened flaps of fur at the belly, pulling them sideways so that transverse tears formed at the top and bottom of the long wound. The fur hung ruched before the glimpse of the pink muscles, which were taut and glistening. A murmur

212

of understanding filled the room. One of them pushed through from the glowing fire and pinned back the fur flaps to the door with tacks. The screams now rose and fell in concert with bands of muscle, and they could see the rhythm and the relationship quite clearly. One of them took up the knife, sensing that they were all close now, that differences were no longer an issue. He pushed the blade through the pink belly wall and pulled it to the pelvis. As a small amount of blood welled the people in the room held back themselves no longer. The blade had cut through the thick heat too. Their moans rose with the animal's. The muscled meat rose and fell with their moans and glimpses of the cavity and its contents for the first time were there. These drew more pity from them, and their grief shook them heavily. The stomach sides were fixed to the wood. It was then as if they took a step back, still shaking, still sobbing, but as if a shout had chorused through the room, from the thick rolling curtain by the open window to all the walls and round.

The secret beauty now held them all. With little further blood. There were its satin tubes hammocked by fine silk sheets, the mineral smoothness of organs in pairs, boldly dark wet undersea sacs in pearl finish, gentle pulses running in loops and waves, ravelled under mists of film, all blossomed against the complete pale delicacy of pink, catching the moves of the light, flowering from the stand of dark pins that leaned back and away and threw their shadows to the jambs so that there was a symmetry now, shining up on the door, and the room tipped so that they were all looking down on it, down a funnel of their hot faces and damp clothes, and rising up the funnel came the savage screaming, no longer modulated, an undying chord of the nerves, rising into the fire at the hearth and interfering with the rolls of thick air.

These occasions have an end, which is often workaday, and it was Penny who reached beneath the ribs and cut across, so that the blood fell after her hand and over the smooth intricacies at the centre of their attention. So that the pulsing slowly stopped.

Jack, elsewhere in England, in an inn. The spirit in the country was good for him. At first he had worried that the tremendous excitement generated by the animals might return people to a state of attentiveness, in which they would be able to see his special operations. Then he had realised that their new pursuits were just pursuits, their prey took them

213

hither and thither, their goals were still lodged beyond some impossible horizon, and therefore none of their paths would ever cross into the country that he inhabited. His England was secure, and as far as he could tell, still empty.

Lying on his four-poster bed, with the television sound turned down, with his suit and shoes on, a can in his hand, he reflected on the weeks that he had spent away from the city. To his surprise his powers had greatly increased as soon as he and Guy and Deany had taken off in the car. He had always regarded the city as the central generator of the situations he required and had not been able to envisage quite how the countryside, in which nothing happened, might ever afford him the crucial vacancies into which he had become so adept at slipping. This had proved to be a specious line of reasoning, based on the lazily constructed notion that pursuits were somehow less feverish beyond the city walls, and that consequently the country folk would retain a degree of attention. As soon as he had dumped his bag in the first hotel room, he had felt obliged to sit down to an expensive lunch in order to test out the state of play. His departure from the dining room had been as impeccable as any of those in his urban operations, as had his leaving the hotel itself two days later. He came to the conclusion that the city had actually confined his powers – the sheer proliferation of possibilities had dissipated the development of his new faculty, and he had been coasting on a succession of small achievements. Out in the roads and hotels the opportunities were continuous rather than episodic, and once he had adjusted to this slightly paradoxical condition he moved from strength to strength with great speed. Indeed such was his certainty that with minimum effort he could maintain an unwavering, phantasmal tracelessness for increasingly long periods.

He drained the can and reached for another. The only thing that got to him about the travelling life, and usually not for long, was that the compelling charade of its variety made him feel more Venusian than usual. In the days when he was merely a limited seer he had used to regard himself, rather fondly, as a visitor from Mars. Now that his powers were so dramatically extended, the planet Earth seemed to him less populated than ever, and had taken on a windswept bleakness that suggested a location much further from the sun than that established by the astronomers. Furthermore, given that his associations to the idea of Mars were red and orange and possibly pleasant gardened cities under domes of translucent rock, he had felt obliged to decamp to Venus,

214

which, unlike the reader, he imagined to be more removed from the solar source than the warrior planet.

When the cold, sterile greenness descended on him, momentarily undermining his generally equable accommodation with futility, he would comfort himself by recalling that he was involved in some extremely promising futures that were still in the process of unfolding. Although he had only been able to bring himself to camp out with Guy and Deany on one occasion, he had kept a careful eye on Guy over the weeks and had become convinced of at least two things. Firstly, Guy's rock had not been dug out of the earth – it came from the same place as Guy's pound notes, wherever that might be. He had been driven to this conclusion partly by Guy's tendency to deteriorate into vaporousness whenever Jack introduced the slightest allusion to geological matters. Jack was also sure that the business with Guy's skin was significant, and was leading somewhere. He found it hard to imagine what the outcome might be, but felt confident that the outbreaks themselves were not random events but part of a continuing process.

Contemplation of a future defined on the surface of another man's body made Jack feel more at ease. He had often noticed that Guy sweated quite a lot, a phenomenon he had dismissed as unremarkable, or at most a predictable extension of the man's perpetual grinning nervousness. During the first couple of weeks under canvas (Guy and Deany's weeks, that is) Jack had observed that, at the end of a long day with map and net, Guy's clothing was consistently damper than Deany's. Deany had got in the habit of coming to his hotels before supper and using the bath, and sometimes he would undress her and fuck her on the bed or floor before she had freshened up. She invariably smelled marvellous on these occasions, and he was tempted to subscribe to the popular idea that this perception demonstrated an essential difference between women and men. His half-hearted efforts to dismiss the idea were not reinforced by the fact that her husband stank. Every evening Guy would stand by the tent, or 'camp' as he called it, waving wearily as Deany and Jack drove off, his clothes thoroughly darkened by perspiration. Having refused Jack's regular but muted offer of a bath or shower, he would peel off his sodden garments, dry himself with a towel and then don his second outfit, which had been drying throughout the day on a line slung between a couple of trees or bushes. The second outfit would be used throughout the evening and the following day. And so on. His odour reminded Jack of the unaired sitting rooms of the very old; it was both sharp and sweet, sickly and homely, quite at odds with what might be expected to issue from a man sleeping beneath the stars.

Deany had refused to take the damp and the stench on board. She attributed it to Guy's being a hard worker. Jack knew that she knew this was bullshit. Within those first two weeks, Guy had broken out in a heat rash on his thighs and upper arms, and this in turn, possibly as a result of being scratched too much, had developed into heat bumps. When the patches of heat bumps had then spread all over his arms and legs, Jack began to feel that something was up. One of Guy's outfits consisted of shorts and a short-sleeved shirt, and the livid stippling of his flesh visible beyond the limits of these garments was so pronounced that even Jack was provoked to a sympathetic anxiety. When, from time to time, he made solicitous enquiries, Guy would irritably explain that anyone working in the field had to be prepared to encounter a great variety of plant life, some of which would inevitably prove mildly noxious to that person, who would have trained himself to ignore minor occupational inconveniences which were commonly exaggerated by those who had not spent any of their working life in inhospitable climes.

It struck Jack nevertheless that Guy had elevated a minor inconvenience into a considerable nuisance by his continual scratching. Despite his assertion that his attentions were focused elsewhere, Guy spent a sizeable part of the day raking his fingernails over his bumps. He did this distractedly rather than determinedly but he applied great friction in his distraction, which surely explains why the bumps began to weep, turn dry, flatten out, and then coalesce into scattered sites of scaly, brittle hide.

Those areas of his body that were not afflicted in this way shortly developed what appeared to be an unstable and arbitrary pigmentation. Within broadly caucasian limits, a range of unusual hues began to declare its elements across the envelope of Guy's skin. At first, and for no apparent reason, he would simply flush all over into a single colour, such as creamy parchment or a palely bilious green. These changes were only recognisable as such to those familiar with Guy's normally healthy tan, for they affected the whole of his body uniformly and could pass muster, case by case, as types of complexion.

Gradually the single colour states became more extreme, so that, to take an example based in fact on the virtual absence of colour, he would be subjected at one moment to a pallor so devoid of tint that his veins became primary aspects of his appearance, and the fibrillations of his muscles suggested another restless, swelling life worming parasitically within him. In the next moment this transparency might be reversed by an angry carmine cloud that would billow up unheralded, bruising over the desolate flesh, blotting out the straining fibres, as if in response to a terrible blow delivered deep down inside, or perhaps to a threat of assault from without that might be averted by the display of its effect.

One day out in the field Guy succumbed to an even more dramatic condition. Jack had been watching him beating around a bush with a stick while Deany simulated, unconvincingly, a figure of alertness and vigilance. Guy was shouting 'Ha! Ha!', a useful enough cry among beaters and baiters of game, but one which in this context suggested to Jack a grotesquely slowed down laughter, unwittingly employed as a commentary on the whole frantic, gruelling enterprise. As Guy walked away from the bush Jack saw that his simmering skin had erupted into a startling variegation of red and white tones. These arranged themselves in pools and blotches which bore no discernible relationship to the features beneath them. Ordinarily, and on a smaller scale, this effect would be described as mottling, and would not seem out of place on the flesh of thighs or buttocks, but the areas of contrasting colour on Guy's skin were too large to justify any comparison with the transient dappling of a chill bottom – they broke across his face in fierce awkward splashes that accentuated and united normally disparate features with complete disfiguring randomness. His arms and legs were similarly daubed, as if some demonic expert in camouflage were preparing him for clandestine operations in a terrain of undifferentiated bodyless flesh.

At the time both Jack and Deany had made little comment. Jack noticed Guy glancing at his arms now and again, and on one occasion Guy had caught Jack studying him. Guy had flicked his eyes away and rapidly composed an expression of stoic annoyance. This expression was designed to refer to what Guy had seen Jack see – it declared that it was not Jack's glance that annoyed him, although it was, but his own momentary diversion by another of the trivial inconveniences so typical of the field and so peripheral to the concerns of the working naturalist.

Jack was reassured by his review of the past few weeks on the road – there was a strong probability that Guy's current dermal displays were continuous with his admirable achievements back at the cottage, those featuring currency and minerals. His training as a seer told him that while the fruition of the process was still obscure, there was no point in his fretting about how he might speed things up: the business

217

had a momentum of its own, and all he could do was lie back in well appointed rooms and wait.

After a couple of days on safari Jack had driven to a nearby town and removed a guide to hotels from a bookshop. His first two rooms had been bland, poky and upholstered in a profusion of unpleasant fabrics. The guide indicated that this need not be the case any longer. A series of handy maps italicised the location of exceptional watering holes through-out the country. He had worried for a while that the camp might not always be pitched within a reasonable distance of one of these places, but he had found that Guy was always grateful for his 'intuitions' about where the expedition might fruitfully head next, and he quickly evolved an advisory programme that drew from overt and covert sources. The latter, the organising factor, was of course the guide itself, while the ostensible bases for his counsel derived from a selective digest of items from television bulletins and newspaper reports. He would make his presentation to Guy casually but regularly, usually in the late afternoon or early evening, and in consequence his lodgings were no longer poky, even if the use of fabrics continued to offend him.

He checked the time and rolled off the bed. The silent TV displayed Ainsley receiving a major tournament award. Jack watched idly as the kid sneered at the duchess, snatched the goblet, then turned contemptuously to the camera, in order to deliver a short message to his public. The message contained only one word, 'Cunts', which Jack was able to lip read without much trouble.

He had invited Guy and Deany over for supper that evening and they would be arriving shortly. He entered the walk-in wardrobe and picked out a suit. A lightweight tropical cloth for a warm night. The thought of the immense but untapped resources of room service still made him feel restless, and he had made something of a hobby of testing its versatility. One of his more mundane practices involved ordering the cleaning and pressing of all his garments, right down to tie and socks and including suit, on a nightly basis. He had no time for the notion that a crisp shirt engenders a comparable mental state, he simply found it intriguing that a machine existed solely to replicate aspects of the home life of people who loved their homes. As a Venusian with no innate nesting instinct he could use the situation to learn a lot about the natives without having to enter their dwellings.

Guy and Deany were hovering near the bar when Jack emerged from the lift.

218

'Want a shower?' he asked Deany.

'Definitely. Give me twenty minutes.' She smiled and took the key. Her hair was dotted with small dark burrs and scraps of leaf.

'Guy. G and t with i and l?'

'That would be most welcome, Jack.' Guy was wearing his long-trouser outfit tonight, so Jack's attention, inclined to its customary perusal of the state of Guy's skin, was drawn to his face and neck. Whatever the arrangement of flushes, their effect was always to make Guy appear startled. Currently a sallow band of paleness ran right across his eyes, separating two vivid scarlet areas that comprised his brow, and his mouth and chin. Despite his fatigued and passive manner, he wore the mask of a man staring wildly out from a place of concealment.

Jack tapped the pile of newspapers he had brought down with him. 'Coach party incident,' he said, and sighed.

'How do you mean?'

'Yes. Bunch of people returning from a garden festival, stopped off at a pub. Having drinks outside and they see one.'

'Where?' Guy enquired urgently.

'Way up north. Can't remember. Burgate, was it?'

'That's the furthest yet. I find it hard to believe.' He gulped at his drink without savouring it.

'Well, yeah. Anyway, they had a sort of game with it, so it says.'

Guy groaned and let his head slump to his chest. 'I don't think I can bear to hear.'

'No. Someone kicked it, with the best of intentions, apparently, and it knocked over the shopping bag of someone's grandmother.'

'Why do they *kick* them? It's beyond me,' Guy muttered, forgetfully.

'So these two groups formed, one that liked the grandmother and the other that liked this person that tried to put it out of its misery. They both wanted to end the suffering, but a competitive element entered the situation.'

'These are rare creatures!' Guy raised his arms to gesticulate but gave up and slumped back in the chair.

'Quite rare. Not as much as they were. The way they breed.'

'We know nothing about them! And people are kicking them!'

'They were kicking it all over the place, apparently. The publican called the cops.'

'At last.'

'No. They broke some tables in the beer garden. So he called them.'

219

Guy sat up suddenly. 'They rescued it?'

'They couldn't find it.'

'It got away.'

'They kicked it to pieces.'

'What?'

'There was nothing left. Obviously there must have been bones or something, but they didn't crop up. Maybe dogs had them.'

Guy gazed at Jack in disbelief. 'Every day, Jack. Somewhere or other.'

'Yep. A lot of these people got arrested. For disturbing the peace. They just took in everyone with blood on their shoes. Which was a good thirty of them, so it says.'

'But where are *we* in all this?'

'Beg pardon?'

'We never get there.'

'Guy – they're scattered around. It just seems like a lot.'

'It *is* a lot. And if it isn't now, it will be very soon. Gestation is clearly remarkably short, and reproductive viability is obtaining before the animal is fully physically mature. If it were smaller this would indicate a short lifespan, possibly under a year.'

'Big things live longer.'

'On the whole. But they also have longer periods of gestation. In this case it's possible that the inability of the parents to tend their young has resulted in their being born in an advanced state of self-sufficiency, bringing a proportionately early fertility. If we make assumptions based on short gestation, it brings a certain urgency to the situation. Unless we can secure specimens soon, from the first two generations, we'll never be able to assess the animal in terms of its original habitat. Its current environment couldn't be more different and its diet will have changed radically. All this could induce different behaviour and growth patterns, and each generation will depart a little more from the true nature of the animal.'

'That's bad.'

'Of course it is. Eke could be dead already, Jack!'

'Still got Ike. Breed him with a girl, when we get one.'

Guy shook his head agitatedly. 'It's not right, Jack. Everything gets blurred.'

'Blurred. I don't know what you mean,' Jack said. Guy frowned and scratched his arm through his pullover. Jack continued, 'You're never going to find Eke, Guy. But the more they breed the more you're going to get a girl. Obvious.'

Guy sat forward and stared at Jack from the livid mask. He spoke softly, but with great insistence. 'It has to be Eke. It has to be.'

'Oh well! I didn't know this, you see! I didn't know we were actually going to throw back the ones that aren't the right one!'

'We shall keep every animal we find. We shall save as many as possible. But if my work is to develop properly I must recover Eke.'

Guy was still scratching at his arm, in his usual distracted manner, with an increasing ferocity that made it seem as if his limbs were animated by a separate intelligence.

'Wow,' Jack said.

The men sat in silence. For a while Jack mulled over the enormity of Guy's declaration, then found himself drawn again to the absorbing matter of his companion's complexion. At the point where Guy had sat forward to disclose the hopeless impossibility of his project, his facial colouring had suddenly changed. The stripe across his eyes was washed away by the creeping apex of a triangular formation of scarlet which seeped down from his brow, maintaining his nose, mouth and part of his chin in their original pigment, but somehow leaching all the colour from his cheeks and neck. It was as if the shadow of one peak of a tricorn hat had fallen across his face, lending the wearer an air of deceptive gauntness and cartoon-like determination. All his vital features were now framed in one form, and the effect was so apposite that Jack began to wonder if there were any literal link between the things Guy said or did and the blotching of his skin that accompanied them.

An interesting theory presented itself – if Guy's skin condition constituted a running commentary on his behaviour and feelings, this should present the observer with a means of reading him off, even though Guy might wish to conceal himself. With a demeanour as bland as his any increase in access would be welcome, especially if the observer had more than idle reasons for wishing to construe his subject in depth. Trouble was the configuration of the markings on Guy seemed random in the extreme; a reliable decoding scheme would have to be built up from a basis of multiple correlations, and who could be bothered to do that? At the end of the day perhaps the most that could be said was that Guy had lost a means of keeping himself to himself. There now existed a visible counterpoint to his everyday style of presentation, and it seemed to indicate a dimension that was scarcely suggested by his usual light,

221

dithering manner. Jack thought that Guy could no longer lie to him, but he still had no way of telling what the truths might be.

'I took one of your shirts,' Deany announced as she joined them in the bar. She had washed her hair and tied it back in a pony tail so that it would not dampen Jack's white linen button-down. Jack smiled appreciatively. 'Fresh as a daisy,' he said, in the archly jovial tone he sometimes dropped into when talking to Deany in Guy's presence. Guy half rose from his seat, which meant that he had to stop raking the flesh of his arm.

'Something to drink, darling? Jack?'

'Let's eat.' Deany turned from Guy to Jack. 'Can we eat?'

'Let's eat,' Jack said.

'Christ, I could eat,' she said, as they walked to the dining room.

'Who knows about wine?' Jack asked, looking up from the list.

'They say red's good,' Deany offered.

'Where'd you hear that?'

'TV. A man had some on a table. Said we should rush out and get some.'

'Sounds biased, but it is a lead.' He flipped to the back of the list.

'That's the high end, Jack.'

'Eliminates risk. I hate it when it cleans your teeth on the way down, don't you?' He extended his gaze so that Guy was included. The naturalist was studying the menu. His lips were arranged in their usual pastiche of a smile, which might have indicated his appreciation of the banter between Jack and his wife, but in fact signalled his inability to derive amusement from banter, period. His eyes registered consternation, which was not his reaction to the great variety of the cuisine, but a distillation of the general dismay with which he daily faced the world itself.

Guy had not looked up, so Jack pulled him in. 'Guy – something old from France, do you think?'

'I don't mind, Jack. Whatever you'd like.'

'Right. We've sounded out the enthusiasts and we're poised to make a choice.' He summoned a waiter and ordered the most expensive item on the list.

'Gee, Jack, you want to clean us all out?'

'It's on me. I'm buying. Sort of.' Deany looked at him quizzically, so he added, 'The whole meal is my pleasure.'

'That's very kind, Jack, but it's really not necessary. You've given us so much of your time, we should be treating you,' Guy said.

'It's nothing.'

Deany was still looking at him curiously. 'Don't go wild, Jack. You haven't been able to work for weeks. Gotta hang on to the savings, yeah?'

Jack very nearly let a startled look out onto his face. He covered his confusion by reaching for a glass of water. Taking a quick sip, he said 'Who saves? Goes in the front of the wallet and straight out the back.' He grinned at her. There was no way she could know about the Ainsley deal, but why was she interested, all of a sudden?

'Well, right. You don't know where it's coming from next.'

'Hey – what's my job? What do I do?' he protested.

'Okay. You do know where it's coming from. But you aren't working right now. Right?'

For a moment Jack wondered whether to tell her about his new powers, but he rejected the idea immediately. Neither she nor Guy would be capable of understanding the mechanics of the thing, let alone the vision from which the operation drew its impetus. They would see it all in terms of deeds, and probably chastise him. He could not afford to be accredited with cunning by either of them.

'I do phone readings,' he said.

'Huh?'

'Yeah. A lot of my people take scans by phone. I don't need to be there, once I know the person.'

The fact that this current pronouncement had some slight substance to it did not particularly ease its passage or lend its inventor a spurious reassurance. He just said it, and thereby stepped over an awkward situation. In fact he had, from time to time, got in the habit of giving on-the-spot forecasts to certain clients by phone, but it had been over a year since he had actually done any.

'What, you kind of feel them out down the line?'

'Most of my clients I know what they're doing right now, at this very moment. And in an hour's time. I don't need to feel them out.'

'That's sad.'

'It's nothing to do with sad.'

'Still, it pays.'

'Yep.'

Round about the middle of the main course, almost through a second bottle of wine, while Jack and Deany were enjoying their fish and Guy was eating his steak. Deany happened to catch sight of the back of

Guy's right hand.

'Got some crap on your hand, Guy.'

Jack and Guy looked. Guy's hand glistened with a partial coating of a glutinous, translucent liquid.

'Fat,' Jack said.

Guy wiped the liquid off with his napkin.

'Got it on the other hand now,' Jack observed.

Guy nodded and wiped his left hand.

'Honey, it's coming out of your skin, isn't it?' Deany asked.

'It's just, it's quite hot in here, doesn't agree with me. Yes, I should take my jumper off.'

He pushed his chair back and removed the garment. His short-sleeved shirt revealed his bare forearms, the left of which was entirely red, while the right was largely greyish. Both bore expanses of cracked, scaly skin, some freshly broken open by scratching.

'God, Guy, it's all over!' Deany gasped.

The thick liquid covered both arms, apart from the scaly patches. It reminded Jack of wallpaper paste.

Deany put down her knife and fork. 'You didn't have that before, did you? This morning? I didn't see it.'

'It's the heat here. It's very close. It just doesn't help it.' Guy was holding his arms out above the table, unsure what to do with them.

'Should you wipe them? Maybe?' She looked around the dining room nervously.

Jack said, 'Just wipe them, Guy. Use the serviette. They got hundreds of them. Go on.'

Guy picked up the square white cloth, dropped his arms below table level and carefully rubbed them down. He crushed the napkin into a ball and was about to put it back on the table when he hesitated, and dropped his hand back to his side.

'What shall I do with it?'

'We'll get another one,' Jack replied, and waved to a passing waiter.

Guy and Deany both said, 'Jack . . .!' but the waiter was upon them.

'Got another serviette for here? Thanks.'

The waiter took the crushed napkin from a reluctant Guy and moved away.

'What do they care?' Jack said. 'It's a factory here.'

'They look okay now,' Deany observed with relief.

'Of course. It's really nothing to get fussed about.' Guy cut at

224

the piece of steak that had been cooling on his plate. His measured movements seemed to insist that the episode was now history.

'I was telling Guy about the coach party item,' Jack said brightly.

'Yeah. I heard it on the radio in your room. Long way from here, right?'

'Soon be all over the place, can't escape from that.'

'Well, that improves our chances, doesn't it?'

'Just what I said to Guy. He didn't agree.'

'How come?' She turned to look at her husband.

Guy stopped eating and pushed his plate to one side. He took a deep breath. 'Look . . .' He let the breath out in a heavy sigh. 'I know you both think I'm a bit, a bit stubborn . . .'

'Darling, have I ever said that?'

'Well, I know things have been going on for a long time, and that it isn't exactly the best life in the world for you.' He stopped her next protestation with a shake of his head. 'So I've made a decision.' Jack and Deany waited expectantly.

'I'm going on the television.' He looked at Jack and Deany expectantly. They both nodded, as if going on the television were the very thing they had been about to suggest.

'There won't be any problem. Ian Costello. Elizabeth Preeny. They'd slot me in.'

'What did you have in mind, Guy?' Jack asked, casually.

'Well, ideally, the news. But one of the magazine programmes would be adequate.'

'Adequate for what, darling?'

'I want to talk to the people of Britain.'

'They've got no conversation, Guy,' Jack said. Deany glared at him.

'What do you want to say to the people of Britain, Guy?' she asked quietly. Her shoulders had hunched up, and she was gripping her cutlery far too hard.

Guy took another breath, and as he spoke, his voice shook. 'They are destroying one of the most vital resources of the planet. At a time of impending ecological catastrophe on a global level they are wilfully eliminating a discovery that may, for all we know, show us a path through this nightmare. They . . .'

'It's not wilful, is it? They have good intentions. They just want to put the animals out of their misery.'

'Nobody likes pain, do they?' Jack said, philosophically.

225

'Deany, please! I do not wish to impugn the people of Britain! I shall explain the situation to them, show them the priorities that the scientists have.'

'What will they do?'

Guy reached for his wine glass and drank its contents in three long gulps. Jack filled him up again, and noticed that his face had become blotch-free, probably for the first time in weeks.

'They'll stop the killing, and hand the animals in. I don't know why I didn't think of it before.'

'You could have rewards,' Jack suggested.

'There are no funds, Jack. People will understand the situation without inducements.'

'Darling,' Deany began carefully, 'do you think they'll collect up all of them?'

'They seem to have better luck than us, that's for sure,' Jack said.

'It is possible that a substantial majority of the animals will be recovered.'

'And Eke. You hope.' Jack looked at Deany. 'That's what he hopes.'

'I want the killing to stop,' Guy said. He ran his hand through his hair, and his arm was no longer grey. 'Once the animals are recovered, I shall strive to establish a conservation area.'

'Where they can live happily,' said Jack.

'It will be a major research facility. At that point I'm confident there would be no shortage of funds.' He emphasised his certainty with a sweep of his left arm, which had lost every trace of its redness. 'The sheer volume of animals will convince the Medical Research Council that the project is eminently worthy of support.'

'Medical?' Jack asked. 'You going to cure them?'

'Of course not. Once we understand the nature of their condition, the implications for the welfare of mankind are immense.'

'Really? It's good for us?'

Guy placed his unmarked forearms on the dining table. Without angry splashes his face seemed suddenly noble, clear, strong. He picked up his wine glass and emptied it in one long draught. Deany blinked in surprise. Guy looked at his companions with great seriousness. His skin seemed to glow, but Jack thought that this was probably a relative effect deriving its impact from sheer novelty.

'We're looking at the future, Jack. We are contemplating the vanquishment of the single most negative aspect of man's existence.'

'Boredom,' Jack said.

'I mean the possibility of understanding, truly understanding, the nature of pain.'

'Economics?'

'Physical pain, Jack. The animals represent the locus of a unique neurological condition. Submitted to the disciplines of neurology, physiology and biochemistry they will eventually surrender their secrets to us.'

'If they won't, we'll torture them!'

Deany spoke before Guy could continue. 'What have you been thinking about, Guy?' Her tone was cautious but accusative.

'I started to see it a few days ago. It sort of dawned on me.'

Guy really looked absurdly healthy, Jack thought. His face was radiating wellbeing, and even the scaly patches on his arms seemed to have grown less livid. Must be the drink. Jack picked up the wine bottle.

'Better finish it off, Guy.' He emptied the bottle into Guy's glass.

'That's very kind of you, Jack.'

'Guy! What dawned on you?'

'I saw a picture, Deany. Of a world without pain.' He smiled calmly, almost compassionately, at his wife.

'Something to look forward to, Deany,' said Jack, who had started to feel something coming up, but was not going to let it deflate the particularly good mood he had been incubating throughout the evening. He noticed that Deany, on the other hand, had suddenly become very dejected. She sat back against the chair, started to speak, stopped herself, then leaned forward again, with her elbows on the table and her head in her hands.

'I don't know what you mean,' she said, looking straight down at her plate, 'a world without pain – it doesn't mean anything. There'll always be pain, Guy. It's . . . it's just experience, it's a matter of degree. You're saying you want to stop having experience?' Still she could not look at him, but shook her head slowly, as if terribly fatigued.

'Deany, look at how we live. Look at our bodies.' Deany looked up, and saw Guy's body, which, in the low light of the dining room, seemed to have acquired a faint aura, a barely perceptible outline of misty, violet light. As Guy gestured, the light flowed with his limbs, creating ghostly outlines in the air. Jack looked across the room and out through the terrace windows, noticing that the sun was sinking behind the distant hills. Only one or two small lamps had so far been turned on, and the room had assumed the shifting, ambiguous shadowiness that enveloped the land outside.

'How can we grow when the very cells of our body must combat unremitting forces whose effect is to deform their very chemistry?'

'What?' Jack said. He signalled to the waiter.

'I don't know what you're saying,' said Deany. 'What forces?'

'Me too,' interjected Jack, who was ordering a very sweet white wine. 'I ordered a sweet one, for contrast,' he explained.

'It's so clear now, it's so clear,' Guy insisted. 'Nobody has looked at the blood – that's where the answer is.'

'Thought it was nerves, you said,' Jack said, trying to keep abreast.

'We mediate via the blood, Jack. This is where these terrible pressures make their impact. We're not just one body, you know.'

'Uh.' Jack managed to express simultaneous curiosity, perplexity and understanding. Deany was simply staring at Guy. She did not move at all.

'Think of the life that's inside us – the actual independent forms. You must have seen blood under a microscope, Jack.'

'On TV once. I can't remember what happened.'

'Well, you remember the leucocytes and the lymphocytes, the white blood corpuscles. They sustain us and protect us. Well,' and he spoke with even greater portentousness, 'they are alive! They are independent! Moving through our bodies constantly!'

'It's disgusting. Somebody ought to do something.'

'But why do we not grow, Jack?'

'We do, what are you talking about?'

'But it isn't enough, is it? And it's so cruel! So utterly cruel! Within our very skin, countless life forms are enduring all the excesses of our civilisation. What protection is there? He looked at them each in turn, pausing for their answer. Deany was crying, and the failing light caught the tears and made them sparkle on her cheeks.

'Not quite getting the connections here, Guy,' Jack said, breaking a silence of several long seconds.

Guy, who had actually been smiling throughout much of his exposition, adopted a grave expression. He studied Deany, apparently quite closely, but showed no sign of discomfort or sympathy. Then he looked straight at Jack, which surprised the latter for Guy rarely undertook eye contact with him for more than a few moments at a time.

Jack, who refused to accept that the ball was in his court, looked back at Guy.

Guy began breathing deeply and regularly. He swallowed, then swallowed again, hard, as though he had failed to repel a rising gorge. Jack saw that the mistiness had evaporated from the light that seemed to hang about his head and arms. Now a distinct and incandescent layer of violet light covered all the flesh that Jack could see. It appeared to continue beneath Guy's shirt sleeves and emerge at his open collar, covering his face and hair yet not obscuring his features in any way.

Suddenly Guy whispered, 'It's very hot.' He took his eyes off Jack and pushed his chair away from the table. Deany gasped. Beneath the violet light Guy's skin oozed tiny silver globules. Every pore seemed to release a perfect glistening sphere, and for two, or three, or four seconds the effect was profoundly beautiful. Guy was wreathed in a shimmering beaded light that caught all the luminosity in the room and multiplied it.

'So hot . . .'

The silver jewels burst and Guy was flaming. The violet glow broke into flickering tongues of fire which played along his forearms and danced on his palms. Fire lapped the lashes of his eyes and quivered on his lips. It scoured the niches of his ears and lightly rolled around every blonde hair on his head.

He looked out from the flames beseechingly. Deany gave a low, guttural groan and fell away from the table in a faint. Jack watched in admiration, partly for his own prophetic achievements. The dining room was utterly silent.

'Jack . . .'

Shit, his clothes'll go up, Jack thought. He seized the bottle of dessert wine and jumped to his feet. Moving swiftly round the table he stood behind Guy's chair and inverted the bottle over his head. As the flames receded he leaned over and stuck the neck down the front of Guy's shirt. The wine sluiced over the naturalist's stomach and darkened the crotch of his trousers. Jack grabbed Guy's right arm by the elbow and swept the bottle down from his shoulder to his wrist, and then repeated this manoeuvre on the other arm. Glancing at the bottle he saw that he had only a couple of inches left so he splashed it over Guy's shoes.

Jack stood back. Guy had been extinguished.

'You're out,' he said, panting slightly.

'Sir . . .?' The waiter appeared at his shoulder.

'Ah! He insulted me!'

The waiter could not muster a response. He tried not to stare at the sodden Guy or the unconscious Deany.

'We're old friends though. So perhaps another serviette. Or three. And another bottle. And the sweet trolley. Yeah.'

Deany came round and Jack gave her a fresh glass of wine. She wanted to drive straight back to the tent but Jack insisted that she and Guy both stay the night in the hotel. It would be his treat. Guy gave in almost immediately. After they had left the table, Jack finished the wine and ate a plateful of fruit trifle with cream. He followed it with a large brandy and the over-large balloon concentrated the vapours so much that his eyes watered as he tilted the glass. Then he ordered a long cigar and held it under his nose for several minutes before lighting it. Some of his best thinking went on at the dinner table, he thought.

'Fucking Ish! What he fucking did!' says Roylana. The crowd have some time to kill and are standing around in their jewelled garments. Holes is over with Butler, got their heads together and murmuring stuff. 'Ish' is split off and strolling out on the far distance. The rest of the team are all of one mind. 'Shit,' says Roylana, who is wearing this all-over mesh that follows her body, stuck with jewels, every type winking, 'had the wind up through my hair, had a nice breeze running, then snat! the fucking boy goes through the wall no permit, no visa! Over the wire with the beads and mirrors! If we wish to do gift offers, okay, then everybody is wired to one plug, no freelunch pussy is to cut from the pack while we're all still doing parcel wrap! This is so true, yeah, Dashy, huh?'

Slopes, in his gem outfit, crusted with brilliants, general sparklefeast effect, even got jasper and lapis hatband, ruby monogram on the cape, garnet dental detail, lots of facet beam, has to agree. Roylana, in her way, has reminded them of 'Ish's' despicable move with the precious stone. After Holes had deliberately loaded that controversial rock with solid unfathomable 'no call for it' material, so as to quash the after effects of the cashflow Pushthrough, the 'Ish' had mixed in this bonanza *value* element without consulting him. Result was a big hoohah on the 'outside', where it seems the rock is discovered to be abloc with ore redeemables cashwise and the outside agent is hot again to stripmine the client.

'I mean shit, Dashy, and then he bursts out with the fuckin *blowtorch!* I mean this is *daywork* we're talking!'

Since the major underground presentation culminating with rock Pushthrough they have been entirely taken up with daywork, a rare pleasure. Basically it is an outside decorating job where they get to try out mixnmatch jewellery effects on the client's outer limit, various accessories in tasteful combinations according to mood. They were cruising around very satisfactorily, on a gradual build, up to when suddenly! thanks to 'Ish', it is all snatched away! the gang gasps! they were saying it with flowers and the boy delivers the greenhouse!

The crowd have nothing against Pushthrough, you understand, well maybe Butler is picky, but what they don't like is where one person slips on the track shoe when the rest still have the lead diver boot. Plus in addition they wish to cleave with John: he launches some tangibles, they'll take the pace from him. This constitutes an all-time company first and they want to get it right, it's that craft thing, that workmanship pride and cetera. Pushthrough is their dream – it's like you spend a million years pulling back the bow and letting it go, thinking, 'What is this, a stringed instrument?' and Tuesday morning without harbinger someone says, 'Oh, here's the arrow.' The fucking arrow at last!!

But after 'Ish' cracked out of turn with the flamethrower display, they feel distinctly a leaky team. Holes is not serene, and Butler is not far behind him.

Butler: 'John, I can hobble that boy. Just say.'

Holes: (raspy) 'Michael. He'd slip the rope. We have to ask. Was there malfeasance?'

Butler: 'He jumped the gun, John.' (refers to flame effects)

Holes: (slow deep) 'History, Michael. Now. Boy is coltish. Sees the jewellery going out, but no heed back. Gets antsy.'

Butler: 'We still have jewellery by the rack, John. We were gradualising, no? (prefers to display jewels from the *in* side)

Holes: (out of a dark pit) 'This whole business. We're always chasing. And all we see is arse.'

Butler: 'So we step it up, John. We have the facility, just say.' (avers there is plenty of good material still in the racks)

Holes: (foghorn in a black shaft) 'He's after rabbits, Michael. Doesn't see the dogs behind.' (implies the client is so busy hunting he doesn't look at the jewel show)

Butler: 'Which is why I say step it up.'

Holes: (chain cranks under sand) 'We rack. He runs. Every time. So.' (prepares big resolve)

Butler: 'You're thinking, John?'

Holes: (electric storm in next county) 'I figure to spring clean.'

Michael Butler reels. As lieutenant he should be cool but this is a boneshaker. He looks to see if the gang picked it up. They are still muttering 'fuck that "Ish"' shit. Turns to Holes, stalling for air. 'Spring clean? John?'

Holes looks to Butler's eyes. He looks with the shark, the flatbed lathe, the big meateaters that died in the sudden freeze, the piercing shell that finds bone regardless of race or creed, the glacier that gravels over you, the shrike that spikes you.

Just for a glimpse John looks at Michael like that. Michael reels.

'Speak English? Michael?'

'I understand completely, John.'

'Want to tell them?'

'Um . . .'

'I'll tell them.'

The crowd see Holes coming.

'Oop,' goes O'Bably.

'Hey,' says 'Dead'. Both these old hands see how the boss has this glare on him. He has this big vector going, this whole *quality*.

Holes gets there, to the crowd, and says, 'Andrew!' and the 'Ish' catches it, comes in from the side, this cruel easy walk he has, and he's nodding at John, to say 'Well, I hear you heard about me, John. That's nice.'

The crowd looks at Andrew, they feel he parked the bus in the shitter. He just gives that so derisive glance under the lashes. Fucking 'Ish' knows he did wrong and he knows some momentous shit is coming.

So Holes nods around the team, still with the *quality*. 'Dead' cuts in. 'John, that fuckin "Ish"! I got diamonds to burn still!'

The crowd gives a general kind of swell of going along with 'Dead'.

Holes: 'This big collection hobby. This rabbit hunt. For shit. We only see arse. So. Make a major motion. Now.' (says pissed off with client, let's action)

They look to each other, what is this?

Holes: 'I go for Pushthrough. Again.'

O'Bably, he loves Pushthrough, lets go a yodel. Slopes does his buglehole blastout, that razz from the rearflap to show both ends burning to go.

Holes: 'No party! Last ditch! I see us back to yesterday soon.' (chiding)

Well that's strong terms from the smokevoiced figure, so the crowd hush it down a piece. Holes is saying how the client is so raced-off with his big collection project he wouldn't notice his dick is in the mincer. You hang out the sapphires, make those fine ruby gashes, give earrings, necklaces, brooches, bracelets, clasps, cuisses and cuirasses, splash it all over, and the sum is nertz – the client steps out of it like they are socks. Plus the client has a whole *new* scheme on the hob, where he proposes the big all-eyes world communications pitch and this gives him the sandboy outlook meanwhile back at the base the crowd are still strapped for a rock pool.

Holes: 'This time no more giveaways. Close down the cashables. Fresh start. Outdross. We spring clean.'

Shit the crowd are bullrushed. It's like everything before this was training. This could be the career acme, the craft peak, the point of the point, the major motion. Woo, they churn around, gladding hands, serious nods, we're ready for it, rubbing the palms, nudge movements, take me to the gate, pave my soles, latch off the hatch, let's basically unfuckinleash.

'So when is that enormous day, please John yeah?' says Roylana, on her tiptoes, lovely arms both waving, she can't believe he means it, can't believe he says, 'I want the team to take full responsibility', after all the passes, the moves, the thousand nights.

'I shall name it. Roylana. You shall be the first to know,' Holes.

'Gotta get me some inoculations!' yells 'Dead', and he holds out his arms, goes naked, goes red, and bursts. Gack everywhere, they're about to go yecch, and he's back, in a neat morning suit, topper, cane, gloves, spats, carnation, best man for the outing.

Joyous roar the gang. Spring clean! Spring clean!

And in this joy, beneath it, is seedling sorrow. No longer will they, our roaring friends, be known by their traces, no longer will they live within mists and masks. We shall find their works in our streets now – hard, clear, separate. They will leave behind their soft, spaceless places, and make their model suggestions in utter utterance.

'I know, finally, people of Britain, that the age-old community of man and beast is still a powerful memory for us all, never far below the surface of the difficult lives so many of us perforce now lead. We recall, filtered down through the ages, reinforced by the images from dramas, paintings and pageants, the marvellous closeness to the horse, the falcon and the dog. Few now know the thrill of the talon on the gauntleted wrist but many enjoy a canine companion, or indeed a cat.

'Indeed, on my own recent excursions in search of my tragic charges, I have been the grateful beneficiary of the unwavering support, both practical and moral, of my setter Cindy. It is these timeless links between the species that I bring to your attention now, at one of those increasingly rare moments in history when the continuing wonder of the natural world is visited upon us in the shape of a new major mammal. Let us not be carried away by our awe – let us instead hark back to the days when there was probably a new animal every year, creatures of many furs and hues, all welcomed into the great selection and taken as proof that life is actually extremely interesting and not sent to try us. I believe we can all find some truth in these notions, and I urge you to respond, for the greater future benefit of mankind, by handing in all found animals to one of the addresses that will shortly appear on your screen. Thank you.'

A warm ripple of applause ran through the studio as members of the crew put aside the apparatus of their trade and spontaneously registered their appreciation. Miss Desperanza felt strangely stimulated but decided not to join in in case she disrupted the concentrated atmosphere at her end of the set.

'Oh, that was terribly moving,' sniffed Patti Allen, Susie Marshall's assistant.

'My dear, you crying,' Miss Desperanza observed, raising her arms while a sound man pulled at the microphone cable that led from the back of her jacket out into the darkness beyond the bright pool of light enveloping her, Susie and Ainsley.

'Animals affect everybody, don't they?' said the sound man.

'Oh, certamente, Zelka effect me with great frequency,' she replied, looking around for her dashing pet. 'She is with someone?'

'Tina still has her, Silvia,' said Patti, but an indignant bark from the far end of the studio suggested that this assertion was no longer accurate.

'Tina! For God's sake!' yelled the floor manager. 'Get it out!'

'Zelka! What does she do? She is so curious!' said Silvia, straining to see between the cameras.

'Jerry, Jerry, I'm sorry! She yanked the lead out of my hand!'

'Well, Jesus, take her outside and tie her to something!'

A moment later a flushed young woman hurried past Miss Desperanza's setup, dragging Zelka behind her. Silvia waved to the dog and cried, 'What did you do, sweetheart?'

'She rushed at Guy Blighton's legs, right after he finished. I couldn't stop her!'

'She didn't bite?'

'Oh no! She found something on the ground there, and started eating it, and then I got her and she didn't want to go!'

'See – she still eats! What did she find, you know?'

'I'm afraid I didn't see – just something by Guy Blighton's shoes.'

Susie interrupted, 'Silvia, I'm afraid we have to start. Take her to Miss Desperanza's dressing room, Tina.'

Silvia shrugged, waved at Zelka again and turned to wink at Ainsley.

The champ, whose normally sulky features had shown some signs of interest during Guy's address, had been watching the more recent proceedings with disdain. Silvia's wink caught him by surprise, and he quickly looked away and stared fixedly up into the lights.

'Five seconds, four, three, two, one. Cue and cut to three.'

'How fitting it is that one of our next guests, on her last visit to this country, also experienced distress with animals. It must all seem a terrible memory to you now, Silvia Desperanza, over here at the moment to attend the opening of a new Eva Kuwait film.'

'Oh yes Susie, *Eva Kuwait Goes Home*, it was a great nightmare when my dog is strock by the champagna in the middle of the falling escaffolds but the meraviglious Jeck Garvin kiss her back from the dead.'

'Yes, viewers may remember the heroic deed of the local seer beside the disastrous supermarket. Well Silvia, the idea of going home, what an exciting thought soon to be widely in our cinemas.'

'In fact the eighteen film of Eva, Susie.'

'Your enduring series is loved nationally and perhaps a hint of the pleasures within this the most recent, I'm sure we would be agog.'

'Pardon?'

'Please tell us a little of the plot and excitements.'

'Si. Some groups of men are climbing through the mountains in a faroff place to look for this most valuable book, si? It is, what do you say . . . dic, dicsh . . .'

'A dictionary?'

'Yes, and most rare, every thing in this dictioner is the same . . .'

'You mean it's all one word?'

'No, no, every word, when you look at it, has the same word beside it. Understand? You look for "automobile" and it says "automobile".'

'How wonderful! It must be very heavy.'

'No.'

'And this is the story?'

'Oh no! Is an element.'

'Ah.'

'Yes. This is just the object of these hardoned men. They are all pursue it for money, they do not love books. Each is from different criminal organisations, and so the safety of the world is under very great threat. So Eva Kuwait must get it first, but when they are all climbing they come over the climaxes of the mountain and there is a whole place below them and it is where they live.'

'Yes.'

'Their home is below them.'

'Which is convenient?'

'But they are living in Italy.'

'So they have found their way back to Italy.'

'No. This is the most peculiar event – they are faroff from Italia. Understand?'

'It sounds very original.'

'You see, there is their house, and their wifes, and their street, everything. It is a big puzzle.'

'And terribly confusing. And what does Eva do?'

'Ah, you must find out!'

'And a great many of us will I'm sure among them our other guest tonight, someone who needs no introduction.'

'Ainsley.'

'Hello Ainsley, the most influential sportsman at large. I understand you have followed Silvia?'

'Yes.'

'What do you think?'

'What about?'

'Her films.'

'Yes, they're good.'

'And?'

'They take you out of yourself.'

236

'What's that like, can you tell us, Ainsley?'

'I should imagine for ordinary people it's a good idea because their lives are shit.'

'Is your life like that?'

'Like what?'

'Shit.'

'I've got everything I want.'

'This must be very gratifying.'

'Of course it fucking is.'

'But the experience of the cinema?'

'It gives relaxation.'

'Which we all need.'

'I thought we were talking about me.'

'How is it for you?'

'I just said.'

'I believe the last of Silvia's films seen by you, Ainsley, was *Eva Kuwait and the Church of the Two Things*.'

'That is correct.'

'And?'

'Do you think my work is effortless, Miss Marshall?'

'I don't quite . . .'

'Answer the question.'

'Well, Ainsley, frequently you move so fast that one cannot evaluate the effort in the various moves.'

'My smash, my blur.'

'Just two examples from a whole range.'

'And superb.'

'Oh yes.'

'And have brought me to the absolute peak where no fucker can vanquish me. Ever.'

'You are without doubt the most accomplished sportsman of our known era.'

'And you think it just happens.'

'I'm sure there is training.'

'Training! How can I train, Miss Marshall? Tell me.'

'Viewers would be fascinated to hear of the behind-the-scenes sessions.'

'Fuck the viewers! How do you think I train, cunt?'

'With people?'

'Who? Who can fucking do it? No one! They just stand there! They serve, I smash, they're fucked. I serve, they can't fucking see it. What do I do, get a fucking machine?'

'Yet you are never off peak.'

'Listen, I'm unfit. How could I get fit? How could I get near my real potential? There is nobody on this shithouse planet who can give me any fucking competition!!'

'We all eagerly await the forthcoming championship with explosive young Panamanian Hector "El Swoosh" Vasquez, seen by many as good.'

'Vasquez! That fucking little smear! His mother still buys his underpants! I'll eat that fucking chimp and puke him down the pisshole! I just hope he can run with his shorts full of shit and his fucking hairoil on fire.'

'You don't anticipate a marvellous match?'

'Jesus fuck! I've never *had* a fucking *match* in my life! These smears queue up and I vanquish them. That's it. Is it any wonder I go to the pictures?'

'The films of our Italian guest must be a great relief.'

'It's something to do.'

'Of course great shock was widely felt after the terrible maiming of two picturegoers and the paralysis of a third in the cheap seats by darts during a showing of *Eva Kuwait and the Two Things*.'

'Scusi.'

'What better moment than to turn again to our delightful and experienced visitor from Europe.'

'*The* Church *of the Two Things*.'

'Forgive me for my error, Silvia. Had you heard of the awful woundings?'

'Si. I saw some photographs of the girl with the arrow in her neck.'

'Dart. Although amusingly you have used the working man's expression for the sporting implement.'

'You know, Susie, it makes you realise, the cinema is so dangerous a place.'

'Yes, Silvia, and I wonder what our prominent sport celebrity feels about this new danger where before it was considered the safe place to be?'

'I can't see anything wrong with it.'

'Oh no! You make a jock!'

238

'What do you want, armed protection? You want a police state? You don't like people to express themselves? You don't know where you're living!'

'In these troubled times all people must follow their urges is your remarkable view?'

'Look, Miss Marshall, why is life shit for all humans? Because nobody does anything any more. There's no excitement. You sit in the cheap seats you take what fucking comes, it seems to me.'

'But Silvia, is life so bad as this, in your native country? Where the cheap seats means taking it in the neck or similar from thrill-seekers?'

'Life is bad, I think.'

'Oh. What about thrill-seekers?'

'They must go with their darts to a pob.'

'That's completely ridiculous. You've got the lights on, people right next to you. You know who you'll hit before you fucking throw it! People want excitement, they don't like to predict everything!'

'Well, that is an encouraging thought for those who are young and meaningless and how very stimulating my guests have been this evening with their unexpected philosophical output: Silvia Desperanza, so charming with her latest and exciting *Eva Kuwait Goes Home* now available and Ainsley, perhaps the most famous person ever to visit this television facility with his upcoming big world championship. Thank you very much.'

'Thank you, Susie! Can we have the seafood man, please?'

'Patti, did you see where my husband went?'

'Hello, Mrs Blighton! He's probably back in the hospitality room, isn't he?'

'You want to point me there, I get lost with all these doors.'

'It's right through that exit, down the corridor, through two lots of swing doors and then fourth door on the right.'

'Okay.'

'Tina! You can take Miss Desperanza's dog to hospitality now.'

'Ainsley, what a wonderful exchange of views! What can I get you?'

'Water.'

'Do you know Mrs Deany Blighton, the wife of Guy Blighton who was on just before you?'

'No.'

'Mrs Blighton, I'm sure you know Ainsley who did a marvellous interview after Mr Blighton.'

'Hi.'

'Hello.'

'Patti, I've got the dog.'

'Just hang on, Tina. She'll be here any minute.'

'I'll give it some water.'

'Mister Blighton! I am so very move with your discourse!'

'Miss Desperanza! That was your dog, wasn't it?'

'You call me Silvia. And Zelka was most fascinate with your legs, I am afraid.'

'No, no! It's always a pleasure! Where is she now?'

'Some girl have her. She must find me, I cannot look, it is so easy to become disorient here.'

'Yes, indeed. Still, this bar seems to be where everybody comes. Can I get you something to drink?'

'You are charming. I would have an cinzano with soda.'

'That's very summery, isn't it?'

'We pitch a tent most nights.'

'Do you eat baked beans?'

'Not a lot. I make my husband take us to a restaurant if there's one anywhere near us. Got to keep our strength up for the hunt. Also we have a friend helping us out, and he likes to stay in a proper room, near proper food.'

'Looks like everybody's seen these things but you.'

'Which has got to be promising. That's what Jack says, anyway.'

'Jack?'

'Jack Gavin, the friend that's with us.'

'I know him.'

'Oh.'

'We met once or twice.'

'He never said.'

'No.'

'Silvia, if you don't mind, what I'd like to ask, something that's actually been on my mind, for some considerable time actually, about one of your

240

films, I suppose everybody asks these things, you must tell me if you're bored by it all, I'm sure you must be, you probably like to get away from it all, whenever you can, but I did see the most annoying piece, I mean, not the film, that wasn't annoying, it was very good, excellent, but they showed this um episode from it on the television, here, when I was last here, in fact.'

'Oh please, Guy! You must ask me! I shall be flatter! I am impress that you are interest in such a little thing.'

'Well, no, I mean, I only saw this clip, they called it, and I was very, very gripped, thrilled! You were in this completely dark room . . .'

'That is *Eva Kuwait and the Powder Room.*'

'Yes. Is it? And there was dust everywhere.'

'Was powder. Put there especially.'

'Oh. Ah! Not dust!'

'No.'

'How did you know that?'

'What?'

'They like biscuits.'

'I saw you both on the television when you first got back.'

'No, we didn't know what they liked back then. We tried a whole bunch of stuff before we found that.'

'I must have read it.'

'They printed that? I didn't think we ever mentioned that. Maybe Guy did. Maybe they saw it when they took photos some time. I guess so.'

'You said your husband wants to get back the original female.'

'Sure. We both do. Keep the link with their habitat.'

'It's hopeless.'

'Thanks. I think we realise that. Well, I do. Guy has his hopes.'

'You should put a price on it. A reward.'

'Who's got the cash?'

'Is it worth much?'

'You don't price an animal, Ainsley. What can you say – a thousand, a hundred thousand? That's why Guy did the TV thing, appeal to people's better nature. To us, to us, it's worth everything, it's our whole life.'

'That's very interesting, Mrs Blighton. To want something so much.'

'Yeah? You never wanted anything?'

241

'If I do, I get it.'
'Gee. Never had a problem in that department, then?'
'No.'

'I knew it.'
'Si.'
'Of course it wasn't a horse. I said that to people then.'
'But she is looking for a horse in the movie.'
'She is? But that wasn't clear, not at all.'
'In the cleep.'
'No.'

'Do you think everyone who has seen one has always killed it?'
'Who knows? It's all we ever hear about.'
'I expect there are people who have caught them and kept them.'
'Could be. But are they going to feed them right? Are they going to keep an eye on them all the time? They have to be supported, you know.'
'I don't think so.'
'No? You got some ideas on this, yeah?'
'They can adapt. They'll eat green stuff.'
'Well, yeah, they're herbivorous. They won't eat meat, that's for sure. So how did you work that out?'
'It's obvious. They're all over the countryside, so obviously they know how to get along.'
'So far. Anyway, be nice if you're right. Be nice if just one person comes through now. Take a little of the pressure off, I can tell you.'
'It's all very interesting.'
'You said that before.'
'I'd like to help you.'
'Really? I thought you weren't a nice person.'
'I'm sure I could help you.'

'Zelka! She is so energetic! Thank you so much, my dear!'
'I'm sorry it took an age, I thought you might be in the hospitality room.'
'No, I find my way here and am so lucky to discover Mr Blighton.'
'Is that where my wife is, do you know?'
'She's having a drink with Ainsley. Susie and Patti are there. Do you

242

want me to tell Mrs Blighton?'

'Thank you. I'll come and find her later.'

'See – she is again by your legs.'

'She's a lovely old thing, aren't you?'

'Not old, only a teenager!'

'Has she ever been in a film with you?'

'Oh no, Eva is such a complete woman, she don't need anybody. Also she must now to stay in England because of what do you say, fortina.'

'Fortina. I don't. . .'

'Because of disease, you understand. Or else each time she return here she is again lock up.'

'Ah! Quarantine, quarantine!'

'Si. It's the same.'

'Of course.'

'But now you must tell me of your sitter.'

'I'm sorry?'

'That you mention in the discourse, you have a sitter dog.'

'Oh dear, I'm afraid that was a bit naughty. I don't actually have a dog at all.'

'You lie! That's a surprise!'

'It just sort of came to me while I was talking. I hadn't prepared it. I just thought people would like to hear that sort of thing.'

'Well, I bet you're right. It's a good idea.'

'I hope so. Can I get you another cinzano?'

'Guy, I must go. I must take phone calls in my apartment tonight.'

'Where do you stay?'

'I got a little place that I have brought. It is quite close.'

'I could give you a lift.'

'Is not necessary, I shall get a taxi-cab. But you are kind.'

'No, really, my car is just down in the car-park. I'd be happy to. And perhaps, if you could put up with it, I could ask you one or two things, if you didn't mind, how they do certain things, it's really so fascinating.'

'No, I love to talk with you, but your wife, she is wondering where you are, no?'

'I'm sure she's enjoying herself. I'll just run you there and come back.'

'It will take just ten minutes, no more.'

'So who is this guy?'

'I can't remember where I heard it, one of my managers perhaps,

I don't know.'

'You could ask your managers, maybe?'

'If it was them. Maybe it wasn't. I know somebody said something. This man had a pair, in fact.'

'What, a male and female?'

'Yes.'

'You've got to remember, Ainsley.'

'Yes, he had a pair, and there was something about how he'd bought them from someone.'

'Why did he want to buy them? Jesus, I wish we could!'

'You haven't got the cash, Mrs Blighton. No, this was some time ago, before they were all over the place. He bought them off someone who had stolen them. Didn't you say they were stolen, originally?'

Guy stood at the toilet bowl relieving the pressure that he had detected in his bladder during the drive. He looked admiringly round the fixtures and fittings. The walls and ceiling of the room were completely covered in copper-toned mirror, and on the floor lay a shaggy ochre carpet, cut to accommodate the pedestals of the toilet and the sink, which, like the bath, were made of cream and brown marble. Four glass shelves ran across the wall opposite the bath, arrayed with dozens and dozens of bottles and jars containing fragrant liquids and creams. Guy wondered at the display, and also at the gravity of the enterprise that it suggested. He imagined that Silvia had enough combinations of various make-ups to cover any character that she cared to play. His gaze wandered up the wall and onto the ceiling, and he shortly found himself looking up at a fore-shortened reflection of himself standing with his dick in his hand. This vaguely embarrassed him, and he started to lose his balance. Abruptly he looked down into the toilet bowl and finished his pee.

The man peering at him from the mirror above the sink struck him as distinctly shabby. He had done his best for the television appearance, acquiescing when Deany had insisted on his taking a shower in Jack Gavin's hotel room and even allowing Jack's room service to launder one of his shirts. Now, however, he suddenly realised that this was probably not good enough. His hair was unkempt, and his pullover was grubby. He turned round and looked in the full-length mirror on the door. His trousers were grubby. His plimsolls were battered and torn. He licked his chapped lips and smoothed his hair with both hands.

In the kitchen Silvia was experiencing a profound inner turmoil. One

244

part of her had been gripped by feelings of an intensity she had not experienced since her late teens. Another part of her was struggling to muster some semblance of an adult resistance to these forces. As she sought for the liqueur bottle and some suitable glasses, images of Roberto kept springing to mind. He waddled towards her across the living room, shaking a mug full of water in which effervesced three indigestion tablets. He lay on the reclining chair gesturing at her irritably and she understood that she was supposed to hand him the newspaper that lay on the floor by his feet, beyond the limits of his ability to lean forward and stretch out. His head was on the pillow beside her, his mouth was open, the pillowslip was dark with dribble.

She walked across the suite with a small glass of yellow liqueur in each hand. Guy stepped out of the bathroom and smiled at her. As she reached the low glass table she started to tremble. Bending quickly she tried to place the glasses on the table top. Her left hand accomplished its mission, but her right hand shook so violently that she drove the base of the liqueur glass hard onto the table and snapped it off at the stem. Zelka, curled by the sofa, whined. Silvia let the broken glass fall onto its side. The liqueur spread across the table and dripped onto the creamy, deep-pile carpet. She stood up and felt uncontrollable muscular spasms coursing in waves from her pelvis down along the back of her thighs to her calves. Guy was walking over to help her. Her throat felt constricted. She clasped at it and gasped like a stranded fish. Her mouth opened and closed and her vision swam in and out of focus. Guy. She undid the top button of her blouse. Her turmoil suddenly evaporated. No more baleful images rose to chastise her. She ran at him. Knocking him back against the bathroom door. She put her arm round his neck and pulled his head down towards her. Thrust her tongue between his lips. His lips were soft, they made her mouth tingle. A great groan welled up from deep within her, driving her tongue further into his mouth. He made small noises. She moved her tongue urgently and pulled at his jumper. The spasms emanating from her pelvis now took over the whole of her trunk. Her body beat against Guy's, slamming his back repeatedly against the bathroom door. Silvia stepped back, seized a fistful of Guy's jumper, at about chest height, and dragged him to the centre of the room. Groaning continually, she took hold of one of his sleeves with both hands and pulled down on it with all her strength. At first the grubby wool stretched until the sleeve extended beyond Guy's hand by about a foot. The neck of the jumper elongated, travelling

245

along his shoulder and part of the way down his arm. Silvia fell to her knees on the carpet, clutching the woollen cuff to her breast. A guttural, coughing moan issued from her mouth. She bent over and put even more weight onto the sleeve. Guy was trying to formulate larger noises of confusion. His mouth opened and closed like a gasping fish. The jumper neck had reached its limit and was cutting into the back of his neck. He bent his head and the jumper rapidly rose over it. Within moments Silvia had grabbed at the descending shoulders and torn the garment away from Guy's half-stooped body. She threw it across the room. Zelka jumped up and barked indignantly. Guy stared at Silvia in alarm and said, 'Silvia!' She got to her feet and fumbled at the buttons of his laundered pale blue shirt but her legs were not sufficiently straightened to keep her at a useful height for more than a few seconds. As she collapsed she snatched at the fabric and applied a violent wrenching motion which sundered the whole shirt front and lay bare the unlaundered offwhite cloth of his vest. 'Oh, Guy!' Silvia muttered, rising up again. She sought the sides of the vest near his belt and lifted them clear of his trousers and on over his shoulders. Guy raised his arms weakly. His eyes were open very wide and he said, 'What . . .?' Silvia pushed her face into one of his armpits. Guy remembered he had had a shower, then his thoughts dissolved and were replaced by further consternation. Silvia had moved her face to the area of his diaphragm and her hands to the buckle of his belt. With the same intense but unwavering determin- ation she tugged at the free end of the belt, drawing it further through the buckle. Guy winced as his waist band cut into his stomach. The ligature was only a temporary imposition – it enabled Silvia to free the belt from the buckle pin and instantly loosen its grip on Guy's corduroys. Guy looked down on the frenzied activ- ity at his waist from what seemed like a great height. He found himself studying the detail of the bronze clasp that supported the impressive coiled mass of Silvia's glossy black hair. As his eye followed the whorled patterns of the burnishing, he could hear, beneath his assailant's head, the snapping of the threads that secured a trouser button as she jerked at the top of his fly. He remembered that his zip was broken and had been secured with a safety pin. He wondered how Silvia would tackle it, or if she would even notice it. He hoped she would not hurt herself, or him. After searching for the zipper pull to no avail Silvia murmured impatiently and tore at

246

Guy's trousers so forcefully that the zipper stitching gave way right down one side. The lesion continued some way into the fabric of the leg, gaining unexpected ground towards the end of its momentum as it moved into the readily rippable grain of the corduroy. The trousers fell to the ground immediately and it was only a matter of a second or two and a firm, swift pull before Guy's well worn and not recently changed underpants followed. Guy thought about how the pressure of work had prevented him from attending to his grooming, and felt relieved that the pants had received such scant attention on their way down. His relief dissolved quickly and was supplanted by feelings of awkwardness and self-consciousness as he considered his nakedness and then horror as Silvia gulped his dick into her mouth. Grasping his buttocks, she moved her head back and forth with great rapidity, whilst continuing to moan and mutter. Guy tried to make out what she was saying and then realised that it was probably Italian. Normally he found it extremely pleasant to have a mouth round his dick, but normally Deany did it, and he would always know, to within five or ten minutes, when it was going to happen. He wondered what his dick would do in this mouth that he had barely met. He realised that things had got to a pretty crucial stage now, and that unless something went very wrong, from Silvia's point of view, the immediate future would hold an ever-narrowing range of options. He also wondered why he had not been able to detect Silvia's interest in him earlier. Most of the time he had spent with her he had been concerned not to pester her too much, despite the fact that there were so many things he wanted to know about. Perhaps she had appreciated his detailed interest in her work. He did not know what to do with his arms. It seemed rude to push Silvia away, in her own flat. He put his hands on his hips for a moment, but this felt wrong, as if he were just standing there while someone, a film star, had his dick in her mouth. He folded his arms across his chest, and while this felt more natural, it did not seem any more appropriate. Below him Silvia groaned 'Oh Guy!' and as he looked down she suddenly pulled away from him and stood up. His dick hung there. Silvia grabbed hold of it, tightly. He looked her in the eye, for the first time. She seemed not to notice him. She turned and moved away, without letting go of him. His dick took the strain. Silvia kept moving. Guy made a noise of complaint, but was then obliged to thrust his hips forward as the limit of his elasticity was quickly reached. He laid his hand anxiously on Silvia's arm, but she paid no heed to his signal. Thinking that he might somehow neutralise her pull, he gripped her wrist, but such were the mechanics of the situation that she was not prevented in the least from administering a rather fractious tug. Guy yelped and jumped forward. His ankles were cluttered with his pants and trousers, but he had had the foresight not to attempt to move one leg before the other. Yet as Silvia tugged again he realised that, first, nothing was going to stop her, and second, he could only avoid a further series of tugs by providing a constant, rather than sporadic, forward movement. He began to shuffle, finding that short paces were indeed possible. His reluctance to be grasped by the dick was paradoxically balanced by his eagerness to comply with his captor. He had never been handled in this way in his life. Ever. It was the most unambiguous and unmysterious predicament in which he had ever been. There was no question of offering resistance, the notion was absurd. Were Silvia now to lead him over beds of glowing coals, the probable discomfort would be secondary to his fervent desire to ensure that the gap between them remained constant within a tolerance of no more than half an inch. At the back of his mind he was quite deeply impressed. Like all men in the world he was habituated to the automatic protection of his parts, and consequently had assumed that others, particularly women, would not, *could* not abuse him in such a terribly simple and straightforward way. This aspect of the chivalric code had obviously not impinged on Silvia's conscience, for she was now picking up speed in her journey across the open expanse of the lounge area and clearly expected an unimpeded progress. Guy trotted obediently and attentively behind, his hands by his sides, quite naturally. They passed through some open double doors into Silvia's bedroom. Guy saw the big bed. The quilt and sheets were red satin. Silvia accelerated and Guy found that he could trot even faster than before. It occurred to him that there was probably no limit to the speed he might attain, thus motivated. He saw himself running behind a red open-topped sports car, Silvia with one hand on the wheel, her free arm stretched back over the folded fabric of the roof, her hand tight around his dick. They were driving through the countryside. His legs were a blur. At the foot of the bed Silvia jerked Guy forward. It seemed she would not reward him for his unflagging provision of compliance by honouring the no-tug agreement he thought they had established. Just before reaching the edge of the bed, she stepped aside and released him. As his knees made contact with the mattress she placed her hand between his shoulder blades and pushed him so that he fell face down onto the satin quilt. The satin was cool and soft, he wanted to close his eyes and sink down. Silvia took hold of his trousers and pants and ran backwards for two or three paces. The garments turned inside out and then jammed up around his plimsolls. Silvia put her weight behind a final heave and managed to remove pants, trousers, socks and plimsolls in one go. With a cry of relief she ran forward and bit Guy's buttock. Guy said, 'Ow!' and rolled over. Silvia put his dick in her mouth again. Her brow moved to and from his stomach. Now that he was on his back and quite comfortable, he found that he was less inclined to think about things that were not actually happening. Although he had started, for example, to contemplate the moulded plasterwork on the ceiling immediately above his head, his attention was soon drawn away to the region of his loins and the sensations that were emerging through the turmoil of activity there. Silvia seemed to have developed her approach: without losing any urgency it had become distinctly more thoughtful, more focused. Her mouth was pleasantly warm and Guy could distinguish the different frictions imparted by her tongue, her teeth, her lips. He looked down at her head, the burnished clasp in her hair, the jacket of her black suit, her bottom swathed in the tight black skirt, her stiletto-heeled shoes. Tentatively he placed his hands on her head. She did not seem to mind. Fearful of appearing presumptuous, he patted her hair in a light, friendly manner. As far as he could tell, she nodded her head, and he took it as a sign of approval. Encouraged by her friendliness, he began to examine her hair-clasp with his fingers. A dark, copper-coloured crossbar protruded from either side of it, evidently acting as a securing device. Guy pulled gently at the bar and it slid free of the clasp. Silvia's hair unravelled and fell down around her shoulders. Guy ran his hands through it, tidying it up and extending it to its full length in every direction. Laid out over his hips and stomach, the hair glistened magnificently and gave off a light perfume that helped to impress on him that his companion, she who knelt and rocked so diligently between his outstretched legs, was actually very feminine. He had been, it need scarcely be said, fully aware of the gender of his companion for some months, but at no time had it occurred to him that he might find her directly, tangibly attractive. He had merely admired her; she had been an exquisite but distant icon, more artefact than flesh. He burrowed beneath her hair and found her neck, which he stroked gently. Silvia looked up at him, and

249

brushed her hair away from her face. Their eyes met for a second time. She squeezed his dick, which now showed every sign of its involvement in an absorbing situation. 'Oh Guy,' she said throatily, 'I must place you within me.' Guy moved his eyes in a way that showed that he understood. Silvia rose to her knees and began to pull at the buttons of her jacket. 'You must help me,' she instructed. With tremendous dexterity she opened at least eight small buttons with her thumb and forefinger and rolled the garment away from her shoulders in one fluid movement. Guy picked up the jacket, shook it out and folded it. There was no bedside table so he leaned over and put it on the carpet. When he sat up he found himself looking at her breasts. So close to him. The bareness. He could touch it. He started to feel embarrassed lest Silvia should think he was just looking at her. She pressed her breasts against him. Against his face. He felt blood drain violently through his body, down through his guts, into a pit beyond his stomach. In the same instant his eyes and lips drooped and his senses began to take their leave of him. Guy rolled his head to one side and brought her nipple into his mouth. As soon as he did so Silvia's whole body bucked against him and the nipple was abruptly withdrawn. 'Oh Guy, help me put you inside!' she exclaimed. Standing up on the bed, she wriggled free of her skirt and despatched her lace pants to her ankles. She then jumped off the bed and, standing naked apart from her high-heeled shoes, took the quilt in both hands and wrenched it from beneath Guy, who fell onto his back as it slid out from under his bottom. He lay on the cool expanse of satin and waited uncalmly. He saw nothing but her nakedness. She was more perfect than a picture in a magazine, more perfect than Eva Kuwait. She crawled towards him at speed, took him in her arms and writhed on him. She entered his mouth with her tongue and forced her head hard against his. He rolled her onto her side, and then, briefly losing his impetus as he slipped on the satin, rolled on top of her. Silvia said 'Guy!' very loudly in his ear. He bent his head back so that he could see her face, and replied, 'Yes?' Again she seemed not to see him, but as he waited for her to respond she took his dick and placed it inside her so fast that he could not remember how she had done it. The sensation of being inside Silvia was intense; not intensely pleasurable, certainly not unpleasurable, just very, very absorbing. Guy at that moment did not want anything else in the world. He groaned with surprise and cried 'Oh God!' Silvia ground her pelvis against him and shouted,

'Oh Guy, now I am in Ravenna!' He kissed her shoulder and moved his pelvis away from hers. She shivered. He pushed his pelvis forwards and was surprised to find that his dick did not move up inside her quite as he had anticipated. It seemed to travel part of the way and then lose momentum. Silvia shook beneath him and rolled her head from side to side. She shouted, 'Si, si, the boats are on the slope of the beach!' Guy moved back again, then, with a little more determination, pushed towards her. As his dick rose through Silvia's close, marvellous warmth, her eyes turned up towards her brow and she dug her nails into his arms. Then his dick eased off again and would go no further. He tried to consider what might be happening, or not happening, and found himself thinking of the dreams where he ran in sand or honey or the ground slipped away from his soles. When he next pushed towards Silvia, he bent his feet at the toe joints and pushed down on the mattress at the same time. Which ought to do it. As his toes took the force translated to them by his thrust, they slipped on the satin, and his dick not only slowed up in mid ascent but then fell back to a lower position. Guy realised that he was working against two factors: the shiny sheet was affording him insufficient resistance and the softness of the mattress was such that he and Silvia were effectively lying on a slope. His attempt to compensate had only exacerbated the problems. Silvia seemed to have picked up some of his unease, for she shouted, 'The streetcars . . .!' and then her voice wavered. Guy said, 'We keep skidding.' Silvia hissed, 'You must do something!' Guy suddenly had a very good idea. He jumped off the bed and rummaged through the pile of his clothing on the floor. 'Where are my plimsolls?' he asked. Silvia lay on the mattress with her hands between her legs, caressing herself, her head turned stiffly away from him. 'My shoes,' he explained. He shook his corduroys and the plimps fell out. He tore at the laces, jammed his feet into the damp canvas and hastily retied the knots. Anxious not to lose the co-operation of his dick, he climbed back onto the bed. Silvia glanced at his footwear and murmured, 'You are so sourceful.' The rubber soles proved to be an excellent investment; he bent his feet at the toes again and as Silvia drew him back inside her he savoured the new, non-slip arrangement with satisfaction and relief. Straightening his legs, he pushed away from the plimps. Silvia screamed briefly and shouted, 'Now it is dusk at Miramare!' Guy felt himself glide into her until he could

251

glide no further. This encouraged him to execute his reverse move as soon as possible but to his annoyance he felt Silvia's hips closely following his own as gravity impelled her to descend the gradient created by their entwined mass. Occurring at the moment when it was most natural for them to sunder, this adhesion disconcerted Guy, who had just begun to relish his ingenuity with the plimps. 'We're still slipping. I don't know what to do,' he complained. Silvia blinked and studied him with hooded, misty eyes. She took a long, deep breath. Guy waited for her to speak. She drew her knees up until they were beside his ears. He squeezed her buttocks encouragingly. With a sudden explosive cry she brought her feet down and arched her back, lifting Guy's thighs right off the bed. Her stiletto heels tore through the sheet and punctured the tough cloth of the mattress with a hollow ripping sound. She arched her back again and ground her heels deep into the cotton waste layered above the mattress springs. The heels sunk in right up to the insteps of her shoes. She dug her nails into Guy's back and hissed, 'Now you drive me, I am fixed like a rock!' Guy lifted away from her, and she placed her hand over the crack between his buttocks. Just as he was about to ease into her, Silvia thrust her finger, with its long, scarlet fingernail, a considerable way into his arsehole. Guy straightened out like an electrocuted man, and yelled 'My bottom!' very loudly. He had, quite unwittingly, thrust himself forwards with some force. Silvia withdrew her finger, stretched out her arms and shouted 'Aiee! Fontana di porca!' Guy drew a deep breath for himself, and he and Silvia began fucking. As they fucked Silvia screamed and shouted and moaned, and Guy groaned and panted. Silvia arched against him and he plimped with great friction as he rose and fell between her thighs. Each time he rose Silvia ran her nails down his back, and each time he flinched and rose higher into her. As he fell back she would sigh, and soon her sighs grew into regular cries which turned into an almost continuous shout. Guy broke out in a sweat, which moistened Silvia's ribs and breasts and flattened the hair on her brow. Her nails cut more and more deeply into his skin and his spine began to burn, the flames creeping round and spreading along his dick. He felt the sweat welling from every pore, and as he looked down between their bodies he saw droplets of liquid running along his chest and falling off his stomach. The heat from his spine continued to spread, radiating out through all his nerves, opening his pores even further, until the

252

waters of his body flowed from every single tiny perforation in his skin. When he closed his eyes he saw bright, sharp colours rippling and kaleidoscoping on his eyelids. He kissed and kissed Silvia, trapping her rolling head with his hands, and his tongue reached deep down into her mouth, and his dick rose through her and its fire lapped up through her insides until she too caught alight and the flame flickered in her throat and took his tongue and for a moment Guy thought he was a circle of fire completed by Silvia. Then the shifting shapes danced out to the edges of his inner eye, leaving a glowing whiteness behind them. He felt as if he were staring down into a hole somewhere inside himself, and as he hung on the lip of the hole he saw thousands of minute coloured grains streaming across into the light, way down at the far end, so far that he could not make out what they were. But as he wished to see the grains more closely, they enlarged within the hole and he realised that some of them were objects and some were mean-ingless shapes. The objects continued to grow and soon the light in the hole was almost blotted out by them. As the last object, a wooden owl, closed the light off completely, Guy heard an extra-ordinary sound in his ears. He started to cry out, to imitate the sound, and, naturally enough, it became much louder. His attention was being quickly absorbed by the new noise, but he managed to look back at the hole, and felt sad that he did not have the time to look longer, and because he was sad the objects in the hole shifted slight-ly and rattled, as if they were impatient, as if they were blocks of ice about to crack from a great floe, and he felt that he really ought to stay to see what was going to happen but Silvia screamed and pressed him and cried 'Oh Guy! Oh Guy! Oh Guy! Si! Si! Si!' and then a long, ghastly and marvellous sound hurtled from him and he shook like snakes and she lifted him up by his hair, his shoulders, his arms, pulling him up and over the bed head board 'Oh Jesus oh Jesus oh Christ' his back searing and smeared with blood and Silvia whimpered and lay flat lay back flat, shivering and then still and then shivering, and he breathing right down to his toes and up through his hair, and then the snakes would take him for a quick reminder and drop him and he slowly fell slow again.

Zelka growled softly at the foot of the bed. Her tail knocked against the bottom bedboard and her mouth could be heard opening and closing. It became clear that she was chewing. Guy felt her damp nose on the sole of his foot and moved his leg away. Zelka whined contentedly,

253

put her front paws up on the bedboard and continued to chew away eagerly. A minute later she growled again and nuzzled insistently at Guy's ankles. Guy murmured, 'Go away, Zelka,' but the dog continued to snap and gnaw in the region of his feet. Guy rolled over and sat up. At the bottom of the bed, all over the sheet, were dozens of dark green, bean-shaped objects, each no larger than the end of a thumb, and covered in a light, viscous film. Guy took hold of one and examined it gingerly. Squeezed between his thumb and fingers it proved to have the consistency of a jelly baby. It lacked any notable features but its meaningless appearance strongly reminded him of something. He felt his stomach suddenly tighten with an obscure dread. His hand flew to his legs and he found himself examining the skin there. For an instant it seemed to break out in small wounds, scattered over his calves, shins and knees. The wounds yawned open and then winked at him mockingly; wet, red eyes in his flesh. He shook his head and looked away. When he looked back the wounds had gone. It had obviously been a fleeting effect of his imagination. Zelka barked at him. He threw the slimy bean across the room, then fell back on the satin sheet beside Silvia's empty shoes and her damp, motionless body. He felt sick with fear.

In that particular swath of the land there were as many unworking as working but affairs had come to a head of a Saturday so it would be tricky to attribute kickoff to a particular section of the community. Unusually the weather set a shining example and this certainly encouraged those who should have been in the malls or at the hedge, clipping, for example.

Some said picnickers among the heaps might have given the early halloo, others thought that anglers at the dank canal may have caught first sight. Rumour had it that the cricketers, the hoarding crews and the traction engine enthusiasts had made spottings separately but within a shortish space of time, and their parties had only subsequently coalesced, perhaps as much as half an hour after abandoning their respective engagements.

It was opined, with the benefit of hindsight, that there had been an auspicious element to the events. The body of the missing child had been unearthed with the latest equipment on the Thursday, evangelists under canvas had given hope to many the previous Tuesday, and starlings had recently blackened the sky after a fire at the shell of the old cordwainers'.

There were those who argued that the heart of the land had been lost, silted over by alluvia of dispossession and disconnection, scoured by the winds of opportunity, leached by the relentless waves of the new freedoms. There was a need for an enterprise with the widest franchise, a cause that would excite the community and thereby reveal to its members that their membership was indissoluble. Through this revived corporation would rise the heart, a force that could never be held too long in check. Now, with the events, the heart was being reborn among the people, delivering itself anew after long dormancy.

Pity, too, was cited among the contributing factors. Those who had argued for the petrified heart held that pity was a vestige of heart that had not wholly succumbed to the scourges of the land. Detected in sentiment, and even in derision, and even in war, its unfettered exercise in common projects could only facilitate the flowering of the fuller compassion that had been mislaid in recent years. The people were drawn by their pity, and their pity drew warmer blood through their hearts.

The older people maintained that they had been partly inspired by their recollections of fêtes and fairs. They recalled the billowing tents, the striped awnings, the bold checks of the trousers of the vendors, the ribbons descending from the high poles, the jolly commerce between children and farm animals, the displays of cakes and jams, the tests of skill with rings, balls or loops of electrified wire, and the hullabaloo from swings and rides.

Also instrumental, contended the amateurs of lore, were more ancient memories, glimpsed through the mists of time. These were the dances round the towns, the dashing with the crowns of flames, the floating of the flowers, the pursuit of the bladders, the dipping of the stump in bitumen, the thunder of a thousand drummers, the larding of the stallions, the exuberance of the songs of hymen.

Yet on the day, it was the ordinary animals that came first over the low hills. A dark and agitated band blurred the line of the horizon, and it soon became possible to discern within it the wide variety of beasts fleeing from the clamour that filled the air behind them. In the vanguard were the dogs. They were toy, house, guard, sheep, guide, pedigree, wearing collars, some coats, some muzzled, many not, trailing leads, some stray, most owned.

Behind and among the laggards of the pack were the cats. Toms and shes abreast, low to the ground, streaking. The formal types were ginger, tabby, tortoiseshell, the eastern breeds, the breeds for fur, and then the innominate hordes with their socks and stars and tips and stripes, some from the saucer, others from the alley.

Mixed with the free-range pets were those burst in alarm from their cages and hutches, the white rabbits lolloping, the golden hamsters scurrying, the tan gerbils bounding, the guinea pigs bustling, the rats and mice undulating like a sea or carpet under the paws and hooves. All ears back, pink eyes in wide fear.

Whinnying desperately from the farms, stables and greater gardens cantered and clopped the ponies and horses. Foam-flecked Arabs rippling in pairs, sweat-flanked Percherons rolling from side to side, mane-flown Shetlands trotting among the greater Danes and other larger dogs, a show Palomino panicked from the ring. Lips rolled back, fearful grins.

The cows at the rear, lowing, at their feet the pigs, squealing. The sounds of the farm rising above the barking, mewing, the shrieking and the squeaking. Swept out from the stalls and sties, the porkers and beefers abandoned their pellets and potatoes, and in the scrum across the yard took in the chickens and cocks, the ducks and drakes, the geese and gander. Alarmed by this hubbub below, the swallows and martins from the eaves swooped up, saw the people, heard their distant clamour, and joined with all the birds of the air from the telegraph wires, the hedges and the nests. The ducks rose but the geese could not, nor the chickens. Some rode the pigs and cows, but the others fluttered in the dust with the lambs from the pasture.

This broad front of consternation flushed all before it, streaming down the low hills away from the town, swarming over the highways and flattening the fences. Voles broke cover and ran with their enemy the ferret. Hares bolted, passing the indifferent jaws of the fox, who had never heard a hue and cry like this.

The hawk soared, over the swarm, and hung. It turned its cold eye into the wind and surveyed the sward. The people had reached the edge of town, they were surging over the broken barriers and into the railyards, across the rubble of the industries, over the balding pitches, between the grassless heaps, through the straggling allotments.

In the town, there has been a concatenation. The weather making the people unsure, cash ejects from several slits simultaneously along West Street, burst mains sluice sports shoes from a stockist's, the soft rot takes all asparagus tips in the fruit market, the complete absence of cars for nine minutes in all streets, the checkout girls weep in a line of thirty suddenly at the largest checkout, many boxes of screws, nails and hooks spill unpushed from high shelves onto the ironmonger's floor, in Deskin Square all mothers turn on their children and slap them smartly, a well-told joke causes the patrons of The Amount of Beer to embrace openly throughout both bars, and before all the hire shops, in every street, as the many screens show the astonishing climax of Ainsley's recent vanquishment of the dago, 'El Swoosh', the teenagers, the young men and women in the crowds, turn and stream to the edge of town, as if with one mind, they would not know why were you to ask them now, they walked east, and met similar groups of like inclination, and chatted warmly with them, and picked up bricks and sticks. The teenagers had a sense of something and the parental generation felt compelled to follow them, mingle with them, and make conversation with them. They spoke of the major differences in their tastes, and their parity in matters of the lack of opportunity. The small shop owners greeted the stream of strollers, handed them brooms, fruit pickers, some four-by-two and two-by-one, rolled parasols, a shooting stick, rolling pins, poles of tents, raspberry canes, canes, rulers, stale baguettes, table legs, cues and cue rests.

Several hundred strode together, some in groups according to their most recent engagement, others drawn from the homes and shops and streets. While all the social classes were represented, and many of the creeds, no divisions along these lines were apparent. Drawn by the throng, sensing the pity beneath it, came managerial groups from the upper floors of stores, the rear rooms of banks and the suites set aside for repose. The mothers took stock of the managers and greeted them familiarly. When the managers joined the other townsfolk, the mothers were encouraged, they left the malls and benches and wheeled their babies and goods to the east with the amiable others. Finding the old among the others, the mothers fell in beside them and were pleased at their openness, speaking with them of their war and their preferred entertainers and their disabling lack of resources. The staff of the bank spoke animatedly with the cleaners of the streets, the investors took the arms of the youngsters from the supermarkets, and those who disliked smoking fell in with pipe puffers and twenty-a-day men.

These groups from the town were drawing near to other groups, groups that had been involved in recreations outside the limits of the town. The cricketers, who had made an early spotting, were the most obviously bloody because of their kit. They explained that a boundary had been pursued by deep fine leg who had been unable to prevent it from crossing the line and rolling into the bushes. In the ensuing search mid-off had found a screechy in the undergrowth and hauled it out. The fellows had gathered round for the usual, which explained the state of their boots and trousers. Unable to concentrate on the game after that, the team had upped stumps and begun to comb the parkland, which is where they were deployed when the greater crowd came by.

A comparable tale from the traction engine enthusiasts involved the chance discovery of three screechy cubs by a group of small children at the rally. The children had been particularly distressed by the plight of the screechies, and had told their father, who had been stoking his gargantuan road roller. The father hated to see his little girls crying so he told them to bring the cubs over to him. Soon more children heard of the discovery, rushed over to see the cubs and were quickly moved to tears. A deputation of fathers approached the owner of the road roller and pressed him to take action. The cubs were placed on a path in the park and the clanking juggernaut slowly passed over them. Although the children were mollified, an air spread through the rally and drove the enthusiasts almost instinctively to the uncultivated land on the far side of the park, where they glimpsed, in the distance, the activities of the anglers.

The anglers, in their despair, for catches were rare, had been casting about in the rank water, snagging on trolleys. The standard short flip from behind, the leaded hooks arc over, break the film and sink. But a codger, sat since dawn, at the first moment of a flip, snags behind him, happens from time to time, gives it the yank, but no give. Grunts, rises, takes a look. It's a screechy! In the eye! No easy job getting it out – penknife, screwdriver. Fingers. A mess made. The codger concludes to hell with it, both eyes out. So with more action at the bank than in the deeps, the fishermen call it a day, bag the tackle, fold the seats, push and poke through the tangles. They had caught sight of the distant whites of the eleven (plus two batted and padded) with stumps, (plus, from the pav, the outstanding nine, four dismissed, five to go out, [one padded and boxed, standing by] two scorers, with pencils, two umpires, with woollies), and over on the scrub, the traction enthusiasts, oily men, little girls and boys, the wives.

At the edge of town the striding town group was encouraged by the sight of the cricketers, engine lovers and anglers converging on each other. When these latter groups looked back to the town and saw the great variety of people coming down the low hills towards them, they shouted simultaneously and spontaneously and rerouted so as to join the

258

larger group. Many mothers had anglers in their families, both husbands and sons, and they waved as the fishermen neared, then hugged them as they closed upon the larger group, swelling it. The elevens saw their sweethearts conversing with the teenagers about Ainsley, and felt warm bonds with those young people, despite the fact that cricket was not the preferred sport of the teenagers. The rally entrants still bore their lunch packages and were happy to share sandwiches and small cakes with the young women from the checkouts, and with the parties of repairers from various repair shops in town.

Even as the several hundred moved over the scrub they were joined by individuals who happened to be in the vicinity: practising athletes, metal detecters and sketch artists. It happened that there was a number of accordionists unknown to each other, in the throng, and these felt moved, at the same moment, to play their instruments, and rapidly one stirring melody was reached and the whole large accumulation of men and women began to sing together and very quickly found agreement on the lyrics. This was due in no small part to the stentorian and initially extemporaneous contributions of the sketch artists, which were then reinforced by the basses among the crews from the hoardings.

The cricketers, particularly the bowlers, were concerned to stay at the head of the thousand, using their keen sight to scan the middle distance. Most of the other types present are content to bulk the throng, but certain factions, such as the teenagers, knowing their own longness or acuity of sight, have filtered to the van, joining the bowlers in their self-appointments as scout and lookout.

This thin line abreast, the eyes and envelope of the assembly, scours the skyline and all terrain between. They are not slow to appreciate the advantages to their number afforded by the band of mixed animals fleeing from them several hundred yards ahead. The fled, flushed beasts have rased the open country and routed its denizens, so that any lingering or outstanding feature, be it plant, plank or pained straggler, will be simple to see.

'Guy, what is there? Look!' cried Silvia as the car sped along the hilltop road. Guy turned and looked down over the scrub that rolled away to the horizon in nearly every direction.

'See! Outside the town!' She pointed out the back window to the buildings on the skyline.

'I'll have to stop,' said Guy.

He pulled in at the side of the road and got out. Silvia jumped out on the other side, followed by Zelka.

'What is it?' Guy said.

'It is many animals, no? Many, many.'

'It's a stampede,' Jack called from the back seat.

'Why are they stampeding?' Guy asked.

'Fire,' Jack replied.

'There is no flames, Jeck.'

'Looks like cattle, doesn't it?' Guy stood on tiptoe and strained his eyes to see some detail through the dust raised by the dark wedge of seething dots far away below them.

'It is so far,' Silvia complained, walking across to Guy and taking his arm. Guy smiled at her nervously and pulled at his trousers, shaking his legs one after the other.

Jack grinned as he watched them. He still could not get used to Guy in a suit, let alone the highly styled lightweight Italian two-piece that Guy had recently acquired. It seemed, and Jack had not pressed his colleague here, that Guy had suddenly tired of his old outfit and decided to throw it away. Silvia Desperanza had been really very kind and helped him to find something a little smarter, the very next day. She had also developed a great interest in his researches, and had been so moved by his appeal on television that she felt compelled to accompany him on his expedition through the country, to give whatever help she could.

'Something is scare them, must be,' Silvia said, looking up at Guy's anxious face. Guy bent down and scratched at his shins. Zelka wagged her tail and barked at him.

'Put her in the car, Silvia,' Guy said irritably.

'But she like to get her leg stretch. All this drive, she is very coop.'

'We don't want her worrying those cattle,' he retorted.

'But they are so worried now, evidamente.'

'I think it's best. In this country farmers shoot dogs.'

'Oh, there is no law?'

'Yes. They're allowed to.'

Silvia took Zelka by the collar and led her back to the car. Guy waited until she reached the door, then shook his left leg vigorously. A number of small, dark green objects tumbled onto his shoes and thence to the ground. He shook the other leg, then surreptitiously pulled his shirt tails out from his trousers and shook the whole of the top half of his body.

'Having a pee!' he shouted, knowing that this would save him from the scrutiny of his passengers. On the road at his feet lay about two dozen of the things. The irony of it was that Zelka was the only one in the group that shared his secret. Her predilection for the things had actually proved very handy. While they were driving along, the things would build up inside Guy's shirt and sleeves, and some would fall down his leg to the pedals. At regular intervals he would discreetly scoop them up from the floor mat and slip them in his pocket. Whenever they stopped he would contrive to drop them somewhere near Zelka, who would dispose of them in seconds. The arrangement had its shortcomings, as when the dog sniffed at his legs and barked demandingly whenever it found him standing up, but its mistress tended to attribute this behaviour to her pet's exceptional gregariousness and Guy's lifelong association with animals, which conveniently obscured the awful truth of the matter.

Guy climbed into the driving seat, unaware of the wry expression on Jack's face. Jack, attuned for so long to the vagaries of Guy's skin, realised that the affair had entered a new phase as soon as Guy had turned up at the hotel the day after his TV talk. All traces of blotching and dryness had gone from his face and arms, and from a distance the naturalist looked quite dashingly healthy. On closer inspection it was still difficult to determine exactly what it was that made him seem far *too* healthy. His fair hair and even tan supported the image of general radiance and his nervous smile continually displayed a set of fairly good teeth that only intensified this picture. It did not take Jack too long, however, to spot the flaw. It was Guy's pores. They were too big. People's pores were never that big, in his experience. Guy's face and hands were stippled with holes of a size that revealed them not as mere marks but definite openings in the flesh. These were what lent him the appearance of rude vigour from afar and disconcerting vulnerability from three paces.

Jack reached over and took the map from Silvia's lap. 'Yeah. We could get down there. Have to drive along the top to the end, then there's a road leads down to the bottom.'

'Do we really need to, Jack?'

'Something's scaring those animals, Silvia said so.'

'Well, yes, but I don't see . . .'

'Guy – I've got a feeling about it.'

'Oh.'

Guy still respected Jack's 'feelings', especially when Jack implied that they were related to the project. Matters of itinerary had gradually passed almost entirely into the seer's hands over the last few days, for

261

two quite different reasons. As a limited seer he could, of course, only depend on short-term readings, but he knew that his patience with Guy was about to be rewarded. By biding his time and never appearing to obstruct Guy's impulses, he had managed to preside over the maturation of a process that would transform his life. He did not, at the moment, have a clear notion of *how* Guy would change his life, but he was definitely experiencing an increase in the number and frequency of readings at his disposal. A reading, when it applied to himself rather than a client, had the effect of setting the course of his behaviour for a limited period. Sometimes it would serve him for a day or two, sometimes for just a few hours. When the period covered by the reading had expired he could return to the standard reactive model, or hope for a further reading. Ideally readings would come to him at regular intervals, each one falling well within the decay phase of its predecessor. His behaviour would then be continually revised and corrected, giving him the sensation of gliding over the back of the future as it passed through him to the past. At the moment this ideal condition was indeed prevailing, and reinforced his conviction that he and Guy were heading for an imminent and fruitful collision. Where before he had based their itinerary solely on the attractions listed in his guide book, he was now finding that his choice of hotel locations and the sightings of creatures were moving towards a state of genuine convergence. In the last few days they had narrowly missed a number of incidents, either arriving too late at a spot that had recently been the site of an atrocity, or finding that they had been only a mile or two away from a scene while it was in full swing. Jack was not sure whether Guy ought actually to find an animal, but he felt it was right that the naturalist should be allowed to get closer and closer to his goal.

There was another reason that Jack had taken charge of the party's movements, and this was closely related to the ominous absence of Deany. Jack had been disconcerted to see Ainsley being interviewed on Guy's TV programme, and his vision of Guy, Deany and the kid meeting over the free drinks raised some distinctly uncomfortable possibilities. That Guy might contrive to strike up a curious relationship with Silvia had not occurred to him, but it looked fairly harmless and seemed to have kept Guy from actually encountering Ainsley. Guy had mentioned, however, that after the transmission he had lost his wife in the studios and had then learned that she was elsewhere in the building, chatting with the champ. Jack had been appalled, blanching inwardly at the prospect of his menage unravelling just as the whole business showed every sign of being about to deliver the goods. He was convinced that the worst had happened, and there was more to Deany's absence than her reaction to Guy's escapade with Silvia. Quite possibly she had no inkling of what her husband had been up to anyway.

Guy was so utterly frail in spirit at the moment that he offered no resistance to the manic element Jack had introduced to the scheduling. They stayed at, or in the vicinity of, a different hotel every night, and spent at least a couple of hours every morning driving to another one. When Guy had expressed concern about losing contact with Deany, Jack had assured him that the hotels would pass on their forwarding addresses so that Deany would be able to locate the party in a trice. By omitting to leave the relevant information behind, let alone bothering to check out of the hotels in the proper manner, Jack had effectively cut his group loose from any tracing operations. The steady improvement in his targeting proved to be more than enough to assuage Guy's anxiety, and Jack was left with the fervent hope that Deany would either give up, get lost or at worst track them down well after the more pressing matters had come to a head.

Guy slipped the car into gear and moved off in the direction of the side road that led to the bottom of the hill.

'We learn so much of unusual nature in this exploring, I think, Guy,' Silvia announced.

'It's a jungle out there, Silvia,' Jack said. In the rear-view mirror he could see Guy frowning.

'Si? Where is that?'

'It's an expression, Silvia,' Guy said testily.

The presence of two helicopters in the sky above them excited the thousand, for the interest of the television companies confirmed that the remarkable mood of the occasion was perceptible to outsiders; it was not an eccentric thing concocted by a closed-minded community. Distributed among the thousand were a number of individuals who recognised that while the passions of the occasion had developed out of an inimitable set of local circumstances, the very nature of these passions linked the thousand to a body of values that had universal, or at least national, application. The insightful individuals mentioned their feelings to those around them, and a sense of dignity gradually spread through the greater group, informing the senses of excitement, purpose and togetherness.

Gaining ground by the minute, the panic-stricken animal herd had gathered unto itself riverside creatures such as the water rat and toad. Moles by the banks bored into the sod ahead of the thunderousness and otters were surprised from their sinuous play. Flushed from copses ran fawns, urgent does nipping their flanks to spur them on. Over the crushed twigs and leaves seethed the separate society of the insects, millipedal clamberings, a fluid of clicking joints and frantic feelers, spiders over the backs of beetles on bugs, ants over lice on mites. For these the twig is a log, the stalk a stiff climb. From their points of vantage, vistas gathered at the summit of a toppled mushroom or a bowed daisy, the land erupts all round in limitless expanses of dark, dead gradient. Colossal trunks blot the upper reaches, whence come the falling sky and the deafening end. Between the mulch and the awesome overheads, are the mid-range obstacles, to be circumnavigated rather than scaled. One such obtrudes presently, writhing on the trampled weeds, screeching at the perfect messages that it receives from every atom of its flesh.

The cricketers raise the cry and the thousand gasp 'Ah!' as one. The walking pace changes to a trot, managers help mothers with their carriages, shopping and children-in-arms, while the halt are propelled by teenaged boys and girls. Reaching the screechy, the thousand encircle it. The most attractive child is pushed to the centre. It touches the screechy on the head. There is a great silence. The thousand catch their breath in the only noise, the long scream. Without organisation, representatives of the trades and services lay their hands on the screechy's limbs, short tail and neck. The beautiful youngster steps away, its eyes misty. The representatives pull the screechy apart. They run their sticky hands over the youngster. The crowd flips out. It goes fucking mad. They start to swear, people who you would never have thought. Things you would never imagine they would imagine. The reps throw the screechy skin up, the limbs here and there, the guts left, right and centre. Effing and blinding the thousand clutch pieces and just shout out madly. They break into another run. Like the animals before them they are plural, wild-eyed, but they are searching, not fleeing.

'Look at those fucking things!' Jack shouted as the herd hurtled past the parked car, raising dust. 'All kinds of fucking animals in there!' Silvia, her hand firmly on Zelka's collar, wound her window up to keep the grit at bay. 'Where do they go?' she asked.

'Can't hear you!'

Silvia raised her voice. 'Where do they go now?'

'Anywhere! Anywhere that isn't back where they came from!'

Guy had twisted round in the driving seat so that he could look through the window on Silvia's side. His back was pressed hard against the door, and he seemed to be on the point of nausea. 'Guy! What's up?'

Guy turned to Jack. He was terribly pale. 'What are they doing, Jack?'

'Everybody's asking me! You're the naturalist!'

'But what do you think?'

'It's a hunt. It's obvious.'

The thunderous roar made further communication impossible. Dust swirled right around the car, cutting down visibility to the point where the occupants could only make out a stream of lumbering, galloping shapes, some of which could be identified by the howls or bellows that cut at intervals across the general cacophony. Zelka contributed to the pandemonium by barking dementedly and pawing at the window. Guy seized Jack's wrist, pulled him towards the front of the car and pressed his mouth to Jack's ear.

'They're out there, Jack!' he cried hoarsely. 'We've found them!'

Jack nodded vigorously. 'Right, right! But we're not the only ones!'

'Why?'

'Give it a few minutes – this is just the front end.'

Guy pushed down on the door handle and fell backwards out of the car. He picked himself up and dashed into the dust clouds. Silvia screamed. Zelka wrenched her collar from her mistress's grip, bounded between the front seats and out into the melee. Silvia screamed again and tried to open the door on her side. Jack grabbed her arm and held her back.

'Jeck – we must stop them!'

'There's nothing we can do, Silvia, they can't hear us and we can't see them!'

'But they will be crosh!'

'Guy's at the back of it. All the heavy stuff has passed.'

'But Zelka – she is not use to such animal variety!'

'She'll be okay. Dogs are cleverer than us.'

'So we just sit? Do nothing?'

'Wait till the dust goes, then take a look.'

Silvia shook her head doubtfully and peered through the window. Jack was about to shut Guy's door when he caught sight of some dark green

265

objects on the rubber mat beneath the pedals. He leaned right over the back of Guy's seat and picked one up, It had a soapy feel to it, and the consistency of a hard rubber. It was about the same size as a golf ball but irregularly shaped, bearing a number of conical extrusions of different lengths which gave it the appearance of a crude Christmas tree star.

'What's this?'

Silvia looked distractedly at the object. 'Is a biscot. Guy give them to Zelka.'

'A biscuit? Why does he do that?'

'He like her. Always he have some in his pockets.'

'They're all over the floor, look.' Jack opened his own door and climbed out. Not only was the floor mat covered in green things of all shapes and sizes but also the road outside. Scattered quite densely near the offside front door, the objects thinned out in a trail leading round the front of the car. Jack leaned on the bonnet and saw that they continued on into the scrub land adjacent to the road. He bent down and picked up three or four more of them. Although all were of the same consistency, and uniformly covered in a thin slime, their shapes, while quite rough, were completely different. Studying them one after another, he was reminded of photographs of that stuff that whales ate – endless varieties of forms, all to no apparent purpose. As he turned them over in his hand he found that each one, at some point on its surface, bore a small area of greater definition. In one case three almost parallel ridges, no more than half a centimetre in length, were clearly discernible, while on one side of another was a shallow depression, unmistakeably semi-circular in shape.

'Bloody funny biscuits,' he remarked.

'Jack, they are nowhere, see!'

He looked up and saw that the dust had settled, although several hundred yards away the cloud thrown up by the stampeding animals still hung in the air. There was no sign of Guy or the dog.

'What must we do, Jeck?'

'Trail'em.' Silvia got out of the car. 'We follow the biscuits,' Jack explained.

'There are so many. Where does he keep them?'

'When we find him, you can ask him.'

Enlivened, the thousand swarmed across the plain of scrub. Their imprecations rose before them, equally from the mouths of mothers and tractionists. The bloody roared 'Shit!' and 'Fuck!', the unsplashed

'Hell!' and 'Damn!', the children 'Buggabugger pissnerpoosnerpees!' Some leashed dogs, shepherds, chows, rottweilers, not running with the wild mixed pack, strained from their retainers. Tossed hats, glove pairs on high, woollies flying up, sticks as batons twirling in air, scored the sky. Steps, whether high-heeled, loafered or steel capped, fell increasingly to unison, all lefts all rights all lefts all rights. The accordionists, having located each other, are the melodic centre now, their brows wiped of perspiration by those adjacent who recognised that two hands are required to maintain the instrument. Here and there constables in their navy dot the thousand. They mop their own brows, opening the fronts of their thick tunics, conversing with the anglers on patience, with the checkout girls on memory, with the teenagers on the husbandry of the body.

The thousand reach the top of a long slope. For some reason – the imperatives of vista, the general requirement of breathers – they pause and survey the lower land. Instantly the sharp-eyed shout 'Covey!'

There below is a group of five.

'Hollah! Hollah!'

'Fuck! Shit!'

'Covey!'

The long run is exhilarating. Gravity is with the thousand. Many raise their arms as if rollercoasting. Unwanted garments scatter the wake of their descent. Parasols and lengths of plumbing are aloft. From all throats come curses and cries. The people are pouring down the side.

Guy was perfectly at odds with himself. The situation below him could not be clearer. He must dash along the valley floor at great speed and collect up that which had evaded him for so long, the source of so much of his misery, the absent agent of his professional undoing. His unflinching singlemindedness was to pay off at last, he could recuperate his abandoned research, his wife would work alongside him again, forgiving him for his obsessions and excesses. But there at his feet lay hell. On the ground around him, trailing off far behind him, back over the hills, the plain, the scrub, back to the car where he had left Silvia and Jack Gavin, there they were, the hellish, hideous exudations of a body gone quite mad. Even as he hesitated before the dash, trying to collect his thoughts, regain his breath, he could feel the slight pressure against his thighs, his back and his stomach as the vileness gathered in his clothing. He shook his arms and more of the things fell from his sleeves. He kicked out with his legs and expelled several more from his trousers. Why did he not feel anything when they oozed from him? How could his pores give vent to things so improbably large in relation to the pinhead apertures from which they emerged? When he could bring himself actually to keep watch on an area of his skin, it proved impossible to determine the precise moment at which an exudation began. Despite their current, abnormal enlargement, the pores never seemed to increase their dilation prior to an appearance of one of the things. It was infuriating – he could stare and stare at a patch of his arm, say, and quite suddenly and painlessly part of it would be obscured by one of the things. He felt sure that they must emerge in miniature and then grow rapidly once exposed to the air, but he could not swear to have perceived this process occurring – it was almost as if they just *arrived* at the surface without having come from anywhere first. If the notion were not utterly beyond the pale, he thought he might be forgiven for concluding that the things were falling onto him from the outside, magically collecting in his clothes after their passage through the air. He knew that this was desperately wishful, and realised that he was clutching at straws. He also knew that the 'he' who was doing the clutching was terribly frail, so violently beleaguered that it might at any moment dissolve into irrecoverable particles.

He tried to push these appalling considerations from his mind and concentrate on the task ahead of him. To his dismay, the harder he tried, the more he could feel the objects accumulating in his clothes. It was almost as if they wanted to monopolise his attention and block him off from doing the one thing that would make any sense of his shattered life. He stared very deliberately at the distant outlines of the creatures at the bottom of the slope and began to breathe deeply through his nose in an attempt to impose some calm on himself. The enormous crowd of people was picking up speed as it came onto the steepest part of the opposite slope. Guy loosened his tie, unbuttoned his shirt and pulled its tails out of his trousers. He attempted to ignore the shower of objects that tumbled onto the grass, but something about one or two of them caught his eye. Before he could stop himself he had scooped them off the ground. Although in most respects both were quite different, he was alarmed to discover that their basic dark green colour was overlaid with patches of red and blue. Furthermore these new colours coincided closely with small but unmistakeably smooth and regular areas on the rubbery surface.

Guy swallowed and suddenly felt queasy. He hurled the things away

268

and looked across the valley. The mob was gaining speed as it closed on the creatures. He was closer to the valley floor than the people but a greater distance from the creatures themselves. He started to run. Accelerating down the slope he hit the flat at full sprint. Even as his legs pounded beneath him he felt the objects working their way down his trousers in a steady stream. They fell from his chest onto his forearms and were batted aside. Miraculously they did not end up under his feet and throw him off balance. After a hundred yards at top speed he felt a searing pain in his lungs which made every breath unbearable, but he ignored it. He would find the energy to run for as long as necessary, and his body would have to cope.

Now that he could see the creatures quite clearly he began to consider how he was going to carry them. Even if he could manage to get two under each arm there would still be one spare. He wondered if he would be able to gather them into a bunch and encircle them with his arms, holding them against his chest. The weight would be considerable. Perhaps two under each arm and the fifth held in both hands, across his knees. He thought it unlikely that he would be able to run very far with that arrangement. The mob still had some way to go, and he realised that he had a decent chance of getting there first. As he redoubled his efforts he could hear, through the sound of the blood drumming in his ears, what sounded like cries of anger from the far slope. The people in the mob were yelling and cursing as they raced towards the creatures. The noise did not seem to be directed at him, rather the shouters were egging each other on, like men in a rugger game.

At least two of the creatures were fully grown. Adults. Guy tried to calculate how long they could have been in the wild, in this area. If they had been born nearby then . . . but they might have wandered from miles away . . . how long had it been since he had lost them – two months? three months? But he didn't know how long it took them to grow up, surely they couldn't . . . not in three months, which means . . . no, that was absurd . . . but . . .

'Eke! Eke!'

Tears streamed down his face and he shouted the name over and over until it became a rhythmic, sobbing howl, shaken up by the relentless jolt of his running. Then he was upon them. Their screams filled his ears soothingly as he tried to up end one of the adults for sexing. A shower of multicoloured objects spilled onto it from his chest and the ends of his sleeves. The creature was convulsing in such a way that its back legs kicked repeatedly, threatening to tear at his hands. He turned to the other adult and crooned softly as he rolled it onto its back. The five screams, piercing in a way that he had once found so unsettling, now blended into a chord that insulated him from the hubbub rolling down from the far slope. 'Eke, Eke,' he whispered, pulling the creature's back legs apart. It was a male. The spell dissolved, he looked up at the wave of men and women charging towards him and was abruptly returned to a sense of urgency. He picked up the two adults first and tucked one under each arm, then, falling to his knees, grabbed two of the cubs. For a moment he could not think how to get hold of the third one. Squeezing it between the other two, he tried to lift it, but the cub just slipped straight back to the ground. He couldn't seem to get enough pressure on it. The curses from the mob were clearly audible now. He could hear shouts of encouragement as well, and had the odd idea that they were directed at him. When he looked up he saw, not more than a hundred yards away, what seemed to be a group of cricketers bearing down on him. Some of them were wearing pads, which were spattered and smeared with blood. They waved bats and stumps and in among them was a variety of men and women brandishing umbrellas and sticks of french bread.

'Shitcake! Shitcake!'

'The fuckers! The fuckers! Hold them fast!'

Guy bent right over and sunk his teeth into the scruff of the third cub's neck. A great cheer rose from the mob. Biting as hard as he could, he staggered to his feet. The cub, which weighed about the same as a cat, trembled and twitched against his chest. He started to run and instantly felt the hairy flesh slipping from his jaws. The strain on his teeth was considerable, and the faster he ran the more untenable the situation became. He closed his jaws even harder, and felt the cub's skin give way. His teeth broke its flesh at several points and the slippage stopped while he still had a sizeable roll of pelt in his mouth. He was now running parallel to the mob, and must keep up maximum speed to avoid being headed off by its far flank. His only alternative would be to climb back up the slope from which he had just descended. The adults under his arms were gradually sliding down his ribs, and soon reached his waist. He pressed his arms against them, hoping they would come to rest on his hips. To his side he thought he could hear clapping and whistling from the mob, and this convinced him that he must change tack and relinquish the possibility of getting beyond its flank. He turned and headed up the slope. As soon as he hit the gradient the cub in his teeth swung away from his chest and drew his head down. He could feel the blood from its neck wound moving around in his mouth and wondered how he might dispose of it. It would be folly to spit and he was certainly not ready to swallow.

The material of Guy's suit was quite smooth and shiny. The adult creatures pinned at his hips began to slide forwards until both their heads were below the level of his knees. Only the protrusion of their haunches kept them from inching beyond his grasp. As he glanced down at them, the one on the left contracted energetically and fell to the ground. Guy instantly put his foot on it. He dropped one of the cubs, picked up the adult, then found he could not get it up under his arm without using his other hand. There was no question of leaving the creature behind. Still biting into the third cub, and breathing noisily through his partly clenched teeth, he dropped both the right-hand side animals, jammed the first adult up into his armpit, and reached for the second. As soon as he had secured it he looked round for the first cub. It had gone. He straightened up violently. The third cub was torn from his teeth by the force of this movement, leaving a piece of furry flesh in his mouth. He spat the lump out and the mouthful of blood that followed it sprayed onto the wounded creature at his feet, and over the profusion of coloured objects that fell from his sleeves and chest. He put his foot firmly on the creature then turned round. Both the other cubs were rolling down the slope, shrieking and shaking, making no attempt at all to check their descent. The mob, now only some fifty yards from him, roared with excitement. Guy blinked the stinging perspiration away from his eyes and made a decision. Two adults was enough. He ascended the slope, the lighter by three cubs, two rolled and one punctured in the nape of the neck.

The swarm of the thousand, with leashed hounds, lively speculation, triumphant huzzah and new relations forged in the heat of chase, swept the flat. All who bore weapons of offence raised them. The language was dreadful. Each person gave vent to strong mixtures of dark words and ideas, as if there were a storm howling in every individual head. A great sense of the awfulness of life, its unspeakable inadequacy, its profound constraints and ravaging differentials, seized the people. Their actions were in some measure reactions.

Correcting this pervasive and unquantifiable wrongness to some small extent, the thousand closed upon the cubs and soon killed them. Complexes of intermingled feelings shunted through the people, salting

271

their blood and adulterating the messages carried to their nerves. Their biologies embraced the diversity and provided a complete support for the concert of deeds and expressions that were then required. Each weapon of offence had to be brought down onto the bodies, involving a great deal of movement around a small central area. Each blow was the occasion of cries, through which were funnelled an anger comparable in its force to the anger often felt in dreams, when the subject stands up in a crowded room to declaim his complete reaction to the sum of all the small and major pains and injustices that he can remember sustaining and all those that he has forgotten. On those volcanic occasions the subject is torn by the torrent that erupts from him, and then finds that these lesions secrete bitter tears. The rhythm of his sobs dissolves the harsh knots of his rage, and eventually the rents give forth softer fluids, the tears of the deeper sadness. The spume and fury are dispersed, but still the laval melancholy wells unchecked from ancient recesses. The subject learns to pity himself. From this pity of self to a pity for all who have been wronged is a short step. The subject weeps for the sentient who share life with him, the millions that he does not know, but whose broken, blocked and unflowering lives he now feels through the stratum of his own despair. This broad, marvellous sympathy contains in its very universality the seed both of its transformation and its return to the swollen, sullen point of its origination. The subject is incensed by the bald, simple badness of all that he has perceived. He trembles with helpless rage at a foulness that seems as inevitable as the weather itself. His instinct is to locate agency behind the scheme. In so doing he lays the foundations for important attitudes and stances. The great journey through the cycle of fire to water to fire may produce piety, or it may produce politics.

As the thousand shared the creatures, finding fury and clarity, the creatures were broken down to paste. The staining of the thousand was thorough, and required that the materials be exploited to the utmost. As with the beating out of gold film, there is little extravagance for the thicknesses are barely measurable.

Once the creatures had been completely distributed, the thousand were able to turn their attention to the larger picture. As their eyes moved from the central area, they were drawn to the far slope, up which struggled the man in the silver-grey suit of continental cut. It would have been second nature to the group to catch up with the man and help him with the animals, but a checkout girl suddenly exclaimed, 'Look!'

Her cry demanded a closer inspection of the scrub between the thousand and the man. Strewn over the trampled weeds, apparently tumbling from the pockets of the struggling figure, were hundreds of small, widely differing items. Fabricated in a durable rubber or plastic and finished in a variety of both bold and subtle colours, the items, mostly fist or tennis-ball size, were extremely intriguing. The thousand scattered and bent to the scrub, eagerly picking up the items and discussing them. Their excitement was so great that soon they spread out along the trail that led back along the floor of the valley, up the far slope to the very top, possibly to the road beyond. The models were examined minutely, regardless of the sense they made. Each one proved to have points of intense interest, and because the people felt that further study would be repaid, all were pocketed. Pockets bulged and stretched, and many of the people clutched two or three objects in either hand as well. The thousand felt that they had always wanted objects like these, and more than one lamented the fact that the shops in the town had never sensed these basic needs and catered to them.

'See how the dogs like them!'

The dogs, unnoticed at first by their restrainers, had snuffled then eaten every item that they had come across. As the people packed their pockets the dogs whined, leaning on their leashes and worrying the fabrics of the jackets and tunics above their heads. Powerfully composed, tautly muscled, each hound pulled towards the greatest concentration of items that it could scent. Although the man in the suit with the screechies had now almost reached the top of the slope, it was clear to both the people and their hounds that a thick trail lay behind him. Now doubly captivated, the people listened to the message in the baying that came from their pets. They slipped the leashes and shouted as the dogs shot from the group. They marvelled as the dogs ran, jaws grounded and agape, shovelling up the items in their path without pause. Collectors now, and hunters ever, the people took to the slope, bagging what the dogs did not gobble. Their clearness, their appraisal, gave them buoyancy.

Guy was slowing up. The access of energy brought about by this triumphant reunion had faded. After an initial mighty uphill burst he had had the sensation of suddenly losing momentum. All vitality drained from his limbs and left him dramatically fatigued. A few seconds later he stumbled and nearly fell. He realised that his trouser legs had become so swollen with exudations that their cloth was stretched to its limit.

273

His thighs were chafing each other and rapidly making it impossible for him to move one leg before the other. The pressure was so great he wondered whether there was any danger to his circulation. A similar condition obtained around his chest and arms, forcing the latter gradually to straighten out, thereby slackening his grip on the animals. Looking over his shoulder he was horrified to see that his lead over the mob had been reduced again. The people were surging up the slope, at least a hundred abreast, led by a pack of dogs.

Lumbering to the top of the slope at last, he let the animals drop to the scrub. They were on level ground and lay howling but relatively immobile at his feet. He bent down, took hold of one of his trouser legs and tore it right up the outside seam. The objects bounced off the pelts of the animals and onto the grass. He opened the seam on the other leg, then struggled to take off his jacket. The sleeves were so tightly packed that he could not remove either arm and was reduced to rolling the garment off his shoulders then squatting down and stepping back onto it in order to wrench his arms free. As the sleeves turned inside out he was able to see the absurd bulging of the arms of his shirt. He tore off the cuff buttons and with some difficulty ripped both sleeves up to the armpit. The only area of pressure left was around his underpants. Unzipping his fly, he gripped the flaps of the y front and pulled them violently apart, from waist band to bottom seam. Then he reached down the back of his trousers and ripped the pants all the way up the back seam. There were now no more catchment points in his clothing, which should mean he could continue his flight unimpeded. He brushed the objects off the two adults and put them back under his arms. Behind him he could hear the barking of the dogs. Although they were more than half way up the slope they seemed not be running at full speed. Their noses were close to the ground as if they were pursuing a scent. As he took off across the flat top of the hill, Guy remembered Zelka's predilection for his exudations, and wondered if this meant he still had a fighting chance.

Jack eased the car out onto the hill top road. He turned to Silvia, who had the map on her lap.

'Can we get round somehow? Over there?'

'You can go right along, I think.'

'We need to look down from the far side, where there aren't any trees.'

'It is like the horse foot, you see?'

274

The road ran around the full sweep of a u-shaped ridge. Guy had disappeared at the bottom end of the u and reappeared minutes later running along the floor of the valley, towards its open end. As far as they could tell, the mob had closed on him but he had managed to get ahead of them, even though he had headed for the high ground again. Much of the land had been flattened by the stampede, but groups of trees on the slope had prevented Jack and Silvia from following his progress further than about halfway up.

High above them a helicopter banked and dropped down in the direction of the far ridge. Jack could see a cameraman strapped into its open doorway.

'Those guys know where he is!'

He slipped the car in gear and moved off round the top of the hill. After a couple of minutes the trees thinned out and it became possible to see the full expanse of the valley again. The mob had mounted the slope and those at the front had almost reached the flat ground. Guy was nowhere to be seen. There were still scattered groups of trees in the way, however, and it occurred to Jack that Guy might be just beyond them, making for the road. He gunned the car and took it fast round the long bend.

'Jeck, there!'

'Shit! What's he doing?'

Several hundred yards away, on an open stretch of scrub, was a scene of considerable activity. Completely surrounded by a pack of vicious looking dogs, his clothing in tatters, Guy kicked and shouted as he struggled to make his way to the road. The dogs leaped repeatedly at his chest, snapping their jaws and barking fiercely. As Jack drew up at the spot closest to the scene, he realised why Guy looked so unstable.

'Look! Under his arms! He's got a couple of animals there!'

'But the dogs, they want to kill him!'

'Not just the dogs! Shit!'

Streaming over the top of the slope came the vanguard of the mob. They were singing and shouting as they ran, and waving all manner of weapons. Seeing Guy, they roared lustily and picked up speed. Jack was taken aback – clearly something valorous and resourceful was required, and he wondered if fate had not made a serious error in casting.

As more and more people poured onto the flat ground they formed themselves in a crescent around Guy and the dogs. It seemed likely that within a minute or two Guy would be surrounded. Jack suddenly had a chilling thought – Guy actually might die, and he, Jack, might actually lose everything that he had so patiently constructed. But what the fuck could he do? Leap in there and end up as dog meat? Fight off the crazed citizens with a rolled-up map? He groaned and drummed his fingers on the dashboard.

'Jeck, there is a breach!'

'What?'

'There – an apertura, in the green.'

Thirty yards from the car, set in the hedge separating the road from the scrub, was an open gate. 'You can go through,' Silvia said animatedly, 'then we save him.'

'We save him?'

'We must save him.'

Couldn't be denied, really. He slammed the car in first, through to second and kept it there. By the time he reached the gate the engine was whining but he felt he needed the flexibility of the low gears. As they shot over the scrub the camping equipment in the back bounced noisily around with the car jack and tools. Silvia undid her seat belt. 'You should keep that on!' Jack shouted.

'No, no! I must be free! You go in backwards!'

'Backwards! You're kidding!'

'No! You go straight to the dogs and pull around. Then we look back to the road!'

Jack was now at the maximum speed the gear would allow, and heading directly for the centre point of the crescent of citizens, where Guy still grappled with the hounds. He had no idea at all what was going to happen next, and no time to be chastened by what would normally be a humiliating condition for a professional seer. As he neared the mob he could hear them cheering, and saw that those without weapons were clapping and waving. For a moment he had the impression that they were applauding the arrival of the car, but dismissed it as absurd.

'Jeck, now turn!'

'Jesus fuck!' As the car hurtled right up to the outermost hounds, Jack wrenched the wheel round and hit the brakes hard. The car sank onto its offside suspension and seemed to pivot around a still front wheel as the long body tore across the scrub, throwing up a shower of dust and macerated weeds over Guy and the dogs. He heard an unpleasant thud and a yelp as the rear wing smacked a cur hard on the arse and propelled it into the snapping, snarling pack. In the infinitely long and eerily silent split second that followed the end of his huge skid, Jack looked over his shoulder and took in a number of unconnected and unconnectable impressions. Everybody was covered in blood. Guy had no blood on him. Guy's suit was in tatters. The dogs were not biting him. Guy was exuding objects at a great rate. The people were pleased to see Guy. The people waved at the car. The dogs were eating the things from Guy as fast as they could. There were questions to be answered here.

The split second expired. Silvia had opened the door. She dived out, ran round the car to the hatch back and pulled it open. Jack was about to follow her but she shouted, 'Jack, no! You stay!'

The thousand recognised Mr Blighton from the television. A manager stepped forward, shouting over the noise of the helicopters. 'Mr Blighton, what an honour for our mixed bag! Your stirring exhortations have moved us in many ways so what a surprise!'

Mr Blighton did not speak, taken aback by the plurality of the thousand, and their obvious warmth. An athlete spoke out now, 'Many of us have keenly collected the items you have so kindly distributed.'

Mr Blighton moved energetically to evade the attentions of the unleashed dogs, and a mother was also moved, 'How all animals take to you, Mr Blighton. Mothers particularly respect this.'

Mr Blighton spoke, 'I have come to save these poor creatures.' Applause from the thousand filled the air, and some laughter based on feelings of mutuality. A young boy, no more than fifteen years of age, pushed his way to the front of the people. A silence fell across the configuration and all that could be heard was the eager chewing of the dogs, the roar from above of the helicopters and, of course, the sound of the screechies. 'Mr Blighton, as a teenager your programmes have given outgoing examples. Most recently we have seen your plea and we wanted to do something to help. Other teenagers in other places will have felt the same. Because of your fine statements we have come together with the older generation and discovered their attitudes and common ground, which you do not expect until later life. The youngsters of this particular grouping would like to salute you.' As the boy stopped the teenagers distributed regularly throughout the assembled crescent of the thousand cheered, cried, 'Yes, Mr Blighton!' and sang parts of a spontaneous song 'Joined to the Old'. As the last verses died away Mr Blighton said, 'But we can all help to extend man's understanding of the deepest things.' The people turned to each other and exchanged unaffected, amiable glances. The lightness of these looks concealed the

277

pride of the members of the thousand, and their sense of the momentousness of this hilltop meeting, heightened by the helicopters. Beside Mr Blighton stood a dark, beautiful woman from a car. She touched the dogs and they fell quiet, no longer jumping at Mr Blighton in order to chew his freely dispensed items. A pit bull pressed its head to her leg, a harrier folded itself about her ankles. Her arm was in Mr Blighton's arm. An angler voiced what the people hardly dared believe, 'Miss Silvia Desperanza! As gorgeous in real life!' Now conversation broke out around the crescent, and members stood on tiptoe to see the star who had given so much pleasure. 'Miss Desperanza!' cried a constable, 'will you say for us the lines from the climax of *Eva Kuwait and the Transparent Box* where she turns to the Spanish businesswoman who may or may not be her longlost sister?' Clapping delightedly the thousand cry, 'Oh yes!'

With a graceful smile Miss Desperanza said, 'Oh Carmen, can you not take this flower into the next room?' Again a hush spread. Then it was as if the thousand were infused with energy. Smiling and with their hands outstretched they moved towards the handsome couple. Stepping among the various dogs they congratulated the naturalist and the film personality equally, touching and squeezing them. The naturalist gave many more items which were received with delight. The screechies were lifted from Mr Blighton's arms and laid among the dogs. Swiftly they were made paste, with first the umbrellas and tent pegs, then the bats and boards. The thousand made sure that the couple were fully stained before the paste was distributed among all their number.

'Guy! You can't do nothing!' Silvia screamed.

Guy was on his knees, shouting wordlessly, scrabbling at the bloody scrub where small pieces of sodden fur were all that remained of the two animals. Silvia grabbed the collar of his jacket and heaved on it with all her might. 'Come! Come!' Her voice was drowned out by the frantic barking of the dogs and the babble of the crowd pressing all round them. Guy pulled away from her and fell face down into the mud. Dozens of coloured objects seemed to erupt from his body, rolling out from beneath the back panels of the suit top, and piling up around his bloodstained, mudspattered legs. Silvia bent over, seized a handful of his hair and pulled it back hard. Guy's head rose out of the mud, and he pushed himself up onto his knees again. Silvia kept on pulling mercilessly at his hair and began to walk away. Guy almost fell, then twisted round and stood up. She led him, half stooped, through the mob, kicking at the dogs that leaped up at his chest. One of her shoes came off in the slippery mess underfoot but she kicked the other off and elbowed her way onward.

Arriving at a point a few feet from the back of the car Silvia released Guy's hair and quickly collected a handful of objects as they fell from the front of his body. She turned dramatically to the crowd, her hair blown back from her face by the downdraught from the helicopters, and raised her arms above her head. The mob, whose members had begun to murmur uneasily when she had apprehended Guy, watched her expectantly. Suddenly with a cry of simulated celebration she threw the objects up and over their heads. Pockets of scuffling broke out as people strained to acquire the doubly endorsed novelties. Her admirers in the front ranks were momentarily distracted and as they turned away Silvia shoved Guy into the back of the car, slammed down the hatch and dashed for the passenger door. Jack stamped on the throttle and the car hurtled across the scrub and back onto the road.

'Oh god, oh god, where shall we go?' Silvia was shivering, she tried to rub the mud and blood from her bare feet but only succeeded in transferring it to her hands and then back onto her calves. She gripped the facia above the glove compartment and braced herself against it, but her arms continued to shake and her teeth chattered audibly.

'We'll find a hotel, Silvia. Somewhere quiet. Then we can sort things out.' Jack felt calm again. The heroic phase had passed, without drawing too heavily on his resources, and now matters had reverted to a territory in which he could exercise his powers with the usual confidence.

In the back of the car Guy started to sob. Silvia looked round and gasped. 'Jeck, we must open the windows!' Even in the driving mirror Jack could see the objects building up around Guy and spilling over onto the back seat.

'No. We don't want a trail,' he said.

'But he will drown!' Silvia insisted.

'I'd rather not throw these things away. People seem to find them a bit too interesting,' he said disingenuously.

Silvia extended a bloodstained hand towards Guy. 'Guy, do you hurt?' He responded with a loud moan and tried to move his arms in what might have been a shrug or flailing of despair. So great was the volume of objects around him, piling up under his bent legs, filling his lap and rising almost to his shoulders, pressing against the rear window, that he was only able to flex his arms to a small degree before they were obstructed in the jumble of exuded

279

shapes. He moaned again and rolled his head from side to side in frustration.

'Poor Guy, you had them in your hands.' Silvia leaned over and pulled dozens of objects from the back seat onto the floor of the car, in an attempt to ease the congestion that threatened soon to engulf Guy's head.

'Fucking helicopters are still with us,' Jack observed. He rolled the window down and stuck his head out. The two news teams were following the car at a height of about three hundred feet, a camera clearly visible in the open side of each craft.

'So they trail us anyway,' Silvia said.

'We'll be in town soon. They won't dare fly low there.'

'How shall we bring Guy into the hotel? We will be inhibited for sure.'

'I don't think so.'

Jack strode through the busy foyer and up to the reception desk. 'What's big?'

'A suite?'

'Yes. Quite high.'

'The Pumice Rooms.'

'Are big.'

'A large lounge area with three adjoining double rooms.'

'And balcony?'

'Of course.'

'You are familiar with the work of Miss Silvia Desperanza.'

'What picturegoer isn't?'

'I can trust you, I can feel it.'

'Our chain aspires to this condition.'

'Miss Desperanza, fresh from nearby location work on *Eva Kuwait and the Catholic Mass*, needs to recuperate in comfort and privacy in spacious apartments.'

'Her privacy is assured.'

'She will be accompanied by her personal secretary, namely myself, and her special effects advisor.'

'Momentarily speaking as an enthusiast, what sort of effects?'

'The usual sort of thing, but produced with revolutionary new equipment.'

'Will she come through the foyer?'

'My next point. Miss Desperanza is still in costume and her contract stipulates that all aspects of the current production must remain the vis-

280

ual and intellectual property of the producing company until such time as the complete feature film has been theatrically exhibited for no less than six days in each house designated by the distributor on a national basis, or, in the case of the failure of receipts, for a lesser period prescribed at the discretion of the distributor.'

'Heaven forbid.'

'An unlikely event, we would both agree, but a certain caution is indicated.'

'May I suggest the rear delivery bays? Adjacent to the underground car park and accessed through our discreet side-street ramps.'

'I'll take the key now, if I may.'

Guy, slumped on a sofa in the lounge, savoured desolation and plenitude. At the centre of his being he could feel a rawness so intense that it was as if his flesh had actually been scoured from within. He marvelled at the scale of the tribulations he had sustained and wondered why he had not collapsed or fallen in on himself, now that the focus of his life had been so decisively atomised. How much more could go wrong?

Much, much more. Things were going wrong now that bore no relation at all to anything he had done, or anything that had ever happened to him. He was being used for something. Something was visiting him and making him into an obscene machine. He tried to turn away from this thing and found himself on the brink of a paralysing, abyssal panic.

Ironically, his arrival at the suite afforded him the first respite from incident since the condition had set in. Now that he was no longer driven at a hectic pace, compelled to beat a path through varieties of worldly adversity, he had the wholly unwelcome opportunity to consider his condition without distraction. The cessation of the flow of external events seemed to mark the end of his involvement with the world itself – a thick curtain had been drawn around his mind, blocking off access to any conceivable future. His life was over, and he was alone with the objects that streamed from his skin.

Guy, for the first time, looked down and did not turn away. He raised his right hand solemnly and saw a perfect hand emerge from it. The hand was almost the same size as his own hand, and its fingers were in the same position as his own fingers, and as he looked the hand tumbled into his lap and from his own hand emerged another hand, very like his own hand but the fingers were splayed and the nails were curved and the palm thrust forward and at the centre of the palm was a featureless dark spot which he wanted to probe with his finger but then from his own hand emerged a dark, melted hand, the fingers collapsed and run together, bunched around something dark that was lumpy and simply mysterious, and then from his hand came a perfect little piece of curtain, a corner, dark blue flowers against a lavender ground, and he stirred, then came balls, one after the other, red, yellow, blue, but linked together somehow, after which a crescent of teeth, they were fangs, layer after layer on the jaw, all dagger sharp, after which a cloud, something like that, but solid, but red, and with fangs here and there, not recognisable as anything, just a thing, but in a way he recognised it but not in a way that he understood, then another cloud, or more like a cloud than anything else, but it was solid, and streaked with dozens of colours, most of them familiar, then the curtain, again, but not a corner, just a piece, the colours were the same, and the pattern, but larger, as though he were closer, as though he had moved closer to it, and after it it came again, but the pattern was closer again, and not only that but now there were sections within sections so that at the centre the pattern was so large he could see the weave of the cloth, the crisscross lines, and then after them from his palm came many perfect tears, they were hard, but well coloured, and several at a time and larger than a proper tear, and there was no sadness, but then there were cakes, round ones with icing and perfect silver balls, but they were sad, they were such terribly sad cakes, in his hand they would have wept had they not tumbled away, but the eye that came, surrounded with golden fur, brown and friendly, it comforted the cakes somehow, because it came after them, and then its nose came, with another eye beside it, the same one, and the nose was very friendly, and it was wet, but then part of two legs came, larger than his hand, two legs, joined at the top but no features at the join, just dark green, and reaching to the knee but no further, and they were soaking, the water shined them and rivulets were visible, coming from the join, they were his legs, then the join, came, his privates, but they were crimson and wet, and angry, and next came his privates swollen and melted, partly a cloud, something like that, and small keen hooks ran this way and that over the stretched skin, then came his feet, one after the other, and they were both kicking, because of the way the toes were bent and held tight together, after which a mysterious thing, a ball and some sticks, he recognised it easily but had no idea but then again, it came, the sticks, like arrows, all sticking into one side of the ball only and the back of the ball had hair now, it was a head, the arrows were all over the face of the head, he recognised the head, then came two

282

hands, they were his, closed around something, it was the head, stabbed with all the arrows, the hands were squeezing it, pushing the arrows deep into the face but hiding the head, hiding it away, and then a wisp came, something starting thin and becoming wider, just a scrap of paper, flattish, grades of green and yellow, crossed with lines, numbers, some letters, nothing he could actually read, but it was recognisable, it was just a piece of map, of anywhere, not as thin as paper, it fell away, then a hole came, surrounded by cloud, dark brown stuff, but it was really a way of showing hole, his eye was drawn to the inside, the tube through, and it seemed a long way through, the tunnel, to the end, there was an end, blocked off, then another head came, with some shoulders and clothes, there was a pullover, perfectly clear, he turned it round to see the face but it was featureless, just dark green, then out of his palm came his head, a fist-sized head, his, he screamed, threw it across the suite, then another one came, his face on it but his mouth wide open, all his teeth bared, his eyes bulging, it was perfect, he could see his tongue, bent back, in the little mouth, and the eyes, when he turned it in his hand, were looking at him, actually at him into his eyes, then came his hand, from his palm, it was squashing down on his face, pushing it aside, he threw it across the room, looked into his lap and found the mouth-wide head and threw that too, then out came his head again, this time his lips were pressed forward, they were swollen, big, red, lips and his eyes were half closed, it was trying to kiss him, it wanted to be kissed, but he threw it away, he shuddered but he could not turn his head away, his real head, and a dog came out, or half a dog, its head and shoulders and golden coat, the rest of its body packed in mud, he recognised the dog, it had a name but he couldn't, then again a dog, same one, more mud, thick all over around it, and its mouth was open and out of it came mud, and he turned it in his hand, the perfect muddy dog, and he saw its bottom, its anus, and mud was coming out of that, not actually coming, but depicted as such, and he could not see why all the mud was involved in the dog, but then out of his hand came a sausage of mud, but not so smooth like a sausage, more like, and he shuddered and threw it hard across the room, it wasn't mud, it was disgusting, but his palm gave out more, a long long piece, of foulness, of excrement, from his own hand, shitting out of his hand, he hated it, it was the worst thing in the world, he moved his left hand to cover it but then a hand came, in a glove, and it was around a shit piece, covering it, then just a bucket came, an ordinary bucket, it could

283

be used it was so perfect, except that the handle didn't move, it was a depicted handle fixed, then after it was a more pleasant bucket, this bucket had bright coloured shapes all over it, and he looked closer and they were shells, fish and the sun, it was a happy bucket, but he felt sad looking at it, but he did not throw it away, it just tumbled to his lap, then came something more, that he had to look at closely, it was a scene, a small scene, that fitted in his hand, a bold gold sun over lovely land, he could see sand, flowers and some food, he had been there, he could not put a name to the place, the food drew his attention, piles of attractive bread in slices, white bread, then they came out, just the bread, and they had, between the slices, sand, and this was, somehow or other, important, he couldn't say why exactly, but after the bread came flowers and inside them, the stamens, bearing the pollen, were covered thickly in white powder, the detail was perfect, the white powder dusted the petals, then came more bread, a loaf in fact, cut across one end, and in it, in the cross section, were the flowers, looked down on, so that he could see the stamens, and this struck him as correct, though he could not find the actual reason for it, but the things were correctly combined, of that he was certain, and after that came more flowers, but in a scene, around a hole, a tunnel, but with flowers bending over it, even with gaps between the stalks so that he could see through it, quite a delicate thing, the detail was impressive, and he had been through this tunnel, sometime, it was a recent event, he peered into the tunnel of flowers and saw a house, part of a house, across the end of it, quite obvious, it was his house, his garden, and he put the tunnel aside, it became unpleasant suddenly, but then, on his palm, immediately after, was a mess of things, in a shapeless lump, or a lump with many different shapes of things in it, he could see wire, hair, and pieces of metal, and he turned it over, it didn't make sense, but it gave him a feeling in his throat, of dread, but he still looked at it, and decided that the metal was pieces of a box, something with a lid, with some wire mesh parts, or panels, but also the wire was to do with another box, not metal, perhaps a mesh box, but all the mesh was burst, and then he realised what the hair was but then immediately came another thing and he knew from it immediately what the rest of the previous thing was, and he felt nausea suddenly, a dread and sadness mixed, and so great that his stomach wanted to chuck up, but he looked in his lap and found the previous thing, the shapeless lump, and held it in his left hand,

and his right hand squeezed the latest thing and tried to cover it but it was detailed and perfect, in perfect detail, and he could even feel the hair on its coat, the texture of it under his finger tips, and the little claws at the tip of its paws, then looking across at what he had thought was the shapeless stuff around the hair and wire he recognised it, it was dread, just the shape of dread and sickness and sadness, so the previous thing was actually perfectly correct, it was a good model, but then he stole a look at the latest thing, opening his hand, and he felt a very simple wish, it just rose up inside him, and in his hand, pushing aside the little creature model, came its head, but only down to above its forelegs, but the head was as large as the whole of the previous model, and it tumbled into his lap, and the wish was still there though, and then came the head again, much the same, but the forelegs were there, he took it and kissed it, held it against his face, but then again came the eye and nose with the golden fur, but it was wet, and under the brown nose was a smiling mouth, and close up against it was his eye and part of his cheek, and around this model was sadness and happiness, in their different shapes and particular colours, making a sort of bed for Guy and the old bear, but sad as this was, and so warm as this was, his wish was still there, and pushing him and the bear aside came again the creature, its head, its forelegs, and now the rear legs, and it was big, nearly the size of a small cat, much bigger than anything from his palm before, and he took it in two hands and turned it over and saw that it had no backside, no tail end, it stopped after the legs and was featureless, dark green, there, but he knew now what to do, he had realised, and he did it and another creature came out and fell off straight into his lap but again it had no backside, he couldn't finish it, he just couldn't finish it, and immediately a lump came, full of teeth, shit and hooks, stuck with fangs and muscles and boils, filled out with fire and wire and pocked with slashes, slits and holes, and it was a perfect lump, he could see that, and his mouth fell open and he put it in his mouth, bit it hard, in his anger, groaned and ground his teeth on it, and tasted the bland rubberish taste, then felt with his tongue the slits and holes in the thing, and these seemed to be important, so he ran his tongue over it, pushing its tip into the slits and then into the holes, and they sucked onto the tip and held it lightly, then he took his tongue out and looked down the holes, but they were shallowish, and he didn't know why they were important, and then out of his open hand came now flowers again, but different, in another little scene, on some ground, growing around a

285

round pit, like a rabbit hole, but it was straight and deep and long, so the model was long and covered in mud, another shit piece, but perhaps really mud after all, to show hole, and depth of it, in the ground, so he looked down into the hole, past the flowers, but it was dark, so he turned the thing towards the balcony window, to get some light, but it was just too narrow, he wanted to put his tongue in it, which he did, and sucked some air out, but that wasn't correct, so he dropped it on the carpet, and the next thing was easier, another creature came, perfectly formed but now with a hole in the backside, not an anus, a hole running through from the featureless, dark green backend almost to the nose, and the tunnel was as wide as his finger, but he did not finger it, or tongue it, he looked down it, and it was a kind of joke, the kind you cannot laugh at, because there was, down the hole, past some hooks, some sadness and some shit, which were just at the top, a group of faces, small, necessarily, but distinct, but dark, of course, but little faces, as if looking up at him looking down, and he felt suddenly cold, very very cold, and his own anus, his real one, drew tight and seemed to push up into his intestines and in these was mercury or some heavy cold stuff, similar, and he was going to throw the senseless thing away, a good riddance to bad rubbish, but then a hand was on his shoulder and said 'Red bed' and he wondered who, but before he could, there came on his hand a bed, fist-sized, quite ordinary, but it was red, and it was Jack Gavin behind him, he need not look because the man was in his hand now, quite rough, he did not need to be perfect, but it was obvious Jack Gavin was the man in his hand, so he need not look at Jack behind him, then Jack said, 'Horse and cart' and immediately it was in his hand, rough but definitely recognisable, and he wondered why Jack said it, but then Jack said, from behind the sofa, 'Watch', and there came a scene, he was in it with Jack, and he was sitting in a chair and Jack was standing in front of him, and he was looking at Jack, but Jack then said, 'Wrist watch', quite firmly, and he saw one of these in his hand, but without perfect detail, and Jack grunted then, which he didn't like somehow, and there was a little shop came, but it had no doors and nothing in the windows, which felt correct, and he didn't need to speak to Jack, he had made it clear to him, but Jack was still behind him and said, 'Pound note' and all that came was slabs, like slate, dull pieces, quickly, one after the other, five or six of them, just falling off into his lap, and then, and he could see this was another joke, a big shit piece, very turdy, followed by some trumpets, banjoes and trombones, slightly melted together, but clear, and well coloured, with a good shine effect, and this was another joke, obviously, then came a fat, pink pig, wearing spotted trousers, with a fork stuck in its back and something protruding from its rear end, and he turned it round and saw that in the pig's bottom was a stick of high explosive, and this was even more a joke, and he smiled this time, and placed it on the arm of the sofa so that it could be seen, and bringing his hand back to his lap he saw on it him in a chair, a rough chairish chair, and this time behind him was Jack, looking down at him, and he smiled again, because he thought 'eyes in the back of my head', and then immediately came just the back of his head, with the eyes under the hair, and he put this one in his shirt pocket, he felt it was worth hanging on to, and behind him he heard Jack move away and cough, there was something about Jack's cough that he understood, but vaguely, and another lump came, and he thought that perhaps the lumps came when he felt vague, and this lump had several things in it, he knew what they were but not why they were together, there was some striped cloth, and the back of a head with hair, and some white china, perhaps from a vase or cup, and wrapped around and about this was some more cloth, but it had ducks on it, and all these things were not strange, he had seen them all somewhere, more than once, also he felt they were very important, so he looked at the back of the head, because that gave him most curiosity, and when it came out again, it was his mother's face, which wasn't such a surprise, he felt it was going to be her, but he also felt she wasn't the point of it, and then the china made him curious, and out came a cup, but it wasn't a cup, it was wider, it was a chamber pot, he had a potty in his hand and he wondered, and then it came, a scene, perfectly clear, the little boy standing on the bed, he was peeing, and in front of him was the potty, and the potty was being held for him, and it was his mother holding it, but not his mother's face, it was Jack's face, which had never happened, he had never peed in front of Jack, but then another scene came, and Guy shook, he shook to see it, it was perfectly clear, Jack was by the little boy's bed, he had the potty in his hand, but he was bending over the little boy and his other hand was in the boy's pyjama pocket, on the ducky hanky, but this had never happened, but it was important, it was so important, then another scene came, it was much clearer, and his whole body trembled, just jerked and started to shake and shake, it was fear, and around the scene was fear, in its shapes, and in the scene itself, there was Jack, and he was bending over the bed, and on the bed was Guy, the proper Guy, and his eyes were open, but Jack's hand was near the pocket of Guy's shirt, as if just coming away from it, or going to it, and in Jack's hand were some keys. Guy's keys.

'The Press are all out in the street.' Jack's voice. Guy looked up, as if looking up because of Jack's voice. The sofa and the floor around it were thick with things. He saw that since he had started looking at his hand the heaps had piled up almost to his breast, carrying his arms up with them. The french windows leading to the balcony were open, and the things had begun to spill out onto the smooth concrete, spreading to within inches of the edge, and obstructed only by the narrow verticals of the safety rail. Soon they would fall into the street, some eight floors below.

Guy looked at Jack. He could feel the things still churning out of his body, concealed by the mounds above them. His mouth was terribly dry. He could not think, perhaps he did not need to. He wondered, if he could not think, why the things still came out of him, but he concluded that there were probably ways of thinking that didn't require his actual attention, they just went on anyway. Certainly at one level his mind had stopped, as if one thought, or one realisation, had frozen in the foreground of his consciousness and was blocking everything behind it.

He looked at Jack, who was standing on the balcony, looking down at the street.

'Jeck, they see you! Come back.' Silvia's voice. He had forgotten about her. She sat on the edge of a shiny, mock-antique chair by the door to the main bedroom. Her face was pale and drawn, streaked with dark, dried blood, and her legs were still caked with mud. So tightly was she gripping the arms of the chair that her knuckles were white.

He looked back at Jack. Jack moved away from the balcony, stumbled on the things, almost fell, but regained his balance.

'Shit!' Jack's voice. Some of the things shot over the edge of the balcony. 'Fuck it!' Jack's voice, angry.

'They trap us, Jack.'

'Yes. Fuckers.'

There was a knock at the door of the suite.

'Who's that?' Jack said to Silvia.

There was another knock, more insistent.

'Who's that?' Jack called out.

Silvia got up and walked across the room. Jack signalled to her,

288

and shook his head fiercely. But the door opened. Deany stood in the corridor. Ainsley was with her. They stepped into the room.

Guy looked at his wife. He felt quite calm. Deany looked round the room. She saw the things on the floor, and flinched. She closed her eyes and took a breath.

'Guy . . .'

'Yes, I know.'

'What?'

'It was Jack. All along.'

'How did you find out?'

'I . . . remembered.'

Jack stood in the middle of the room, quite still, smiling with his mouth, but not with his eyes.

'Ainsley . . . this is Ainsley . . .' She turned and gestured towards the arrogant young man in pale blue tights and shorts.

'I know.'

'He told me. Jack sold them to him.'

Guy felt his heart thump violently in his chest. The mound around him pulsed as a great quantity of things streamed out of his body, a flush of fearful hope made into its shapes and pushed from every pore. He looked at the champion.

'Have you got Eke?'

'Who's Eke?'

'An adult female. Did he give you an adult female?'

'Yes. She had babies.'

'Is she still alive?'

'Of course. She eats biscuits.' The champion looked at the things piled around Guy. 'What's all this stuff?'

Guy pushed some of the things away from his chest, and watched them roll down the slope that now completely obscured the outline of the sofa. 'They're . . . you know, whatever comes to mind.'

It was quiet. Silvia stood by the door, shivering, her arms held tightly across her breasts. Jack had not moved, only his smiling lips shifted slightly, sometimes exposing his teeth, sometimes parting as his tongue flicked over them.

Guy cleared his throat and then spoke in a thin but determined voice. 'Well, I want her back.'

'They cost me money, Mr Blighton.'

'He gave him twenty thousand, Guy,' Deany said, 'for a pair.' Her voice too was weak, but calm, and cold.

'These creatures belong to science, they're not people's property,' Guy said.

'That's rubbish, Mr Blighton. You took them out of the jungle, and they became saleable. That's the way it is.' Ainsley strolled across the room and picked up some of the things from the mound. Guy was beyond prevarication. 'All right,' he said flatly, 'I'll give you the money.'

'Guy – we don't have it,' Deany protested.

Ainsley was on his knees at the edge of the mound, turning the things over with his hand. He picked one up and studied it closely. It was one of Guy's scenes, a cricket ball set in mashed potato beside a sheaf of propelling pencils. 'What does it mean, this one?' he demanded, looking round the room for an answer.

Guy peered at the fist sized scene. 'It's a ball, isn't it?'

'I can see that. But why did you make it?'

'I didn't make it. Well, I did.'

'Of course you did.'

'I don't know what they mean, most of them. They just come to me.'

The champion snorted, then shook his head disparagingly.

'Ridiculous.'

'Why?'

'They're very good. Very pleasing. Intricate. And you don't even know why you made them. Typical.' He put the scene to one side and continued to sort through the pile. The exchange had come to an end. Jack glanced at Deany, then thought the better of it. He addressed the floor instead. 'Well.' He looked up at the ceiling. 'I'll be going.' He took a pace towards the door, then turned to Silvia. 'We should go, Silvia.' She frowned. Jack said, 'We have to get you some shoes.' Still frowning, Silvia limped to the open door. 'I see you, Guy.' She searched his face for some response, but Guy seemed not see her at all. She turned to Deany and nodded quickly. 'And Mrs Blighton.'

Deany watched Jack walk out of the room. Only a faint tremor in her cheek belied the still malevolence of her expression. As he closed the door she turned her back and bared her teeth in a silent snarl.

Guy was looking at his hand. Jack was fucking Deany on a carpet. He knew the carpet, it was in his house, in the sitting room. Beside them, in a roughish chair, a man was watching them. He wondered about the man, and then the scene came again. The man was him, he was looking at Deany being fucked on the floor by Jack. This had never happened. But he looked hard at the scene. He saw the shapes of horror around his body, clinging to his clothes. He had never imagined this. Another scene immediately came into his palm. Jack Gavin's penis was in his wife's mouth, just those parts of their bodies, nothing more, and his head, a model of it, was near those parts, and he had a carrot in his mouth. His eyes looked in the direction of the penis and the mouth, but beyond them, the eyes had no expression. He crushed the rubbery thing in his hand, but he knew that he was about to make sense of it all. The pressure of another thing forced his hand open again. It was just part of his face, nothing else. His eyes were closed, but he could see through the eyelids, to the eyeballs beneath. No. The eyeballs were on the lids. Both things at once. Seeing and not seeing. And he understood. He looked at his arms and his chest. Things were streaming out so fast they appeared to be joined in chains. He looked at the fresh layer forming on top of the mound. So much of his life, little moments, was there. Moments seen and denied, unfinished ideas, abandoned thoughts, aborted pictures, snippets of just now, faded figments of back then, little cowboys, little spacemen, little explorers, little husbands, and all in beds of terror. The shapes of terror clinging to everything, the colours of terror bleeding into all the figures, all the views, all the things seen, everything mixed, melted, and run together, nothing quite clean, nothing quite bright.

Then to his hand came smiling Jack, in evening dress, white gloves, dapper, with his hand held up, curved in a peculiar way, a particular way. And Guy recognised it. Jack, conjuring, spiriting something away, some cards, a ball, whatever, and we all watch his right hand while his left simply does what must be simply done. And we never see it. And we give him all the room he needs. Yes, it is magic, he thought. Jack has found another land, where no one ever goes. And it's all quite simple, if you know how. If you want to know.

Jack fell from his hand as something started to break through the skin of his palm. He winced. It had never hurt before. A thing was rising up out of the flesh. The pain was excruciating. He thought he might faint. Small figures, in a group, fist-sized, standing close together, arms around each other, a party pose, in cheap colours, badly applied, some waving, another with a bottle, others drinking, seven of them in all, one woman, with long black hair, head held up, chin jutted out, towards the camera, if there was a camera, it felt like it, standing in the middle of the group, the men around her, six men, various types, one old and scrawny, one rakish, another smart and managerial, a dishevelled barroom type, but the most imposing figures were at either end, and his eye was drawn to, on the one side, badly blurred, a gaunt, unsmiling man with craggy features and empty eyes, and on the other, perfectly sharp, staring straight out at him, a young man, hair slicked back, eyebrows a fine line, his expression distant and direct, inviting and challenging, and, to a degree, cruel. Guy knew this poorly rendered group, from somewhere, he could not place them, but he knew they brought with them the end.

He looked down at his chest, and his arms, and an instant before it stopped, he felt it, and it stopped. The things were still there, he could see them, they were his, for him, but they were no longer visible, not in the same way. And then fleetingly he saw himself, in evening dress, dapper. In one hand a hat, in the other a rabbit. But putting it back in. He had Jack's trick. In his mind's eye.

'Right,' said Ainsley, standing up, 'I'll take these ones.'

Deany gaped at him. 'You what?'

'These.' He held out an armful of things. 'Ten of them. The best ones.'

'They're Guy's.'

'I know. He doesn't need them all, though. Do you?'

Guy stood up and kicked his way out of the mound. 'Let's see them.' The champion handed the things over for inspection. Guy found a fighter plane covered in lettuce, three men holding a used car, part of a thought about humidity in relation to seed dispersal methods, his elder brother crushed by a savage grandfather clock, blue melted to twenty-three, yearning for a radio programme, valour obscured by an old parking ticket, a pharaoh in some shadows, the corner of the suite near the bathroom door showing part of lintel and ornamental moulding of ceiling, a group of officials stand around a marshal felled by an ineptly hurled discus.

'They're very personal.'

'Two thousand.'

'What?'

'By the piece. Ten at two thousand.'

'I'll have to think.'

'Twenty grand, Mr Blighton. Must ring a bell.'

292

'Two thousand five hundred.'

'Guy!'

'They're unique, Ainsley. Every one different. Not like the animals.'

'The animals and three grand. I'll send them to you.'

'I'll pick them up.'

'Suit yourself.'

'You could give me the three thousand now, and leave with the things.'

'You think I carry money like that?'

'Yes.'

'Maybe you're right.'

The pressmen turned in unison as Silvia suddenly cried out and pointed behind them.

'Zelka! Oh Jeck! She comes!'

'What's she got?'

'God, she has killed something.'

'It's one of the animals.'

The Saluki dropped the creature at her mistress's feet then jumped up to lick Silvia's face.

'It's not dead at all. Listen,' said Jack.

'Miss Desperanza! A photo, please!'

'Hold the animal, Silvia, and Mr Gavin put your arm round her!'

'And one hand on the dog's head, Mr Gavin!'

'Mr Gavin, can you hold a couple of the sculptures, sit them on Silvia's shoulder? Yes!'

'Smile, Mr Gavin!'

'Mr Gavin, what are your plans for the sculptures now? Will you distribute through the gallery system?'

'We shall exhibit, of course. When we have found suitably spacious premises. The sculptures will, however, be disposed of by auction. We feel that this is our only means of ensuring the appropriate degree of security.'

'You're worried about unscrupulous collectors?'

'I don't need to tell you that it's virtually impossible to insure work of this quality these days. We certainly do not take lightly the dangers attendant on the maintenance of a major collection.'

'Is there any truth in the rumour that Miss Desperanza and yourself have recently dined together several times?'

'Miss Desperanza and myself both find that six hours after lunch we are obliged to take refreshment, on a daily basis.'

'We are just colleagues who have share some accidents together.'

'Where are the sculptures now, Mr Gavin?'

'Apart from the few thankfully recovered by yourselves, gentlemen, the bulk of the collection is presently held in a secure facility. You won't be wanting me to tell you the location, I'm sure.'

'Silvia, one last question! Shall we see Eva again soon?'

'Well, of course. Now I am to work on a wonderful movie in this next month.'

'And called?'

'Is *Eva Kuwait and the Force of Gravity*. Is a western with modern physique.'

'She means physics. Gentlemen, thank you. We have to go.'

Jack raced across the underground car park to Guy's car. He opened all four doors and the hatch back.

'What do you think?'

'It is almostly completely fool.'

'How many?'

'Oh, Jeck, there is hundreds.'

'Hundreds! Silvia, there's a thousand there, easy. Maybe two. Jesus.'

'Where shall we sit? And Zelka?'

'Throw the camping stuff out and stick the dog on top in the back. And don't let her eat any!'

They drove away from the hotel, out of town.

'Jeck, you are crying. I didn't think you are like this.'

'I'm looking forward, Silvia. It makes my eyes water.'